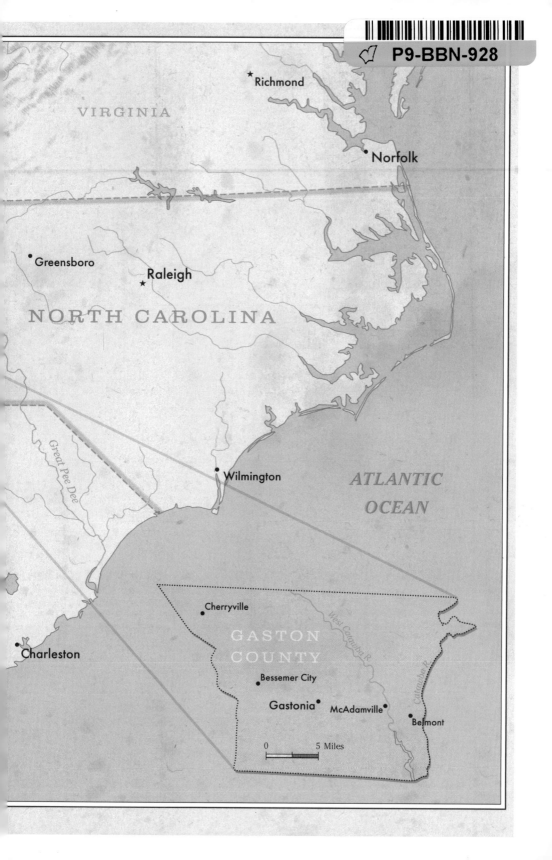

Richmond

VIRGINIA

Norfolk

Greensboro

Raleigh

NORTH CAROLINA

Great Pee Dee

Wilmington

ATLANTIC
OCEAN

Charleston

Cherryville

GASTON
COUNTY

West Catawba R.

Bessemer City

Gastonia McAdamville

Belmont

Catawba R.

0   5 Miles

The Last Ballad

ALSO BY WILEY CASH

This Dark Road to Mercy

A Land More Kind than Home

The Last Ballad

WILEY CASH

WILLIAM MORROW

An Imprint of HarperCollinsPublishers

This book is a work of fiction. References to real people, events, establishments, organizations, or locales are intended only to provide a sense of authenticity, and are used fictitiously. All other characters, and all incidents and dialogue, are drawn from the author's imagination and are not to be construed as real.

FIRST EDITION

Designed by Bonni Leon-Berman
Endpaper map by Nick Springer, copyright © 2017 Springer Cartographers LLC

Library of Congress Cataloging-in-Publication Data

Names: Cash, Wiley, author.
Title: The last ballad : a novel / Wiley Cash.
Description: First edition. | New York, NY : William Morrow, an imprint of
  HarperCollins Publishers, 2017.
Identifiers: LCCN 2017007053 (print) | LCCN 2017011098 (ebook) | ISBN
  9780062313119 (hardback) | ISBN 0062313118 (hardcover) | ISBN 9780062670731
  (large print) | ISBN 9780062313133 () | ISBN 0062313134 ()
Subjects: LCSH: Domestic fiction. | BISAC: FICTION / Literary. | FICTION /
  Suspense. | FICTION / General.
Classification: LCC PS3603.A86525 L37 2017 (print) | LCC PS3603.A86525 (ebook) |
  DDC 813/.6--dc23
LC record available at https://lccn.loc.gov/2017007053

17 18 19 20 21 LSC 10 9 8 7 6 5 4 3 2 1

For my daughters Early Elizabeth and Juniper Rose

GASTON TRANSOM-TIMES

THURSDAY, APRIL 4, 1929

Were you there, friends? Were you one of the patriotic, law-abiding AMERICAN CITIZENS who witnessed mob rule at the Loray Mill yesterday? Any man who loves this country and its one-hundred-and-fifty-year history of FREEDOM could easily see the difference between our STARS AND STRIPES and the bloody red flag of Communism, the flag of the Bolshevists who want to destroy our government, the flag of anarchy, the flag of dark Russia where men do not believe in religion or the sanctity of marriage. PEOPLE OF GASTON COUNTY, WILL YOU ALLOW FRED BEAL AND HIS MOSCOW ASSOCIATES TO SPREAD THE DOCTRINES OF BOLSHEVISM ANYWHERE IN AMERICA AND ESPECIALLY HERE IN OUR BELOVED NORTH CAROLINA?

Before Governor Max Gardener called in the National Guard yesterday the mob at the Loray Mill ran wild in all of its fanged terror, ready to harm, ready to kill, ready to destroy. Chief of Police Orville Aderholt and his officers, who were few in number but loyal in their duty, had spent hours trying to quell the mob. They maintained law and order as best they could, but they were quickly overcome, for Fred Beal and his gang had told the strikers to use violence, to attack the officers, to kill anyone who stood in their way. The troops arrived, men who believe in liberty, freedom, and our Constitutional government, and the mob saw it would be defeated and dispersed.

WE ASK EVERY MAN AND WOMAN IN GASTON COUNTY TO ANSWER THE FOLLOWING QUESTION: WILL I ALLOW THESE COMMUNISTS TO GAIN CONTROL OF GASTON COUNTY, THESE COMMUNISTS LED BY MEN LIKE FRED BEAL WHO DO NOT BELIEVE IN OUR GOD, OUR CONSTITUTION, OR OUR GOVERNMENT?

THE LORAY MILL STRIKE IS ABOUT MUCH MORE THAN A FEW MEN ATTEMPTING TO JOIN A UNION FOR BETTER WAGES. IT WAS NOT ORGANIZED FOR THAT REASON. IT WAS STARTED TO MASK THE BOLSHEVISTS' DESIRE TO OVERTHROW THE GOVERNMENT AND DESTROY PROPERTY AND TO KILL, KILL, KILL.

THE TIME IS AT HAND FOR EVERY AMERICAN TO DO HIS DUTY.

CHAPTER ONE

Ella May

Saturday, May 4, 1929

Ella May knew she wasn't pretty, had always known it. She didn't have to come all the way down the mountain from Tennessee to Bessemer City, North Carolina, to find that out. But here she was now, and here she'd been just long enough for no other place in her memory to feel like home, but not quite long enough for Bessemer City to feel like home either.

She sat on the narrow bench in the office of American Mill No. 2—the wall behind her vibrating with the whir of the carding machines, rollers, and spinners that raged on the other side, with lint hung up in her throat and lungs like tar—reminding herself that she'd already given up any hope of ever feeling rooted again, of ever finding a place that belonged to her and she to it. Instead of thinking thoughts like those, Ella turned and looked at Goldberg's brother's young secretary where she sat behind a tidy desk just a few feet away. The soft late-day light that had already turned toward dusk now picked its way through the windows behind the girl. The light lay upon the girl's dark, shiny hair and caused it to glow like some angel had just lifted a hand away from the crown of her head. The girl was pale and soft, her cheeks brushed with rouge and her lips glossed a healthy pink. She wore a fine powder-blue dress with a spray of artificial, white spring flowers pinned to the lapel. She read a new copy of *Gentlemen Prefer Blondes,* and she laughed to herself and wet her finger on her tongue and turned page after page while Ella watched.

How old could that girl be? Ella wondered. Twenty? Twenty-five? Ella was only twenty-eight herself, but she felt at least two, three times that age. She stared at the girl's dainty, manicured hands as they turned the pages, and then she looked down at her own hands where they rested upturned in her lap, her fingers intertwined as if they'd formed a nest. She unlocked her fingers and placed her palms flat against her belly, thought about the new life that had just begun to stir inside her, how its stirring often felt like the flutter of a bird's wing. She didn't know whether or not what she felt was real, so she'd decided not to say a word about it to Charlie, not to mention a thing to anyone aside from her friend Violet.

Charlie had blown into Bessemer City that winter just like he'd blown into other places, and Ella knew that one day he'd eventually blow out the same way he'd come in. He didn't have children or a family or anything else to tether him to a place where he didn't want to be.

"I hadn't never wanted a child," he'd said after they'd known each other for a month. "I just never found the right woman to care for a child the way I want it cared for." He'd come up behind Ella and spread his palm over her taut belly as if trying to keep something from spilling out. She'd felt his hand press against the hollowed-out space between her ribs and her hips. She was always so racked with hunger that she found it hard to believe that her body offered any resistance at all. "But who's to say I'm always going to feel that way?" he'd said. "I might want a family of my own just yet." Maybe he'd meant it then, and, if so, she hoped he still meant it now.

Perhaps it was the soft thrash of wings against the walls of her belly that made Ella think further of birds, and she considered how her thin, gnarled hands reminded her of a bird's feet. She placed her palms on her knees, watched her knuckles rise like knobby mountains, saw her veins roll beneath her skin like blue worms that had died but never withered away. What was left of her fingernails were thick and broken, and it was laughable to imagine that someone like Ella would ever spend the time it would take to use a tiny brush to color such ugly things.

She resisted the urge to lift these awful hands to her face and allow those fingers to feel what waited there: the sunken, wide-set, dark eyes; the grim mouth that she imagined as always frowning because she did not believe she had ever smiled at herself when looking into a mirror, and she had only seen one photograph of herself in her lifetime, and she was certain that she was not smiling then. She recalled the photograph of a younger version of herself taken more than ten years ago; she and John and baby Lilly posing for a traveling photographer inside the post office down in Cowpens, South Carolina. John with his arm thrown around Ella's shoulder, his face and eyes lit with the exaltation of the gloriously drunk, Lilly crying in her arms, what Ella knew to be her own much younger face blurred in movement as it turned toward Lilly's cries at the exact moment of the camera's looking. John had purchased the photo, folded it, and kept it in a cigar box that rattled with loose change and the quiet rustle of paper money when and if they had it. Ella had removed the photograph and gazed upon it from time to time over the years, but never to look at her own face. She'd only wanted to see the face of her firstborn, the girl who was now a tough, independent young lady who mothered her little sister and brothers more than Ella had the time or the chance or the energy to. John had left her—left them all, for that matter—over a year ago, and Ella assumed that he'd taken the cigar box with him because Lord knows he'd taken all that money, but the only thing that Ella missed now was the photograph.

She looked over at the young secretary where she sat reading. No,

Ella wasn't pretty, not like that girl. Pretty took the will to be so and the money to do it and the time to see to it and the sleep to maintain it, and Ella didn't have any of those things. The woman lowered the book to turn a page. Her eye caught Ella's. The girl's gaze shifted toward the closed door of Goldberg's brother's office.

"It won't be much longer," the girl said. She didn't look back at Ella. Instead she returned her eyes to her book, but Ella nodded her head *yes* anyway. She sat and listened as the girl turned pages and laughed softly, cleared her throat, yawned, laughed again. Ella closed her eyes and tuned her ears to the goings-on behind Goldberg's brother's closed door, but she couldn't hear a thing.

Her shift had just started, and she'd only been at work for a few minutes when the foreman, whose name was Tommy Dobbins, sent her down to Goldberg's brother's office. He'd put his fingers in his mouth and whistled until she looked up and spied him several rows over from the spinners she'd been tending. He'd pointed at her and crooked his finger and mouthed the words "Come here."

Ella walked down the line away from Dobbins while she stared at the dozens of white strands of yarn where they coiled around the spools, her eyes searching for a break or a weak spot that would require her to twist the broken ends together before the strand could continue on to the bobbin. From there the doffers would come behind her and remove the full bobbins and replace them with empty spindles. After that, spoolers would combine several strands into yarn. If a strand broke on Ella's spinners, then the tension failed, which meant the hank clock wouldn't register any output, which meant Ella's pay was docked for any amount of time the little dial on the hank refused to tick. She needed to keep the dials moving, and any interruption, even if it was the shift supervisor himself, ran the risk of cutting into her pay. And that was how she spent twelve hours a night, six nights a week: eyeing hundreds of strands of yarn at the same time while worrying about the tiny hands of a clock that dictated whether and how much her children would eat.

She came around the far end of the line and checked the strands on the other side on her way to where Dobbins leaned against the railing at the top of the rickety wooden stairs. She stopped in front of him and waited for him to explain why he'd called her away from the frenzy of the spinning machines, but Dobbins just rubbed his eyes with his thumb and index finger, and then he looked down at a pocket watch he wore on a leather strap. He wasn't tall, but he was broad-shouldered, and although he was only forty years old his red hair had long ago faded almost completely to gray. He closed the watch and slipped it into his pocket.

"Goldberg's brother wants to talk to you," he said.

Everyone knew there were two brothers, two Goldbergs, but the smaller and slighter of the two was the one who came into work each day, the one who signed their paychecks, the one most likely to call them into his office and chastise them or promote them or fire them altogether. This man had always been known as Goldberg's brother; the other, more mysterious brother, simply as Goldberg.

"Can it wait?" Ella asked. "I don't get a break for another six hours. It's going to set me back on the hank if I come off the line."

Dobbins looked over Ella's shoulder at the other workers. "Dinah and Molly can tend your spinners."

"Dinah and Molly can't run all them machines," Ella said. "This stretch-out makes it so we can't even keep track of our own. It's going to set all of us back."

"Don't matter," Dobbins said. "Go on down. He don't like to stay late on Saturday nights. He's got a family to go home to."

"So do I," Ella said, "and this is going to set me back."

"Don't matter," Dobbins said again. "Go on. He's waiting for you."

"I'll tell him you told me to come off the line," Ella said. "Wasn't my idea."

"Go on down," Dobbins said.

Ella wanted to crane her neck and look toward the far end of the floor, where Violet worked along with the rest of the colored spinners, but she didn't want Dobbins to ask her any questions about who she was looking at. She wondered if Violet was watching her now.

She walked down the first flight of stairs to the landing, Dobbins's footsteps falling hard behind hers. She gained the landing and turned to follow the next flight of stairs, and as she did she looked up toward the second floor and saw Violet's face peering over the railing. There were other faces too—the rest of them white—but Violet's was the only face she saw. Dobbins's eyes must have followed hers to the second floor because all the faces disappeared at the same time.

She reached the bottom floor where the opening room led toward the loading ramp. The air here was warm and soft, clean. A bird flashed through her line of vision like something that had been thrown from one side of the world to the other. Dobbins stood beside her, removed his watch from his pocket, and looked down at it again. He sighed.

"Go on back up when you're done," Dobbins said. "Unless—" But he didn't finish.

Ella walked the length of the mill toward the office at its far end, her eyes locked in front of her instead of grazing the faces of the men and women who worked at machines and the boys and girls who looked no older than her own and who pushed carts full of spindles and swept heavy, lint-choked brooms across the floor.

Aside from sanctioned breaks and shift changes, Ella had left the line only once in the years she'd worked at the mill, and the thing that had caused that leaving now passed through her mind. A new doffer boy, whose name she later learned was Giles Corley, had tottered on his toes when reaching too far for a full spindle and found his hand caught up and nearly yanked off in one of the operating belts that snaked through the mill and powered the machines through a system of pulleys. By the time Giles and the spinners around him realized what had happened he was holding a bloody appendage to his chest and three of his fingers had dropped to the floor and disappeared.

Ella didn't know if he had screamed—it was too loud to hear a boy that size scream anyway—but the recoil of his hand away from the belt and toward his body had caught her attention, and without thinking she lifted the hem of her dress and knelt to the floor and started searching. Others searched too, but it was Ella who found them: three little fingers tucked against the base of the brick wall at the end of a trail of blood that had already begun to turn a deep brown on the dirty floor. She scooped up the fingers and carried them to the boy, who stared at them like creatures from a nightmare. He didn't seem able to muster any interest in reclaiming his fingers, so Ella held them in her closed hand while she tended the spinners and she and Giles waited for Dobbins. When he arrived she showed him the boy's fingers.

"I found them on the floor," she said. "Over there by the wall."

"Goddamn," Dobbins said. He took a white handkerchief from his pocket and opened it, gesturing for Ella to drop the fingers inside, which she did. He closed the handkerchief and twisted it so that it formed a little satchel. Blood bloomed through the cloth. "Goddamn," he said again.

The boy never returned to work. At first Ella assumed it was because the mill did not have much use for a one-handed doffer, but other forces had come to bear. A trip to the doctor who'd tamped the bleeding and tossed the three fingers and sewn the hand shut had uncovered the fact that Giles was only twelve years old. The boy, who was clearly in shock, had told the doctor his correct age, to the great disappointment of the mother, who stood beside him and did her best to focus on the loss of her son's blood and fingers instead of what the loss of his three dollars a week was going to mean to her and her husband and their brood of young children.

Ella had seen the boy twice since the incident. A few days later she passed Giles and his angry mother and father on their way out of the mill's gate as she and Violet headed inside for the night shift. The dirty, frayed bandages that covered the boy's hand had come untethered and were spotted with blood. Ella thought she saw blood on the fingers of his good hand too, but when she looked at his face she realized that what she'd mistaken for blood on his fingers was actually chocolate, the same chocolate that smeared his lips and cheek. Word later came through the mill that the boy's parents had gone to Goldberg's brother looking for some kind of settlement that would equal the loss of three fingers, but instead they'd been turned away with the offer of a chocolate bar wrapped in foil and a promise "to think on it for a few days." According to Goldberg's brother the mill had taken the word of the boy's parents when they'd vouched for him being fourteen, even though one glance at Giles Corley would have revealed otherwise. The mill had been willing to look the other way, and now they refused to look back, and so it went. Nothing about that surprised Ella.

She saw Giles Corley again a few months later—much thinner and perhaps a little taller—when she turned a corner in downtown Bessemer City late one afternoon before her shift, and someone ran smack into her chest and knocked her down. She reached for the knife she kept folded in her pocket and lifted her face to confront the offender, but her eyes paused for a moment when they registered the boy's mangled hand and missing fingers. He looked down at her with desperate, hungry eyes. He stuffed something into his pocket, stepped over her, and ran on down the alley. She turned and watched him go, his feet kicking up dust where the asphalt turned to gravel as he disappeared into one of the settlements that ringed the town.

Now, outside Goldberg's brother's office, Ella closed her eyes and crossed her ankles and leaned against the wall, the mill causing her body to vibrate so that her bones rattled beneath her skin. She considered how the only thing worse than stepping off the line was missing a shift, and that's what she'd done last night, and she knew that that was why she was sitting where she was sitting now.

She'd spent almost all of last night on the porch with her three-year-old daughter, Rose, asleep in her arms, singing and humming all the songs she'd ever known until she had run out of songs and begun to make up new words to old melodies. The air had been chilly, but Rose's body had burned like a cinder against Ella's chest. Sweat had soaked through the girl's bedshirt, but her coughing fits had finally given way to sleep.

Ella had been able to hear the rest of her children stir inside the cabin, where they lay atop pallets on the floor, and she pictured eleven-year-old Lilly with one-year-old Joseph, whom they all called Wink, nestled in the crook of her arm. Nine-year-old Otis would have his back turned to them, his thumb in his mouth, something no one ever saw except Ella, and then only when he slept. When she heard one of the children move or cough, she stopped humming the melody she'd been humming to Rose, and she listened until the child settled to sleep again. Willie would have been four years old by now, and Ella turned her attention to the soft, high-pitched whistle of Rose's lungs and remembered holding Willie this way before he'd died from the same whooping cough disease. The thought had made her hold Rose more tightly against her chest. She wanted to keep her daughter on this earth and in her arms for as long as possible.

Ella had spent most of the night out there on the porch envying horses for their ability to sleep standing up. She'd worn a man's coat over her shoulders, the waxed canvas duster the only thing John had left behind when he disappeared, aside from little Wink, who'd just begun to grow inside her when John closed the door for the last time. She'd never had the chance to tell John he was a father again, but it wouldn't have mattered. He'd said he wouldn't live among niggers anymore, said he was sick of millwork, sick of the children themselves being sick. He'd said other things too, but Ella had decided to forget those things on her way to forgetting him. She didn't care that her neighbors were colored; it wouldn't have mattered anyway because there was nowhere else for her to go. As far as working as a spinner at American Mill No. 2, Ella knew that the work she did was dirty, dangerous work, knew that the nine dollars she earned for a seventy-two-hour workweek wasn't worth the work itself. But she did it because there was nothing else to do. If there were something she could do to keep her children healthy and alive then she would've done it a long time ago, especially now that she might have another child on the way.

The American Mill No. 2 was the smallest mill in town and the only one to employ blacks and whites in the same jobs, albeit in separate areas of the mill. The Goldberg brothers had fled Latvia in 1915 after the German invasion, and they'd slowly made their way south from New York before settling in Bessemer City, where they'd purchased one small mill and then another before buying a Main Street home large enough to house both brothers' wives and children. In the years that followed, the brothers busied themselves with the twin pursuits of spinning cotton and weaving themselves into the fabric of the white, Protestant populace that owned and operated the mills in Bessemer City.

But no matter how long the brothers and their families lived in town, they never forgot the first night in their new home, when sometime before dawn they awoke to the orange glow of the six-foot-tall wooden cross afire in their front yard. They also never forgot the next morning's visit from the Christian Ladies' Association, a group largely composed of the wives of local ministers. The women appeared unannounced that Saturday morning, cakes and flowers and casseroles in hand. They walked single file up the walk, past the blackened grass and the charred, smoking remains of the cross their husbands had left behind. The women did not glance at the wreckage, nor did they glance at the oldest Goldberg brother, whose sweat-soaked, soot-covered clothes did little to hide his hulking frame where he stood in the yard, axe in hand, the cross's still smoking cinders gathered about his feet.

The message to the Goldberg brothers was clear: they would be considered white but not American, and because they were white but not American, the town had a different set of expectations for the brothers and the way they would run their mills. They expected the Goldbergs to buy the low-quality cotton passed over by the other mills, which they did, and they expected the Goldbergs to lack a certain allegiance to the codes of the South's race-based society, and this was true of the Goldbergs as well. But the people of Bessemer City also expected the Goldbergs not to treat their workers any better than any other mill treated theirs; not to pay them a better wage, perhaps even a lower wage as workers at No. 2 were relegated to work near blacks. The brothers owned American Mill No. 1 as well, and although it was all-white, the conditions there weren't much better than where Ella and Violet worked. Both mills were small, poorly lit, stuffy, and cramped, the lint-choked air enclosed by low ceilings and dirty floors. Machines rattled and whirred in a deafening hum around the clock, stopping only for maintenance or repairs, when some small-handed woman or child would be brought in to stand on a box or a ladder and close his or her eyes before reaching deep into the gears in order to investigate what had gone wrong. They were expected to be quick about it, and they always tried to move fast, for no other reason than the fear of losing an arm or a hand or a finger or three.

Ella kept her eyes closed, her head leaning against the office wall, and she hummed the tune that had been stuck in her mind since she'd held Rose in her arms the night before. "Little Mary Phagan" was a true song about a young girl who'd been murdered by her boss at a pencil factory in Atlanta, and something about the melody had stayed locked inside Ella's head. She didn't think for a minute that Goldberg's brother or Dobbins or anybody else at American would ever murder her, but she knew for certain that working there might kill her just the same.

Ella had been singing the song for years, and last night, after she tired of the original words she began to create her own. "She left home at eleven, when she kissed her mother goodbye" became "We leave our homes in the morning, we kiss our children goodbye." Afraid that Goldberg's brother's secretary would take notice, Ella hummed the next line as quietly as she could: "Not one time did the poor child think she was going to die."

She slid her right hand into her pocket and fingered the union leaflet that she'd kept hidden there for the past month. She took it out and unfolded it on the bench beside her, then removed a stub of pencil from behind her ear and turned the paper to its blank side, where she'd written a few new lines that had come to her mind. She hummed the old line again, felt its rhythm, let its syllables roll over tongue. She wrote, "While we slave for the bosses our children scream and cry." She looked at the line she'd just written, thought about Rose at home right now, the good chance that her cough had gotten worse, the horrifying possibility that she was wheezing and gasping for air, Lilly pounding on her back and Otis tearing up the road to Violet's mother's house for help. She pushed the thought from her mind. She inhaled, fought the urge to cough, and turned the leaflet over and—for what was surely the hundredth time—read the words that were printed on the other side.

The Gastonia Local of the National Textile Workers Union

Invites All Workers to Join the Struggle for Equality.

We Demand:

An End to Piecework and the Hank Clock—A Standard Wage—A 40 Hour/5 Day Workweek—$20 Weekly Minimum Wage—Equal Pay for Equal Work—An End to the Stretch-Out—Sanitary Housing—Reduced Rent—Recognition of the Union

Seven miles east in Gastonia, the seat of Gaston County, the day shift at the Loray Mill had voted to strike on April 1. That evening, hundreds of workers had marched to the gates of the largest and most important textile mill in the state and kept the night shift from going inside. By the next morning Ella had heard that West Gastonia, especially the Loray village, had transformed into a carnival overnight. Children played in the street. Women cooked food on their porches. Men strummed guitars and blew on harmonicas. They drank whiskey and slung rifles across their backs.

Two days later the governor called in the National Guard. Women were beaten. Soldiers pressed guns to men's heads. The strikers' first headquarters had been destroyed by a nighttime mob. The union commissary attacked, the food stores ruined.

The first leaflets had begun trickling through the mill in early April, carried by whispers and subtle passes from hand to hand. Ella had held on to the first one she'd seen, had kept it with her ever since. Another leaflet had come through American just a few days ago. Union members were being forcibly removed from the Loray village on Monday, May 6, just two days away. All workers in the surrounding area were invited to a rally on Sunday evening. The union would even pick you up, take you there.

Ella looked again at the list of union demands. She had a decision to make.

Goldberg's brother's voice spoke from behind the door, and Ella wondered if, godlike, he'd been able to sense that her mind had just wandered from her job at American to the strike at Loray. She folded the leaflet and slipped it into her pocket, slid the pencil back behind her ear.

"Janet," Goldberg's brother said. The young secretary closed her book when she heard her name. She set it down on her tidy desk and stood and smoothed her dress. She opened the office door and stepped inside. Ella could hear their whispered voices. She closed her eyes again, uncrossed her ankles.

"Mrs. Wiggins," the secretary said, "Mr. Goldberg's ready for you."

Ella stood and approached the door. The secretary squeezed past her, stepped back behind her desk, and gathered her book and the purse that she'd hung on the back of her chair. Ella could see Goldberg's brother at the desk in his office, pen in hand, writing something in a thick ledger. He finished writing, capped his pen, closed the ledger, and looked up at her.

"Come in," he said, his voice clear but quiet, his foreign accent almost unnoticeable. He straightened his glasses, pushed them up on the bridge of his nose. He did not stand, but Ella already knew that his body was thin and angular. Although he was past middle age, his face appeared youthful despite a well-trimmed beard and dark hair that glinted with oil in the soft, yellow light. He wore a bow tie and suspenders, his brown suit jacket left folded across the back of the chair in which he sat. He seemed like he should be standing in front of a classroom instead of sitting in a tiny office on the trembling floors of a cotton mill.

For the first time in years, Ella pictured the dark, one-room schoolhouse back in Sevierville, Tennessee, heard the voice of her mother as she begged her father to let Ella and her older brother Wesley go to school for a few days in September before her father needed them on the farm full-time. Ella was six years old and had never had a moment of schooling. Neither had Wesley, who was almost fifteen.

The schoolmaster's name had been Mr. Musial, and when he introduced himself Ella had misheard him, and although she never spoke his name she always thought of it as *Musical*. Mr. Musical had been short and thin and well dressed like Goldberg's brother, but unlike Goldberg's brother, Mr. Musical had a violent limp that wrenched his face into a grimace when he walked. Ella and Wesley had heard that he'd served in the Civil War, and she'd imagined that he'd been a hero and had suffered his injury in battle, but in reality an angry horse had taken a bite from his thigh and gangrene had set in; he'd lost the leg just above the knee and had never even shot the rifle he'd never learned to load. The schoolchildren did not know, no one in the small community actually knew, but Mr. Musical's leg was made of wood from the hip down, his knee joint nothing but a shiny metal socket that swung wildly no matter how slowly he walked or how much he struggled to control his gait.

A chair sat in front of Goldberg's brother's desk, but he did not ask Ella to sit down so she did not sit. He pushed himself back from his desk and put his hands in his lap. His thin lips formed a straight line.

"I'm glad you joined us for your shift this evening," he said.

"Yes, sir," Ella said. She did not look at him when she spoke, choosing instead to focus on the other things on his desk aside from the ledger and ink pen: a small wooden globe with etchings too faded to read; an empty mug; a half-eaten sandwich of some kind; a shiny red apple.

"I say that because you missed last night's shift."

"Yes, sir," she said again.

"Mrs. Wiggins," he said.

"It's May." Her eyes darted to his for a moment, returned to rest on the half-eaten sandwich.

"What?"

"It's May. Ella May."

"I've got Wiggins written down here."

"It's May," she said again. "I told Dobbins to change it, but I guess he didn't."

"Why have you been missing your shifts, Mrs. May?"

"Shift," Ella said. "I just missed the one last night."

"No," Goldberg's brother said. He leaned toward his desk, picked up a clipboard, flipped through a sheath of papers. "No, you missed one in January and one in March."

"It's been a long time since March," Ella said. "Even longer since January."

"That's not the point," he said. "Why are you missing shifts?"

"I got a sick little girl at home. She gets bad at night, and I had to stay home," she said. "I asked Dobbins to put me on day shift, but he won't do it. Maybe I should've asked you."

"Dobbins handles shift change requests," he said.

"Well, he didn't handle mine," Ella said. "And now he told me to come down here, and that's just going to set me back even more."

Goldberg's brother leaned back in his chair, placed his hands in his lap again. Ella stared at the sandwich, tried to judge what kind of meat rested between the slices of bread.

"You have a sick little girl," he said.

"Yes, sir."

"Please look at me, Mrs. May. I can't tell whether or not you're being truthful unless you look at me."

She lifted her eyes to his, saw that he stared at her intently, saw that her missed shift must mean a great deal to him, but she knew it meant even more to her, because she would not be paid. "Why wouldn't I be truthful?"

"I don't know, Mrs. May. People often don't tell the truth when they lay out of work. Sick means drunk. Sick means gambling. Sick means lazy. I don't know what a sick little girl means."

She felt blood rush to her face, knew that her cheeks were flush with color. Her guilt, or whatever it was she had just felt, faded. She imagined throwing herself across the desk, reaching for his neck, his eyes. "*Sick* means my little girl's sick," she said. "That's what it means."

He stared at her for a moment, then lifted a wastebasket from beneath his desk and swept the sandwich and apple into it. He returned the wastebasket to the floor.

"What if all my employees had sick children, Mrs. May? What about me? What if I had a sick child at home and decided that I couldn't come to work? Who'd run this mill?"

Ella had never seen Goldberg's brother's family, knew nothing about them aside from their existence and the existence of the older brother. She had never been inside the Goldberg's large brick home and she had never met anyone who'd been inside it either. She envisioned electric lights and running water and warm blankets and bedsheets and a pantry full of food and a cooler full of ice, a pair of soft, warm slippers tucked beneath a neatly made bed. A baby might cry out somewhere upstairs, and a nurse or a maid or a young cousin would ascend a grand, curved staircase and open a nursery door and whisper something kind and reassuring to the child inside.

"Yes, sir," Ella said.

"Who'd run this mill?" Goldberg's brother asked again.

"Nobody."

"That's correct: nobody. And you know who runs your spinners when you decide to lay out on a shift? Nobody." He leaned forward again. "But I can assure you of this, Mrs. Wiggins: it'll be much easier to find someone to operate your spinners than it will be to find someone to run this mill. I expect you'll keep that in mind next time you find yourself with the desire to stay home."

ELLA THOUGHT THAT no one should ever have to look upon a sad place like Stumptown, but she knew that if someone were ever forced to look upon it, then the quiet, silvery moments before dawn would be the best time to do it. That's what she thought of now as she and Violet stumbled down the muddy road that branched off the Kings Mountain Highway and rolled toward the settlement like an artery forgotten by its heart. The sky directly above them was dark, the sky behind them pink with the stirrings of dawn. There were no shadows yet because there was not enough light to cast them. The tarpaper shacks that huddled close to the road with their crooked porches and lopsided doors and low, tin roofs were nothing but dark forms looming beneath cottonwoods and willow trees. The scrubby patches of garden could not be seen at this early hour in this weak almost-light, nor could the clumps of geraniums that lined the walks that led toward porch steps or the clotheslines strung across the porches themselves. At this hour, at this time of morning, Stumptown could be anything one could imagine it to be.

Ella heard the tinny scratch of "Carolina Moon" floating from the phonograph inside Fox Denton's house on the other side of a dark stand of trees. She hummed along.

"You going to stop in, say hello to Fox?" Violet asked. Ella smiled, quit her humming. "Ain't you interested in making a friend?"

"I got enough friends," Ella said. "Too many, maybe."

Fox Denton, an old man who lived alone, was the only white resident of Stumptown aside from Ella and her four children. He worked as a machinist at Margrace Mill in Kings Mountain and never said a word to anyone, white or colored, but that didn't keep Violet from teasing Ella every time they passed his house, which they did twelve times a week on their two-mile walk to and from the night shift at American Mill No. 2.

"Just seems like you'd want to meet him after all this time," Violet said.

"I got enough friends," Ella said again.

"Ain't none of them white."

"All of them poor though," Ella said. "We got that in common."

"That's true," Violet said.

They kept walking. The birds began to move through the trees on either side of the lane. Fox Denton's music came from behind them now. Ella cocked her ear to listen, found that she could no longer hear the song although she still felt it. She closed her eyes, opened them slowly, sang:

> Carolina moon keep shining,
> Shining on the one who waits for me.
> Carolina moon I'm pining,
> Pining for the place I long to be.

She stopped singing. The women kept walking. Neither of them spoke.

"Ain't nobody waiting for me," Violet finally said. "Nobody but the bill collector."

"I know that's right," Ella said.

"You write any new songs?" Violet asked.

"I been working on one."

"What's it about?"

Ella smiled, said, "It's about this shit life we're living."

Violet laughed. "Sounds pretty," she said. Then she said, "You could make a few dollars."

"Come on."

"I'm serious," she said. "I've told you, you can sing, girl. You know they got people over in Charlotte that'll pay twenty dollars for a hillbilly record."

"I ain't no hillbilly," Ella said. "Not no more."

"Millbilly then," Violet said. "Call yourself whatever you want. Just get over there and get yourself paid."

"We'll see," Ella said.

They stopped in front of the cabin where Violet lived with her mother and her younger sister Iva.

"Wait here," Violet said. "I'll be right back."

"You think it'll help her?"

"I wouldn't give it to you if I didn't," Violet said. "And you better hope something helps. You can't miss no more work."

"I can't lose another baby either," Ella said. "I asked Dobbins to put me on days so I could take care of Rose at night, but he won't do it. I told Goldberg's brother too. Something's got to change."

"I'll be right back," Violet said. "I got to be quiet. They're still asleep."

Ella watched Violet walk up the porch steps and disappear inside the tiny cabin. A weak light came from inside.

Violet was twenty-five, unmarried, and without children. Her sister Iva was twelve years old and as close to a daughter as Violet would have unless she had one of her own, but Ella knew that a sister was no substitute for a being who was born of your own body. Violet was Ella's best friend, but that didn't mean Violet could understand what it was to lose a child and then fear that you might lose another.

Ella waited for Violet to return, and while she waited she thought about death: her children's, her own. She assumed and assumed correctly that she had more life behind her than she had ahead, and when she tossed that thought around in her mind she saw the faces of her four living children and imagined their world without her in it. So far, only one child, two-year-old Willie, had died and slipped from her life forever, and it was hard for her to imagine that one day her children would think of the final act of slipping away from life when they thought of her.

Ella and John had buried Willie ten miles east, in Ranlo, because they'd been living there and working at the Rex Spinning Company when he died. They'd buried him in the municipal cemetery because they had not belonged to a church and no church had offered a piece of earth in which to place the tiny pine coffin.

It had been five years since Willie's death, but Ella still traveled to the cemetery at least once a month on her Sundays off. She and John had not been able to afford a tombstone, so John had chiseled the letter W on a field rock and placed it at the head of the grave. Ella had maintained it since, sweeping it clean, dressing it with what she could find, what she could afford.

That fall she had set aside what little money she could in the hopes of buying one of the felt poinsettias she'd seen in the window at Falls Hardware in downtown Bessemer City. She finally purchased one before her shift on a Saturday afternoon, three days before Christmas. The next morning she walked and hitched to Ranlo with the felt flower wrapped in tissue paper and a shiny new baseball in her coat pocket. Willie had died too young for Ella to know for certain whether he loved baseball, but his older brother Otis loved it more than anything on earth, so Ella figured that Willie would've loved it too. She'd done everything she could to keep Otis from finding the baseball after she'd bought it, went so far as to wrap it in oilcloth and hide it up under the cabin's eaves, where she prayed it wouldn't get wet or loose itself and fall to the ground.

The Sunday she'd visited the cemetery had been unseasonably warm, and she'd removed John's old jacket and left it on a bench while she picked weeds and used her hands to sweep the field rock. After that she spent close to an hour arranging and rearranging the poinsettia and the baseball on a cleared patch of dirt in front of the rock. She'd brought along a small glass jar to house the flower, but the jar just seemed to swallow it instead, and so she decided to curl the poinsettia's metal stem around the baseball to keep it from rolling away, the felt flower peeking out above the white leather like a red burst of sun.

The weather had changed by the time she returned to the cemetery a few weeks later in January. The sky had spit snow all night long but had stopped near dawn, and only an inch or so remained when Ella arrived in Ranlo. Her footprints were the first set of tracks in the cemetery, and she looked forward to seeing the red flare of felt against the snow-covered ground. But when she arrived at Willie's graveside she found that the poinsettia and the baseball were gone. She stood there for a moment, staring down at the hump on the ground where the field rock lay covered in snow. She looked around at the other graves, searching each one for a flash of red, for a glimmer of the baseball's bright white leather. She turned and saw the tracks she'd left on her way in, retraced them in her mind, came to terms with the fact that the snow had not caused her to lose her way. Although Ella knew that it was Willie's grave that she stood before, that did not stop her from kneeling and brushing the snow away and using her finger to trace the chiseled *W* in the cold stone. She ran her hands through the snowy grass, hoping to find what she knew for certain was not there.

She stood, turned around, walked beside the footprints she'd just made. The caretaker's tiny shack sat by the cemetery's entrance, a thin wisp of smoke slipping from its chimney. She knocked on the door and waited, listened for a moment, knocked again. Inside there was the crash of something metal falling to the floor. The sound was followed by mumbled words of frustration that Ella wasn't able to discern.

The door swung open, revealed an old man in spectacles and long underwear. He squinted into the sunlight and buttoned a denim coat over his chest, did his best to part his thin, white hair with his long, crooked fingers.

"Yes, ma'am?" he said.

Ella looked at the old man, and then she turned and looked back in the direction of Willie's grave, hoping again that she had made some kind of mistake, that the poinsettia and the baseball hid somewhere out there in the snow, waiting for her to find them. The man straightened his spectacles, folded his arms across his chest, and tucked his hands under his armpits to keep them warm.

"My son's grave's been robbed," she said.

"Ma'am?" His eyes went wide, the blue pupils smoky with cataract.

"Somebody stole things off his grave," she said. "I need to know what happened to them."

The old man turned his head so that his right ear was closer to Ella. She realized that he could not hear well, and she repeated what she'd just said.

"Oh," he said. "Scared me. I thought you meant his grave was dug up." He smiled as if the fact that such a ghastly violation had not occurred should serve as the end of the matter.

"A felt poinsettia," Ella said. "And a baseball. They've been stolen."

"I clear all the graves after the New Year, ma'am," he said. "Always have." He sniffed, scratched at the side of his nose.

"But they cost me a lot of money," Ella said.

"I'm sorry, ma'am," he said. "That's the rules."

"Nobody told me the rules."

"Well, I'm sorry, but that's the rules."

"What did you do with them?"

"The rules?"

"No," Ella said. "My son's things. What did you do with them?"

"I probably threw them away, ma'am."

She knew he was lying, knew that he'd probably sold them for much less money than it had taken her months to save. Something broke loose inside Ella's chest, and she fought the urge to cry out. When she turned and looked back over the graves it seemed as if the world had turned with her, and she feared that she might collapse from the dizziness of it.

"Everything?" she asked. "You just throw everything away."

The old man sighed and peered into the shack behind him. "You can come back here and look," he said. "See if you can find what you're looking for. I doubt it's here, but you can look."

As soon as Ella stepped through the door of the tiny shack, she knew that the old man had long been a tenant of the tiny shack and would no doubt die inside its walls. It was heated to stifling and reeked of sweat, urine, and some kind of liniment. A metal cot sat in front of a sooty stove, where a fire licked at the grate. Rotting books and newspapers and circulars were stacked waist-high against the walls. Ella followed the old man past the stove into a tiny storeroom full of tools and equipment. Wooden shelves hemmed them in on either side and housed all manner of things: crucifixes, dolls, placards, faded artificial flowers. Ella was hardly inside the storeroom when she knew for certain that Willie's poinsettia and baseball were not among these things, but she looked anyway, took her time and pored over each article as if it might morph into a thing she recognized.

She finally selected a red, water-damaged paper carnation that looked nothing like the felt poinsettia that had cost her a day's pay, but still she closed her hand around it and slipped it into the side pocket of John's old coat. The man's eyes followed her as if he knew that the flower she'd taken was not the one she'd described, but neither of them said a word by way of explanation or conjecture.

Ella left the storeroom, was halfway across the old man's living quarters when she heard him call to her. She turned and saw that he was on his knees, his hands feeling around for something tucked into the filth beneath his cot. She watched him until she found what he'd been looking for. He stood and held something out to her: an old baseball, oil-stained and swollen, riddled with what appeared to be teeth marks from a dog.

"I imagine it ain't as nice as the one you're looking for, but it's yours if you want it," the old man said. "I'm awful sorry."

Ella nodded, took the baseball, surprised by how heavy and large it felt in her hand after the memory of the fresh, unused ball she'd purchased for Willie.

Once she was outside she did not look back toward Willie's grave. She went left instead and followed the path out of the cemetery's gates. There were no cars on the road, everyone either at church or at home because of the snow. Ella had walked only a mile when she found herself standing beneath the snow-dusted boughs of a pine tree, her chest heaving in sobs. She held her hands over her eyes, caught the reek of the old man's shack where it had infused itself into the baseball he'd just given her. She sniffed, wiped at her nose, blinked warm tears from her eyes.

She hadn't told her children about the poinsettia or the new baseball, and she decided that she'd give the old man's ball to Otis as soon as she arrived home. It was as nice or nicer than any baseball Otis had ever owned, and she found herself thinking, Something, something will come of this. It was not the waste that it now seems. But even as her mind said this, she found herself pulling back her arm and pausing for just a moment before throwing the baseball as far into the woods as she could. She removed the paper carnation from her pocket, tore it apart in her hands, the paper disintegrating like a dead leaf. She opened her palms and watched the tiny scraps of red paper fall onto the snow. She didn't want charity or kindness or relief or pity. All she wanted was what she'd worked for.

She stared down at what was left of the carnation, her body registering the anger and humiliation and pain as they left her as slowly as an extinguished fire leaves a room so it may be reclaimed by the cold. Her breathing slowed, lifted like steam in the frigid air.

This is fitting, she'd thought. This is what happens. The cemetery is where you leave things behind. You aren't supposed to go home with anyone in your arms or anything in your pockets.

THE LIGHT INSIDE Violet's cabin winked off, and Violet opened the door and stepped out onto the porch. The morning had brightened in the short time Ella had been waiting, and she could see Violet clearly as she walked toward her across the neatly kept yard, the dirt walk swept smooth and clean, the clumps of flowers that lined it damp with dew and glimmering against the morning. Violet's body seemed to hum in the soft light. She held a Mason jar in each hand. She stopped where the grassy yard turned to muddy gravel and offered Ella one of the jars.

"This one's honey," she said. She offered the other. "And this one's whiskey and a little something else."

"What else?" Ella asked.

Violet smiled. "An old Stumptown secret."

"Mother used to give my brother and me ginger and moonshine," Ella said. "Horehound candy if she could find it."

"Well, you ain't no hillbilly no more, remember?"

"Yes," Ella said. She smiled. "I remember."

"You still thinking about going to that rally in Gastonia today?" Violet asked.

"Only if Rose is better when I get home," Ella said. "I can't leave her here sick on my only day off."

"I can look after them," Violet said.

"I was hoping you'd go with me," Ella said. "Could use the company."

"Girl, you trying to get me killed? Ain't no way that many white folks going to welcome a colored girl from Stumptown."

Ella considered removing the crumpled union leaflet from her pocket and holding it before Violet's eyes, jabbing her finger at its demand of "Equal Work for Equal Pay." Instead, she said, "I heard the union says white and colored are the same."

Violet snorted. "So? So what? Saying it and meaning it are different things."

"It's still *something* to say it," Ella said. "No white folks around here say it but me."

"What's Dobbins going to think about you missing last night's shift and *then* joining the union?"

"I didn't have no choice about missing that shift," Ella said. "I might not have a choice about the union either."

"What's Charlie going to think?"

"You know Charlie," Ella said.

"Everybody knows a man like Charlie," Violet said. She shook her head, gestured toward Ella's belly. "You ain't told him yet, have you?"

Although she held the Mason jars, Ella's hands instinctively moved toward her flat stomach. The whiskey splashed inside the glass. "No," she said, "I ain't told him. I don't know for sure yet."

"You're pregnant, girl," Violet said. "Any fool can look at you and tell that, but I guess Charlie ain't just any kind of fool. He's a special kind."

"I'll tell him when the time's right." She turned away from Violet, stepped onto the road.

Violet called after her. "Better tell him soon. Time ain't never right for a man like Charlie."

Ella walked on. The sky lightened above her while the air around her cooled. She descended the road toward the end of the lane where her cabin sat. Sleep clung to her bones like a heavy coat that pulled her toward the earth. Behind the cabin, willow trees hid a spring-fed pond, and Ella could always feel and smell the water before taking the last bend in the road and seeing the clapboard shack where she and her children lived. She took the steps as quietly as she could and opened the cabin's door, stepped over the pallets where her children lay sleeping in the front room.

Ella bent at the knees, lowered herself to the floor. She covered Rose's foot, tucked the blanket around it. Outside, birds stirred in the trees as morning broke over Stumptown. The only sound inside the cabin was Rose's raspy, labored breathing. Ella brushed the girl's hair from her forehead, gently placed her hand over it. The fever had passed. Ella closed her eyes, allowed herself a quiet sigh.

When she opened her eyes she saw that Lilly had been watching her. Ella smiled. Lilly smiled back.

"Hey," Ella whispered.

"Hey," Lilly whispered back.

"How was she last night?"

"She coughed a lot, but she didn't have no fever."

"Not now either," Ella said.

"Good."

"Did you sleep?"

Lilly nodded her head. Yawned.

"Good," Ella said. "See if you can sleep a little longer." She reached into her pocket and showed Lilly the jars of honey and whiskey. "Got this from Violet. She says it'll fix a cough. I'll mix it up and leave it by the stove. Give it to her when she wakes up: just two spoonfuls. She ain't going to like it, but make sure she takes it. There'll be something for you to eat too."

Lilly nodded her head again, watched Ella as she got to her feet.

Ella stared down at her daughter for a moment, saw her ex-husband's thin nose and light blond hair. The girl was beautiful, sweet, in spite of looking like John.

"See if you can sleep a little longer," Ella said again.

Ella made a fire and fried a piece of fatback. It would cool in time for Lilly to wake and feed the children. She looked to find four day-old biscuits waiting in the cold oven. She mixed a little of the whiskey into the honey, left it on the stove. She put the jar of whiskey back into her pocket.

In the back room Ella closed the door and latched it behind her. The room was dark, this half of the cabin shrouded in the shadows of the trees that hung above it, but there was light enough to see the outline of a body beneath the thin blanket atop the skid. The window by her bed was open, and she could hear the spring babbling in the woods.

"I know you ain't sleeping," she said. She kicked off her shoes and stepped barefoot onto the cool floor. She slipped her dress over her head. "I know you been out there somewhere all night, barely beat me here."

Charlie sat up in bed and looked at her.

"I run on winged feet," he whispered. "Like Cupid."

"Cupid's got wings on his back."

"I got two sets, girl," he said. "That's how come I'm so fast."

"I need to start locking my window," she said.

"I'd just come down that chimney like Santy Claus."

She stifled a laugh, covered her mouth so she wouldn't wake the children.

"You'd better bring presents if you come down that chimney," she said.

"I will," Charlie said.

"I don't got a chimney."

"Then you'd better leave this window unlocked."

THE FIRST TIME Ella had ever laid eyes on Charlie Shope was back in February when he'd catcalled her from the back of a Model T flatbed as it rumbled past on the Kings Mountain Highway. She and Violet had been crossing the field that separated Stumptown from Bessemer City on their way to work the night shift. The weather was cold and damp. The sky was white. The man's legs were covered over with a blanket. His feet dangled off the back of the truck. A battered suitcase sat beside him. An old guitar rested on his lap. Ella and Violet watched him get smaller and smaller as the distance between them and the truck grew. He tipped his hat and blew a kiss, and then he was gone.

They walked in silence for a moment.

"What in the hell was that?" Ella had finally said.

"That was a white man in a truck," Violet said.

"I know that," Ella said. "Who's he think he's whistling at?"

"You, white girl." Violet forced out a laugh. "You think he was hollering at me? Shoot."

Violet had stopped walking, had stared at Ella. Then she looked behind her in the direction of Stumptown. A few roofs were visible on the far side of the hill. She looked toward the forest on their right, the leafless trees wispy in the distance. Then she turned her eyes to the road where the truck had just passed. The air was cold. It smelled of wood smoke. Their noses ran.

"What in the world else was he whistling at?" Violet asked. She took a handkerchief from her pocket, blew into it.

"I don't care," Ella said. "I just mind my own business."

Violet smiled, put the handkerchief back inside her pocket.

"Come on, girl," she'd said. "We're going to be late. Neither one of us can afford that. This world ain't going to pay you in whistles."

The second time Ella saw Charlie Shope was the very next night, in the spinning room at the mill. He sidled up to her where she stood on the line, took off his hat, and held it over his heart. He was small, not much taller than her.

"I seen you yesterday," he said, his voice barely reaching her over the noise of the machines. "Crossing the field with that colored girl."

Ella acted like she didn't hear him. She kept her eyes on the strands as they coiled around the bobbins. He leaned toward her, cupped a hand around his mouth.

"I seen you yesterday!" he hollered. Ella looked up as if she'd just realized that someone had spoken to her.

"Yeah?" she said. "You saw me? Good for you."

"Yeah," he said. "You seen me?"

Ella looked at his sweaty brown hair, his ruddy face, the gap between his front teeth when he smiled.

"Where do you work?" she asked.

He stood up as straight as he could. "Down in the carding room for now."

She shook her head, allowed her face to register a smile. The doffer boy came through, and she and Charlie both stepped back as he lifted the full bobbins from the spinners and replaced them with empty spindles. Ella moved quickly behind him, fixing the strands to the bobbins. Charlie followed her.

"I'm just in the carding room for now," he said.

"What's 'for now'?" she asked.

"The carding room," he said. "I'll be weaving here soon, and I make most of my money with my guitar anyway."

"Okay," she said.

He stopped following behind her, asked, "Did you see me out there on the road yesterday or not?"

"If I seen you I don't remember it," she said. "And if I remember you I done forgot you already."

"That's okay," he said. "We got all the time in the world to get acquainted. I'm going to marry you."

Ella laughed and looked over at him again, noted the greasy cowlick he'd smeared down on his forehead.

"I already had me one husband," she said. "Took me ten years to run him off. I ain't got that kind of time anymore."

"All right, honey," he said.

She fought another smile.

"Heard Dobbins is heading this way," she said. "You better go on. You don't want to get fired your first night in the carding room, especially when you ain't even in the carding room."

"Hell," he said, "it'd be worth it if you keep talking. What's your name?"

"Busy," she said.

"Okay, Busy," he said. "I'm Charlie. Charlie Shope. But here soon you'll just be calling me sweetheart."

The third time she'd laid eyes on him was five nights later, when his face appeared on the other side of a row of spinners.

"When do you go on break?" he'd hollered.

"No time soon," Ella said. She moved down, kept her eyes on her work. He followed her on the other side.

"I'm serious," Charlie said. "When?"

Ella stopped working, looked up at him. He smiled. "I get fifteen minutes at ten P.M.," she said. She went back to her work.

"Perfect," Charlie said. "You know Mose?" he'd asked. "The old colored man down in the opening room?"

"I seen him before," Ella said.

"I spent all week saving up a quarter dollar for him to go outside for a smoke and a nip with the boys."

Ella laughed, said, "Takes a disciplined man to save that much money."

"You can tease," he said, "but at ten P.M. the clock'll start ticking on that quarter."

A few minutes after 10 P.M. she found him in a dark corner of the opening room, hunkered down between huge mounds of raw cotton. He stood when he saw her, and then he smiled and let his body fall backward and disappear into the white fluff.

"You've never experienced such comfort," he said. Ella could barely see him in the near dark. Just a shadowed space with eyes and teeth sunk into all that whiteness. She laughed when he coughed, picked a stem from his mouth, flicked it toward the floor. He reached up for her and she took his hand, allowed herself to be pulled toward him, allowed him to kiss her, to run his hands up and down her back, through her hair, but she laughed and pushed his fingers away each time they fondled the buttons on her dress.

Afterward he climbed out of the cotton and lit a cigarette. He drew on it and then held it out to her. She stood and dusted the cotton from her dress and smoothed back her hair, pinned it into a bob at the nape of her neck.

"You ain't supposed to smoke in here," Ella said.

Charlie laughed, took another drag. "You ain't supposed to kiss on strangers in here either."

"I suspected you for a rule breaker first time I seen you," she said.

"See," he said. "I knew you'd seen me."

"I just remember some hobo whistling like a fool from the back of a truck."

He reached out and brushed the cotton lint from her dark hair.

"You're pretty," he said.

"And you're a damn liar."

He laughed. "You're sweet too."

"And you're a damn liar," she'd said again.

ELLA WOKE TO the sounds of her children's feet moving across the floor in the other room. She'd dozed a little after climbing into bed beside Charlie, but her body had not released itself into sleep. She heard Lilly at the stove, heard her hush the children while serving the fatback and biscuits. She heard Rose cough, heard Lilly say, "Take this," followed by Rose's whimper and the sound of the spoon scraping honey from the glass.

She slipped out of the bed and opened the door and stepped into the front room in her bare feet. The children all sat on their pallets eating biscuits and gnawing on the tough strips of fatback. They looked up at her.

"Hey, babies," she said.

Wink cooed and waved both hands at her, a stream of drool spinning from his lip like the beginnings of a spider web. He reached for Otis's shoulder and tried to pull himself up, but he fell and rolled backward onto the quilts. They all laughed. Ella sat down beside Otis and picked up Wink, set him in her lap. She rubbed her nose against his head, felt the soft fuzz of his hair on her lips, looked down at his grasping baby hands. She touched Rose's face, felt the fatback grease on the little girl's lips, used her thumb to wipe it away. Rose leaned away from her.

"How you feeling?" Ella asked.

"Happy," Rose said, which was what she always said unless she felt sad.

"I'm happy that you're happy," Ella said. She touched Rose's face again, and the girl allowed herself to be touched. Ella cupped her cheek.

"When you leaving?" Lilly asked. She used biscuit crumbs and sopped up the little bit of grease on her plate that was left behind by the small piece of fatback she'd allowed herself.

Ella sighed, let her lips brush Wink's hair again. She inhaled, breathed in the scent of his babyness. "Here soon," she said.

"Where you going?" Otis asked.

"Gastonia," Ella said.

"Why?" he asked.

"Different reasons," she said. "Work. Money. Different reasons."

"Can I go?"

"No," she said. "You stay here. Help your sister with these babies."

"No baby," Rose said.

"That's right," Ella said. "You're a big girl." She lifted Wink into the air and bounced him up and down. He laughed. "I've only got one baby left. The rest of y'all are grown."

She helped the children get dressed in the nicest, cleanest clothes they could find. Otis sensed the reason why.

"We going to church?" he asked.

"Violet's going to take you with them," Ella said. "And then you're having lunch at their house. Probably a ham or a chicken. Something better than this old fatback."

"They don't do nothing but sing in that church," Otis said.

"If singing's all I had to do to have myself some ham and chicken I'd consider myself a lucky boy," Ella said.

Lilly picked up Wink. Ella kissed them all, pulled them to her. She watched as they went out the door, and she listened to the sound of their feet going down the steps.

She went back into the other room and sat down on the edge of the bed. She closed her eyes. Exhaustion crept over her body like a fog. Charlie stirred beside her as soon as she lay down. Her back was to him, but she knew he was awake and staring at the back of her head.

"You ain't still thinking about going to that rally today?" he asked, his question more of a statement than a query. His warm breath was in her hair, on the back of her neck.

"Sunday's my day off," she said. "I reckon I can go where I want."

He sighed.

"What do you want with a bunch of communists?" he asked. "Governor already called in the National Guard. Beat up a whole bunch of people. That strike won't get you nothing but killed."

She pictured Rose's tiny feet and skinny ankles sticking out from beneath the blanket that morning. She thought of how Wink had cried when her milk dried up when he was just three months old. She thought of the biscuit crumbs sitting in the empty pan atop the stove, the fatback's grease the only thing left behind in the skillet, the apple and half sandwich Goldberg's brother had thrown away before her eyes. Her nine-dollar pay wasn't coming until Friday, and most of it already gone to rent and store credit.

"Well, I reckon me and these babies are going to die if we keep living this way," she said. "So what's it matter?"

"It matters to me," he said.

She kicked off the sheet, sat on the side of the bed, turned toward him. "What should I do, Charlie? Wait on you to bring it home? You can't even keep a damn job."

"You know millwork ain't my thing."

She laughed, looked toward the window, put her elbows on her knees and her face in her hands. "It ain't my thing either, Charlie. If you got something else in mind for me to do, then tell me, and I'll do it. Otherwise, this union's my last chance."

"I don't want a girl of mine out there running around with a bunch of Yankee reds."

"Well, I ain't yours," she said. She looked up, folded her arms across her knees. "And this ain't your bed or your house neither. If you think any different I reckon it's time you move on."

She heard his hand slip from beneath the sheet. Instead of closing her eyes, she stared at the wall where the light moved across it. She was prepared for a slap or a punch, so it was only the surprise of his hand reaching around her to caress her belly that made her flinch.

"Come on," he said, "you're my girl."

Ella wasn't afraid of him any more than he was afraid of her. They'd gone at it before. He'd hit her. She'd hit him. Two weeks ago he'd shown up drunk in the middle of the night, looking for her ex-husband, a man she hadn't seen in over a year. Charlie had pulled a knife on her when she'd come outside, and she'd chased him off into the woods. Charlie was the kind of man to which nothing good could happen. He was a rough sort. She knew that she was a rough sort too, but she worked hard and took care of her children, and she deserved some measure of softness, a moment of kindness, to be touched softly and kindly every now and then: Charlie Shope was the only measure of those things that she could find. They were both nearing thirty, both mired down in the kind of poverty they'd never see the end of. She'd been married before—she reckoned she still was—and she had four children she'd managed to keep alive.

Charlie's finger traced a circle around her navel as if branding her, and she thought of the tiny life taking root on the other side of his touch.

"You're my girl," he said again.

"I'm nobody's," she said.

"Come on," he said, "sing me a song."

"I'd rather you just get the hell out of my house," she said, but even as she said it she knew it wasn't much of a house: more like a two-room shack with a cookstove over in one corner of the crowded front room. In the chilly back room there was nothing but a low skid and a window always left unlocked unless she was mad. No, it wasn't much of a house, but it was hers as long as she could make rent. That was something to be proud of.

"Did you know the communists think whites and coloreds are the same?" he asked.

"I know we're all poor, if that counts for anything," she said. She stood from the bed, curled her toes into fists. "And I work with coloreds, and you used to. And you go to them for liquor and who knows what else."

"It ain't the same," he said. "It ain't the same as believing it."

"Well, I got to believe in something," she said. "Might as well believe in the union."

"Union ain't going to save you," he said. "There ain't no kind of life in these mills." He leaned on his elbow and propped his chin on his fist. He watched her dress. "Music's how I'm going to make my name."

She smiled, laughed just so he'd hear it.

"Keep on," he said. "You'll see. You won't catch me running around with communists. And you won't catch me making the rich man richer by working in his mill."

"If we could all just make the big bucks strumming an old guitar like you, Charlie, we'd close the mills down, wouldn't we?"

"Keep on," he said again, "but I'm telling you, your voice and my music, we could make a damn sight of money. Leave this old place, go to Nashville."

"I ain't going to Tennessee," she said. "I ain't crossing those mountains again."

"St. Louis then," he said. "Hell, anywhere but Bessemer City, North Carolina."

She pulled her dress over her head and stepped into her shoes and cinched the buckles. He watched her until she picked up his overalls from the floor and tossed them at him where he lay. He dodged her throw, and his overalls sailed over his head and fell to the floor on the other side of the bed. He pointed to his guitar where it rested against the wall in the corner of the room.

"Let's play something," he said.

She picked up the guitar by its neck and raised the window. Charlie watched her from the bed. She leaned out the window and lowered the guitar until she felt it touch the earth. She dropped it with a hollow thud.

"That's just being ugly," he said. "Ain't no reason to be ugly."

A FEW HOURS later, Ella stood alone at the crossroads of West Virginia Avenue on the edge of downtown Bessemer City. The sun shone directly overhead. There were no clouds. The American Mill sat just one block over, and she couldn't help but wonder what Goldberg's brother would think if he happened to drive by and see her standing in the sun on the side of the road waiting for a group of strikers to take her to Gastonia. She doubted that he'd even recognize her, although he'd just seen her the day before. On the other hand, Dobbins would know her for sure. She'd be fired for even thinking of attending a union meeting.

She stepped away from the road and stood in the shaded, high grass beneath the trees. It was spring, and it felt like spring. The limbs above her were thick with bright green leaves. Ribbons of wisteria twined through the branches, the heavy fragrance mingling with the damp, musky scent of the wet earth. Across the street, clumps of azaleas lined the road into downtown, the pink and purple flowers already beginning to wilt. The sight of the withering blooms and the scents of wisteria and mud laid a delicate finger upon Ella's memory. Something stirred inside her as if attempting to fire a childhood recollection, perhaps something she'd promised herself she would never forget. She closed her eyes, breathed deeply, took in the scents, but all she could think of was what might happen next, and she could not uncover the shadow of nostalgia that lurked in the corner of her mind.

Instead, she thought again of Mr. Musical and the week she and her brother Wesley had spent sitting side by side on a weathered wooden bench in the small, hot schoolhouse, the schoolmaster scrawling numbers and figures on a dusty chalkboard. Ella's own life had been a series of additions and subtractions, and she wondered how Mr. Musical would condense it all into some kind of equation that would make sense to her six-year-old self: her childhood minus her father's failure as a tenant farmer equaled the family's move to the smoky lumber camps deep in the Blue Ridge. More minuses: Wesley's leaving for Detroit; the flu that killed her mother, followed so quickly by her father's death from a falling tree. Those minuses equaled her all alone at sixteen standing in the train station in Bryson City, where she somehow added John Wiggins when she was supposed to have added a ticket north to a life with Wesley and his wife like he had promised in his letters.

In her mind, the equation of her life spread across the chalkboard, more minuses than pluses, more losses than gains. Her and John's move from the mountains to the tiny town of Cowpens, South Carolina, and her first job in a textile mill coupled with the plus of

Lilly's birth, another plus almost two years later when Otis arrived just as they had to move again, this time to the scarred, ruddy soil and lint-heavy air of Gaston County, where her losses had racked up so quickly and so painfully in so few years. All this time and all this traveling made Ella feel as if years and years had somehow slipped by without her having the chance to count them or even mark them as they passed. She'd been swept along in a current that she could not control, and all of it had brought her here to Charlie, to the American Mill, to the union leaflet in her pocket, to this new life growing inside her. She thought about what Charlie had said that morning, about how the strike might get her nothing but killed. He might have been right, but she might have been right too. She would die if she carried on this way, and then where would her children be? She'd already lost Willie, and she knew that her unborn baby wouldn't have any better chance than the others had had.

She heard the sound of an automobile and stepped toward the road. An old truck passed. Three colored boys wearing nothing but overalls sat in the back, the oldest one holding a fishing pole. The youngest boy waved. Ella waved back. The other two boys did the same. She watched the truck until it rounded the bend in the road that led toward Stumptown.

If she left now and returned home, she'd catch her children right as the church doors opened. Maybe they'd go down to Violet's house for something to eat. Or maybe Charlie would come over and sit on her porch and strum his guitar and they would sing something together. Lilly and Iva and Rose would trade the stuffed dolls they'd made from old stockings. Otis would disappear into the dark woods and come back an hour later with wet clothes. Wink would sit right there on Ella's lap and take it all in.

She turned to her right and looked down the road that led to Gastonia and the uncertainty of the strike. She could go or not go. Those were her only two choices, but, in that moment, neither of them seemed any good.

That's when she saw it: the specter of the huge black truck belching smoke above the eastern horizon. Once she'd seen it she couldn't look away. She feared it might be a nightmare vision that her sleeping self had sent to her by way of warning.

As it drew closer, Ella saw the faces of two women peer at her from behind the dirty windshield. The truck creaked to a stop at the crossroads, lurched forward, and stopped again. Its engine shook the ground. The driver, a girl who didn't appear a day older than fifteen, opened the door and looked out at Ella where she stood on the side of the road.

"You waiting for a ride?" the girl asked. She had olive skin and dark eyes, thick, wavy, brown hair, and an accent Ella had never heard before. She wondered if the girl came from another country.

"I'm heading to Gastonia," Ella said.

"For the rally?" the girl asked.

Ella nodded. A woman in the passenger's seat leaned across the driver and looked down at Ella. Her pale face was thin and pinched, her hair tucked up under a bell-shaped hat. She could've been thirty or sixty.

"At which mill do you work?" the woman asked. She was from the North.

"American," Ella said.

"Which one?" the northerner asked.

"Number Two."

The two women in the truck looked at one another. The younger one said something to the northerner that Ella couldn't hear, and then she looked down the road in both directions as if hoping more people would materialize. She looked at Ella.

"Where's everybody at?" she asked.

"I don't know," Ella said. "Church, maybe. Home. I don't know."

"You ain't got friends?" the girl asked.

"I got a couple," Ella said.

"You couldn't bring none of them?"

"I tried," Ella said. "None of them were interested."

"You want to join the union?" the woman from the North asked.

"I don't know," Ella said. "I figure on learning something about it first."

"You a capitalist?" the girl asked.

Ella looked down at the clothes she wore: the same white dress she'd worn the day before, one of two she owned that didn't embarrass her; the soles of her dusty black shoes caked in mud; her loose stockings, the hole in the left knee that the women couldn't see. She looked up at the girl.

"No," she said. "I don't have the cash money to be capital about nothing."

The girl smiled. She turned and looked at the passenger.

"There's room in the back," the older woman said.

"We've got a few more stops to make," the girl said. "Pick up a few more interested parties. I just hope they got more friends than you."

Ella walked alongside the truck. High, wooden rails lined its bed. It gave the impression that a dog pen had been set down atop it.

The truck was so tall, it wasn't until Ella reached the open tailgate that she discovered that the truck's bed was empty. She stood there a moment, the smoke and heat of the exhaust gathering about her. She considered whether or not to climb in, whether or not to go around to the driver and ask to ride in the cab with the two women. But the gears grinded and shifted, and the truck jolted forward. Ella reached up and grabbed the railing and pulled herself inside on her belly.

The truck lurched through the crossroads, and Ella raised her eyes and looked up as she passed beneath the twining wisteria. She felt speed gather around her, knew that they were following the Kings Mountain Highway west in the direction from which she'd come. If she had stood and looked to the south, she could have seen the red mud road that led down into Stumptown, could have marked Fox

Denton's crumbling shack as the truck passed by it. But she did not stand, and she did not look. Instead she closed her eyes and leaned her head against the rails.

She waited until the truck had slowed and made a right turn that carried them north. Once she knew for certain that Bessemer City was behind her, she opened her eyes and stood and looked out over the roof of the truck at the road before her. The wind blew her hair back and made her eyes water. Tears streaked her cheeks. The wind wanted her to sit down, but she refused.

CHAPTER TWO

Lilly Wiggins

Sunday, December 25, 2005

Edwin, I want to tell you up front that I do not write very many letters. I do not write much of anything these days, so please forgive my handwriting. I am much more likely to send an email than I am to pick up a pen and write a letter and then search this house for an envelope. Yes, old ladies do write emails. It is 2005, after all, so do not be surprised if you happen to receive an email from your aunt Lilly one day. Although I would prefer to telephone you as I always have, I do not resent technology like some old people pretend to. Those same old people who complain about the Internet are kept alive by medicine and machines that did not exist even five years ago. They'd prefer to lick a stamp with their crusty old tongues than hit "send" on the computer. Don't even get me started on stamps. As I write this now I am already combing my mind for a place in this house where I can find a stamp or two to make certain this letter reaches you. If I send it. I will probably send it. I hope I do, anyway.

Needless to say, I arrived safe and sound tonight despite your worry about me driving home after dark on Christmas. The roads to Asheville were empty, which I guess is what one should expect on Christmas night.

This evening, when the two of us were standing on your porch before I left and we heard the panther cry from the zoo down in the park, it brought back many memories that I had not thought of in a long time. I did not tell you about these memories then because I did not know how to tell you about them, but I want to tell you now.

You may remember that your mother and father often took you to the zoo when you were a little boy, but you may not remember that I would go along with you when I visited, especially after you lost your mother and Otis was working and could not take you. But sometimes your father would come with you and me. During those trips to the zoo, Otis was the same as he always was. Quiet, with-drawn, especially after he lost your mother. My little brother did not change very much during his lifetime. Perhaps none of us change very much.

Edwin, it was remarkable for me to hear that panther cry out there in the dark tonight. So many things came back to me.

I always listened closely to how you spoke when you were a little boy. Would you have your mother's soft, low-country drawl, or would you have your father's twang? At the zoo, what were you, two, maybe three years old, you'd point to the panther and say "line" just like your father said it, just like I would've said it if I weren't thinking so hard about speaking and acting "properly," something that you were expected to become back in the 1930s if you were a young woman who attended a normal school in order to make a life as a teacher. But you were just a boy and you were not interested in speaking "properly," nor should you have been, and you would point to the panther and say "Line! Line!" and your mother would laugh and say, "Yes, baby, 'lie-yun,'" extending the word to two full syllables when you were able to get the job done in only one. This is not to say that your mother did not have a beautiful voice. She was a gorgeous woman, inside and out. You can't say that about very many women who are as striking as your mother was. Secretly, though, I was happy that you spoke like your father, that you spoke like me when I am able to forget myself.

Tonight, after we heard the panther roar, you told me that you felt bad for it. You said you were afraid it roared at night because it was lonely in that cage all by itself. And then you said something about the sadness of even an animal spending Christmas alone. Forgive me, Edwin, I'm being sensitive, I know I am, but there was something in the way you said it, the way you looked at me or did not look at me, that embarrassed me, that made me feel that perhaps you thought that about me and that was why you invited me down to spend Christmas with you and Sarah and Owen. And I wondered if, every time I call you on the telephone, you hear my voice and mistake it for the cry of loneliness.

Don't worry about me, Edwin. I'm not lonely. I have more friends here in Coventry Village than I've ever had in my life, and there's a lot to do that keeps me busy.

So don't worry about me, and certainly don't feel bad for me like you feel bad for that poor panther down at the zoo. I'm not lonely. Besides, if I were lonely I would not roar. I would sit very quietly so that no one would know I was alone.

I suppose it was serendipitous (if I'm using and spelling that word correctly) that you asked me what you did. You asked me to tell you something about your father, something about my own mother and my father. I promised you that I'd think about it, and I can tell you that although only a few hours have passed, I have been thinking about it ever since.

You have told me before that you did not know your father well, that you knew your mother much better, although you lost her when you were eight and Otis passed only ten years ago. I've often wondered how well I knew Otis. Like you, I've often wondered how well I knew my own father in the short time I did know him. I only knew my mother for a short time as well, and sometimes I wonder how well I knew her even though every day of my life was spent with her right up until the day she was murdered. I'm assuming you do not know much if anything about her death. We have never spoken of it, and I don't know what Otis told you about her. He did not talk about her. None of us did.

We experienced some amount of shame for being Ella May's children. It was not shame that we felt naturally or that she had caused us to feel. Other people put this shame upon us, but it was shame nonetheless. It made us quiet. It kept us from asking too many questions about Mother, about her life, about how and why she died. It kept us from talking about her, even to one another. I don't know the extent of what Otis told your mother or anyone else for that matter. But you asked me, and I think you should know. You have a family of your own now, and Owen will not be five forever. One day he may ask you the questions you asked me tonight. I want you to have answers for him. I can't give you all the answers, but I can give you some of them. Your grandmother Ella May, my mother, was murdered during a strike at a mill in Gastonia in 1929. No one knows who did it or why, although I have long suspected that at the time everyone knew who did it and there were many reasons why.

Have you ever read any books by the North Carolina writer Thomas Wolfe? He was born in Asheville in 1900, the same year my mother, your grandmother, was born just over the mountains in Tennessee. I never knew Mr. Wolfe, but I knew his mother for a short time when I was younger. Perhaps I'll tell you about her someday. His oldest brother Fred used to live there in Greenville, but exactly where I don't know. Maybe it was Spartanburg. I don't remember. I ask you about Thomas Wolfe because his most famous book is called *Look Homeward, Angel*. There is a line in the novel that asks, "Which of us is not forever a stranger and alone?" I've thought about that question a lot since the first time I read the novel, which was many, many years ago. I especially think about it when the past is on my mind, when I am trying to remember things about my life that I think I've forgotten but secretly fear I never knew. Being unable to remember parts of your own life can make you feel like a stranger, and I figure that strangers are alone more often than not.

Tonight, your questions about your father and our family were serendipitous because I was thinking much the same thing after what I'd decided to do during my drive down to see you this morning. I have made the drive down from Asheville to Greenville many times in my life. I have seen the same trees and road signs and buildings many times. Perhaps I have grown numb to them in some way. Perhaps I have driven past the exit sign for Cowpens many times without fully recognizing what that place meant to our family, what it means to me, to you. That is where your father Otis was born in 1920. You probably know that. Your mother probably told you if your father did not, but surely he did. It is only a few minutes away from where you were born and raised in Greenville.

Cowpens, South Carolina: I always thought that was such a strange name for a town when I was a young girl and I would over-hear Mother mention it, which happened rarely. She did not have good memories of it, but that's where Otis was born just eighteen months after me, so I suppose she had at least two good memories of our time there. I do not know why my mother and father went there or why they left the mountains. I think my father must have heard something about the mills there, about how easy it was to get a job, and Mother did not know what else to do but follow him. She was pregnant with me when they left the mountains, so what else could she do? Cowpens is the first place I remember, but I was not born there. It is embarrassing to say this, but I was born in a mule-drawn wagon on the way down to Cowpens from up in the mountains around Bryson City. I grew up hearing Mother tell about it, and I can almost hear her tell about it now, all these years later.

Today, when I saw the exit for Cowpens, I pulled off I-26 and drove through town, thankful that I'd left home early not even knowing that I would have either the desire to see this old place or the cause to ponder questions like the ones you asked me tonight. I'm so happy that I allowed myself this one flourish of nostalgia because it brought back things I thought I had forgotten.

I wondered what I would see of the town, and as I suspected there was not much of it to see. Downtown is mostly a collection of antique stores and civic buildings. Nothing so different from any other little downtown. The mill there, the Cowpens Manufacturing Company, I assume it was the mill that Mother worked in almost ninety years ago, was closed. A chain-link fence enclosed the entire property, and the trees had grown so wild and thick that you couldn't see anything on the other side. I wish I could've seen the mill though. It may have reminded me of Mother, may have reminded me of something about my life in Cowpens that now I will never know.

I was very young when we lived there. I remember a field, thick with strawberries, and I believe there may have been a strawberry patch near the place where we lived, and my father would take me out in the morning and we would pick strawberries and eat them where we stood.

Aside from the strawberries, I can recall apples, but I do not believe there were orchards near our house because most of the orchards are farther up in the mountains. But I remember apples, and it seems like I remember a man who delivered apples. I remember a man who gave me apple slices.

Mother would wake me up late at night when she got home from the mill. She'd make me something to eat because Daddy never learned to make anything. I can remember her doing that, cooking, preparing food. And I believe I can remember her being pregnant with Otis. She worked at the mill the whole time she was pregnant. My father did not work in Cowpens. At least I cannot remember him working. He never cared much for work.

Your father was born on April 10, 1920. I remember waking up one morning and a little baby boy named Otis just being there as if he had always been there. I slept right through it. I don't know if Mother had any help with the birth. She may have done it all herself. Knowing Daddy, she probably did.

In South Carolina, Mother and Daddy were like they always were, like they always were no matter where we lived: she'd run him off, let him come back. Run him off, let him come back. My father was a good-looking man, and he knew it. He probably always had somewhere he could go. He was always into things he should not have been into, and for some reason I think that is why we left Cowpens not long after Otis was born.

I remember Mother waking me up and carrying me outside wrapped in a blanket and laying me down on a wagon's seat while she and Daddy loaded the few things they wanted to take with them. I could hear the mule's reins clink together when it shook its head. I could hear its feet stomp on the dirt road. They must have just purchased it from somebody because I do not remember us owning a mule. The night was cold and dark. Mother and Daddy did not say a word to each other. I remember hearing Otis cry out, and then hearing the sound of Mother soothing him back to sleep. She sat in the back of the wagon with your father in her arms, and Daddy climbed in beside me and took the reins in his hands. I remember laying my head on his lap and staring up at the silhouette of his face against the dark night sky as the four of us passed beneath it. I do not remember seeing stars up there, but that does not mean there were not any to see.

We went to a farm after that. Mother worked in the field there, and there were black people there, the first black people I had ever seen. Daddy did not want to be there because blacks worked alongside whites, and we all lived together in a big bunkhouse, all the women and the children, black and white, the older children taking care of the younger ones. The men lived in a different house, even if they were married.

Daddy left us there and went ahead to North Carolina to find somewhere for him and Mother to work, and it was just the three of us on that farm until he sent word for us to join him. I do not know how long we were there, and I cannot remember much about it except my surprise at seeing black people for the first time. I remember wondering if the color could be wiped from their skin, and then, when it warmed up, a bunch of us went swimming in a little pond that must have been somewhere near the farm. I wondered if the black children would turn white after they got wet, but of course they did not.

The woman who owned the farm was an old woman named Miss Rose. Mother must have thought a lot of her because that is who my sister Rose was named after. Do you remember your aunt Rose? She passed when you were just a little boy, and none of us saw her very much because she lived so far away in upstate New York. But that is where her name came from: an old woman who ran a farm where blacks and whites worked together and slept side by side.

We were not there long before Daddy came back and got us. We moved to North Carolina. Lowell first, and then a few other small towns where there were cotton mills. Mother always worked. Daddy worked sometimes.

Mother gave birth to another baby boy when I was about five years old, which means your father was almost three. The baby only lived a couple of years. His name was Willie. I remember him, but not well. I can remember him crying, and looking down at his little red face, and I can remember your father pointing at him in Mother's arms and saying, "Baby cry," and Mother saying, "Yes, sweetheart, 'Baby cry. Baby cry.'"

I don't know exactly why Willie died. I was too young for Mother to explain it to me, and I do not know where we lived at the time, so I never knew where they buried him, but I think about him often, and I always feel a great sense of sadness sweep over me when I do. I am sorry to be telling you something like this in a letter, but it feels good to tell someone about it now as I am thinking of things with a sense of clarity and purpose with which I have not thought of them in a long time.

Your aunt Rose was born a few years after Willie died, and by then we had moved to Bessemer City, North Carolina, in a little community called Stumptown where our neighbors were all black. It was just like being back on Miss Rose's farm, so maybe that's how Mother thought to name this new little girl Rose.

The clearest memories of my life before Mother passed away are of the years that we lived in Stumptown. I know that Daddy lived with us off and on there, but I do not remember him as well as I remember other things, other people. Mother had another baby, her last one, in 1928 when I was ten, and he was healthy. His name was Joseph, but we always called him Wink because he blinked his eyes one eye at a time, and it always looked like he was winking. You have probably never heard of him, but your father just doted on him. That was *his* little brother, but they took him away after Mother was killed, and they sent Rose, your father, and me to an orphanage at Barium Springs near Statesville, North Carolina. None of us saw Wink for a long time after that. Years. By the time we saw him again he had no idea who we were.

There were five of us in a tiny, little two-room cabin there in Stumptown. Daddy would have made six, but he was gone much of the time, and before Wink was even born he left and never came back. I never saw him again, although I know he died in 1967. How I found out about it I don't remember. I think your father may have told me. Maybe it was in the paper and someone showed it to him.

After my father ran off, Mother spent a lot of time with a man named Charlie Shope. Just how she met him, I don't know. He was a mean little man, an awful sort. We all hated him. But I suppose Mother was lonely, and I understand that now in a way I did not understand it when I was a child. Maybe I know more about being lonely than I first thought.

Mother with four children to look after, one already passed away, working a full-time job at the mill there in Bessemer City, which back then meant she worked six days a week, probably seventy hours, maybe more sometimes if they needed her and she needed the money. She always needed the money. I don't know how much she got paid, but I imagine it wasn't much. We went hungry a lot, and we were cold in the winter and hot in the summer.

I did not mean for this letter to turn into a "poor me" letter. There were good times. We had fun, especially your father and me. We had to look after Rose and Wink because they were so little, but we still had fun. We would play games, swim in the pond out behind the cabin, fish, panfry whatever we could catch. Your father was always trying to lure the neighbors' chickens into traps he made in our yard. He once caught one while Mother was at work. I scolded him, but he said it was the chicken's fault for coming into our yard, and I guess it was. He killed it, and I fried it for dinner. We begged Rose to keep it secret from Mother. She'd have worn us out if she'd known we'd killed and eaten one of the neighbor's chickens. More than any-thing, it would have humiliated her to know that her children were hungry enough to do such a thing, especially because our neighbors would've given us anything we ever needed if they had it to give. They looked out for us. We all looked out for one another.

My best friend, I guess she was my only friend at the time, was a little black girl named Iva Gingles. Her older sister Violet was mother's best friend. If I was ten, Iva was probably twelve or thirteen. Earlier, I told you I was born in a wagon on our way from Bryson City to Cowpens. Can you even imagine that? When I think about it I think less about myself being born and more about Mother giving birth. Here she was, a teenager that had never left home before, had never been any farther from home than the church or the general store, pregnant by a man she could not have known that well, a man she may have never gotten to know. It amazes me, honestly. It always has. Everything about my mother has always amazed me.

She was never able to remember the exact day I was born. She never wrote it down. I know it is hard to conceive of that now. I remember when Owen was born and I visited Sarah and you while she was still in the hospital. I remember knocking on the door to her room, and while I waited for a nurse to finish up with something, I stood in the hallway and stared at the form you had clipped to the door with all of Owen's information filled out on it. It was the form the county would use for his birth certificate. I have never told you this and I am embarrassed to tell you this now, but I was jealous of Owen because he would have a document detailing everything about the day he was born. I chose not to say anything to you about it then because the last thing new parents need is advice, especially the advice of an old woman who never had children of her own, but perhaps I will say now what I wanted to say to you and Sarah then: Hold on to that paperwork, that birth certificate. Make sure Owen sees it often, especially when he is young. Those official pieces of paperwork may not mean much when you've seen them and you know they exist, but when you do not have them it is easy to imagine yourself as being somewhat less than validated in this world. I know there will be a slip of paper documenting my passing, but there will never be anything that marks my beginning, and something about this feels so fleeting to me, and it makes my time on this earth seem all the more impermanent. That sounds crazy, I know, but it is something I have spent much of my life thinking about: what it means to be on this earth, what it means to leave it, what of us is left behind once we are gone.

When I was younger I was deeply hurt, deeply affected by not knowing the exact day of my birth. "It was June. I know that for a fact" was all Mother would say. She would say, "You can pick any day you want to be your birthday. A lot of folks get stuck with numbers that don't suit them, and they pay for it for the rest of their lives." But that was just mountain talk, all that stuff about signs and "haints" and old-time ways I suspect she never believed in.

One day, a few years before Mother passed, I was at Iva's house. I can remember being amazed that Iva could read. Mother had been trying to teach me, and Iva had been trying to help, but I struggled. You have to understand that, back then, a lot of people could not read. White, black, it did not make any difference. My own father never learned to read as far as I know, but Iva could read. She could write too. I remember thinking that was about the greatest thing in the world.

There is one particular memory I have, one of the clearest of all my memories, which makes me wonder if I made it up, but surely not. Iva and I were sitting on the edge of her mother's porch late one afternoon playing with some dolls we had made out of old stockings. Rose and Otis sat out in the grass by the road. Your father had found a puddle and was trying to float a little boat he had built from sticks with one of our old stockings for a sail. Rose was right there beside him.

As you can imagine, it was unusual for whites and blacks to live so close together back then, and it was even more unusual for us all to play together the way we did, but we didn't know any different. By the time we were sent to the orphanage after Mother died, all the children there had heard about us, who we were, who Mother was, what she had done. They had heard about how we lived with black people in Stumptown, and I remember some of the children at the orphanage whispering "nigger lover" and things like that when they were close enough for me to hear it. I had never once in my life heard that word. I had no idea what they were talking about until I made friends with a little redheaded girl named Lucy, my first friend at Barium Springs. She said "nigger lover" meant that you were friendly with colored people. I wanted to say, "Good Lord, Lucy, colored people are the only friends I ever had until you."

In this memory I am sitting on Iva's mother's porch watching a little old black woman come up the road at dusk. She walked right by Otis and Rose and stopped in front of Iva and me where we sat on the edge of the porch, our feet dangling off the side. The woman had on a purple dress and a hat that almost matched it, a big handbag on her forearm. When she spoke she spoke only to Iva. She would not look at me, which I remember thinking was strange at the time, but since then I have come to understand her reasons. I have forgotten what her name was, but Iva knew her. The woman said her daughter had just given birth to a son that morning. She reached into her handbag and pulled out an old family Bible and asked Iva if she would write down the baby's name and the day of his birth inside.

I tried not to stare at that old lady while Iva went inside the house for her pencil or whatever it was she needed. My eyes traveled down through the trees to the road where Otis and Rose were playing on the edge of the yard, and I watched them splash in that puddle for a little bit, but no matter how hard I tried not to, I couldn't keep my eyes from falling on that old woman. Her skin appeared to be as frail as old newspaper and just about as thin. She must have felt me looking at her, because her eye caught mine and she lowered her head and stared at the cool, dark dirt beneath the porch.

"Miss," she whispered.

"Ma'am," I whispered back.

And then the screen door slammed behind me and Iva was back on the porch. She took up that old woman's Bible and scrawled out that baby boy's name in just about the prettiest script I have ever seen, even though I was not able to read a word of it. Instead, I pretended that she was writing my own name—Lilly Wiggins—and my own birth date—whenever that was—inside that Bible.

The next morning, after Mother got home from work, I slid out from beneath my blanket and followed her to the stove. She was pregnant with Wink then, and I remember thinking about how hard it must be for her to bend down to the oven with her belly as big as it was. I believe Daddy must have run off as soon as he learned she was pregnant. Your grandfather was not a good man, Edwin. He could be nice sometimes, but he was never good.

I told Mother about the birth of that old woman's grandson, and I told her about what I had seen Iva do. I asked her why we did not have a Bible with my name and my birthday written down inside it. She had just gotten the fire going in the oven, and she was rolling out dough for biscuits. Rose and Otis were still asleep just a few feet away from us. When Mother finished rolling out the dough she cut the biscuits, and then she looked at me.

"Lilly," she said, "it was just you and me and that man who called himself your daddy in that wagon on the way down the mountain. And there wasn't hardly food or money to go around for two of us, much less three." She opened the oven door and slid the pan of biscuits inside. "If you think I was worried about toting along some Bible then I don't think you know your mother as good you should.

"Besides," she said, dusting her hands on the front of her dress, where her pregnant belly seemed to reach toward me, the dry flour and the cotton lint coming off her fingers like snow, "you don't need no Bible to tell you that you exist in this world."

And she was right, Edwin. You exist whether it is written down or not, and you are dead whether it's written down or not too. If I decide not to send you this letter, that will not mean that the things I have written down never happened, that they are somehow less significant because I am the only one who has seen these words. If you never show Owen his birth certificate or if you lose it and have to send away for a new copy, that will not mean he does not exist or that his life matters less than it would have otherwise.

Maybe this is what I was thinking when I went out to the Bessemer City cemetery on the morning after they buried Mother. Hundreds of people had attended her funeral, and there had been great heaps of flowers piled atop her grave, but the next day, before I arrived, someone had returned and taken all those flowers. I may have realized it then, and I definitely know it now, but those flowers had not been arranged for Mother. Those flowers had been arranged for the newspapers and photographers who took all those pictures of me and Rose and Otis and Wink standing before her grave. Less than twenty-four hours later there was nothing on her grave but a rock to mark the spot where they'd laid her to rest. About thirty years ago, the AFL-CIO erected a huge stone marker there. They paid for it and everything: a huge, expensive monument saying something about who Mother was, what she did. They spelled her last name incorrectly, Mae instead of May, which is ironic considering how much money they spent and how important they said she was to them.

On this morning, the morning after she had been buried, there was nothing there but that rock. It was just a quiet place, with the earth still soft from her being put inside it. No words, no tombstone, no monument marking that she had ever existed, but she did, and she made me exist too, even though it was never written down. Here I am, Edwin, and here you are too.

If Otis never told you any of this it is because it hurt him to talk about it, about Willie's death, about losing our mother, about losing Wink after we were sent to the orphanage. And there was the shame of it too, the shame of being Ella May's child. After she died newspapers across the state called her a communist for being involved with the strike, a loose woman for not being married, and any other number of terrible things. There were years when we did not want anyone to know who we were. I made myself forget. Your father chose not to talk about it. Rose moved away to a place where no one had ever heard of us or knew the name Ella May.

But shame can work the other way as well. Once, years and years ago, when I first moved to Asheville, I was seeing a man who worked as a pharmacist for one of the drugstores downtown. He was very kind and very successful and the only son of a lovely old family, and I knew for certain that we would be married. And then, one evening, the woman who managed the boardinghouse where I lived knocked on my door and told me that the pharmacist was downstairs. I was surprised because it was a weeknight and I had not been expecting him. I found him on the porch, still in his white smock. It had grown dark out, and I remember thinking how white his smock appeared beneath the porch light.

I will be quick about things: he told me he didn't want to see me anymore. He did not give a reason, although I suspect he had met someone else. I had been grading student papers, essays about "What I Will Do Over My Summer Vacation," and I had tucked my pencil behind my ear. I had hoped he would find it charming, but after his news to me I thought of the pencil and was humiliated because I had put it there on purpose to get his attention. He left, and I never saw him again.

I was devastated, Edwin, just devastated, and how I cried. He was the first man I had ever really loved, and I believe that at that moment I knew for certain that I would never marry. The funny thing is that I rarely think of the pharmacist now, but throughout that summer I was convinced that my life was over. I was only twenty-nine. Twenty-nine.

Months passed. Summer ended, and before I knew it I was heading back to work at the elementary school where I was scheduled to teach fourth grade for the second year in a row. One evening, I was in my room organizing my teaching materials, getting ready for school to start, when I came across a photograph the pharmacist and I had taken together at Lake Lure the previous fall. The two of us were sitting on a rock and holding hands, our legs crossed, both of us smiling. I wore sunglasses and he wore a straw derby and white jacket. We made a nice-looking couple. The photograph was in black and white, and you could not tell that the trees behind us were alive with color, but they were. I stared at the photograph, and the same feelings I had felt that night on the porch returned: the deep hurt and sadness, the disappointment, the certainty that so many things I'd expected of my life would not come to pass.

And then, I do not know how, I seemed to step outside of my body. I looked back at myself where I sat on the single bed in my small room in a boardinghouse in the mountains between the place where my mother was born and the place she had died. How had I come to be here? I wondered. How had I come to have the things I had? The dresses, the shoes, the books, the radio that sat on the shelf across from me that I would turn on in the evenings to hear music or a baseball game or the news while I sipped tea and looked at a magazine. I asked myself these questions on the way to realizing something important: I was twenty-nine years old, and I had outlived my mother by one year. I had outlived a woman who had never slept on a bed this comfortable in a room this warm, who had never worn a dress as nice as the dresses I often gave away after a season, who had lost one child while keeping four alive. It all felt so self-indulgent, this worry over a man, this longing over a photograph in which I wore sunglasses as if I were some kind of Hollywood starlet. In short, I was ashamed not of who my mother was, but of how much stronger she was than the woman I had become.

I want to tell you about her, Edwin, and I'll tell you everything I know, which isn't much, but maybe it'll be enough for you to understand something about who she was, about who your father was, about who we are now.

CHAPTER THREE

Verchel Park

Monday, June 3, 1918

Perhaps a friend would have said, "Verchel, what's a woman like that want with a man like you?" But Verchel didn't have any friends, didn't hardly speak to a soul aside from the younger brother with whom he lived once he'd lost the use of his right hand after getting it caught up in a machine at the Cowpens Manufacturing Company. Since the accident he'd spent his time convalescing in his brother's front room and using his good hand to spoon corn bread and buttermilk into the mouths of his twin niece and nephew. Besides, if a friend had sought to warn Verchel about Miss Myra Stebbins née Olyphant, what would that friend have said? That a forty-four-year-old widow wanted Verchel's money? He didn't have a cent. His land? His fancy house? He didn't own a thing. The only thing she could have wanted of value was his soul, and Verchel had already given that to God after Miss Myra's father, Pastor Olyphant, had called him into the baptismal waters of the muddy creek that ran behind Spartan Baptist where it sat alongside the highway to Greenville.

So what did a woman like her want with a man like him? There were whispers that Miss Myra had considered all three options available to women of her age and station—spinsterhood, widowhood, and matrimony—and decided that the latter suited her best, but after a year of marriage there still remained many mysterious things Verchel Park did not know about his wife. But he figured he knew her well enough to know that she'd be interested in the case of a young girl sitting all alone in a mule-drawn wagon at dawn. The only thing that could interest Miss Myra more than a young girl in danger was a fatherless child, so when Verchel discovered that the dirty blanket the girl cradled in her arms held a tiny newborn baby, he felt certain that he had a story worth telling his wife that evening while they sat on the porch after dinner.

The wagon had been left in the alley on the west side of the general store. The early morning sun had not yet found the shaded street where it sat tucked between the store and the Cowpens Community Bank. It was June 1918, the morning air cool in the early South Carolina summer before the real heat arrives. The bony old mule that had pulled the wagon did not look as if it would survive the morning. As Verchel passed the girl in the wagon he felt an awkward, confusing urge to make small talk, almost considered saying, "That old mule could use some oats," but he did not know anything about mules or what they ate, and he did not like small talk. The girl did not appear to be interested in small talk anyway. Her face was pale, her cheeks dirty and sunken. Her dark hair had come loose and fell in strands around her face. Verchel didn't realize that she held a baby in her arms until he heard it let out a cry. And he didn't realize that someone aside from the baby accompanied her until he turned left at the corner of the alley and followed the sidewalk to the front of the store.

A man sat on the front steps as if he'd been sitting out there all night. The sun hadn't risen quite high enough for Verchel to make out the man's face, and Verchel didn't get a good look at him as he passed him on his way up the steps. All Verchel could think to do was to say a kind "Good morning" to the stranger without staring at him too long before getting out his key and unlocking the door as if it were any other morning, which it was, of course, until he got home that afternoon and told Miss Myra about the stranger and the girl with the baby out in the wagon.

"What did he buy?" she asked.

"Nothing but some powdered milk," Verchel said. "Two boxes of it."

"That must mean that girl's milk hasn't come in good yet, or the baby won't nurse, one."

And then, at Miss Myra's prodding, Verchel rehashed the full scene: the half hour the stranger had spent on the front porch steps after Verchel turned the sign from CLOSED to OPEN; the way he'd stalked up and down the aisles, picking things up and setting them down; the way he'd stood at the counter, his dark hair covered by a wide-brimmed hat and his face just as dirty as the girl's out in the wagon, his eyes looking over Verchel's shoulder at the tins of tobacco; the dirty hands that tossed the boxes of milk on the counter; the question he'd asked Verchel about whether or not the store took paper money.

"That's how I knew he was a stranger for sure," Verchel said. "Anybody from town would've knowed Mr. Haney'll take paper money if you don't work at the mill. Anybody from town would've knowed that."

Verchel told Myra that after the subject of the mill had come up, the stranger inquired about work in town, and Verchel told him that folks who didn't own their own business all worked for the mill in one capacity or another.

"Do you think he's looking for work?" Miss Myra asked.

"I can't say," Verchel said. "He just asked me what folks did."

"Well, I hope he can find some work if he needs it, especially with a wife and that little one to care for," Miss Myra said. "It won't do to have a girl with a baby that young and him not being able to find work." Her eyes narrowed and her thin lips pressed themselves together and all but disappeared. "I'm correct in saying they were married?"

Verchel laughed an awkward laugh, but he caught himself and stopped when he saw that she actually expected an answer. "Gosh, Miss Myra," he said, "I didn't ask him. It wasn't none of my business."

"The moral health of our community is the business of us all," she said. "That means you too, Verchel Park."

And the moral health of his community as well as his household is exactly what Verchel was considering when he made the decision not to share with Miss Myra the last question the stranger asked him before leaving the store that morning. After paying for his powdered milk, the stranger had stood at the counter for a long time and looked all around the store, and then he'd asked Verchel the question that seemed to be the real reason he'd been waiting on the steps since dawn.

"Is there any place for a man to get a drink in this town?"

VERCHEL HAD NOT had a drop of liquor since his accident inside the mill, and until meeting and marrying Miss Myra he'd believed himself just as useless as the lifeless hand that he kept pinned against his chest.

"You need to march right back to Mr. Haney and reclaim your job at the mill," Miss Myra had said on their second night as a married couple. He was sitting on the porch steps because they had only the one rocking chair she'd brought over from her father's house to furnish the porch on their new home, and she sat in it now, her black dress pulled up just enough for the late-afternoon sun to catch a glimpse of her white ankles. She held an open fan in her other hand and used it as if dusting the stifling air around her face.

Verchel had thought for a minute about what she'd said, and then he sighed and looked down at his hand where it rested limp and lonely in his lap. The gears that had ravaged his hand had crushed his palm like a rock, popping the bones into tiny bits of gravel that had never grown back together. He often thought of it now as a puppet's hand that he had never learned to use. He and Myra had never spoken of his injured hand or the accident that caused it, but he felt certain that she had noticed it by now, especially because he'd positioned his wrist right by her head while propping himself up during their blink-of-an-eye marriage consummation.

She'd collapsed the fan with a *pop* and dropped it onto her lap.

"You need to shake that thought right out of your head, Verchel Park," she'd said. "You're still a young man at forty. There's not a thing wrong with you."

"I'm not saying there is," Verchel said, although he was really forty-one and couldn't figure out how Miss Myra had subtracted a year of his life. "It just don't take a fool to know that I can't work inside no mill. You need two good hands for that."

"Well," she said, reopening her fan and raising it to her face, "there has to be a job down there for a man with just one good hand, and you need to go down there in the morning and find out what it is."

And that's how Verchel came to just about the only job he could come to in the employ of the Cowpens Manufacturing Company: working as a clerk in the mill's store. He'd tried his best not to picture himself as a man who goes crawling back to a job he'd basically cast himself from by his poor choices, and he found this an even more difficult prospect because everyone he came into contact with seemed to know the story of the circumstances in which he'd destroyed his hand. Mr. Freen, who'd managed the mill store for as long as Verchel could remember, sure didn't make things any easier on him.

"Now, you know Mr. Haney don't like a drinker," he said. "I don't say that to mean nothing against you, because only the good Lord knows what a man does when he ain't at work. But I mean to tell you that Mr. Haney needs to know what a man does while he's at work, and he has a right to know. I don't plan on keeping a thing from him neither."

Verchel had just nodded his head as if he agreed, mostly because he did agree. He wanted to tell Mr. Freen that he was a changed man, a married man, and a religious man to boot. But admitting to a change in oneself meant admitting that a change had been needed in the first place, and Verchel just couldn't bring himself to make that kind of admission to anyone but Miss Myra, and she'd never asked but somehow seemed to know just the same.

So he'd shown up early and stayed late, worked hard, and kept clear of suspicion. Mr. Freen seemed satisfied with Verchel's work ethic and his ability to run the till, stock the shelves, keep the store clean and straight, and have the afternoon dope wagon ready to go for the boy Wilfred to push through the mill for the second-shift employees' afternoon refreshment.

After a few months it wasn't an uncommon thing for Verchel to be in the store all by himself. And soon he took over the morning shift, with Mr. Freen coming in to spell him at lunchtime and the two of them working together until 2 P.M., when Verchel went home and left Mr. Freen to close up between the second and third shifts at the mill.

He was making ten dollars a week now, more money than he'd ever made—much less made consistently—in his entire life. And he was able to save it too, but only because Miss Myra collected it each Friday when he walked in the door, and dispensed it in equal portions each morning when he left so that he might have the funds for a bologna sandwich and pork rinds for lunch each day.

Once she'd been able to propel Verchel back into the community, she set her sights on the community itself. Along with a few of the farmers' wives from her father's church, Miss Myra had formed the Spartanburg County Ladies' Improvement Society, and she and the women regularly made trips to the local saloons to hand out literature about the evils of alcohol and the effects a drunken father, husband, son, brother, or nephew could have on a household and a community. At each establishment (there were only three in town and one out on the highway toward Greenville) she threatened the proprietor with the possibility of her founding a full-blown anti-saloon league if certain conditions weren't met: they weren't to sell liquor to mill employees, churchgoers, town officials, or married men, a rule that Verchel suspected of being pointed directly at him. What he also felt pointed at him were the eyes of the men and women in town as he walked to and from work during the week; he imagined that all of them were either cursing him under their breath for his wife's attempts to influence the tide of public opinion or silently mocking him for, first, being liquored up enough to nearly lose his hand in the mill, and then being repentant enough to marry a woman who was hell-bent on making certain such a thing could never happen again. Either way, Verchel figured that the town viewed him as hamstrung by his own incompetence.

But aside from those with a taste for liquor, it was the young women and the motherless and fatherless in the community who Miss Myra believed were most in need of her assistance.

Even if Verchel had wanted to recount the full version of events involving the mysterious stranger to Miss Myra, which Lord knows he didn't, he couldn't have done it no matter how hard he tried. That wasn't because he didn't remember things: the girl and the baby waiting out there in the wagon; the stranger's beady, close-together eyes, his sharp nose; the flash of expectancy in his face colored with something like malice as he waited for Verchel's answer about where to find that drink.

Verchel could have recounted those things, as well as the slow light coming through the windows and the dusty smell of the store, but those things were always there, so they didn't bear mentioning or even remembering because they'd be there every day.

No, what Verchel couldn't recount was the one thing he couldn't quite remember, even when he tried to recall it that night in bed where Miss Myra breathed heavily beside him and tossed slowly in her sleep like a great ocean liner beset upon by swells. And the thing he couldn't remember was this: his response to the stranger's very simple question.

There'd been something that had crossed Verchel's lips about Cowpens being a God-fearing community of sober men and women, a place where hardworking millhands and harder-working farmhands split their time almost equally between their physical toils at the job and their spiritual lives in the church. He'd even mentioned his own wife, Miss Myra Stebbins Park née Olyphant, who along with other women in the county had started an improvement society that was doing awfully good work, don't you know, the kind of work a once-depraved place like Spartanburg County, South Carolina, desperately needed done so that it could ascend to its rightful register as a sanctified, purified land where a man who'd once craved a drink no longer thought of it, much less needed it.

But the thing about it was that Verchel's heart just wasn't in it; his words were both unconvincing and hollow. And the stranger knew it, and Verchel knew that the stranger knew it as well, and that's why Verchel told Miss Myra some of what the stranger had to say, but also why he made sure not to tell her all of it.

But Verchel tried his best to hold his head high and celebrate his own personal victories regardless of whether they were shrouded in half-truths, obscured truths, or complete untruths, and he decided that he would no longer view his life as a struggle not to crave whiskey; instead, he chose to view his life as a life that no longer needed it.

VERCHEL HAD ALL but forgotten about the stranger and the girl in the wagon with the baby when Miss Myra asked about them one evening after dinner the following April. They sat out on the porch just as they did most evenings, her in the one chair and him on the steps smoking a cigarette, the one thing he looked forward to each day.

"Have you seen that girl?" Miss Myra asked.

Verchel took a drag from his cigarette.

"What girl?"

"The one that showed up in the wagon with that baby last summer," Miss Myra said.

"No," Verchel said. "Not that I can recollect."

"What about her husband? Have you seen him?"

"Not that I can recollect."

Miss Myra rocked in silence for a moment, her eyes taking in the empty gravel road that ran along the edge of their yard.

"I bet he took a job at the mill," she finally said. "It's a wonder you haven't seen him come in the store."

"I reckon so," Verchel said.

"You should go on down to the mill and look for him," Miss Myra said. "Check up on that girl and that baby. Maybe see if there's anything the ladies and I can help with while they get settled."

"It's almost been a year. I reckon they're settled by now," Verchel said.

"Well, you go and see about them," she said. "It's not too much to ask, is it?"

But it is too much to ask, thought Verchel. He didn't have a reason to step foot inside the Cowpens Manufacturing Company, and even when he tried to think of a reason, his mind wouldn't let him do it. The last thing he wanted to do was find himself inside the mill's noisy walls, walking along the rows of machines, staring through the combed cotton for the face of a man he'd seen only one time. It wasn't just the stranger's face that he'd be forced to behold; it would also be the faces of his former coworkers, many of whom had been the ones to help him gather himself after the accident, the same ones he knew had been questioned after they'd carried him out and taken him to the doctor: How had he been acting before it happened? Had anything seemed strange about him? Had anyone been close enough to smell his breath?

But Miss Myra's request ended up taking care of itself. On Thursday of that next week, Verchel heard the sound of the store's front door opening, and he looked up and saw Mr. Freen coming through instead of the boy Wilfred.

"Go on ahead and count the drawer," Mr. Freen said. "Wilfred's done come down with this danged flu, and I need you to take the dope wagon down to the mill today. Maybe tomorrow too."

It wasn't until then that Verchel realized that something could actually be more humiliating than showing his face inside the mill; this higher level of humiliation would be accomplished by him showing his face behind the dope wagon while he served chilled pop, cold sandwiches, and hot coffee to his former coworkers.

BY THE TIME Verchel had entered the mill behind the dope wagon and seen the same girl he'd first seen holding a baby at dawn from atop a wagon seat, he'd sold two Nehi drinks (a peach and a grape), two Coca-Colas, four bags of pork rinds, and two Moon Pies, answered three questions about his now-useless hand and one question about his married life, and told two different women how his wife, Miss Myra, was doing. After all that, he was actually relieved to see the girl, especially to see her instead of her husband, because it meant he could spend a moment speaking with someone who knew nothing about him or his time at the mill or what he'd been doing since leaving it.

Verchel saw that they'd put her to work as a doffer, changing out the full spools for empty ones, work usually reserved for the very young, the very small, or both. From looking at her, Verchel had no idea how old she was—maybe seventeen, maybe younger—but he knew for certain that she was small. Her brown hair was braided and pinned up behind her head, and her thin dress could hardly hide her narrow shoulders and thin waist. It seemed impossible that a body so small could have given birth to another. But there was something about her that made him fear getting too close, something that told him she would just as soon spit in his eye as say hello.

When he saw the girl she was in the middle of a bank of spinners, yanking off the full spindles and sliding the empty ones into place. She pushed past the women on the line, not looking a single one of them in the eye. Verchel stopped the dope wagon and watched her, then he looked around to see if anyone was watching him. He waited for her to reach the end of the line.

"Hello," he hollered, trying to raise his voice above the crush of machinery, waving his good hand and keeping the other tucked up close to his body for fear that something would grab ahold of it and not give back what was left. The girl looked up at him as if she were surprised that someone might be addressing her. Then she nodded and gathered the full spindles in her arms and set them on a little cart. She turned her back to Verchel and pushed the cart toward another line of spinners.

Verchel, not knowing what else to do and not knowing enough about the girl to chase after her or to ask after her once she was gone, called out the only question that came to his mind.

"How's your baby?"

The girl stopped pushing the cart and turned to face him. Where her brown eyes once seemed to look past him, Verchel now felt as if they penetrated him.

"Who are you?" she asked. Her voice was clear and strong, deeper than he assumed it would be.

"I'm Verchel Park," he said. "I work at the store. My wife wants to know how your baby is."

"What business is it of yours?" she asked.

"It ain't my business," Verchel said. "It ain't me who's wanting to know. It's my wife."

"That's not what you said first," she said.

"What do you mean?"

"*You* asked me how my baby is. You didn't mention nothing about your wife."

"Well, I'm mentioning her now," Verchel said.

"What business is it of hers, then?"

"I don't know," he said. "She just wanted me to ask you."

The girl looked at him for another moment, then she spun around toward the cart and lifted two full spindles and replaced them with two empty ones. She pushed the cart on ahead of her.

He didn't know what else to do, so he left the dope wagon and hurried to catch up with her, looking around all the while to make sure no one he knew had spotted him talking to the girl across the banks of spinners that separated them.

"I saw y'all when you first got to town last year," Verchel said. "I was at the store, and I saw you out in the wagon with your baby and that mule."

"We ain't got no mule," she said.

"You had one then."

"We ain't got no mule."

"Well, you must've sold it," he said.

"Nope. Died."

"Well, it was living when I seen you," Verchel said. "And I told my wife when I got home, and she thought I should ask after you, ask after your little one."

"And what is it your wife wants to know?" she asked.

"Well, how y'all are getting along, one," Verchel said.

The girl looked up the row where the dope wagon sat waiting for Verchel's return.

"Give me one of them Coca-Colas and I'll tell you," she said.

"Okay," Verchel said. He smiled, acknowledging that the girl had gotten one over on him. "Okay."

He left her and returned with an ice-cold, sweaty Coca-Cola in his good hand. The girl eyed the bottle. He offered it to her across the top of her cart, and she closed her fingers around it and tipped it back, emptying it in just a couple of swallows, the fizz of it causing her chest to jump. She handed the empty bottle to Verchel.

"We're getting along fine," she said.

"And your husband?"

"We're getting along fine," she said again.

"Whereabouts y'all living?"

The girl looked at Verchel, a slight smile playing across her mouth. She nodded toward the dope wagon again.

"How about one of them Moon Pies," she said.

WITH THE GIRL'S directions, Verchel found the cabin easily enough later that afternoon after he'd returned the dope wagon to the store and left for the day. The family lived in an old shack on the edge of a piece of property still owned by the McGarrity family, a people who once made their lives from the land but now made their lives somewhere other than Spartanburg County after leaving this partic-ular soil behind. The girl had described the place perfectly: a dogtrot shack with bleached boards and a metal roof burnished brown by the sun.

The trees along the road were mad with crows. The birds ruffled the leaves like a heavy wind, and their cries seemed to bore into Ver-chel's ears. He could almost smell the creek water from where he stood at the top of the road, hidden behind a clump of wild blue and purple hydrangea, sweat running from under the brim of his hat and catching in his eyebrows before he brushed it away. From this van-tage point he could see the house perfectly, see that its two windows were covered from the inside by dark curtains, that its front steps leaned away from him toward the slope where the land rolled down into a green holler.

After dinner he told Miss Myra about seeing the girl, how good she looked, how happy she seemed to be working such a good job in such a nice little town as Cowpens clearly was.

Miss Myra had all kinds of questions: "What kind of work does her husband do?" and "Where do they live?" While he knew the answer to the second question, it took him a few days to know the answer to the first with anything approaching certainty, although the final question the stranger had asked Verchel on the morning they first met was certainty enough.

The shack where the girl and stranger lived formed a kind of triangle between Verchel's house and the store, and so it was only a matter of minutes by which Verchel was late on his way home each evening, minutes of tardiness that could be and were always explained by his having to push the dope wagon back to the store, unload it, count the money, and organize things for the next morning's shift. The boy Wilfred hadn't yet returned to work, and the way this flu was spreading there was a very good chance Verchel's tenure behind the dope wagon would be long, if not permanent.

He took to spying on the shack each afternoon on his way home, assuming his perch by the road behind the wild hydrangea, and watching the doors on either side of the dogtrot to see if they ever opened. That's where he was on the third day, what happened to be a Wednesday, when he saw the stranger come out of the door on the left side and stand on the porch steps in the bright sunlight and take in great gulps of air as if the shack's interior were filled with water rather than darkness.

The stranger stood for a moment, hatless and shoeless, blinking his eyes in the bright, hot sun like he'd just woken from a long sleep and didn't know the day or season. Verchel was close enough to see the stranger's eyes, but far enough away not to worry about being seen himself. He watched as the man nearly skipped down the porch steps and into the knee-high, weedy grass before turning right and disappearing down into the holler where a creek gurgled out of sight.

If one were to have asked Verchel if he held his breath until the stranger reappeared from his trip to the creek he would've said no, but anyone passing by would've disagreed, for Verchel stood still long enough to have a succession of things land on him without him or them noticing his or their presence: ladybugs, dragonflies, a dollop of robin droppings, and a single leaf from a maple that drifted nearly twenty-five feet before coming to rest on his right shoulder like an angel or a devil that might or might not soon whisper advice into his ear.

But one thing is for certain, and that is that Verchel did eventually exhale and then inhale a breath large enough to fill his lungs twice after seeing the stranger crest the hill on his way back to the cabin. The man hopped up the porch steps with the same gaiety with which he'd descended them, and he'd disappeared inside the same black hole of an open doorway. Verchel's eyes saw these things without their being registered by his mind because his mind's eye was too busy beholding and later re-beholding a particular image: the two large, heavy jugs the stranger had grasped in either hand.

THE FOLLOWING AFTERNOON Verchel did not return to his perch by the wild hydrangea in order to look down at the old shack and wait for the stranger to reappear, because now he knew all he needed to know. That evening, when he returned home an hour or so earlier than usual, he explained it by the slow day at the store and the slower day behind the dope wagon. And then he sat on the porch steps and brooded over his lone cigarette while Miss Myra went on and on about the good, county-wide work the Ladies' Improvement Society was doing.

"We've started calling on the homes of the ill and the ill-bred," she said, explaining how one of the wives in her group had convinced her husband to let them commandeer an old wagon and two even older mules for the purposes of gallivanting around the county to pay visits upon unsuspecting wanton souls. "It's amazing how many people need the assistance of a group like ours. It's amazing how many dark souls need the light of Christ to shine upon them."

Verchel sat and listened, concentrating only on his cigarette and the palpable darkness that clouded both his lungs and heart.

IT WAS BEHIND the counter at the store on Friday that Verchel made the kind of decision he'd never made before: the decision to take action instead of waiting for action to take him. The man who stumbled into both machinery and marriage with his eyes closed would no longer stumble blindly, but would instead move with calm conviction toward wherever his heart led him, and it was back to the dogtrot where he was led that afternoon on his way home.

Once he assumed his familiar post by the hydrangea, there were a number of decisions that needed to be made: Which door to knock on? How to go about discussing what he'd come to discuss? How to broach a subject that a stranger might be too suspicious to broach? How to remind a man of who you were when he might not remember having ever laid eyes on you?

These questions were answered—or more clearly put, these problems were solved—when Verchel did not see the stranger appear but instead felt something of the stranger's presence: the cold steel tip of a rifle's barrel pushed up against his spine.

"So," the stranger said, his voice sounding both familiar and foreign, containing something of the mountains that rose toward North Carolina on the northern edge of the county, "you a revenuer or a snoop?"

"Neither," Verchel said. "Neither. I'm a friend."

"I don't got no friends," the stranger said.

"Me neither," Verchel said.

After that introduction Verchel knew he'd finally stumbled upon a spirit that would elucidate his own. That day he made the first of what would become regular visits to the stranger's house on his way home. The time he'd once spent hiding behind the hydrangea was now spent sitting in the cool, dark recesses of one of the two rooms that comprised the dogtrot shack. Sometimes Johnny Wiggins would let Verchel hold the baby girl named Lilly in his lap, and the little babe would turn her head toward the ceiling and stare backward at

Verchel as if she were looking into his past and didn't know quite what to make of who he'd been or who he'd become.

Often, the two men would talk: Verchel telling Johnny about how his hand had come to be the tiny, shriveled thing resting on his lap after one wrong step at the mill; about how his life had been changed, brightened, and saved by Pastor Olyphant and specifically by the man's daughter—Miss Myra—the greatest woman and human being he'd ever known. Johnny's side of the conversation was always less romantic. He complained to Verchel that he'd grown tired of humping his product out to the highway thrice a week in the middle of the night to meet his distributor, and he wanted to know if Verchel knew anyone who had a car. Johnny nodded at little Lilly where she sat on the floor, playing with a pinecone, and told Verchel that another baby figured to be on the way and that times were about to get tough and money tight.

Verchel was doing his part to assuage Wiggins's fears of financial ruin: the few dollars a week that Miss Myra gave him for lunch at the store now found their way into Johnny's upturned and expectant hand, and instead of crunching on pork rinds and using his tongue to scrape white bread and bologna from the roof of his mouth, Verchel now knocked back and nearly coughed up the crystal-clear rotgut that Wiggins had been cooking creekside at the bottom of the holler.

As the weeks passed and the spring turned into summer before waning toward autumn, Verchel opened his pocketknife twice to notch new holes in his belt so his pants could be cinched tighter around his shrinking waist.

"Are you feeling all right, dear?" Miss Myra asked on more than one occasion, doing her best to look into Verchel's eyes for any kind of sickness. For it was late 1919 and the Spanish flu had proven more powerful than the war.

"Aw," Verchel would answer, "I'm as healthy as a man can be."

"Your clothes fairly hang on you," Miss Myra would say.

"I'm feeling fine," Verchel would promise. "Mighty fine. I don't know that I've ever felt finer."

And, aside from stomachaches brewed by the wild mint and sassafras he ate by the roadside on the way home from Wiggins's house in order extinguish his liquor breath, Verchel did feel fine. As a matter of fact, he couldn't think of a time when his mind seemed clearer, freer, more all-seeing than it did these days, especially on the long weekday afternoons he spent inside Johnny Wiggins's shack. For Verchel's waist wasn't the only thing shrinking; the dope wagon profits were getting smaller as well. Verchel now zipped through the mill at near-breakneck speed. The only thing that would stop him or slow him down were the few brave souls who'd leap in front of the cart in order to enjoy an ice-cold soda or reach out their hands in an attempt to grasp the cart as it passed by so they could fork over a few cents for some sweet or savory treat.

As he always had, Verchel did his best not to make eye contact with any mill employees, and the one employee he'd first sought out was now the one he least wanted to see. The girl, whose name he'd learned was Ella May Wiggins, would often appear on the other side of a loom or deep in the recesses of the card room. She'd risen rapidly in responsibility and rank, but she'd gotten stuck in the second shift, going in at 2 P.M. and knocking off around midnight every day except Sunday. Whenever he saw her, Verchel averted his eyes, pushed the dope wagon without stopping, and found himself wondering if she knew that he'd spent so much time inside her home, sat beside her husband, bounced her baby girl on the sharp cap of his knee.

Usually Verchel and Johnny would nod to one another by way of hello, and then Verchel would fork over a couple of coins into Johnny's dirty palm. Then they'd each take to a straight-back chair and sit in silence for a few minutes, passing a jar of clear liquor back and forth between them, the baby girl either playing on the floor or sleeping on a makeshift pallet. She had Johnny's light eyes and hair, but something about her stillness and quiet nature marked her as being Ella's girl.

Sometimes Johnny would be entertaining a couple of women by the time Verchel arrived at the house—women Johnny called friends—and sometimes Johnny and his friends would have a few drinks and leave the room and go across to the other side of the shack and stay gone for long minutes at a time, nothing but giggles and the occasional stifled sigh making their way across the dogtrot to let Verchel know that someone else was at home aside from himself and the baby girl, the odors of the women's soft powder and sweet perspiration hovering about them both.

In many ways it was those two women—or at least two women like them, as Verchel could hardly differentiate between such women—that caused the first and what would be final rift between him and Johnny Wiggins. It was a Friday afternoon in the spring of 1920, the air sharp and crisp, although the late day had turned somewhat warm after the cool morning. Johnny had gone across the dogtrot with two women, and Verchel, as usual, had stayed behind with little Lilly, who by now knew his face and his voice and almost seemed to recognize the little songs he'd sing between sips of shine. The newborn baby boy named Otis slept on a spread of quilts by Lilly's pallet. Verchel hadn't even known Ella had given birth, and when he'd remarked on the presence of the little baby, all Johnny had said was "That's my son."

Verchel watched Lilly now from where he sat in his chair as she stood on her own two skinny legs and reached up toward the table where a shiny red apple—the last of a bushel they'd spent the past few afternoons eating—sat just out of reach. Verchel suddenly found himself making his own wobbly attempt to stand on his own two skinny legs, his pocketknife swinging open in his hand, its blade stabbing at the apple. He returned to his seat, and with his bad hand he held the apple up close to his body and then cut as nice a slice as he could manage.

When Verchel held the small wedge of apple out toward her, Lilly ambled over to Verchel's chair. She closed her tiny fingers around the apple slice and lifted it to a mouth that had slowly grown full of pearly-colored teeth in the short time Verchel had known her. He watched as she sucked the juice from the apple slice, the fruit turning soft and pulpy in her hand, the peel lifting away like a ribbon before she shoved the slice into her mouth. She didn't swallow it, but turned away from Verchel and walked over to the mess of quilts where her brother slept. Verchel watched as she used her finger to spoon the apple mush from her mouth and spread it across her brother's lips. The baby startled when she touched him, opened his eyes, licked at the sugary pulp. When Lilly returned, Verchel cut another piece of apple for her, watched as she fed it to her brother like she'd fed him the first piece. Verchel picked up his cup and knocked back what was left in it.

As his knife cut another slice of the apple, something of Verchel's past life flashed before his eyes: he recalled what a pleasure it had been to spoon corn bread and buttermilk into the open mouths of his twin niece and nephew all that time ago while his mind, body, and spirit healed at his brother's house, and he thought of how he had hardly laid eyes on them in the time he'd been married to Miss Myra. The more he turned it over in his mind, the more he understood that leaving work early and spending the late afternoons in a dogtrot shack with a no-good, philandering moonshiner had less to do with the liquor he craved and more to do with the life he actually wanted. He wanted Wiggins's life: the rosy-faced toddler who stood before him now, drool and apple juice streaming from her mouth; the sleeping newborn baby boy; their small, tough mother Ella, who toiled like a mule six days a week at the mill.

All of this culminated with a clear conception of the pleasures Miss Myra's love had taken from him: the joy in the company of small children; the bite and flushed feel of a good, stiff drink.

So perhaps that's why he said what he said when Johnny opened the door and stumbled inside the room, one of the two women close behind him, both of them drunk and giggling as if they'd never be sober or somber again. Verchel waited until Johnny collapsed into the other straight-back chair and pulled the woman down onto his lap.

"You ought not do them that way," Verchel said.

"Who're you talking about?" Wiggins asked.

"Your wife," Verchel said. "These babies here."

"What 'way' you got in mind?" Wiggins asked.

"You know," Verchel said. He folded his knife and slipped it back into the front pocket of his trousers. "I've watched you."

"And what would you recommend I do? What 'way' would you have me follow?" Wiggins asked. "Yours?"

"There's worse ways than mine," Verchel said.

"Maybe so," Wiggins said, "but it'd be hard to find them. What's worse than a man who prays to the Lord on Sunday morning with liquor in his veins?"

"I'm a sinner," Verchel said. "I got no qualm saying it."

"You're worse than a sinner," Wiggins said. "You're a coward."

"Now hold on," Verchel said, his heartbeat picking up, his mind flashing forward to the prospect of him and Wiggins coming to blows.

"You're a henpecked coward," Wiggins said, his teeth clenched on the other side of a dangerous smile. The woman in Wiggins's lap moved as if attempting to stand in order to get away from whatever it was that was about to happen, but Wiggins held on to her hips so that she couldn't scramble free.

"You watch your mouth. My wife's a fine woman," Verchel said. "A great one."

"And why's that?"

"Because," Verchel said, "because she does the Lord's work. Uplifts this community. That's why I come looking for you. She wants to uplift this family, just like she uplifted me."

"Well, I sure as hell don't need no help getting uplifted," Wiggins said. He popped the woman's backside with the palm of his hand, and an exhalation shot from her mouth as if something had burst inside her chest.

"We all need grace," Verchel said.

"Your wife can't give you that. All she can do is fool you into believing you don't want the things you actually want. That ain't grace," Wiggins said. "That's trickery.

"But that one over there," Wiggins said, his head nodding toward the door that led across the dogtrot, "she's the kind of gal you need, all the grace you can handle. And I'll tell you this: she likes you. She told Sarah here that she thinks you're cute."

At that, Wiggins snaked his hand up Sarah's back and, closing his fingers around the nape of her neck, jostled her a little as if trying to wake her.

"It's true," Sarah said. "I heard her say it. Just now, when we were all over there—"

"See?" Johnny said. "I told you." With his free hand he reached out and clapped Verchel's shoulder, and then he reached beneath his seat where a milk crate housed a collection of Mason jars. He unscrewed the lid on one of them and took a long drink, and then he passed it to Verchel, who did the same. "Now go on over there and ask her yourself what she thinks about you."

As Verchel swallowed down what would be his last bit of liquor for the day, he discovered that his head felt empty. The feeling was a good one: the warm liquor threading through his blood; the sweet scent of the woman named Sarah encircling his head; the knowledge of the other woman waiting for him in the other room; his new understanding that grace wasn't something Miss Myra could give, but was instead something he must go out and claim for himself. He felt a hand in the small of his back push him forward, and although he knew the hand belonged to Johnny Wiggins, Verchel also knew the hand was unseen and therefore unknown, and he decided to go where it led him, and where it led him was across the way and into darkness.

As Verchel passed across the dogtrot the momentary explosion of blinding sunlight carried his mind back to the time he'd had his picture taken—the only time he'd had it taken—the summer after he and Miss Myra were married. They'd come into Cowpens, where a traveling photographer had set up shop inside the post office, and the two of them—dressed in the wedding clothes they'd worn that fateful Sunday morning—had taken their places before a dark swath of fabric that hung from the wall. While the photographer readied his equipment, Verchel felt Miss Myra's hand come to rest heavily upon his shoulder, her whispered voice falling just as heavily upon his ear.

"Now, sit up straight, dear," she'd said just before the brilliant flash of the bulb cemented their images as husband and wife for time immemorial.

Well, that's that, Verchel had thought.

And now this was this: before him a blond-haired woman bent at the waist in the dark room, her left leg atop the low mattress skid, her long fingers either rolling up or rolling down a white stocking worn thin enough to show her pale white toes through its tip. He'd seen this woman an hour ago in the other room, but seeing her now—in a state of either undressing or redressing—was to see her in a manner he had not seen a woman before.

When she raised her eyes to Verchel where he stood in the open doorway—the light playing across her face and flickering through her eyes—Verchel saw something of a performance in the way she stood there letting his eyes take her in, and he thought of the actress Betty Compson, whom he'd beheld at a movie house in Spartanburg the previous summer. The woman before him carried the same bright yellow curls that tumbled over Compson's shoulders and draped across her chest and the same wide eyes that had looked out from the screen and found Verchel where he sat alone in the dark, dusty theater.

But he'd never heard Betty Compson's voice, which he imagined as high-pitched and sweet, so it was a surprise when this woman's raspy tone shattered the stillness of the scene.

"You need something?" she asked.

"Johnny told me to come over here," Verchel said.

"You got any money?"

"You ought not be living this way."

"You got any money or not?"

"I done give it all to Johnny," Verchel said.

"Well," the woman said, sliding her foot off the skid, standing up straight and running her hands down the front of her dress, "if that's how he wants to work it."

Verchel swallowed hard.

"They said you like me," he said.

"Okay," the woman said. She lifted her dress and slid her undergarments to the floor and kicked them aside. Verchel watched her, his mind not quite registering what occurred right before him.

"They told me you said that: that you like me."

"Okay," the woman said again.

"And I like you, and I want to share the good news of salvation."

"Share it," the woman said. She lay back against the skid, her legs parted enough for Verchel to see the shadow between them. He didn't move. She sighed and scooted to the edge of the skid and stood and walked toward him. "Are you too drunk?" she asked. She took his hand. "My God," she said, "you're ice-cold." She led him over to the skid and undid his trousers. "My God," she said again, "you're shaking."

When she pushed him toward the bed, Verchel felt his body falling as if it might never stop, and even after his back came to rest atop the skid he felt his fall continue through the bed and into the floor beneath it, down through the earth, where he tumbled toward its hot, fiery belly. He fell with such velocity that he didn't notice when she climbed atop him, didn't notice as the skid and his body gave with her weight, her movement.

He lay there staring at the darkened rafters without seeing the ceiling, without seeing the wisps of blond curls that swung in and out of his line of vision, without hearing the dull scrape of the bed skid against the wood floor, without registering the encouraging, almost demanding, words of the woman atop him, who clearly wanted this thing to be done.

But what he did hear was the approaching hoofbeats that bore down upon his skull and trampled their way into his brain. At first he thought it might be the pale rider, commonly and better known as Death, but he couldn't figure out what could've killed him so quickly: the whiskey or the woman or the way his body felt as both things coursed through his veins.

But it wasn't Death that Verchel heard because Death doesn't sing like an angel, doesn't announce his coming with song. No, what Verchel heard above the hoofbeats were the voices of angels as they sang strains of "Glory, Hallelujah."

What he heard next were the shouts of voices in the room across the way: Johnny Wiggins screaming something aloud that Verchel couldn't decipher over the scrape of the skid across the floor and the words of the woman above him and the sound of something wild coming from his own throat. And then there was silence around him so that the noises in the other room were suddenly louder: along with Wiggins's voice came the screams of the woman Sarah, who'd been seated on Johnny's lap, and along with her cries came the cries of little Lilly and her baby brother.

Without a word, the woman climbed off Verchel and picked up her undergarments and walked toward the door and opened it. Verchel raised his head and peered across the dogtrot into the dark, gaping maw of the other room. He stared for a moment, his eyes adjusting to the spinning of this room and the bright light of the sun and the blackness of the room into which he gazed.

From deep in the dark void a pale face appeared and floated toward Verchel so that he believed himself to be hallucinating, because even in his state he knew faces could not float, could not detach themselves from bodies and hover above the earth. And then the darkness took shape and walked from the room and became whole and separate in the sunlight: the pale face and the black shape were those of Miss Myra. In her arms she carried the screaming baby boy. Miss Myra and the baby were followed by several other black figures, and Verchel had a vision not of angels that had come to save his soul, but of crows that had come to pick his body apart.

Miss Myra stopped in the open doorway, her eyes never once leaving Verchel's. The woman Verchel had been with now slowly backed away from the door as if she could disappear into the shadows of the darkened room. She bent at the waist and stepped into her undergarments one leg at a time and pulled them up under her dress.

The baby continued to cry, and Miss Myra looked at the screaming, red-faced infant in her arms, tears streaming down his cheeks, his tiny fingers opening into and closing around the nothingness before him. Miss Myra looked back at Verchel. He sat up slowly and propped himself on his elbows. He wanted to stand, but his trousers were still gathered around his feet and he was afraid he might fall. Miss Myra whispered into the baby's ear in an attempt to soothe him. She patted his back. She bounced him in her arms. She stared at her husband.

"Oh, Verchel," Miss Myra finally said. "What are we going to do with them? With you?"

CHAPTER FOUR

Ella May

Sunday, May 5, 1929

The truck, piloted by the young girl with the strange accent, left Bessemer City and headed north. In the town of Cherryville a handful of crumbling brick buildings housed a few mills just outside of the small downtown. The truck came to a stop, and Ella stood and looked over the railing and gazed at the collection of buildings. The streets were still and quiet, the lone strip of sidewalk empty and dusty. Ella wondered if everyone had fled in advance of the strike organizers' arrival, and she recalled her first sight of the truck just an hour earlier, how it had terrified her, how it had elicited only fear when the one thing she'd needed was hope. Doubt flared in her mind.

She remained peering over the rails when the truck reached Lincolnton, a larger city ten miles to the northeast. Unlike Cherryville, Lincolnton's downtown streets teemed with people, and Ella wondered if it was court day, and she recalled the times as a young girl back in Tennessee, back before her family moved to the lumber camps, when her father would load her and Wesley into the wagon and take them into Sevierville to watch the farmers and the businessmen and county men converge on the square for court day. Her father would park the wagon and find a seat on one of the benches near the courthouse. He'd drop a few pennies apiece into her and Wesley's upturned hands, and then he'd light his pipe and talk with other farmers while she and Wesley ducked in and out of the general store and the confectionery, conspiring on how best to spend their pennies.

But today was Sunday, and court did not meet on Sundays in the Sevierville, Tennessee, of her childhood, nor did it do so here in Lincolnton, North Carolina. No, the crowd before her had gathered only to confront the truck in which she rode, and by the time Ella had embraced this realization—the realization that the crowd was composed entirely of men, no women or children in sight—the girl behind the wheel had already decided that no one in Lincolnton would be traveling with them to the rally in Gastonia.

The dozens of men—dressed in suits and overalls and shirtsleeves and trousers—waited in the middle of the street as if forming a barrier to the truck's passage. Their numbers spilled over to the sidewalks. Others watched from inside buildings and leaned from windows. The truck picked up speed as the first projectiles struck its sides and crashed onto its bed: bottles, bricks, lengths of pipe that clattered like blasts of thunder when they landed beside Ella. Impulse told her to gather these missiles, stand, hurl them back toward the men who'd thrown them, but as things continued to fall like hailstones around her she could do nothing but cower in the driver's-side corner of the truck bed.

She did not remove her hands from her head or open her eyes or raise her face until she felt certain that the last of the launched weapons had landed in the truck or somewhere outside it. When she looked toward the open tailgate she found a man struggling to climb inside. His face, handsome if not for its anger, was red with exertion, his blond hair ringed damp where his bowler hat had blown from his head during the chase. Behind him swarms of men ran after the truck screaming all manner of curses about Russia and communism and whores and Reds. The man who clung to the back of the truck kept his eyes on Ella. He grasped the railing and tried to climb inside, but his foot slipped off the bumper. He spat at Ella.

"You damn union bitch," he said. "You damn commie bitch."

He tried to climb inside again, but by the time the sole of his shoe met the tailgate, Ella already held a brick above her head. She first smashed the fingers of the man's left hand where they had wrapped themselves around the railing. He screamed, unclenched his fingers. His foot slipped from the tailgate again and for a moment it looked as if he would fall, but he managed to cling to the truck, his ruined left hand flailing for a hold. Ella brought the brick down on the back of his right hand where he'd kept it flattened against the bed. The bones crunched like a pinecone crushed underfoot, and in the brief moment before he tumbled from the truck and cut somersaults in the road Ella saw the fear of death touch the man's eyes.

She sat down, surrounded by shattered glass and dusty crumbles of red brick and rusted pipes that rolled around the bed as the truck bounced along. She watched the horde of men surround the fallen man where he lay prone in the road and help him to his feet. She felt no relief in seeing that he had survived. She felt nothing for him, nothing for the other men. Not fear or intimidation and certainly not pity.

THE TRUCK SLOWED again when they reached the town of High Shoals. Ella allowed her body to shift, to let her right shoulder come to a rest against the railing as the truck turned onto a shadowed lane. Bottles and other things the men had thrown still rolled around the truck bed. The brakes squealed, then hissed as the truck came to a stop. The engine vibrated so that Ella's hands appeared to tremble of their own accord. She looked down, watched her hands for a moment, made her hands into fists to stop their shaking.

Ella heard the sound of one of the truck's doors opening and slamming shut. She couldn't tell which one. Then the sound of the other door doing the same. She imagined the two women being yanked from the truck and pulled into the trees by men who'd been waiting for them. She wanted to stand, to look over the railing, to leap to the road and break off at a sprint and put as much distance between her and the truck as she could. But the same survival instinct that had fueled her to act in Lincolnton now forced her to remain silent and still. She picked up a length of pipe that had rolled to a stop at her feet. She waited, tried to hear over the engine, the truck trembling beneath her with its own impatience.

The appearance of a face at the tailgate startled her, and Ella raised the pipe as if she might hurl it at the person she saw. It took a moment for her to recognize the face as belonging to the girl who'd been driving the truck.

The girl smirked at Ella. "I come in peace," she said. She looked down the lane behind her, where the late-day sun found the road through the heavy trees. She turned back to Ella. Her eyes searched the otherwise empty truck. She spoke over the noise of the engine. "Seems like plenty room," she said. "I thought I'd let Velma take a turn behind the wheel."

The girl climbed up into the bed just as the truck lurched forward. She fell to her knees, pivoted, and kicked at the back of the cab, barely missing Ella's left shoulder. "Goddammit, Velma!" she screamed. She looked at Ella. "Sorry," she said, "but goddammit, Velma!" She kicked the back of the cab again. A knock came from the other side. "She can't drive for shit," the girl said. She turned so that she and Ella sat side by side facing the open tailgate. They watched the view before them shift while the driver attempted a series of maneuvers to return the truck to the main road.

The girl removed a tin of tobacco from her dress and rolled a cigarette. She gestured toward Ella, but Ella shook her head.

"Don't smoke?" the girl asked. Ella shook her head again. "Nasty, ain't it?"

"Don't bother me," Ella said. She allowed her shoulders to relax, her spine to resettle itself. She released the breath she'd been holding. "You go ahead."

The girl took the length of pipe from Ella's hand and tossed it off the back of the truck. It bounced on the road. She struck a match, drew on the cigarette, and then stared at it. "Yep," she said. "Nasty all right." The fingers of her free hand traced along the floor. She picked up a piece of broken bottle and looked at Ella through it, her eye suddenly large and grotesque behind the glass. "Got a little hairy back there, didn't it?"

"You could say."

"I saw that man take a tumble," the girl said. She tossed the piece of glass onto the road. They had picked up speed. Trees and fields rolled away from them. "You must know how to handle yourself."

"I ain't trying to get killed," Ella said. "Didn't sign up for that." She caught herself. "I ain't signed up for nothing yet."

The girl smoked and stared out the back of the truck. They passed an old car that was headed north. They watched it until they could no longer see it. The girl finished her cigarette and tossed it the same way she'd tossed the glass. "Shoot," she said. "Ain't nobody getting killed."

Her name was Sophia Blevin. She was nineteen. She'd grown up in Pittsburgh, but she'd been born in a country somewhere called Ukraine, which, to Ella, explained her strange accent. Her father was a history professor at one of the universities in Pittsburgh. Her mother was a Unitarian minister.

"She ain't what you think of when people down here think *minister*," Sophia said. "She ain't holy rolling. She's in it for the people."

Sophia had been raised on a commune in New England before

moving to the smoky steel town where her parents found a growing movement of intellectuals, organizers, and anarchists. She'd joined her parents in strikes in Passaic, New Bedford, and Johnstown. The strike at Loray was the first she'd worked without them, but she hoped to make them proud.

"They sent me because Pop got hit in the head with a bottle at New Bedford and Mother's running a mission for pregnant girls. They stayed put for this one, which is too bad because this here's going to go down as the most famous strike in American history."

The truck sped east down the highway toward Gastonia now, the wind moving overhead like a jet stream, the sun beginning to slip from the sky. Ella watched explosions of sparks as Sophia burned through a book of matches trying to light another cigarette.

"Might be a sign I should quit," she said. Her last match sputtered, went out. She looked up at Ella. "You believe in signs?"

"My mother did," Ella said.

"You?"

"Maybe," Ella said, suddenly afraid of sounding ignorant, seeming "country" to the ear of this girl whose parents were intellectuals, who'd traveled all over the country organizing people just like Ella. "But I probably don't."

"Well, I believe in signs," Sophia said. "At least I do today, anyway."

She tossed the tin of tobacco from the truck, flipped open the pack of rolling papers, and, one by one, released them to the wind.

Ella watched the papers fly, recalled an image long buried: her mother kneeling at the fireplace, holding scraps of paper to the fire on a New Year's Eve. Ella and her mother would write wishes for the following year: a new dress, a doll, a Bible. Wesley and her father never joined them, even gently teased them about this superstition. The ritual had always been something Ella cherished, that burst of mystery when the paper caught fire, the wish burning itself from possibility into hope as it escaped up the chimney.

The year before they moved to the lumber camps, their last New Year's Eve as tenant farmers in East Tennessee, Ella's father finally joined her and her mother in their yearly tradition. He'd never learned to read, but Ella watched as he and her mother whispered back and forth before he scrawled out his New Year's wish and folded the paper over what seemed a dozen times, as if it could keep his wish safe. He tossed it onto the flames. As the fire consumed the paper, Ella knew that she would never forget the only word she'd ever seen her father write aside from his name: *Work.*

Ella imagined her handwriting printed across Sophia's rolling papers as they took flight. She saw words like *Rose, rest, happiness, food.* She closed her eyes, imagined the warmth of her parents' fireplace, imagined just one of her potential wishes coming true.

"What about you, Ella May?" Sophia asked.

"What about me?"

"That's what I'm asking," Sophia said. "What about you? All I know is that I met you at the crossroads and that you'll stand up to a bully when push comes to shove."

"There ain't a whole lot about me."

"Hell," Sophia said. "There's a whole lot about everybody."

Ella stared west. She imagined the great mountains foggy and rain-damp in the distance, the blue ridges rolling away in great swells. She opened her mouth, paused for a moment, gathered the story of her life around her as she would lift the hem of a long dress before stepping across a stream. She did not think, did not stop to look at Sophia. She simply began to speak.

She imagined her brief life unfolding there in the back of the truck like a story written across a great scroll of paper. The scroll unfurled itself and rolled out the open tailgate, across the mountains toward Tennessee, all the way to the tiny schoolhouse outside Sevierville. There Mr. Musical bent to the rough pine floor, took up the scroll, held it to the weak light coming through the dirty windows, sniffed and nodded to himself, then set about recording the great equation of

Ella's life at the front of the empty room, his pendulous wooden leg swinging as he shuffled along the length of the blackboard.

She told Sophia about her family's life on the tenant farms, then the lumber camps. The music of her mother's voice around the camp-fire, the great steaming cauldron of clothes, the smell of pine tar and sap and the reek of the sawyers' sweat. The deaths: her mother's, her father's, Willie's. John's sudden appearance in her life and the many disappearances that followed. The countless mills in both Carolinas. Life as the only white family in Stumptown. Losing Willie, her fear of losing Rose: the weight of her children and their lives upon her heart. The jangle of Charlie's guitar, the sensation of her voice filling her chest and lifting from her throat to meet his music. She told Sophia about waiting at the crossroads, her nervous hand fingering the union leaflet she'd been carrying in her pocket, the many mo-ments that led to the one they now shared in the back of this truck.

Sophia smiled, looked to the road as if still pondering the stories she'd just heard. She looked back at Ella. "Hot damn," she said. "And you sing too?" She laughed, slapped her knee. "Hell, girl, we hit the jackpot with you. You might be the one we've been looking for."

THE EARLY EVENING sky was dark enough for stars to be seen.

"Look at them stars," Sophia said, her neck craned, her face turned directly toward the sky. "We don't got those in Pittsburgh."

Ella noted Sophia's smooth neck, her olive skin. It was obvious to Ella, obvious to anyone who might see Sophia, that she had never worked in a cotton mill. She was too healthy, too happy, too at ease in the world and too in love with being alive in it.

Ella had passed through Gastonia—by far the largest city in the county, at almost twenty thousand people—on only a handful of occasions, but she knew it ran on textiles. Everyone across North Carolina, perhaps everyone in the South, knew this about the place that had come to be known as "the City of Spindles."

Centuries earlier, the area had been settled by Native Americans because of its proximity to a meandering river they called Catawba. The river's south branch and countless creeks that flowed west toward the Blue Ridge foothills proved especially valuable to the enterprising white settlers who were overrunning the land by the eighteenth century. Whiskey comprised the first wave of industry, bootleggers using waterpower to run their stills and the dense forests to keep them hidden. But it was soon discovered that the swift current was enough to power machinery, and it wasn't long before the men who once used water to grind corn for whiskey decided that the same power could fuel a revolution in the area's other primary product: cotton.

The county's first textile enterprise, the Mountain Island Mill, began operation on the Catawba in 1848, when the county was two years old. Other mills followed. Between the Civil War and the end of World War I, Gastonia's population tripled and the number of textile mills jumped from four to just under one hundred. Tenant farmers laid down their shovels and escaped the parched land that had never been and never would be theirs. Mountaineers from southern Appalachia left the lumber camps once there were no more trees to be felled, no more ridges to be cleared, no more logs to be floated downstream. Millhands in the South Carolina upstate believed and believed incorrectly that life might be a little better, a little easier, just a few miles north. Ella and John had followed that migration from the North Carolina mountains to the South Carolina mills, had caught the tail end of the snake as it coiled around itself and led them back across the border into Gaston County. Ella had believed that an easy life would eventually be theirs because John had said it would be so, but this was back when she believed the things he told her.

The piedmont mill barkers who stood atop stumps in the lumber camps and in knee-deep mud on the tenant farms had promised safe, sanitary housing in mill villages. Children would be educated at mill-sponsored schools. Souls saved at mill-sponsored churches. Paychecks cashed for scrip at mill-owned stores. It soon became apparent that the circularity of life in these villages differed little from what these former loggers and farmers knew about a life lived close to the land: you were forever in debt, forever hoping for the windfall that never came, forever thinking of ways to move on to another place as soon as you could save the money to do it.

Things were no different at the Loray Mill, the crown jewel of North Carolina's textile industry. Loray had been built in 1900 and touted as the largest textile mill in the world, and although local investors had funded it, northern interests took note of the abundance of cheap labor, the proximity to raw cotton, the railroads that now crisscrossed the South like lashings. Of particular interest was the looming threat of war and the incredible ways in which it fueled the country's need for cloth.

Loray's profits exploded. Demand rose. The barkers went farther into the mountains. More men and women and children tumbled down the hills, swathed in expectations of riches and lush living. The war passed, demand fell, work was hard to come by, although people like Ella chased it from mill to mill, from small town to small town. All they found was filth and disease and the kind of poverty they couldn't get away from once it took hold of them. American Mill No. 2 in Bessemer City, Rex over in Ranlo, the Cowpens Manufacturing Company down in South Carolina, Loray here in Gastonia: it didn't matter where you looked, Ella thought, it was the same overwhelming force bearing its weight upon the same powerless group of people; people just like her. The Loray Mill was in Gastonia, but it could have been anywhere in the South. It was all the same.

The truck in which the three women rode left the fields and the trees of the darkened countryside behind, and now the open highway had turned into Franklin Avenue. Streetlamps glowed with a dull light. Brick storefronts with glass windows lined the boulevard on either side. They passed people on foot. The sparse automobile traffic grew heavier. The air smelled of gasoline and exhaust and the myriad scents of cooking food as they passed a section of Franklin known to locals as Greasy Corner. Sophia stood and looked over the truck's railing. She whistled, pointed south. "There she is."

Ella stood, faced the direction in which Sophia stared. The colossus of the Loray Mill rose before them, its six stories of red brick illuminated by what seemed to be hundreds of enormous windows that cast an otherworldly pall over the night. The mill stretched across several city blocks, its central tower looming like a giant eye that stood sentinel above the surrounding village and its muddy streets, weed-choked lawns, and clapboard houses. From what Ella understood, life in the Loray village wasn't much different from life in the dilapidated cabins of Stumptown, except that the Loray village, like the mill itself, was nearly all white.

"Ella, it'd mean a lot if you could speak at the rally tonight," Sophia said. She looked at Ella. "People here need to know that our message is getting out. You coming from another mill in another town is a big deal. People need to see a stranger who's on their side."

Sophia's request hit Ella like one of the bricks or bottles that the men had thrown at them back in Lincolnton. Her head swam, and she gripped the truck's railing to keep from stumbling. She forced a laugh that gave her cover to catch her breath. "I don't know what I'd say," Ella said. "I can't imagine." But as soon as she said it she regretted it; she'd come this far and she needed this girl's help, needed the promises outlined on the leaflet she still carried in her pocket like a talisman.

"Hell, tell some of the story you just told me. You could sing something too."

Ella thought of the song she'd been writing. She slipped a trembling hand into her pocket and felt the folded leaflet. "I might could say something, might could sing too," she said. "I've been working on a song about the mill, but it ain't finished yet." She reached for the pencil she'd kept behind her ear, but it was gone. It must have come loose during the fight back in Lincolnton. "You got something I can write with. I might could finish it real quick."

Sophia smiled, reached into a pocket, and pulled out a thick stub of pencil. Ella took it in her hand, thought of how its thickness reminded her of one of Giles Corley's fingers.

The truck came abreast of Loray, turned left, and crossed the railroad tracks, headed north as if leaving town. Sophia turned and looked back at the mill, its lights floating in her eyes.

"We're going to shut that place down," she said. "You watch, Ella May. You're going to help us do it."

The busy thrum of Franklin Avenue gave way to small houses and grassy fields. The truck stopped on the side of the road by a simple, newly constructed A-frame. A hand-painted sign that read *Gastonia Local of the N.T.W.U.* hung above the small porch that sheltered the single door. Behind the headquarters, a white tent housed the commissary. The rumble of the truck's engine died away, followed by a cough of exhaust and a brief tremble that traveled up Ella's spine. The noise of the evening rose to meet her. A couple dozen men in overalls and women in homespun dresses stood talking by the building. Others were gathered in the grass around it. Children chased each other and played in the fields. The sound of a guitar came from somewhere Ella couldn't see.

"Well, come on, Ella May," Sophia said. They climbed down from the truck. The driver came around to meet them. Her name was Velma Burch. She was from New Jersey and was a veteran labor organizer. She was only forty years old, but the gauntness of her face and the streaks of gray hair beneath her bell-shaped hat made her seem much older.

"Ella May's a singer," Sophia said, "and she said she'll sing something for us tonight."

"Well, Beal wants them to sing," Velma said.

"Who's Beal?" Ella asked.

"And she knows a whole bunch of colored workers," Sophia said.

She raised her eyebrows, smiled in a way that made it clear that a secret thing had just passed between her and Velma.

"Beal's not going to know what to do with that," Velma said. "Best tell him about the singing first."

"Who's Beal?" Ella asked again.

"Who's Beal?" Velma asked. She widened her eyes and opened her mouth in mock surprise. "Why, he's the strike leader, right Miss Blevin?"

"Yes, indeed, Miss Burch," Sophia said. "He thinks he's the strike leader."

"Yep," Velma said. She turned back to Ella. "He's the strike leader all right."

The three of them looked toward the field across the road, where a stage had been erected. Poles had been set into the ground and a man on a ladder was lighting lanterns. Dense woods crouched behind the stage. It looked like a cow pasture that was about to be employed for a tent revival.

"What are you going to sing for us, Ella May?" Velma asked.

Ella looked down at the union leaflet on which she'd written new lyrics.

"I've been working on the words for a few days," Ella said. "It's to the tune of 'Little Mary Phagan.'"

"That's about the girl getting murdered at the pencil factory," Sophia said. "But she changed the words."

"That might not be a good one for a meeting," Velma said.

"It's just the melody," Ella said.

"Look here," Sophia said. She plucked the leaflet from Ella's hand, held it up to Velma's eyes, turned it so that she could see the handwriting on the once-blank paper. "She wrote the words on this side." She turned it over so that the black print that outlined the union's demands could be seen. "And I wrote the words on the other." She looked at Ella. "It's almost like we're sisters."

AN HOUR LATER Ella stood on the edge of the field, the world around her dark but for the oil lamp that hung above the head-quarters' door.

To the south, a steady stream of people crossed the railroad tracks and made their way up the road from the Loray village. Cars and trucks sat parked along either side of the road in long rows. Men in nice suits with cameras in hand took notes and snapped pictures of the strikers. Exploding flashbulbs cast long shadows that stretched toward the railroad tracks behind them.

"Beal likes a lot of media." Ella looked to her right, found Velma standing beside her, the woman's jaw moving as she chewed. She held something wrapped in wax paper. "He says it's free press, even though nothing's *free* about it. Everybody knows the newspaper's tied up with the mills and the government." She popped something else into her mouth, balled up the paper, stuffed it into her pocket.

Ella watched Velma chew and swallow, watched her pass the back of her hand across her mouth. A glowing heat in Ella's stomach sig-naled its emptiness. She couldn't remember her last meal.

"Sophia told me there might be something to eat tonight," she said.

"We eat after the meeting," Velma said. She cleared her throat, ran her tongue over her front teeth. "People stick around for food. If you feed them first they'll get their bellies full and go home."

They watched the crowds gather, watched as more cars and trucks passed and searched for empty places to park. Velma nodded at people as they passed by, smiled, said hello to the ones she knew, kept her silence when newspapermen drew close.

The field began to fill with people. Velma swatted at a mosquito on her arm, looked at the dollop of blood it had left behind. She wiped her hand on her dress and nodded toward the field. "Hard to believe we're going to fill this whole field with tents that aren't here yet."

"When should they get here?" Ella asked.

"I don't know," Velma said. "Yesterday? Evictions begin tomorrow at dawn in the village. They're going to look to us, and I'm going to look to Beal, and I'm going to say, 'We're all looking at you, Fred.'"

"Maybe they'll get here tomorrow."

"They're always getting here tomorrow," Velma said. "Everything's getting here tomorrow: tents, food, supplies. It's all getting here tomorrow." She seemed to catch herself, seemed to want to unsay the things she'd said. She looked down, toed at the gravel with her shoe. "We like to keep things moving during the meetings," she said. "So, if you hear your name you be ready to get up there and tell your story, sing your song."

Ella closed her hand around the leaflet in her pocket. It had grown tissue-soft from her sweaty palm. Velma crossed to the other side of the street, disappeared into the crowd. Ella followed. She passed through clouds of cigarette smoke, caught snatches of conversations about the strike, about the next day's evictions, about the union. She kept moving until she reached the right-hand side of the stage. Three stairs led up to the platform. The moon had risen on the other side of the trees. A form passed through its light, stopped in the middle of the stage, rapped its knuckles on the podium. It was Sophia. She rapped her knuckles again, waited for the crowd to quiet. She welcomed everyone to the meeting.

Ella did her best to focus on the things Sophia said—something about the union's efforts to reach Gastonia's young people, about mothers and fathers bringing their children to the meetings, what to do in the morning if you found yourself homeless. She glanced around her, where men and women and a few small children had pressed in close to the stage so they could hear everything being said. Ella noted the man standing to her right. He slid his hands in and out of his pants pockets. He caught her looking at him, nodded at her, and smiled. He reached into his breast pocket for a pack of cigarettes. Ella noted his shaking hands. He pushed his red hair away from his eyes before lighting his cigarette.

The man was young, only in his thirties. He did not have the hardened look about him that the rest of the strikers had. His face was full, pale and soft, almost childish. His navy blue suit was so worn that the material appeared shiny at the knees and elbows.

"Tonight, we've got Mr. Carlton Reed, a reporter from the *Labor Defender,* here with us all the way from New York City," Sophia said onstage. "And of course we're going to hear from Mr. Fred Beal himself." There was clapping, whistles from the audience. Sophia paused, waited for quiet. "But first, we want to remind you that one of the best things about these meetings is the opportunity it offers us to fellowship with one another and welcome new friends. One of those friends is here with us tonight."

Ella had been staring at the redheaded man's shaking hands and did not realize that Sophia had been referring to her until someone whispered in her ear. "You ready?" a voice asked.

Ella saw Velma standing beside her.

"Don't be nervous," Velma said.

"I can't help it," Ella said.

"The stage has been checked. It's all clear."

"Checked for what?" Ella asked.

"Dynamite," Velma said.

"Dynamite?"

"Shhh," Velma said. "Wasn't anything there." She nodded to the skirt that enclosed the stage's underpinning. "At a meeting last week, somebody stashed a bundle of it under the stage. They lit it too, but the fuse was too wet after the rain."

Ella did not know whether she wanted to run or if she wanted to fall to her knees and lift the skirt around the stage and peer beneath it. Velma must have sensed her fear.

"Don't worry," Velma whispered. "It's been checked. There's nothing there." She smiled. "Not when we got started anyway."

Ella heard Sophia say her name. She turned to the stage at the sound of it.

"Tonight she's joining us from down the road in Bessemer City," Sophia said. "Ella May's a believer in this struggle, and we're hoping she'll go home and organize the American Mill. She's got a family at home to support, just like many of you, and she's here to do her part. Remember her name, brothers and sisters, and make certain you shake her hand tonight. Ella May, you want to come on up?"

The audience could have applauded, or they could not have applauded: Ella was never able to remember. What she could remember was suddenly finding herself walking across the stage in front of all those faces. She didn't look at Sophia, but she felt the girl standing nearby like a distant star that pulled Ella into its orbit. She remembered what Velma had said about the dynamite, wondered what it would feel like to have the stage explode, to lift itself beneath her, toss her into the air over the crowd. She shook the fear from her mind, took hold of the podium with both hands just as Sophia had done.

"Thank you," she said. "And thank you for letting me be here tonight." She opened her mouth, waited. She wanted to turn toward Sophia to ask what to say next, but instead she searched for Velma in the crowd. All the faces looked the same. She touched the leaflet in her pocket. Eventually, more words came. "I ain't from here. I'm from up in the mountains in Tennessee." A whistle came from the back of the crowd, and someone clapped his hands and hollered, "Johnson City!" The people in front of the stage turned at the sound. Some of them laughed, a few of them applauded. "Bristol!" a woman's voice called out. More laughter, more applause. Ella felt that a game had begun, and the crowd cheered as a list of towns, cities, and counties in Tennessee were shouted out: Knoxville, Cocke County, Erwin, Elizabethton, Greeneville. Ella waited until the crowd grew quiet and the laughter and applause died away.

"Is that everybody?" she asked. The audience erupted in cheers. "I don't want to leave nobody out." She laughed then, and she felt the tightness in her stomach leave her body. Her heart slowed.

"It feels good to hear the names of all them places," she said. "I ain't visited all of them, and I'll probably never see the Tennessee hills again, but it feels good to hear those names, so thank you.

"I reckon I ended up here the same way most of you did. The mills sent men up into the mountains, told us all about the good life down here." Boos lifted from the audience, and Ella acted surprised that someone would boo such promises. She heard laughter, and she watched as the people in the audience slowly came into focus, and she felt as if she were looking into each individual face and seeing that they'd been made the same promises she'd been made, and there was nothing to do now but laugh at the absurdity of their own belief in those promises and the men who made them. "They talked about how much money we'd make, didn't they? About how fine our homes would be, what nice things we could buy in town. My husband—the man who was my husband, anyway—he wanted to go. He said, 'It sounds good,' and I said, 'Well, let's go then.' I've worked in one mill or another ever since, a lot of them here in Gaston County. I figure one mill ain't too different from another: they're all bad as far as I know.

"I work at American over in Bessemer City now. I work six days a week for nine dollars, but it ain't enough."

Ella stopped speaking, let her eyes linger on a young woman standing just a few feet away. She wore a homespun dress and held a sleeping baby in her arms, and as Ella stared at her she noticed how the woman swayed back and forth.

"I've got four kids at home," Ella said. "I had five, but I lost one of them when he was just a baby." She pulled her gaze from the baby in the young mother's arms and stared out at the audience, searched the faces again until she found an older woman with a little girl standing beside her who could have been her granddaughter. "I got a little girl sick at home right now. I asked the foreman to put me on days so I could be there to care for her at night, but he won't do it. I don't know why. I'm doing my best for the babies I've still got. But it's hard. You men might not know it the way we know it, but it's hard.

"That's why I come out to learn about the union tonight, and that's why I wrote this song. I ain't never sung it before, so forgive me if it ain't no good. It don't have a title yet."

She stepped away from the edge of the stage, closed her eyes for a moment to find the melody, imagined herself becoming the girl she'd been all those years ago in the Champion Lumber camp in the hills outside Bryson City. She opened her eyes, then her mouth, and she sang as if it were just she and her mother out there by the fire. It was twilight. Warm, soapy water ran over her hands. Her father was still working up in the hills. The tree that would fall and kill him had not yet fallen. The flu that would drown her mother's lungs had not yet found her. She had not yet met John Wiggins. Willie had not been born, would not die.

We leave our homes in the morning,
We kiss our children good-bye.
While we slave for the bosses,
Our children scream and cry.

And when we draw our money,
Our grocery bills to pay,
Not a cent to spend for clothing,
Not a cent to lay away.
And on that very evening
Our little son will say:
"I need some shoes, Mother,
And so does sister May."

How it grieves the heart of a mother,
You, everyone, must know.
But we can't buy for our children,
Our wages are too low.

It is for our little children,
That seems to us so dear,
But for us nor them, dear workers,
The bosses do not care.

But understand, dear workers,
Our union they do fear.
Let's stand together, workers,
And have a union here.

She finished her song, caught her breath, stepped away from the podium. She felt someone beside her, felt Sophia's hand close around hers, felt their fingers intertwine. Sophia lifted their hands together, and when she did Ella's senses awakened to the noise coming from the crowd: people cheered, whistled and pointed, called her name and chanted union slogans. Flashbulbs popped and illuminated ghostly white faces as if lightning had threaded itself through the audience. Ella's legs were numb, her feet affixed to the stage. Sophia led her down the steps, the two of them clinging to one another's hands. Ella followed her into the dark night on the edge of the crowd.

Sophia spun to face her. "That was amazing, Ella. Just amazing. How'd you remember all them words?"

Ella had forgotten about the leaflet in her pocket. She reached for it now, pulled it free. "I didn't expect I'd remember them," she said.

Sophia looked at the leaflet as if it were a holy thing. "We're going to bust this strike wide open, Ella," she said. "You keep on writing them songs. We'll organize your colored friends. This will be over before Loray knows what happened." She smiled, and Ella felt something warm and safe spring up between them.

A man's voice came from the stage behind her, and Ella turned. The man onstage was tall and thin, his brown hair slicked back in a deep sheen. He wore a dark suit. "That was some fine, fine singing," he said. "And what a story. What a struggle."

"Is that Fred Beal?" Ella asked.

"No," Sophia said. "That's Carlton Reed. He's big-time with the party up in New York. He knows his stuff."

Reed smiled at the audience, put his hands on either side of the podium, leaned forward as if he might leap over it.

"Friends, I'm a reporter," he said. "And as a reporter I've always got my ear to the ground." He held on to the podium, but now he leaned away from it. "I've got to listen to both the rich and the poor, the high—" He raised his hand as if he were measuring his own height, and he looked to his right, south toward Loray. The audience laughed. "And the low," he said. "I must listen to everyone, or I'll hear no one.

"And this is what I've heard: tomorrow, the high and the rich are coming to kick you out of your homes. The high and the rich are doing their best to discredit you. They scream words like *communism* and *Bolshevism* and *Lovestoneiteism*," he said, purposefully stumbling over the last word.

Ella pictured Charlie in bed that morning, the angry frustration on his face, the things he'd said about communism and the strike. Charlie was neither high nor rich. He was poor just like her and he couldn't even read, but he'd trashed the union just the same.

"But you don't care about Russia, do you? We're not in Russia, are we? We're in the United States of America!"

The audience cheered, and Reed took a moment before he raised his hands to quiet them.

"What does Russia have to do with Gastonia?" he asked. "With this strike? I'd say nothing. I'd say nothing at all. But you wouldn't know it if you read the *Gaston Transom-Times*." He laughed. "They've even got a few men here tonight, taking notes about what we're doing out here in this field where we're talking about equality and workers' rights. Look around you now," he said. "You'll know them right off. They're the ones in the fine suits."

"That's a fine suit *you've* got on, Reed!" a voice from the audience yelled. The crowd gasped and turned toward the voice as if ready to pounce on the man to whom it belonged, but both the voice and the man seemed to have been swallowed by the night.

"Distraction," Reed said. "That's the practice of the *Gaston Transom-Times* and its moneymen-bosses over at Loray. They're just throwing around accusations and rumors in the hopes of distracting you from two things: your empty bellies and your empty wallets."

The audience around Ella erupted into laughter and cheers. She found herself clapping along with them. She knew she belonged here in the midst of this shared experience, not just the rally but her whole life and all the poor men and women and children who had passed through it.

"You hungry?" Sophia whispered. Ella turned, looked at her new friend. "Dinner's going to be served when this is over, but we could go on up and get in line."

Ella was starving, and she pictured the cold stove and empty skillet back home in Stumptown, pictured her children relieved and smiling to be at Violet's mother's house, their bellies probably fuller than they'd been in days. Her heart swelled at the thought of their happiness.

"I need to get on home," Ella said. "Back to my babies."

The night had grown cool. Dew settled over the grass. Sophia took a deep breath, raised her face to the clear, dark sky, and forced the warm air from her lungs. It lifted like smoke. "There's them stars again," she said.

"I need to get on home," Ella said.

Sophia lowered her face. "The roads ain't safe at night," she said. "Loray's got people. They're likely to follow us, run us down once we get outside town."

"I can't stay here tonight," Ella said. "I got nowhere to go."

"There's plenty of room," Sophia said. "We'll get you settled, and I'll carry you home to those babies tomorrow."

"My shift starts at six P.M.," Ella said. "I got to be home before that."

"Shift?" Sophia said. She laughed. "Girl, you ain't going back inside that mill. You're union now."

The crowd around them exploded in applause. Ella turned, saw the redheaded man with the shaking hands stride across the stage. He shook hands with Carlton Reed, clapped him on the back, waved at the audience.

"Who's that?" Ella asked.

"That's him," Sophia said. "That's Fred Beal."

DINNER WAS SERVED inside the headquarters. Cold bologna sandwiches. Cold coffee. Stale Moon Pies. Ella waited in line behind Sophia. Exposed electric bulbs hung from the ceiling and cast soft yellow light on the uncovered heads of the men in overalls and women in dresses. The room was warm, the people's voices loud and excited.

"It's not always going to be like this," Sophia said over the noise. "Better food's on the way. Things just got hung up, that's all."

"I'm sure it's fine," Ella said. She didn't tell Sophia that it didn't matter to her what they served or how much or how little they offered her. She was starving, and any amount of anything was more than she'd hoped for before she left Bessemer City. "It's kind of the union to offer it."

"Oh, it's not us," Sophia said. "It's the Catholics. Monks from over in Belmont."

"Catholics," Ella said. She'd never met a Catholic, did not know if she'd ever even seen one.

"Yeah," Sophia said. "The Protestants won't touch us. The churches around the village and most of them downtown are on Loray's dole. They'd rather see us dead." Sophia stopped and looked around. Ella did the same. She realized that people were staring at her. "You're famous now," Sophia said. "I'm standing beside a celebrity."

The line of strikers shuffled forward, and Ella and Sophia drew closer to the table where the food was being served. Two monks wore cassocks, something she'd never seen before. The first, the younger of the two, was balding. He wore tiny spectacles on the end of his nose and stared through them at the sandwiches he carefully wrapped in wax paper. The monk offered a sandwich to Sophia.

"Thank you, Father," she said.

Ella waited, watched the monk wrap a sandwich for her. She received it, bowed slightly, thanked him as Sophia had. The older of the two monks, his hands trembling, poured black coffee into tin cups. He handed one to Ella. He was short with a round, red face and a full head of gray hair. He smiled. Ella could not help but smile back at him.

"Thank you, Father," she said.

"Bless you, child," the old monk said.

Beside him stood a man handing out packages of Moon Pies from a crate stashed beneath the table. He held one hand behind his back as if he were a mannered attendant. Unlike the two monks, this man didn't wear a cassock. Instead he wore denim pants and a white collared shirt, the collar of which was nearly hidden by a long dark beard. Beneath the beard a tiny straight-back chair, something fit for a doll house, hung from a leather strap around his neck. Ella looked at the man's face. His eyes were dark, shiny, his skin red with sunburn. Although the man's eyes did not rise to meet hers, something about his face stirred a memory in Ella's mind. He held out a Moon Pie and she reached for it, closed her fingers around it, felt that it was old and stale. She knew that she would eat it without hesitation.

The man's fingers grazed Ella's, and he pulled his hand to his chest and touched the chair where it hung from his neck. He bent to the floor, rummaged through the crate of Moon Pies as if waiting for Ella to continue on.

Ella saw Sophia at the end of the line, saw her nod toward the bearded man and touch her own chest as if the chair hung there instead of around the man's neck. "He's a strange one, isn't he," she whispered once Ella was close enough to hear her.

They searched the cramped, poorly lit room for a place to sit. The few chairs and even fewer tables were already taken. Sophia made her way across the room and sat on the floor where a group of women had gathered by the door. Ella followed. They settled themselves and nodded at the women around them by way of hello. The women nodded back, gave no sign that they recognized either Sophia or Ella as having been onstage earlier in the evening.

A jar of yellow mustard was being passed around. When it came to Sophia, Ella watched her roll her sandwich as if she were rolling a cigarette, and she dipped each end in the jar, coating it in mustard. She passed the jar to Ella, who'd already opened her sandwich and had the two pieces of bread and the slice of bologna sitting separately on her lap; she used her finger to spoon out a dollop of mustard on each, then used the same finger to spread it. She ate slowly, first the individual slices of bread and then the bologna, pausing after each swallow. Ella noticed that Sophia had moved on to her Moon Pie by the time she'd finished the first slice of bread.

"I got a colored friend up in New York City," Sophia said. "He'll come down and help us organize your friends over in Bessemer City. We'll keep it quiet, at first. Ol' Fred ain't going to like it one bit, but he'll like it fine when we're done."

Ella knew it was all happening too fast. A different variation of the same wave that had swept her down from the mountains to the mills had now swept her into the union. She felt herself clamoring to stand against its surge, her feet struggling to touch the bottom, her lungs gasping for breath.

"I got to work," Ella said. "I've got babies. I can't lay out of work to organize."

"Don't you understand what you did tonight?" Sophia asked. "Getting onstage, saying your name, where you work, where you live. There ain't going to be no job for you to go back to, Ella May." She ate the last bit of her Moon Pie, took a drink of coffee, made a face as she swallowed it. "The union is all you've got now. And we'll support you. There's relief funds on the way. You and your babies are going to be taken care of, I promise you."

Ella remembered what Velma had said before that evening's rally about supplies arriving late, if ever. Her face grew hot, and the food she'd just eaten turned sour in her stomach. She'd been a fool to come here, to be so easily swayed, to write the song she'd written and to sing it in front of people she did not know. Her life had been altered, and now it could never be repaired. Charlie had been right.

Light passed across Ella's face, and she looked to see that the door to the office in the back of the building had opened. Carlton Reed and Velma stepped out, followed by Fred Beal, who held on to the door as if preparing to close it again. Sophia got to her feet.

"I'm going to go talk to Beal about you right now, Ella May," she said. "You don't worry about a thing except signing your name to a union card."

As soon as Sophia left for Beal's office, Ella felt the enormity of what she'd done that evening. The weight of it was a physical thing, and again her mind turned toward her children. Her palm passed across her stomach. She picked up the wax paper that had covered her sandwich and opened it across her lap. She set the Moon Pie in the middle of it, wrapped it tightly and neatly as if it were a Christmas present. She would quarter it and give it to the children when she returned home.

She had not yet touched the small tin of cold coffee. Ella drank it now, and it settled in her stomach like something that would not stay there long.

She looked at the people around her, most of them women. Her eyes fell on a young girl a few feet away in a dark blue calico dress, her long brown hair pinned up in a thick braid. Although her cheeks were sunken, the soft light cast her face in sharp, beautiful angles.

"Oh, he asked me everything he could think of, you know," the girl was saying. "He wanted to know where I was from, if I was married, if I had me a sweetheart back home. Who my daddy was. All that."

"That's just because he wanted to be your daddy," said a woman with sallow skin and thin white-blond hair. She laughed, and her smile revealed a row of discolored teeth.

"I can't say he didn't try," the girl said. "I can't say he ain't still trying."

"That's old Pigface for you," the woman said.

At the mention of the name, several of the women broke into laughter and covered their mouths with their hands and looked around at one another with knowing glances. An older woman sat beside the sallow-faced girl. She swallowed the last of her sandwich and wiped her mouth with the back of her hand. Her thin fingers smoothed back wisps of her gray hair. She looked around at the younger women, stopping for a moment on Ella's face as if she already knew her to be a stranger.

"I know Percy Epps did right more than try with the whole lot of you," the old woman said. She narrowed her eyes as the others lowered their gazes. "And that ain't right. It ain't right for a woman to have to give herself away just so she can get a job that don't hardly pay enough to live on." She sat up straighter so that she could better take in the great number of people packed into the small building, the dinner line still snaking out through the door. "That's what this here's all about. We're all striking so girls don't have to live that-a way."

The other women remained quiet. The sound of wax paper being crumbled replaced the old woman's voice. Something had come over the group that hadn't been there before she spoke.

"Pigface is the devil all right," the pretty girl in the calico dress said. Her eyes and face had darkened as if a shadow hung there.

The gray-haired woman sighed, and then she placed a hand on another girl's shoulder to steady herself as she got to her feet. "If he's the devil that would mean we're all in hell," she said. She dusted off the back of her dress. "And I don't think we're there quite yet."

The pretty girl raised her eyes to the old woman, who now stood above her.

"Hetty, you really think it'll happen?" she asked. "You really think they'll turn us out tomorrow?"

Hetty looked down at the girl with a look that seemed to carry both surprise and pity.

"Why, yes, girl," Hetty said. "That's exactly what's going to happen."

"What'll we do?" asked the sallow-faced girl.

"What can we do?" Hetty said. "Walk out? We done that. Organize ourselves? Start a union? We done that too." She sighed. "The way I see it, we got two things left to try: we can feel bad for ourselves, or we can fight." She reached down and opened her hand, and the girl reached up and placed hers inside it. Hetty squeezed the girl's fingers, gave her hand a little shake. "I plan to fight," Hetty said. "I hope you do too. I hope you all do."

ELLA SLEPT ON the floor inside the headquarters that night, her back to the wall, her head resting on her hands, her mind returning to Stumptown and the faces of her sleeping children. Sophia had found an old blanket—a wiry, woolen thing that was so stiff it seemed never to have been unfolded—and Ella had used it to cover herself.

A handful of people had remained outside the headquarters all night, passing around thermoses of coffee and flasks of whiskey. Ella had fallen asleep listening as they recounted stories of the Loray strike and the other strikes they'd heard of: Lawrence, Passaic, Pineville. They'd talked about the threats they'd received since joining the union, the violence they saw when the National Guard arrived, the potential of what was to come.

She woke in the night to what she thought was the scratch of Rose's breathing, but when she opened her eyes she saw a mouse dragging a piece of mustard-coated wax paper across the rough plank floor just a few feet from where she slept.

The next time she woke it was to the sound of laughter on the street. Ella raised herself to her elbows, felt the bones in her back and shoulders shift into place, looked around the dark room at the shapes of sleeping bodies where people had arranged pallets on the floor. She searched for the forms of Velma and Sophia, but it was too dark to see them and too quiet to search them out. Instead she stood quietly and opened the door.

Outside, night felt closer than morning, although morning was near. Several groups of men stood in silhouette on the road in front of the headquarters. None of them seemed to take note of her.

She tuned her ear to the dark field across the street. The chirping of crickets rose from the grass. She heard the sound of faraway water where it ran over rocks in a shallow, muddy gulch that cut along the field's far edge. For a moment, in this cool almost-night with the rolling water and the crickets in her ears, Ella felt transported back to the mountains. She closed her eyes and imagined that if she were to open them she would see dawn creeping through the low clouds enshrouding the lumber camp.

A burst of laughter rang out in the quiet street. Ella opened her eyes. Instead of the lumber camp's denuded hills she saw the same dark figures of strikers clustered in groups of twos and threes. Out on the road, the glowing, orange tips of cigarettes. The shapes of shotguns propped on shoulders. The men's whispered voices.

Ella crossed the gravel road, stood on the edge of the field. The stage remained, but someone had removed the skirt from beneath it and taken down the lanterns.

She looked at the building behind her. Beal had instructed them to meet at the headquarters at 7 A.M. to march down to the village, where they'd wait for the evictions to begin. Ella did not know what time it was, but the sun had just risen, and she knew there was plenty of time for her to be alone before the crowds gathered again.

She walked south in the direction from which she'd seen Loray workers coming the night before. She crossed the railroad tracks, studied the yards of the boardinghouses and small shacks as she passed them. She reached Franklin Avenue, where Loray rose before her. The morning was still dark enough to see the lights burning behind the windows, the downtown streets quiet enough to hear the incessant thrum of the great machines at work inside.

Ella stepped onto the curb, walked west. How long would it take her to reach Stumptown? Three hours? Four? She'd been gone almost twenty-four hours, which was the longest she'd ever been away from her children. If she left now she could easily make it home before noon, have a few hours with her babies before her shift started. Her body ticked with desperation to see them, to touch them and hear their voices.

They were used to spending their nights alone, but she'd told them she'd be back. Violet would have made sure they had something to eat for dinner. Lilly would have gotten them ready for bed. The children would be waking now: Lilly searching the cabin for something to eat; Otis stoking a fire in the oven in expectation of breakfast; Rose coughing the damp night air from her lungs; Wink swaddled in thin blankets, his fingers closing around anything he could reach.

Morning in downtown Gastonia was different from morning in Stumptown: Across the street, a boy unloaded bound newspapers from the back of a running truck and stacked them neatly on the sidewalk. Cars and trucks rolled past. A man pushed a covered vegetable wagon down the center of the street. Lights winked on behind glass windows inside businesses that were preparing for the day's work. Ella drew closer to Greasy Corner, where the smells of frying eggs and bacon, toast, and coffee filled her nose and stirred her hunger.

Ella had walked far enough that she could see an end to the downtown streets and sidewalks as they gave way to countryside. She stopped, looked back toward Loray, where smoke rose from cookstoves down in the village.

She heard voices and looked toward the shadows at the end of an alley. Fred Beal stood talking with a tall, thin man in a black suit and a black stovepipe hat. A silver star gleamed on his lapel. The man must have felt Ella's eyes on him because he raised his head, still listening to Beal, and looked at Ella where she stood at the alley's mouth. He nodded. Beal noticed, and he looked up at Ella too, raised his hand to her. The men walked up the alley toward her, their heads bent, their voices just beginning to reach her.

"It's the law, Mr. Beal," the man said. "I'm sorry, but there's nothing I can do about the law. Mill owns those houses. You know that."

"But it doesn't own the people inside," Beal said.

"I agree," the man said. "But they can't just stay there if the mill wants them out. The mill has a right to remove them. I'll have some men on hand to see that it's done carefully and respectfully. But I need your people to be careful and respectful too, Mr. Beal."

"I've made clear to them that there is to be no violence," Beal said. "But we've been attacked before, Chief Aderholt. You saw what happened to our old headquarters. You saw how the commissary was destroyed."

"And I hated it," Aderholt said. "It just made everything worse, and we can't have it get any worse than it already is."

"You've got a few ruffians on your hands too, Chief. Roach and Gibson, to name only two."

"I've spoken with them about the complaints," Aderholt said. "And I've given Roach some time off to get himself together, and Gibson knows I'm watching him. Passion's running high, and not everyone has acted as professionally as they should have, but you need to take responsibility for your people's behavior too."

The men had moved out of the shadows. They stopped in front of Ella. Aderholt nodded toward her. "Is this the one?" he asked.

"Yes, sir," Beal said. He smiled, put his hands in his pockets. "This is the one. This is Ella May."

Ella stared at Aderholt while he stared at her. He was older than she'd assumed. His skin was fair, his eyes dark. Wisps of white hair protruded from beneath his black hat. He touched its wide brim, nodded.

"Miss," he finally said.

Aderholt turned back to Beal.

"Mr. Beal?"

"Yes, Chief?"

"Let's not have anyone hurt or, God forbid, killed this morning." Aderholt looked behind him, where sunlight poured onto the road, shone against the windows of the shops and restaurants along Franklin. "It's too nice a morning for that." He turned and walked back toward town. Beal and Ella watched him go.

"He's a fine man," Beal said. "He has to toe the city's line, but he's done everything he can to help us."

"What did he mean?" Ella asked. "When he said, 'Is this the one?' What does that mean?"

Beal smiled. "Word's out about you, Miss May."

"What word?" Ella said. She felt heat rising in her face, and she didn't yet know if it came from anger or embarrassment, but she knew that whatever Beal said would decide it for her.

"You made quite the impression last night," Beal said. "With the story you told and your song. It all made quite the impression on Loray, on the newspapers too. They're saying we brought you in from Nashville, paid you big-time money to get up there and sing."

"I ain't from Nashville," Ella said. "I ain't never even been to Nashville. I'm from Sevierville."

"It doesn't matter, Miss May," Beal said. "The mill wants people to believe that you're not real, that your story's not real. They want everyone to believe that you're an actor or a singer or anything other than a mill mother with sick babies and an empty wallet.

"But we're going to fight against lies like those," Beal said. "Your story's true. People need to hear it. Your singing too." He lit a cigarette, turned his head, and blew smoke up the alley. "You were wonderful last night. And that song. It was wonderful."

"Thank you," she said. She spoke the words just in time for the sound of them to merge with another sound. A westbound train that neither she nor Beal was prepared to see or hear burst from the morning's silence and bolted past at the end of the alley. The rush of it blasted a gust of wind toward them. Beal stumbled, ducked as if someone had hurled something dangerous at him—a knife, a stick of dynamite, an unspent bullet—and in a quick sweep his eyes strafed the alley as if that dangerous, unseen thing were now rolling toward him, where it would stop at his feet. He caught himself, smiled at Ella, straightened his suit. They stood without speaking and waited for the train to pass.

The last car slid by. The quiet morning returned.

"Where do you think that train was headed?" Beal asked.

"Spartanburg," Ella said.

"Spartanburg." He said the word as if testing it before deciding whether he would ever say it again. "You ever been to Spartanburg, Miss May?"

"Yes."

"What's it like in Spartanburg?"

"Like here, I reckon," she said. "Not too different from any other place where they got mills. No better. No worse."

"What were you doing down in Spartanburg?"

"Passing through," she said.

"On the way to Bessemer City? To the American Mill?"

"No, sir. I worked other places before I worked at American."

"Where?"

"A bunch of different mills," she said.

"And what's it like at American Mill Number Two?"

"I reckon it's about like it is here at Loray," she said.

"No better, no worse," he added.

"I'd say that's right."

"And you heard about our strike, so you came over to Gastonia?"

"Yes, sir," she said. "I got Sundays off. I don't go back until six tonight. But I need someone to carry me home. I reckon I could walk if I had to."

"You came last night to decide on the union?"

"Yes, sir."

"Please," he said. "Don't call me sir. I'm hardly older than you. Please don't make me feel any older."

"All right," she said.

"And have you decided?"

"No, sir," she said. "I mean, no, I ain't decided. Not yet."

"You could become the face of this strike, Miss May. Loray's already heard about you. And they're scared. Your story, your music: it's all made for the newspapers. You could be what turns the tide for these people."

"I'll lose my job if I join the union," Ella said. "I got to get paid, Mr. Beal, Fred. I've got babies to support. I can't be out of work."

"We can pay you to organize workers. Come to the rallies. Speak. Sing like you did last night."

Ella was silent. She'd spent enough time in front of men who promised work that she knew it was best to say as little as possible, best to wait for them to begin talking of money first.

"How much do you make a week now, Miss May?"

"Nine dollars," she said.

"We can pay nine twenty-five, maybe nine fifty. I'll know soon."

"I could think about it for ten dollars," she said. "But I can't live here in Gastonia. I can't bring my babies over here."

"Nine fifty and you can stay in Bessemer City except for rallies and meetings," Beal said. "You can organize there with our leadership, eventually open a local chapter. But there's one thing I'll need you to do that'll require you to leave home."

"What's that?"

"We're sending a group to Washington in a few days," Beal said. "They'll be meeting with senators. I want you to go. No one can portray this struggle better than you did last night."

Ella had never been north of the Smoky Mountains in Tennessee. Her heart thrilled at the idea of it: riding on a train or in a car, watching as the countryside unfolded before her. But she quickly calculated what that kind of freedom would cost: A trip to Washington would mean days and days away from her children, and she didn't know if she could manage that. Violet would be there to help, but it was her absence in their lives that terrified her. And if she took the time to make such a trip then she had no doubt it would mean the end of her job at the American Mill. She could explain missing a shift to care for a sick child, but she couldn't explain a trip north with a group of strikers.

"I'll have to think on it," she said. "I don't know what I'm going to do just yet."

"I understand. Your life's been hard," he said. "And I'm sorry. I'm sorry about the child you lost. I can't imagine the pain of that."

Ella stared at Beal for a moment, considered telling him what she'd been thinking since first feeling another new life stir inside her. She'd decided that giving birth to a child is nothing but an invitation to lose it, and that was what she'd feared each time she'd heard the first newborn cry of one of her children. The weight and space of the child in her arms carved out a similar weight and space in her heart. The mere idea of that space being rendered empty and weightless was almost too much for her to bear, even now, especially here on this sidewalk in the early morning with a strange man speaking to her.

Beal must have registered Ella's reticence because he cleared his throat and dropped his cigarette, stubbed it out with his shoe.

"What do you think of our strike so far?" he asked.

"I think it's white," Ella said.

Beal laughed. "It is white, isn't it?" He looked at the ground where his cigarette lay smoldering. "It is, come to think of it."

"If I work for you I want to organize colored workers," Ella said. "For ten dollars a week I could organize a whole lot of them who'd walk off their jobs at American if the union would support them the same way it's supporting white folks over here in Gastonia."

Beal stared at her. Ella wondered if he was assessing something about her, trying to make sense of who or what he was seeing.

"You wouldn't be working for me, Miss May. You'd be working for the union, for your fellow workers, for yourself."

"Well, if I work for myself and whoever else you mentioned I want to organize colored workers. I'll do it for ten dollars."

"Sophia didn't mention this to me," Beal said. "But, knowing Sophia as I do, I can't say I'm surprised. How'd you come to know so many Negroes?"

"I couldn't get no recommendations from the mills I worked at around here. I missed too much work when my baby took sick. And the mill down in South Carolina—" She stopped, considered how to proceed. "I had a little trouble there. American Number Two was the only one in the county that'd take me on without no recommendation. And it's the only one that has white and colored working together. So that's how I come to know them."

She stopped speaking, prepared herself for the comments that a man like Beal might make about a white woman living among colored men, her white children playing alongside colored children: breathing the same air, touching the same things, eating the same food. But Beal didn't speak.

"They ain't no different from me," Ella said. "I knew that before I worked with them, but I know it for sure now."

"What kind of trouble did you have in South Carolina?" he finally said.

"I'd rather not say," Ella said. "My husband got into something, but he's gone now."

"Passed away?"

"Just gone," she said. "The what-for and the where-to don't matter."

"It's not my business anyway, is it?" Beal said. He cleared his throat. He looked around as if checking to see if anyone stood nearby. "The Negro question is a sore subject for people in this part of the country," he said. "Most of them don't think well of Negroes like you do, or like I do. This strike is for equal rights and equal pay, but most of these strikers aren't quite ready for what that really means."

"They'll be ready soon enough," Ella said. "Especially if they don't got nowhere else to live."

"Maybe," Beal said. "Maybe not."

"They're getting turned out today," Ella said. "And I know the tents ain't here yet."

Beal cocked his head and peered at Ella as if wondering how she had come to possess such information. He smiled. "You've been talking to Velma." He shook his head, looked toward the end of the alley. He gestured for Ella to follow him. The two of them took the alley away from Franklin Avenue. Beal turned right and they walked along between the railroad tracks and the backs of the businesses that fronted Franklin. Beal turned left and climbed up the embankment, and then he looked back and offered Ella his hand. She acted as if she didn't notice the gesture. They scrambled over the railroad tracks and picked their way down the embankment on the other side. Beal entered the woods, held back limbs so that Ella could follow him. She smelled mud, cold water.

When she stepped from the trees she saw the gulley she'd been able to hear from outside the headquarters that morning. The water ran clear and fast along a rocky creek. The land rose before her. She couldn't see it, but she knew that on the other side of the hill was the field where she'd been onstage the night before, the headquarters just across the road.

"I received assurances that the tents are arriving on the train this afternoon," Beal said. He swept his arm across the expanse of the meadow.

"Everybody's going to live out here?" Ella asked.

"Yes," Beal said. "We're prepared to see this strike through. If that means housing and feeding evicted workers then that's what we're prepared to do." He held his hand above his eyes, looked toward the sun as if judging the time by its place in the sky. "Are you going to help us, Ella?" He dropped his hand, looked at her. He waited. "Nine seventy-five a week if you'll help us organize Bessemer City. Let things stabilize, let our numbers grow, let us reclaim some power from the bosses. We can welcome colored workers after that. We'll need you to make it happen."

"Nine seventy-five a week," she said. "And I stay in Bessemer except for rallies and meetings and the trip to Washington, just like you said."

"Yes, just like I said."

"All right," Ella said. She held out her hand and Beal took it. They shook.

"Welcome to the Gastonia Local of the National Textile Workers Union," Beal said.

"Thank you," Ella said. She felt herself smile, tried to fight it. "I'm glad to be here."

He reached into his pocket and removed an old watch on a thin chain. "I hope you're ready for your first official act of resistance as a member."

Ella followed him through the field. They stopped where the creek narrowed, spotted a large rock in its middle, used it to step across. They crested the hill. The stage sat on their left, the headquarters just ahead. Perhaps one hundred men and women had gathered. Ella saw

Sophia and Velma, recognized the old woman Hetty from the village the night before. An old man stood beside her.

Beal crossed the street. Ella followed behind, too insecure to walk beside him with the people's eyes upon her. Beal stopped and surveyed the crowd. He ran his fingers through his red hair; it parted naturally at his pronounced cowlick. Ella walked past Beal and joined the other strikers, tried her best to blend in as if she'd been there all along.

"Friends, today is a test," Beal said. "You're being evicted from your homes simply because you want a better life for your family. You have the money to pay the rent, but Loray has said, 'We do not want your money as much as we want your soul, and if you do not give us your soul then you can no longer live in your home.'

"What they want is violence, brothers and sisters, and we won't give them violence. Our words and our actions are more effective than violence, and more powerful.

"Mothers," he said, "go home, and when the mill's gangs come, hold your children in your arms as tightly as you can." He smiled. "For all we know they'll take your babies and force them to work an eighty-hour week!" The crowd hesitated to laugh at first, then did so quietly.

The women cut their eyes at one another, turned their faces toward the village, began to slip away silently.

"Men," Beal said, "I need you here to guard our headquarters. As much as the bosses want you out of your village, they want you out of your union even more. So draw your guns, but steel yourselves against firing them. We do not seek violence, but we will not shrink from it."

A cheer rose from the men, and in that cheer Ella heard the long night of whispers and rumors and sips of whiskey culminating in some kind of darkness that now rubbed against her body. Something about the morning made it seem that a fight would be unavoidable. She left the crowd, followed the women and children toward the village.

Sophia fell in step beside her.

"I just talked to Beal," she said. Ella smiled. Sophia laughed, threw her arms around Ella's shoulders. They both stumbled, nearly fell. "I knew you'd do it, Ella May. I knew it."

"I ain't done nothing yet," Ella said.

"You said *yes*," Sophia said. "That's plenty for now."

"Why'd all the men stay back there?" she asked. "Why's it all women doing the marching?"

"Beal says the mill's men are less likely to beat up on women."

"Most men I know would rather hit a woman than a man," Ella said.

"Beal doesn't want anyone carrying guns down in the village," Sophia said. "He says it doesn't send a good message, but the men won't listen, so they can't come."

"You're telling me that the men keep all the guns and stand around by themselves at headquarters while the women march? That don't make no sense."

"There's a lot about this strike that doesn't make sense, Ella," Sophia said. "You'll see that soon enough. But it can be fixed, and we may have to be the ones who fix it." She hugged Ella again, then ran ahead and disappeared into the crowd.

Ella walked with the strikers as they turned down Dalton on the east side of the mill. Clouds of white breakfast smoke drifted from cookstoves and rose above the sagging rooflines of the small, un-painted mill shacks. The muddy streets were pocked with graveled divots where water pooled. Weeds choked out the grass in the patches of yard. Aside from the women on foot, the streets were largely quiet and empty.

When the group turned right on Fourth Avenue it stumbled upon a crowd of strikers who had gathered in the street in front of a di-lapidated shack with broken shutters and a haphazard set of steps that led up to the porch. They stood watching as a dozen or so men in overalls and work clothes moved empty-handed into the house through the flung-open front door and then reappeared carrying beat-up furniture and old, lumpy mattresses. They dropped the items in piles on the lawn, piles that spilled over the edge of the yard and down into the crowded street.

Ella's eyes fixed themselves on a woman in a blue gingham dress who stood with a crying, pink-faced baby in her arms. The woman's hips rocked from side to side as if she were either trying to quiet the child or contemplating whether or not to spring upon the men. Sophia stood whispering to a group of strikers. She led them up the porch steps and inside the house. A few moments later the strikers reappeared, sitting in chairs that were being carried by two men instead of one. Sophia was rolled up inside a mattress. When the men dropped her on the lawn the mattress uncoiled itself; she stood up and ran back inside the house. But it soon became apparent that nothing could stop the men from carrying out the furniture and piling it by the road. Heaps of it were strewn everywhere. A few of the women cried, especially the younger ones, new wives and even newer mothers, but Ella watched as the older women stood back, their arms folded across their chests, their eyes locked on the men's faces.

"You proud, boy?" one woman asked a young man who couldn't have been older than fifteen. "Boss Guyon got your palms greasy enough?"

The boy lowered his face and brushed past her. He walked back into the house.

Another old woman lifted the crying baby from the girl's arms and held it in front of one of the men.

"Here, Cass," the woman said. She pushed the baby into the man's arms as if it were his own. "You got babies at home and food to spare. Take this one home with you. It ain't got nowhere to live no more, thanks to you."

The man took the child into his arms. It was wailing. The man sighed, carried the baby back to its mother. He moved up through the yard and went back inside the house.

Over the next few hours, the men cleared the houses on one side of Fourth Avenue, and then they crossed and moved down the other. By midmorning, furniture, clothing, and people cluttered the yards in huge piles. But soon, once the shock of homelessness had worn off, the strikers began to celebrate their removal, as if not having a roof over their heads had given them one less thing to worry about. Some of the men who'd spent the morning guarding union headquarters had left their weapons behind and come down to the village to join their families in sorting through their belongings. Even the handful of police officers who were on hand to make certain that heightened tensions didn't give way to violence seemed relaxed. As Aderholt had promised Beal, the police had kept their distance.

Ella found Velma in the crowd.

"Have you seen Sophia?" Velma asked.

"Last time I saw her she was getting carried out of a house inside a mattress."

"She's something, isn't she?" Velma said. "Dumb and passionate, and too young to realize both can get her killed." She smiled. "But she's something."

The mood of the crowd that milled about Fourth Avenue changed as the company men made their way through the yard of a shack whose rotted boards seem held together by some kind of magic. Standing sentinel on the porch was the woman Hetty, with whom Ella had eaten dinner the night before.

Hetty stood on her steps alone. Ella and a group of strikers watched the company men approach Hetty's house, Hetty's arms down by her sides, her body rigid. It was not until the first man's boot touched the steps that Hetty thrust the upper half of her body inside the shack's open door. She emerged with an old rocking chair, which she lifted above her head and hurled toward the men. The lead man ducked, and the rest of them scattered in different directions with shouts of "What the hell!" and "Goddamn!"

Hetty, her arms now empty and her chest heaving, stood and

watched the men as they composed themselves. They moved past her and through her home's open door. She followed them inside as if she'd been hired to do their work.

For the next few minutes, the crowd watched the men carry belongings out of the house and deposit them on the curb. Inside, Hetty moved from room to room and tossed whatever she could lay a hand to out into the yard. When she finished she took hold of a hammer and busted the glass out of the few windows that weren't covered over with pine boards. By the time her home had been emptied she was on her knees, the hammer still in her hand, using its claw to pry up the floorboards just inside the door.

And that was when one of the mill's men—a slight man in overalls—bent at the waist and laid a hand on Hetty's shoulder and asked her to stop destroying the mill's property. He didn't have the chance to move his hand from her shoulder before Hetty swung the claw end of the hammer toward his leg and pierced his calf muscle through the denim pants.

Two policemen pushed through the crowd and bounded up through the yard as Hetty pulled the hammer free of the man's leg and prepared to swing at something, anything, else. The man screamed and fell to his knees and rolled out of the doorway. Blood soaked through his overalls and dotted the steps. One officer hooked Hetty beneath her arms and the other tried to corral her wild, kicking feet.

"You sons of bitches!" she screamed. "You sons of bitches! Tell Pigface to come down out of that mill and carry me out of this house his damn self. Let him see what I got for him!" She reared her head and spit into the face of the young, scared officer above her. "I know you. I know you, Paul Bradley," she said. "I know your people. They're going to be ashamed of you for hurting a old woman!"

"We're doing our jobs," said the policeman who carried her feet. "Don't listen to her, Paul." They carried her across the street toward a patrol car.

"Turn her loose!" a man yelled. Ella looked up to see Hetty's husband barreling toward the police who were carrying his wife. A rifle was in his hand. When the policeman holding Hetty's feet turned and saw the old man bearing down upon him, he let go of her and drew his pistol. The shift in weight surprised the man named Paul. Hetty slipped from his grasp and spilled onto the street at his feet. She yelled out when her head hit the road but no one was watching her anymore. They were all watching and waiting to see what her husband would do.

"Drop that rifle, old-timer!" the policeman with the pistol said, but the old man either did not hear him or was not willing to listen, because he held on to the rifle and kept running toward them, his eyes on Hetty where she lay on the street. "Drop it!" the policeman screamed.

A loud crack like a tree limb snapping rang out against the morning. Hetty's husband collapsed in a heap on top of her. The moment she felt the weight of him she screamed and struggled to get to her feet to discover exactly what had made him fall. The policeman leaned over the old man and grabbed his shoulders and turned him so that he stared up at the blue sky. Hetty's husband lay there beside her, his eyes wide open, a cut that seemed to have collapsed the bridge of his nose forcing blood to pulse in streams down each side of his face.

"Emmit!" Hetty hollered. Blood shone on her neck and hands. It stained her dress. She spread the blood across Emmit's torso as she touched his body, searching for a bullet wound that wasn't there. "Wake up, honey," she said. "Baby."

"He's dead!" someone screamed over Ella's shoulder. "You killed him!" Ella turned to see a young woman with her hand held over her mouth as if she could cram the words back inside before the policemen heard them.

"He ain't dead," the policeman said, "but he will be if he moves." He holstered his pistol and picked up Emmit's shotgun where he'd dropped it before being cracked across the face with the butt end of the pistol. In what seemed to Ella's eyes to have been one fluid motion, the man broke the shotgun and saw that both barrels were loaded. He snapped it closed, raised it toward the gathered crowd.

"Somebody run and get Beal!" a man's voice cried out.

The policeman pointed the shotgun in the direction from which the voice had come.

"Nobody move," he said. "Not one of y'all." He scanned faces as if expecting someone to step forward to tell him how to handle the situation. The morning had gone silent. "Now, dammit," the policeman said. "We tried to be fair with y'all. We tried. And this here's what happened."

Ella noticed that the shotgun's barrel quivered in the policeman's hands. The young policeman named Paul Bradley stood beside him, staring down at the gun as if his partner might turn it on him at any moment. A man in the crowd took advantage of the stillness, and he turned and took off at a sprint up the road toward headquarters.

"Hey!" the policeman with the shotgun yelled after him. "Freeze!" But the man kept running.

The officer named Paul watched the man flee. Paul looked at his partner and then took off up the street in pursuit.

"Paul!" the officer called. He watched him for a moment before he realized that he was alone. He turned his attention back to the crowd, where two more men fled: one cutting behind Hetty's house and disappearing into a grove of maples, the other turning and bounding down the hill toward Garrison Boulevard.

In this manner the situation was defused, the matter settled. The strikers peeled away in hot-footed singles at first, and then the women—who did not fear the law and violence in the same way the men did—drifted off in groups of twos and threes, their children pressed to their chests or held close by their sides.

Not knowing what else to do, Ella waded through the crowd and turned up Fourth Avenue where it skirted along the mill's southern edge. She'd go back to the headquarters, find Sophia, and ask about that $9.75 Beal had promised. Then she'd demand a ride home to her children.

Here, in this part of the village, the company men had already finished clearing the houses. The street was full of people and their personal effects: chairs, mounds of clothes, broken furniture, and piles and piles of cast-iron skillets, washtubs, cookpots, and dolls missing faces or with faces missing eyes or mouths. All told, almost a thousand people had been turned out of their homes. As Ella shouldered through the crowd she wondered how Beal was going to move these people and all their things across Franklin Avenue and into tents that were yet to arrive.

Perhaps what unsettled her most was the beauty of the day: a clear, warm morning that smelled of gardenia and honeysuckle. The dew-damp mud road sat drying in the sun. This was the weather that Ella would pray for if she were ever to look forward to a day at a fair. How ironic, almost cruel, she thought, that it should come on a day like this one.

As Ella broke free from the edge of the crowd, a Model T stake-bed truck rounded the corner and lurched down the street toward her, its tires brushing against the mounds of strikers' belongings that had been left on the curbs.

In the driver's seat was an older, mustached man with dark eyes. Beside him sat a heavy, jowly man, a derby pulled low and tight on his head. He smiled at Ella. She saw the soggy, chewed cigar clenched between his teeth. Percy Epps. Pigface. The man the girls at dinner had spoken of the night before. She knew him now without ever having seen him before. Two bird-faced men with sunken eyes and straw-colored hair leaned over the rails surrounding the truck bed and stared down at her.

Furniture and boxes and crates clogged the street behind Ella, and the crowd was too thick with bodies for her to turn around. Before she realized it had happened Ella found herself penned in the middle of the street by the piles on either side of her, her only choices being to climb one of the banks of mattresses, clothing, and chairs or to turn and force her way through the mass of people.

Before Ella had the chance to make a decision, the driver leaned on the horn. Its squeal made her flinch, and the driver looked over at Percy Epps. Both men laughed. The truck ground to a halt barely five feet in front of her, its body rumbling and twitching like a leashed animal.

The driver leaned out of the window. "Clear this street!" he yelled. No one moved. He leaned on the horn again. "Go on!" he said. "Get out of the damn way unless you want to be run down!"

The truck sat still, its engine vibrating beneath the hood. Ella saw a stream of shiny black oil trickle out from beneath its body, as if it bled. Ella didn't move, didn't say a word; neither did the people in the crowd behind her. The driver killed the engine, so that the only sound heard was the noise of the mill where it hummed unseen. Epps opened the truck's rickety door and took his time climbing down from the cab. He removed the cigar from his mouth, sighed, looked all around him at the row houses as if he'd never seen this street before and couldn't quite believe how sorry it all looked. He put the cigar back between his teeth and walked around to the front of the truck. He ran his thumbs along the inside of his pants waist as if adjusting his paunch so that it would fall comfortably over his belt. Ella caught the gleam of a silver revolver holstered under his left arm beneath a thin corduroy jacket. He stopped in front of her and pulled the cigar from his mouth again. He smiled, nodded at Ella.

"Miss," he said, "is something wrong with your ears? Or your legs?"

Ella was surprised by his voice, which attempted to hide something like the twang of eastern North Carolina. An image of curing golden leaf tobacco flashed through her mind, something she'd seen in cigarette advertisements, and she imagined that Epps was a long way from home and that something he did back there had caused him to flee west toward Gastonia, to Loray. She knew she was trembling, and she knew he could see it. He stood close enough for her to smell the wet tobacco in his soggy cigar.

"I think I recognize you," he said. "What's your name?"

In the question Ella heard more than the same simple query that Sophia and Velma had asked her just a day earlier. In Epps's question she understood the danger of divulging the only thing she possessed: anonymity.

"My name ain't important," she finally said.

"Your name ain't important?"

"Not to you," she said.

"No?" Epps asked. His tongue poked around his mouth, moving the cigar along his lips.

"You think your name's important to Fred Beal, that dandy Yank who's down here telling you how to work? When to work. What to do instead of working."

He was speaking directly to Ella, but his voice and his words were meant for the crowd behind her. Even as she stared into his eyes Ella could feel Epps looking past her at the strikers around her.

"But I reckon y'all gave up your names when you became communists," he said. He looked behind him at the two men leaning over the truck's rails. "Boys, I guess we got a bunch of nameless nobodies on our hands," he said. The men smiled at the same time like children responding to a parent's cue.

Epps turned back to Ella.

"Is that who you are?" he asked. "A nameless nobody?"

Epps stepped closer, as if trying to smell her, and this allowed Ella to smell him: hair grease, sweat, the scent of oiled machinery.

"I already know your name, Miss Wiggins," he whispered. "I don't know where you came from, but I know who you are, and you can rest assured that I will never forget your face."

He stepped away from Ella and took in the people behind her.

"I'm sure you good church folks have heard of the Book of Life," he said. "God's got every one of y'all's names writ down there. Every last one of you, whether you believe in Him or not, whether you fear His wrath or not. Well, I've got a Book of Life too. And all y'all are in there." He stopped speaking and stared at the crowd for a moment. Ella watched his eyes as they moved across the faces behind her. "I got you writ down there, Mamie Stihl. And you, Zachary Goshen. Lydia Roberts and Sadie Grant; Sadie, I got both you and that baby of yours in there."

He kept his eyes on the strikers for another moment, then he pulled the cigar from his mouth and flicked it to his left, where it landed atop a mattress. Suddenly there was the sound of something exploding. Ella saw a cabbage rolling off the truck's hood. It fell to the street. A smear of rotten leaves coated the truck's windshield and obscured her view of the driver. Epps turned toward the truck at the sound. The crowd roared with laughter, cheers.

But every voice fell silent when Epps turned back to face them, the silver revolver clenched in his right hand.

"Who threw that?" he screamed. He waited, but no one answered.

He raised the revolver and pointed it at the crowd, swung his arm back and forth so that it passed within inches of Ella's face. In that moment she wondered if death had found her. Every moment of her life had led to this one, and the only thing she could feel was surprise that death would come for her now, when she was so far from her children, so much farther from East Tennessee, where death had found her mother and father.

"Clear this damn road!" Epps screamed. "Now!"

Something whizzed past Ella's ear. She wondered if it was the sound a bullet would make as it flew by, but she realized the direction was wrong, and then she saw a second cabbage, this one more firm and less ripe, smash into Epps's face. He dropped the revolver and lifted his hands to his nose. When he pulled his hands away and looked at them, Ella saw that his lips were covered in blood and white flakes of cabbage had spattered across his face. His hat had been knocked to the ground. He wiped at his nose, bent to pick up his gun and hat from the road, but before he could grasp either, a cane chair crashed onto the truck's hood. Epps fell to his knees and cowered at the sound of it. The crowd laughed.

Suddenly all manner of things sailed through the air over Ella's head toward Epps: sticks of furniture, vegetables, bottles, shoes, and rocks. They caromed off the hood, windshield, roof, and the men's arms as they raised their hands to cover their heads and faces. The sounds echoed through the street.

Epps holstered his gun, and—still bent at the waist—shuffled toward the passenger's door and climbed inside. The truck rumbled to life and rolled backward away from Ella as if the world were moving in reverse, as if a tide were receding, and although Ella had never seen the ocean before—would never see it—she pictured the dark tide that had flushed her from the mountains and carried her east here to Gastonia, and she realized that it was possible for a tide to recede, to turn back, to relinquish its pull on your life.

One last bottle sailed overhead and crashed to the ground, scattering its shards along the road. The voices of the people behind Ella grew louder, and she turned to face them.

"That's the singer," someone said, and "Bessemer City," another said. "Seen her with Beal this morning," and "That there's Ella May."

CHAPTER FIVE

Brother

Friday, April 12, 1929

He had not known it was Gaston County when he arrived in mid-April, had not even known it was North Carolina through which he'd trudged a day earlier. He'd spent a clear, moonless night sleeping in an open field, and when he woke covered in dew he slung his satchel over his left shoulder and picked his way through the rocky eddies of a shallow run of river. Once on the other side, the sun now cresting the horizon, he kept the river on his right and followed the shoreline north, his clothes drying in the warm morning air.

Hours later, the sun directly overhead, he'd walked west until he saw a crossroads where a boy stood beneath a persimmon tree, staring down into a ditch that ran through the high grass alongside the road. Although he was some distance away, the boy must have heard his approach, because he turned and looked at him; then he went back to staring at whatever was at the bottom of the ditch.

"Hello, friend," he said. He waved, but the boy's back was turned and he could not see him as he approached.

The boy turned again and looked at him but did not say anything. He wondered if the boy was mute. He was much closer now, and he could see that the boy was no older than ten, barefoot and in overalls, the legs of which had been rolled to his mid-calves. His face was dirty, his blond hair the color of straw.

The boy did not look at him again, not even when he stood beside him and peered down at a black-and-white mutt that lay panting, its dry tongue lolling from the side of its mouth. Specks of blood spattered the white fur around its lips. More blood glossed the dry grass around the dog's anus. The animal appeared calm. One of its eyes, the only one he could see from where he stood, rotated in the orbit of its socket and repeatedly looked at him, the boy, the sky, and then the tall blades of grass that stirred overhead in the breeze.

"This here your pooch?" he asked the boy.

The boy nodded his head.

"What happened to him?"

The boy shrugged.

"You just found him here?"

The boy nodded his head again.

He looked up from the ditch and touched a branch of the persimmon tree, trailed his fingers through its yellow blossoms. He took in the landscape around him. The river was somewhere behind him, so he did not turn in that direction. Instead he looked toward the bright green trees on the other side of a field, and for a brief moment he wondered what grew in the field and when it would be harvested. The day was clear, but he smelled something in the air. Something damp, clammy, perhaps born of river mud.

"Where are we?" he asked the boy.

The boy lifted his eyes from the ditch and looked around as if getting his bearings.

"Gaston," the boy finally said.

"Gaston," he repeated. He looked down at the boy. "Do you mean Gaston County?"

The boy shrugged.

"Mama just says 'Gaston' when she says 'here.'"

"You and your mama live close by?" he asked.

The boy nodded his head, lifted his arm, and pointed down the road that seemed to lead south.

"Your mama got any work needs doing?" he asked.

"She'll shoot you," the boy said.

"Excuse me?"

"She'll shoot you," the boy said again. "She said she'd shoot the next man who come up from the river." The boy looked at him. "You come up from the river, didn't you?"

"I did."

"Well," the boy said, turning his gaze back to the dog, "she'll shoot you sure enough."

"Huh," he said. He looked south, in the direction the boy had pointed, but there was nothing to see.

"I think some old jalopy come through here and run him over," the boy said.

It took a moment for him to realize that the boy was speaking of the dog. The dog hadn't moved, apart from the one eye that still looked around at all it could see of the world.

"You think he's paralyzed?"

"What's paralyzed?"

"Means 'he can't move nothing,'" he said.

"You a doctor?" the boy asked.

"No," he said. "I ain't no doctor."

He dropped the satchel at his feet and held his right arm against his chest and reached down into the ditch to stroke the dog's rear flank with his left hand. The mutt's pupil widened. Without raising its head, its eye searched for the source of the touch. It growled, but its growl was low, even.

"I think some old jalopy come through here and run him over," the boy said again.

"It's okay, buddy," he said to the dog. He rubbed the dog again, stopped, looked up at the boy. "What's your pooch's name?"

"Roscoe," the boy said.

"It's okay, Roscoe," he said.

It happened quickly, so he did not see if the mutt's teeth came anywhere near him, but he felt the dog's body tense for just a moment before it yelped and sprang toward his hand. He fell back onto the road. The dog resettled itself as if it had never moved.

"You see that?" he said.

The boy bent down and stroked the mutt's head, whispered something into its ear.

"Guess he ain't paralyzed," the boy said.

"I guess not." He stood, dusted off the seat of his pants. "There a town close by here?"

"There's some castles over there," the boy said, pointing west.

"Castles?"

"Yep," the boy said. "Castles."

The dog closed its eyes, tongued its lips over and over. The boy continued to stroke its head.

"How far you think them castles are?"

"I don't know," the boy said.

"How long would it take to walk to there?"

"I don't know," the boy said again.

He wondered if the boy was lying about the castles, or if they were something he'd heard of but had never seen. He picked up his satchel, looked west.

"Which way's them castles again?" he asked.

Without taking his eyes from the dog, the boy pointed west again.

"All right," he said, slinging his satchel over his shoulder. "I hope your pooch feels better soon."

He set off down the road. He'd walked a minute or so when he heard the boy's voice behind him.

"Hey!" the boy called.

He turned and looked at the boy. The boy cradled the dog in his arms. Its body was turned in a way that he could see fresh blood where it soaked the fur around its tail. For a moment he feared that the dog had died in the boy's arms, but then he saw it move.

"Why you got that chair around your neck?" the boy asked.

He looked down at the tiny wooden chair where it hung from the leather strap in the middle of his chest. He lifted his hand and fingered it for a moment before letting it go. He looked up at the boy, considered the difficulty of explaining the story of the chair, where it had come from, what it meant. He decided against it. Instead he raised his hand, waved.

"Blessings," he said. "Blessings to you, friend, and Roscoe there too."

The boy turned, carried the dog south, in the direction he'd said was home.

HE WALKED WEST with the satchel's strap over his left shoulder, the chair bouncing against his chest with each step. Years had passed since he'd threaded this same strip of leather through the chair's spindles and tied it around his neck, since he'd learned that he could effect great change with a small seed that continued to yield an enormous crop in not only his life, but also the lives of others.

It had been late summer in 1920, just outside of Augusta, in eastern Georgia, when he saw her for the first and only time. Of all the things he could not or would not remember about his previous life, before he became a wanderer, this was the one memory to which he had fiercely clung. He'd been standing on the sidewalk outside a barbershop. He'd asked the barber if he could sweep the floors and wash the windows for whatever change the barber could spare, but the barber had told him that he smelled awful and was indecently dirty, and that the sheriff would be called if he did not leave the barber and his patrons in peace. He'd been hoping the barber would change his mind, for it was a small town and he'd run out of businesses in front of which to beg, but the longer he stood there, his hands shaking and his throat dry, the more he doubted the barber would budge and the more the threat to call the sheriff seemed certain to be carried out.

What finally caused him to turn away from the barbershop's window was the reflection of her black convertible Packard with its top down as it rolled past on the street behind him. A banner stretching along the side of the car read JESUS IS COMING SOON—GET READY. An older woman sat in the driver's seat, gripping the steering wheel and staring straight ahead. On the back of the Packard's folded top perched the most regal young woman he'd ever seen. Her skin was white and fine, and her dark, shiny hair was piled atop her head. She wore a white dress with long sleeves, and she held a megaphone and called out to people on the street. She waved, handed out flyers, said, "Hope to see y'all this evening!" in an accent that sounded distant and strange, but her voice rang true and clear, and he wanted to hear it again.

He left the shop's window, walked to the edge of the street, and stood in the Packard's wake. He watched as it rounded the corner. A half-dozen flyers lay on the sidewalk on the other side of the street. He crossed over and stepped up onto the curb and picked up one of them.

SALVATION AND HEALING ON OFFER THIS EVENING

Sister Aimee Semple McPherson Brings the Good Word

Public Fairgrounds 7 o'clock

"White and Colored Are Equal Before God and Beneath My Tent."

Perhaps it was the haunting image of her sitting atop the Packard that took him there that evening. Perhaps it was mere curiosity. He could hear her voice and the shouts of the crowd before he entered the fairgrounds. As a child and as an adult he'd attended tent revivals in fields just like this one, had found himself moved by the spirit on quite a few occasions, had even slipped a coin or two into the offering plate as it made its way through the audience. But even with those experiences he was not prepared for what he found: an open field full of what seemed to be hundreds if not thousands of farmers and businessmen and housewives and children, white and colored alike, all of their arms raised, their hands upturned, many of them dancing or twitching or simply running in place, their eyes closed as if to shut out the world. Beneath the tent, this woman, this Sister Aimee Semple McPherson, stood atop a stage in a silken white dress and long white gloves. If he had not known this was a revival, he would have thought her a sorceress and the crowds before her the victims of a powerful spell.

Sister, for that was what she'd told the crowd to call her, spoke of her childhood in Canada, how the spirit of God had come upon her as a teenager as a warning against even entertaining the idea of evolution. She told of how she'd met an Irishman named Robert James Semple at a revival just like the one she now led, how his clean mind and pure heart had so impressed her and had so delivered her unto the Lord, and she realized that the Lord had delivered them unto one another.

She and Semple had traveled as missionaries to China, where he'd died of an illness, but not before giving her a daughter. She'd come home from China, raised her child, given birth to a second child after remarrying a kindhearted, decent man. She did her best to embrace domestic life, did her best to be what a woman should be, but it would not stick. She felt a call to wander the land like John the Baptist, a peripatetic prophet in a black convertible driven by her elderly mother while her children stayed at home with her husband. She'd preach and heal. She'd change the world with her kindness and sense of justice and her cry for the equality of all people.

Never before had he heard someone tell a story that so closely resembled his own. He too had tried to embrace domestic life, had tried and failed to be a worthy Christian and good husband, had tried to stay clear of whiskey and loose women and the men who peddled both. He had failed. He had hurt innocent people. He had destroyed lives. He no longer gave a damn about being holy. He just wanted to be good, and there, in that field outside Augusta, *good* is what he decided to be.

He did not hear Sister speak again until 1921, and by that time he had walked much of Georgia and South Carolina, offering kindness where it could be offered, helping the helpless, preaching the equality of all people regardless of race. In all that time, in that year and a half, he had not touched a drop of liquor, a deck of cards, or the exposed skin of a woman.

On the day he heard Sister's voice for the second time he'd found himself with a little money in his pocket, and he'd taken a seat on the porch of a country store near Sumter, South Carolina, where he'd just unwrapped a pork sandwich. The tinny drone of a radio whined from inside the store, and as its operator switched through the few stations it could pick up from over in Columbia, he heard Sister's voice beckon to him. He leapt from his seat and went inside and begged the store's owner to leave the dial where it lay. Then he leaned against the counter, his sandwich growing cold, and listened to the voice of the woman who'd changed his life.

She and her mother had made it all the way to Los Angeles, California, and there she planned to build a grand temple that would save the world. What she needed now were prayers, prayers and donations, to ensure that the power of God could continue to touch lives with even greater speed than she'd been able to achieve these last few years on the back roads of America. For a donation of five dollars, Sister herself would send the faithful patron a personalized letter and a small replica of the hundreds of chairs that would one day fill the Angelus Temple.

He checked his pockets and found a little over four dollars. He hadn't held a steady job in years, and money meant nothing to him aside from the ease of buying food, and there was plenty of that in the fields he passed and the woods through which he walked on his travels.

He asked for a pencil and wrote down the postal address in Los Angeles, then he pondered the uneaten sandwich on the counter beside him and the unopened, sweating glass bottle of Coca-Cola that sat beside it. He calculated what he'd just paid for each. He refolded the wax paper around the sandwich and asked for his money to be returned, but the store owner would only let him return the Coca-Cola, and even that he accepted begrudgingly. He ate the pork sandwich and waited while the store owner opened the till and counted out the money for the Coca-Cola.

When he finished eating he asked the owner if there was anything a good man could do to earn honest money for a good woman's cause. For the rest of the afternoon, he unloaded boxes in the storeroom and stocked shelves. That evening he swept out the store and swept the porch and the porch steps. For all of this work, work that had felt both natural and fulfilling, the store owner gave him a dollar, which, combined with his existing funds, was plenty of money to buy an envelope and postage to send five dollars to Sister Aimee Semple McPherson.

He took the envelope and the stamp from the store owner. After a brief consideration of where he would be a month from that date—he figured he'd shoot for Greenwood, South Carolina—he scratched out a note in the best penmanship his left hand could muster.

Dear Sister,
    I saw you at a revival out side Augusta. I send you these hard earned 5 dollars and hope your dream comes true. I

look forward to getting a letter from you. I look forward to getting that little chair too.

Your friend...

(Here he paused, his pencil hovering above the page. He smiled, decided to sign a new name, a name he'd gone by ever since that day.)

... in peace and justice,
Brother

WHAT THE BOY at the crossroads had thought were castles were actually the buildings of a Catholic monastery. Brother crested a hill and spotted a monk in a cassock hoeing rows of what looked to be cabbages in a small, neatly turned field. He waved to the monk. The monk stopped hoeing and stared at him for a moment. He leaned against the hoe and wiped at his brow. Then he raised a hand to shield the sun from his eyes so that he might see Brother more clearly. He waved back.

The small order of Benedictine monks at Belmont Abbey were quiet, holy men, benefactors of the small college of the same name that the order had founded in 1876. On the campus, a couple hundred Gaston and Mecklenburg County farm boys in suits and ties wandered from classroom to classroom in search of the mysteries of a proper liberal arts education. Meanwhile, the monks, whose cloistered lives allowed them almost no awareness of the comings and goings of the students, prayed, studied, maintained the life of the monastery, and volunteered their time in the local mill communities. They took Brother in without hesitation or question. They did not ask his name or who he was, and that was fine with him because he did not want to be who he'd been.

The monk he'd first met in the field that April day was Father

Gregory, a gouty, red-faced old man who'd come from Pennsylvania. Brother spent most of his time with Father Gregory, working in the garden, cleaning the monks' quarters, walking the abbey's grounds, listening to the gurgle of the small fountain in the courtyard.

Brother slept on a cot in a closetlike room in the monastery's basement. Here, while listening to water pass through the pipes and the sounds of the forest outside the basement door through which he was allowed to come and go as he pleased, he would lie awake until sleep found him, the tips of his fingers touching each angle of the tiny wooden chair that sat upright on his chest. He pondered the promise he'd made to himself to be good, to know good, to do good.

And then he saw Ella May Wiggins, and his memory of beholding Sister coupled with the dark guilt of his past life caught up with him there in a crowded field in Gastonia. Like Sister, this woman Ella stood atop a stage with a vast audience spread out before her. It was a cool evening in early May, not long after dark. Brother stood with Father Gregory and Father Elian on the edge of the crowd, shoulder-to-shoulder with gaunt-faced millworkers, policemen, and newspaper reporters. He and the two monks had traveled the few miles to Gastonia to help feed the strikers who they had learned would be evicted from their homes the following morning. He had expected to help them, but he had not expected to see Ella or to feel her story uncoil itself in his heart.

And then she sang, and Brother was struck dumb by the beauty of it.

CHAPTER SIX

Claire McAdam

Friday, May 10, 1929

The train had departed Washington, D.C., at 10:35 P.M. By the time Claire and her friend Donna had settled themselves in their bunks it was near midnight and they were drawing close to Manassas. Claire's body still pulsed with anger and hurt, and she'd been unable to fall asleep after the argument she'd had with Donna. Claire slipped her hand from under the blanket and felt around for the train schedule she'd tucked beneath her mattress. She unfolded it and held it to the faint moonlight that trickled through the curtained window by her bunk. On the schedule she saw the name of the great battlefield that her fiancé Paul's father had spoken of, the place where Paul's great-grandfather had fought the first real battle of the Civil War, when it seemed the whole campaign would be short and certain.

Claire recalled the face of Paul's great-grandfather, a man whom she'd never met and had only seen in the huge oil portrait that hung in the Lytles' keeping room in the family's old plantation on the North Carolina coast. She'd imagined the gray-bearded man in the portrait sitting atop a powerful white horse on a muddy battlefield strewn with the bodies of young southern boys.

Claire rested her head on the stiff pillow and lifted her left hand so that the diamond on her engagement ring caught the light. She tried to ignore the heavy breathing coming from the bunk below her, but the sound of Donna's peaceful sleep annoyed her.

Donna's father's connections had been what allowed the young students from the North Carolina College for Women to travel to Washington, and it had been his personal friendship with Senator Lee Overman that had secured them a tour of the city by one of the nation's most powerful congressmen.

"I grew up in Salisbury believing that Lee Overman was the greatest man alive," Donna had told Claire on the train ride to Washington the day before. They'd been sitting beside one another in the dining car. Claire had been writing a letter to Paul. She'd promised him that she'd send him a piece of mail with D.C. postage.

"My daddy always told me that Senator Overman was the only man in Washington willing to protect my 'southern womanhood,'" Donna had said. She'd gathered her thick red hair into a ponytail and fastened it. Claire envied Donna's beauty, the ease with which she moved and spoke and acted. Claire was twenty-one, but she still perceived herself as a quiet, passive child with mousy brown hair, who lived with an acute fear that someone might be judging her. It made her feel very small. She'd sensed Donna's eyes on her, and she'd scribbled a sloppy heart at the bottom of Paul's letter before signing her name.

She had batted her eyes at Donna and dropped her voice into a low-country drawl. "And how can the senator expect to protect the womanhood of a saucy number like you, my lady?"

Donna had looked at her without smiling; then she'd turned toward the train's window.

"My daddy used to say, 'Donna baby, Lee Overman would lynch every damn nigger in this country if he had to.' And as I got older I knew what that meant, and it scared me to hear my father talk that way. It still does."

It was clear that Donna did not think much of Senator Overman or her father or the men's connection, but it had not kept Claire from feeling proud that morning before their tour when Donna had introduced her to the senator as "the daughter of Richard McAdam, owner of the McAdam Mill in Belmont." The senator had smiled at the mention of Claire's family name.

"I know things are rocky down in Gaston County with the strike," the senator had said. "Give your father my best, and tell him we're doing everything we can to put an end to this trouble."

"I will," Claire had said. "I'll let him know." She had nodded and smiled, but she'd had no idea what the senator had meant.

Overman was old and white-headed, and he'd shuffled along before the group of young women and their chaperone and pointed out everything they'd hoped to see: the Washington Monument; the Capitol Rotunda; the White House, where the senator had promised that President Hoover was in residence at that very moment, since the two men had spoken that morning.

Their last stop of the day had been the Lincoln Memorial. Their chaperone, Mrs. Barnes, had stood with her back to Lincoln, as he sat on the chair that seemed so much like a throne. The monument was barely seven years old. Its white marble shone glossy and smooth in the late afternoon light.

"People don't ever believe this story," Mrs. Barnes had said, "so none of you have to believe it either."

The girls had all stopped talking and turned and looked toward Mrs. Barnes. Some of them had even drawn closer to hear her more clearly. She was an old woman, perhaps as old as seventy, and she rarely spoke, except in the classroom, and even then she spoke in such a way that the girls had to focus their ears to fully understand what she said.

Claire had been standing by Senator Overman, who was certainly older than Mrs. Barnes, and when she began her story with her back turned on Lincoln, the senator seemed to sense something in her tone that hinted that her story might be his own story as well. He'd stopped midsentence, stopped telling Claire about witnessing the completion of the statue's body just a few years earlier. He'd dropped his hands where they were gesturing and drifted toward Mrs. Barnes, who stood on the edge of the shadow cast by the portico above them.

"It was early April 1865," Mrs. Barnes said, "and I was just three years old, but my birthday was coming up in June, and I'd already been told that my daddy wouldn't be there. My sister, Margaret, who I called Sissy—called her that until she died—had already told me that Abraham Lincoln had killed my daddy at a place called Chancellorsville. It sounded like a far-off place, and I had no idea where it was. I don't think I even knew what *killed* or *dead* meant then. I was so young. But I knew those words made Sissy and my mother sad, and I hated Abraham Lincoln for doing those words to my father, for making my mother and sister feel that way.

"Richmond was already burning. Our boys had set the fires themselves during their retreat: the bridges, the munitions, the harbor. Maybe they didn't expect for it to keep burning after they'd left. It was after midnight on the second night of the fires when we finally left our home and made our way down Bank Street toward my mother's sister's house, my aunt Jess. Her husband was away at the war too, but he would come home that summer. She was lucky. He was lucky too.

"We were coming down Ninth Street right by the Capitol. Parts of the city glowed in the distance, and you could smell the smoke and all the different smells of the things that were on fire. We were coming down the hill right by the Capitol and it was all right there before us, the whole city on fire, burning right there before us.

"We turned east on Bank Street. I don't know who recognized him first, my mother or Sissy, but I know it wasn't me because I didn't know what he looked like. I was carrying my doll and a little parcel of clothing that Mother had given me. There were some stockings and a pair of shoes stuffed down inside there too. I remember I was crying because Mother wouldn't hold my hand. Her arms were full, and she couldn't have held my hand if she'd wanted to. Sissy's arms were full too, and I was too young to understand that to hold my hand would've meant that they would have had to leave something behind. I cried and cried. I was mad, but I was scared too.

"Now that I think of it, Sissy was the one who recognized him out there on the steps. He had his arms folded across his chest. He had on a dark suit just like you see in photographs of him. No hat, nothing on his head. He was just standing there all by himself, watching. I remember seeing the light from the fire shine on his face where he was sweating. It was a warm night, probably even hotter because the city was burning, and he had on a jacket and a tie. He'd probably just come up from the river.

"But I know it was Sissy who first whispered his name. Mother hushed her as if saying it again would get his attention, would draw his eyes away from the fires to look at us. But when I understood who he was I called out to him. I wanted to ask him why he killed my daddy. I wanted to tell him how sad I was that my daddy wouldn't be coming to my birthday party in June. That he wouldn't be able to sing me camp songs or bring me candy like he'd done the first time he'd come home from the war. I wanted to tell him those things.

"And he must have heard me when I called his name. You may not believe it, and you don't have to believe it, but he turned and looked at us from where he stood right there on the steps on the south side of the Capitol, Richmond burning all around us, the smoke almost choking us to death. He looked right at us, and I swear he nodded his head. What he meant in doing that, I can't say. It could've meant *hello* or *good evening* or *nice to see you,* but I know for a fact that it did not mean *I'm sorry,* and sorry was the only thing I wanted him to be."

Claire and the other girls stood there staring at Mrs. Barnes's back while she looked out over the mud and grass that led toward the Washington Monument, her black hat pulled low and her black coat pulled tight around her against the late afternoon chill.

Claire's heart had swelled at the romance of the story, but it was Donna who'd broken the silence, the spell that Mrs. Barnes's story had cast, a story that had enraptured the old senator just as much as it had enraptured Claire. Donna's white skin was soft and beautifully pale in the waning light, and when she turned to stare at the monument behind her, the setting sun caught her coppery hair and burned it a brilliant red. Donna leaned toward Mrs. Barnes and raised her hand and pointed at Lincoln.

"Was he that tall?" Donna asked. A few of the girls had laughed.

Mrs. Barnes composed herself, then turned slowly, her eyes alighting on Lincoln's face for just a moment.

"No," she said, "of course not. Don't be silly."

Minutes later the group was making their way down Independence Avenue when they heard someone call the senator's name from the other side of the street. Claire looked up to see a man in a dark suit darting through the traffic, horns honking and tires squealing to a stop. A dozen gaunt-faced men and women in mismatched second-hand clothes followed behind him, their eyes wide with terror. The oldest of them could have been fifty; the youngest of them, a skinny wisp of a girl, couldn't have been any older than ten.

The man who'd called out to the senator stood before Senator Overman and the group of young women as if he hoped to block their route to the Capitol. The rest of the ragtag party gathered behind him. All of them were panting, trying to catch their breath. If it had been any colder their breath would've steamed before them like horses that had just pulled sleds across fields deep with snow.

"Senator," he said, "my name is Carlton Reed. I'm with the *Labor Defender.*"

Claire caught his northern accent, noticed his expensive suit. He talked fast, as if he knew the senator had better things to do and was already planning his escape.

"Sir," Reed continued, "I have with me here today a few members of the Gastonia, North Carolina, local of the National Textile Workers Union, and we're in town to—"

"I know who you are, son," Overman said, "and I know why y'all are here."

"Sir," Reed said, removing his hat, "you may be aware of the Montana senator's inquiry into the southern textile mills. Well, today's hearing was canceled after our party arrived, but we had the good fortune to meet with Senator Wheeler and Senator La Follette of Wisconsin, and my question to you, sir, is why does it take two northern senators to initiate an investigation into—" But Overman stopped him, went so far as to place his big, open palm on the man's chest and give him a gentle push so that Claire's group would have room enough to pass them on the sidewalk.

"I understand, son," the senator said, "and I applaud your efforts, but if you'll excuse me I'm engaged with a group of proper ladies from North Carolina."

"We're proper ladies from North Carolina too," a woman in the textile group said. She stepped out from behind Reed and blocked the sidewalk.

"Ella," Reed said. He touched the woman's shoulder, but she took another step away from him so he could not reach her without following. She was a small, thin woman in a dingy white dress. She wore a man's long coat and a black knit cap that was pulled tight enough to nearly cover her eyes.

"We're all proper," the woman said. She took her hand from her coat pocket and motioned toward the people behind her. "And we're hungry and tired and poor too."

"Ella," Reed said again.

"I see," the senator said. He stepped back and looked at the group as if appraising them. "It looks like you strikers are all decked out in your union-issued finery."

A few of the group, the women especially, looked down at their clothes. One of the men tugged on his lapels and buttoned his suit jacket.

"Senator, are you suggesting that these men and women are in costume?" Reed asked.

"What I'm suggesting is y'all go home to Gastonia and call off this strike and get back to work," Overman said. "Quit playing these games. Quit allowing the communist to dictate your lives." He turned to the thin, young striker who'd been standing quietly. "And you, young lady, you need to return to school."

At that, the woman named Ella flew toward the senator and perhaps would have knocked him down had Reed not grabbed her by her shoulders.

"School!" she shouted. "School?!" She tried to buck free of Reed's grasp but he was too tall and too strong. She kept yelling at Overman, her voice coming out in a husky scream. "Let me tell you something," she said. "I can't even send my own children to school. They ain't got decent enough clothes to wear and I can't afford to buy them none. I make nine dollars a week, and I work all night and leave them shut up in the house all by themselves. I had one of them sick this winter and I had to leave her there just coughing and crying."

Ella's voice dropped and she was quiet for a moment. She looked from Overman to the faces of the girls from Greensboro. Her eyes met Claire's, and something cold and wretched shot through Claire's heart. Ella shrugged Reed's hands from her shoulders. She looked over at the young girl whom Overman had commanded to return to school. The girl wore a dirty white dress and loose gray stockings. She was shrouded in a long black coat that seemed to have been cut for someone twice her size. Her face was sharp, her eyes sunken, ringed in pink.

"And this one here," Ella said, putting her arm around the girl and pulling her toward her. "Binnie here's fourteen years old, but you wouldn't know it by looking at her, would you? This girl here ain't been to school in years. She makes five dollars a week, and that's more than her mother and daddy make. She used to have a brother who worked in the mill too, but tuberculosis ate at him till he died."

The senator sighed loud enough for everyone in both groups to hear him. He rolled his eyes and looked over the heads of the girls from Greensboro and toward the back of the group, where Mrs. Barnes had been standing silently. He mouthed the words *I'm sorry* and turned back to Reed.

"Sir," Senator Overman said, "I appreciate your plight, but let me advise you and your people in saying that the streets are not the place to solve issues like these. I suggest you all return home, and, sir, I suggest you return to New York City and leave these people alone." He looked at the group of college women. His eye caught Claire's. "Ms. McAdam, I'm sure your father's people don't carry on this way," he said. "I apologize that you came all the way to Washington to encounter this behavior."

The senator brushed past Reed, and Claire and the rest of her party followed him. The group of strikers parted, and the girls walked between them, up Maryland toward the Capitol. Claire kept her eyes on the sidewalk. The woman named Ella coughed, cleared her throat. "You ladies enjoy your visit to your nation's capital," she said.

They walked in silence behind Senator Overman. A chilly wind tumbled down the steps on the west side of the Capitol and into Claire's eyes. She felt the sun on her back, saw her shadow thrown out before her. She heard someone sniff, did not realize it was herself until she felt the tears streaming down her cheeks. She looked to her right and found Donna walking beside her, tears streaking her face as well.

"My father's people aren't like that," Claire had said. "Those aren't my father's people. My father takes care of his people."

Claire felt Donna's arm around her waist. She leaned her head on her friend's shoulder.

A FEW HOURS later in their sleeping berth, Claire lay on the top bunk in her nightgown and flipped through a copy of *Vanity Fair*. Donna sat on the bunk below, spreading cold cream over her face, her hair pulled back in a ponytail.

"You would've thought Overman could've shown a little more kindness to those people," Donna said.

"What people?" Claire asked. She looked at an advertisement for the film *Coquette* that featured Mary Pickford in a beautiful peach chiffon party dress, a smile on her face as she gazed over her shoulder at a number of male suitors. Claire could not imagine anyone aside from Paul ever desiring her.

"Those strikers from Gastonia," Donna said. "He treated them like trash."

Claire studied Mary Pickford's dress, noted the beautiful floral design that had been sewn on the front. "Well, did you see how they were dressed?" she asked.

Claire heard Donna gasp, heard the jar of cold cream land on the floor. Donna stood, and Claire saw that the two were now eye-level. "Are you serious, Claire?" Donna asked. Claire smiled but did not speak, did not take her eyes from Mary Pickford's face. Donna put her hand over the advertisement so that Claire could not look at it. "It's not funny. It's not a joke."

Claire closed the magazine and laid it on her chest. "I'm sorry," she said. "It's awkward for me, that's all. My father owns a mill. Those were millworkers. It was awkward."

Donna shook her head, lowered herself to her bed. "Well, I'm sorry it was awkward for you, Claire."

Claire sat up on the edge of her bunk and let her feet dangle over the side. "I told you, Donna, my father's people aren't like that. He treats his people better than that."

"Are you even listening to yourself?" Donna asked. "You talk about your father's employees as if he owns them."

"Of course he doesn't own them," Claire said. "Of course not. He says they're his people because they're like family. Everyone lives in the village together, Donna. It's like a big family."

"And you and your parents live in the big house that looks down on the rest of the family," Donna said. "Just like on Paul's parents' plantation. I bet they viewed their slaves as family too."

"That's not fair, Donna," Claire said. "And you know it. Paul's mother and father had nothing to do with that. That was years ago."

"Look down at that diamond on your finger, Claire," Donna had said. "You can thank Paul's family for that. All of them."

NOW CLAIRE LAY in the dark berth, spinning her engagement ring on her finger. She considered what Donna had said, and she pictured Paul's face, his family's home in Wilmington, the portrait of his great-grandfather that hung in the sitting room. She thought of Manassas and wondered what she'd missed of it by not looking out the train's window. Could she have seen the field across which Paul's great-grandfather had ridden the white horse of her imagining? She pulled back the curtain and looked through the window. Out there, the blackness was barely decipherable from the black things impressed upon it. Nothing but dark shapes passed her. She inched her body closer to the window and cupped her hands and peered through the warm tunnel of her fingers: outside, a quiet town somewhere near Manassas, perhaps Manassas itself; the train passed the station without stopping; a Main Street where hours ago the shops had been closed for the night; trucks parked and waiting against the curbs outside of buildings.

She lay back on the bed, looked at her ring again. She'd met Paul three years earlier, when he was in Greensboro on business. His parents owned considerable tobacco interests in eastern North Carolina, and Paul, who'd graduated from Chapel Hill the year before, oversaw sales at his father's direction.

Claire closed her eyes, allowed her mind to carry her back to the cool October evening in 1926 when she and Donna and two other sophomore girls from their dormitory had crossed the quadrangle at dusk on a chilly Saturday evening. They'd stood on the corner where Spring Garden and Tate streets meet, giggling, watching the red and orange and yellow leaves drift down around them and stir in the wind about their feet. The four of them had waited nervously for the streetcar that would take them downtown to the O. Henry Hotel. The young men from the local armory were holding a fall dance for the women's college. Claire thought of the dress she'd worn, a pale blue silk gown Donna had loaned her. She thought of the boys she'd danced with that night, most of them forgettable, certainly none of them more memorable than Paul, who then was nothing more than a freckle-faced boy with a low-country drawl and homebrew on his breath who'd tried to kiss her on the dance floor in front of her friends. How they'd all laughed, howled really, at the telling and retelling of it on their way back to the dorm that night, their shoes kicking up dry and dying leaves, Donna even corralling the leaves into piles before picking them up and tossing them into the air, singing, "We're the queens of autumn!" How Claire had lain in bed that night and pictured Paul's face, the bodies of the dancers moving all around them, the pulse of the music pounding in her chest, her heart beating somewhere beneath it.

But the things that Donna had said before bed soured the memory, and Claire wished she could remove Donna from it. Donna knew nothing about Paul or his family. She certainly knew nothing about Claire's parents. Claire was certain that her parents were exceptional people. Her mother was kind and gentle and openhearted.

Her father was honest, worked hard, and treated his employees well. He'd joined the army during the war, even though he was wealthy and did not have to and would have never been expected to fight.

Claire's parents loved her, and they seemed to love Paul. After all, they were throwing a huge engagement party for them at the club in Gastonia in two weeks. Donna would be there and Paul's parents would be there too. Donna would see how wrong she'd been to say the things she'd said.

Claire adjusted her pillow, listened to the train move along the track, felt it rock beneath her. She tried to clear her mind, tried to drift off to sleep, but something kept needling her—Mrs. Barnes on the steps at the Lincoln Memorial; the smell of the woman Ella's breath on her face; the things Donna had said about the strikers and Claire's parents; the image of a slightly younger Donna tossing oak leaves into the air; Claire's parents' quiet house that overlooked the mill and the lake back in Belmont; and the uncertainty of the long, silent days that stretched out before her until she could marry Paul in the fall and have the rest of her life begin.

Claire sat up in her bunk, pushed the covers down to her ankles, and slipped her feet free of the sheets. She made as little sound as possible when she climbed down, reaching her foot into the darkness for the flat of the sitting chair by the bunk instead of stepping on Donna's mattress. Once she made it down she slid open the closet door. She pulled her gown up over her head and swapped it for the dress she'd worn that day, her own warmth still nestled in the fabric around the armpits, the scent of the city still clinging to the fabric. She stepped into a pair of slippers and opened the door, did her best to block out the light coming into the berth so that it didn't cross Donna's face. She stepped into the hallway.

While her eyes adjusted to the sudden brightness, Claire's fingers reached for the wall to steady herself as the train rocked beneath her. The late hour, the soft carpet under her slippered feet, the knowledge that she'd left her room fresh from bed without making up her face or hair fed something in her that she couldn't quite put a word to. No one knew where she was right now. Not her parents, not Paul, not even Donna, who was still asleep in her bunk. She wondered if it was excitement that she felt? Danger? Was it freedom? She followed the hallway to the dining car, the lights blazing inside as if a meal service were about to begin. The breakfast plates and cutlery had already been set, and in the corner beside a tray stand, a young Negro porter in a dark vest and matching bow tie polished silverware with a white rag.

"Miss," he said. He nodded his head, looked away from Claire as soon as his eyes met hers. He could have been Paul's age, perhaps a little older.

"Hello," Claire said.

His seeing her in slippers and with an unmade face had embarrassed her, but his looking away from her had embarrassed her even more. She considered turning and walking back down the hallway toward her room, but she feared both offending him and appearing younger and sillier than she wanted to appear. Instead, she walked farther into the car and stopped near its middle. She gazed around her at the set tables.

"First service isn't until six A.M.," he said, "but I might could find you something if you're hungry."

"What time is it now?" Claire asked.

He reached into his pocket and looked at a watch.

"Quarter after one," he said. "We'll stop in Charlottesville in a few minutes."

"Do you mind if I sit?" Claire asked.

"No," he said, "not at all. Want a cup of coffee? I could find some coffee."

"No," Claire said. "But perhaps a glass of milk, if it's not too much."

"It's not too much at all," he said. "Would you like it warmed?"

"No," she said. "Cold is fine."

"Please, have a seat," he said. "I'll be back."

"Thank you," she said. The man nodded and left the dining car opposite the way she'd come. She sat down in a booth on the west side of the train and scooted toward the window. Lights burned outside. She wondered if it was a small town. She wondered how far they'd already come. Her eyes focused on her reflection. Her brown hair appeared darker than she knew it to be. Her face nearly glowed.

The conversation she'd just had was the longest she'd ever had with a Negro. Unlike Paul, who'd grown up on the plantation before so many of his family's tenants had left to find work in the cities and jobs up north, she hadn't grown up with Negroes. She had never been able to approach them with the cool, natural ease with which she'd witnessed Paul and his father move and speak among them.

The porter walked back into the dining car and set a glass of milk down in front of Claire. Beside it he placed a small plate with a cookie sitting atop a napkin. Claire looked up at him. She smiled.

"Thank you," she said.

"You're welcome," he said. He stood there, his hands down by his sides. "What's your name?" he asked.

The question surprised her. She looked up at him, considered his face. She pictured Donna sleeping in the bunk, thought of the things she'd said about Paul's family, about her own family. What would she think to see Claire sitting here in the middle of the night talking to a Negro as if it were the most natural thing in the world?

"Donna," she said. "My name's Donna."

"Donna," he said. "My name's Hampton."

"Hello, Hampton," she said.

"Hello, Donna," he said. "Please, let me know if you need anything else." He turned and walked back to the tray stand.

Claire took a sip of the milk, tried to keep her hand from shaking. Her heart pounded in her ears. The milk calmed her. She set it on the table, spent a moment catching her breath. She picked up the cookie, bit into it. She couldn't tell what kind it was. A sugar cookie perhaps. She brushed the crumbs from the tablecloth and dabbed at her mouth with the napkin. She could feel Hampton's eyes on her. She looked up at him, and he dropped his gaze to the silverware he'd been polishing.

"Trouble sleeping?" he asked.

"Yes," she said.

"Is your room comfortable?"

"Yes," she said. "It's quite nice. I just have a lot on my mind to-night."

He smiled, set the piece of silverware on the tray, and picked up another. He was tall with soft brown eyes and dark skin. She watched him work, and she felt her eyes grow heavy. She felt warm, relaxed. She picked up the cookie and took another bite. She drank more of the milk.

She ran her hand along the windowsill and watched the reflection of it moving in the dark glass. She felt something catch her fingertips. When she looked closer she saw that a hair had been painted onto the metal. She wondered where it had come from. Had the painter dropped it and then covered it over? Had he known he'd left part of himself behind? She used her fingernail and scratched at the hair until it came free and disappeared into the shadows beneath the window. The place where the hair had been was shiny, the metal left exposed.

She looked up at the porter. He'd been watching her, but for how long she didn't know.

"Do you have to stay awake all night?" she asked.

He smiled and looked down. He placed a fork on the tray and picked up another.

"Yes," he said. "I come on in New York and work through until the breakfast service begins."

"That's a long time," she said.

"Yes," he said. "It can feel like a long time."

"Is it hard?"

"The job?"

"No," she said. "Is it hard to stay awake all night?"

"Sometimes," he said. "It gets easier. You get used to it."

"I couldn't do it," she said.

"You're doing it now."

"That's true," she said. "I suppose I've been awake as long as you have."

"You could do it easily if you were working," he said.

"Yes," she said, "I suppose I could." But she wasn't certain. She'd never had a job, and the fact embarrassed her even though there was no way he could have known this.

"It's nice at night," he said. "But it's too quiet sometimes. I don't usually get to talk with nice people like you."

She smiled, perfectly aware that something, although she wasn't quite sure what, was happening between them. "You're from New York?" she asked. He looked up at her, nodded, looked back down at the tray of silverware. "What's it like?"

"You've never been?" he asked.

"No," she said.

"That surprises me," he said. "You look like someone who would enjoy the big city."

"What's it like?" she asked again.

"It's busy," he said. "And loud and dirty. It's wonderful sometimes. Sometimes it's awful."

"It sounds amazing," she said.

"Sometimes it is," he said. He polished the silverware in silence for a moment, stared intently at his hands as they worked. "Where are you from?" he asked.

Claire watched his hands and the white rag move across the knives and forks and spoons as he polished them. She felt herself stepping from her own life back in McAdamville and into Donna's.

"Salisbury," she said. "My family's from Salisbury, North Carolina, but I'm finishing school in Greensboro."

"My family's from the South as well," he said.

"Where?"

"Mississippi," he said. "But we left there a long time ago."

The train had slowed, but she hadn't been aware of it until she saw the lights outside her window.

"Is this Charlottesville?" she asked.

"Yes," he said. He stepped out from the behind the bar. "I have to go," he said. "There are a few passengers boarding."

"Okay," she said.

He looked at the table before her. The cookie was gone, and she'd drunk half the milk.

"Do you need anything else?"

"No," she said. "I don't think so."

"Okay," he said. He nodded. "Good night."

He turned to go, but she called after him.

"I may still be here," she said.

He stopped and faced her.

"Just so you're not surprised," she said. "I may still be sitting here when you come back."

He smiled.

"Okay, Donna," he said.

"Okay, Hampton," Claire said.

She watched his back until he disappeared down the hall toward the other car. She sat for a few moments, sensed that something about the train had changed. She was somehow aware of the new people who'd just boarded, people who were awake and moving while the others slept, although she couldn't see or hear any of them.

After a few minutes, she heard the familiar sound of the cars bunching together, and the dining car stuttered forward, and then it allowed itself to be pulled along smoothly. Claire wondered if Donna had slept through the stop, or if the sudden jolt had woken her. She wondered if Donna would whisper her name, hear nothing, and believe that Claire had slept through the stop at Charlottesville.

She tried not to look toward the door through which Hampton

had exited, although she caught herself staring into the window and trying to use it as a mirror so that she wouldn't have to look directly across the dining room. She waited, and after what seemed like a long time she made up her mind to return to the sleeping car, to sneak back into her berth, climb back into bed in her dress, and sleep for the few hours before they arrived in Greensboro.

She moved away from the window, but before she could stand she sensed that someone had come into the dining room. So she relaxed and tried to hide the fact that she'd ever considered leaving. She picked up the glass of milk and drank down what was left of it.

When she lowered the glass it revealed a white man standing in the doorway of the dining car. For a moment, Claire mistakenly believed that she still wore her sleeping gown, and she dropped the glass onto the table, where it rattled against the plate, and she pulled the collar of her dress tight around her neck. Instead of the sound startling him the same way it had startled Claire, the man simply looked toward her, and then he turned and looked behind him in the direction he'd just come.

He wore shirtsleeves and suspenders. His thick, dark hair was brushed back from his forehead. He was perhaps forty, certainly no older than fifty.

The train moved through a turn at a good clip, but the man stood as if he were outside the train and hadn't even noticed it as it passed. He nodded at Claire.

"Good evening," the stranger said.

"Hello," she said.

The man walked toward Claire and stopped beside her table.

"A fellow night owl," he said. He smiled. "Do you mind if I join you?"

Before Claire had the chance to think about his question, much less answer it, the stranger sat down across the table from her.

"You don't mind?" he asked after he'd already settled himself.

"Of course not," Claire said, and then, "I was just about to return to my room."

"Well, I won't keep you," he said. "You go back to your room whenever you'd like." He looked toward the window. "Nothing like a train at night," he said. "You agree?"

"Yes," Claire said. "Did you just board?"

"No," the man said. "I boarded in D.C. I've been in my berth, working."

He sat back, folded his hands in his lap, and stared at Claire with a cool, distant smile. His eyes fell on the empty glass of milk.

"Trouble sleeping?" he asked.

"No," she said. "I mean, earlier, yes. But I'm feeling tired now."

"Are you traveling with family?"

"What?" she asked. The stranger's questions, which she realized were normal, predictable questions, seemed to be delivered in such a way that she didn't quite understand them.

"Are you traveling with family?" he asked again.

"No," she said. "I was in Washington. With my classmates. I'm in college."

"Wonderful," he said. "Wonderful." He felt around in his pants pockets, removed a billfold, and set it on the table. On top of the billfold was a silver badge with an eagle cresting the top of it. A banner unfurled itself across the badge's middle, but it was turned and caught the light in a way that kept Claire from being able to read it. The man searched his pockets until he found a pack of cigarettes.

"Cigarette?" he asked.

Claire looked at the pack where it rested on the table. She felt emboldened by her anonymity. It was the middle of the night. Mrs. Barnes was old; she had probably been asleep for hours. Even if she were to wake she probably wouldn't shuffle down the hall and come to the dining car this late at night. Were they to find her smoking, none of the girls would mention a word about it to anyone. She wondered what Paul would think to see her here, alone, speaking to a colored man close to her own age and having a cigarette with an older man, a stranger in the middle of the night. She was going home.

Her life would change soon, and she did not know what lay ahead, but this moment in the middle of the night was exciting and uncertain and tinged with danger, and she could not help herself.

"Yes," she said. "Please."

The man picked up the pack and gave Claire a cigarette. Then he shook another free of the pack and put it between his lips.

"Now, if only we had some matches," he said.

Hampton walked back into the dining room. He slowed when he saw someone sitting with Claire. Something changed in his face. Something must have changed in Claire's face as well, because the stranger turned to see what had caught her eye.

"Oh, good," the stranger said. He lifted his cigarette toward Hampton, raised his voice. "Matches?"

Hampton stood still for another moment, and then he walked toward their table. He took a book of matches from his pocket, struck one, and held it over the table. The stranger didn't move, and it wasn't until he looked at Claire and raised his eyebrows that she remembered that she held a cigarette between her fingers and realized that the match had been struck for her. She put the cigarette to her lips and leaned toward the flame, drew on it. Claire chose not to look up at him, and from the corner of her eye she saw the flame's reflection in the train's window. She imagined someone standing outside the train and seeing this burst of light upon her face as the dining car rocketed past in the middle of the night.

The match had burned down more than halfway, but Hampton simply moved it across the table toward the stranger. The man leaned toward it and lit his cigarette as well. Hampton shook the match to extinguish it. He placed the book of matches on the table. He balled Claire's napkin into his fist and picked up the empty glass and plate.

"Anything else?" he asked without looking at her.

"No," Claire said, but what she wanted to say was "I'm sorry."

He nodded and walked through the dining room and disappeared the way he'd come. She watched him go, her hand resting on the table before her, the lit but unsmoked cigarette burning between her fingers.

The stranger tapped an ash into an empty coffee cup that had been left out for the breakfast service. He leaned across the table toward Claire.

"Was that boy bothering you before I came in?"

"No," she said. "He was in here when I sat down. He left when we stopped back there, at Charlottesville."

"You sure?"

"Yes," she said. Her face had grown warm, as if she'd been caught doing something that she should not have been doing. She feared that she was blushing. "I'm fine. Really."

The stranger looked at her for another moment. She held his gaze in hers. She thought that to look away would mean that she'd been caught in some kind of lie, and she hadn't lied; she simply hadn't known what to say.

"So," he said, flicking his ash into the coffee cup again. "What were you and your classmates doing in D.C.?"

"Sightseeing, mostly," Claire said. She looked down at her cigarette, then brought it to her lips.

"What did you see?"

She inhaled, looked at the stranger, watched his face as the smoke spread between the two of them.

"Just the usual things," she said. "The things everyone sees: the White House, the Capitol, the monuments."

The man raised his eyebrows and gave a half smile as if he'd been expecting to hear what Claire had just said, had been expecting to hear that she'd only seen and done the things that tourists always saw and did. Claire looked down at the coffee cup between them. She turned it toward her and peered at the ash inside.

"Senator Overman gave us a long tour today—well, yesterday," Claire said. She set the coffee cup upright, raised her eyes to the stranger's.

The stranger cocked his head and smiled.

"How interesting," he said. "I just met with Senator Overman. You must be with the group of young ladies from North Carolina."

"Yes, sir," she said.

"What's your name?"

Claire remembered what she'd just said to Hampton, and now she spoke without hesitation. "Donna," she said.

"Donna what?"

"It's not important."

"It's not important?" the stranger repeated. "Come on. You're a southern gal, aren't you? Riding in a fancy dining car in the middle of the night, getting tours from senators? Names are always important to girls like you."

"Abernathy."

"Donna Abernathy," he said. "Where are you from, Donna 'It's Not Important' Abernathy?"

She couldn't stop herself.

"Salisbury," she said.

He cocked his head, looked at her.

"I know your daddy," he said. "Carter Abernathy."

Claire choked on the smoke in her lungs. She coughed, reached for the glass of milk, but remembered it was gone. She dropped the lit cigarette down inside the coffee cup instead, heard the gasp of its extinguishment. She tried her best to remember Donna's father's name, certain that she must have mentioned it, weighed the possibility of there being two Carter Abernathys in a town the size of Salisbury. She nodded her head, coughed again.

"Sure enough," the stranger said, smiling. "I know your daddy. Good man." He smoked, looked out the window. "Lot of Klan down there in Salisbury." He laughed to himself. "If you want something handled down in Mississippi or Louisiana, all you have to do is tell the police. In North Carolina, it takes the Klan to get a thing done right." He stubbed out his cigarette, offered Claire another, but she shook her head no. "I saw your father last year during the march on Washington. He had a lot of North Carolina knights with him. It was something to see: twenty thousand men from around the country marching in white on the streets of our nation's capital. Very impressive."

He looked across the table at Claire as if waiting for her to respond in some way, to say something about Donna's father or Salisbury or the Klan or her family's long friendship with Senator Lee Overman, but Claire couldn't think of anything to say.

"Are you a police officer?" she finally asked.

The stranger looked surprised. He smiled, lit another cigarette, tipped an ash into the coffee cup.

"Your badge," she said. "That's the only reason I ask."

He smiled. "I'm a detective of sorts, which is like a policeman."

Claire wondered if he would say more, but he didn't. The dining car was quiet. The stranger reached out and brushed a crumb off the tablecloth that Claire's cookie had left behind. She wanted to get up and go back to bed, but she didn't know how to extract herself from the situation she'd created.

"Do you live in Washington?" she asked.

"No," he said. "I live wherever my work takes me."

"Where is it taking you now?"

"To Gastonia, North Carolina," he said. "I understand you met some strikers from Gastonia."

"We did," Claire said.

"Did they have the singer with them?" he asked.

"I'm not sure what you're talking about."

"A woman named Ella May Wiggins," he said. "She's some kind of hillbilly singer the union hired."

Claire remembered the woman Ella, her dingy dress and over-sized coat, her gaunt face and husky voice. The way she'd glared at Claire and the other girls as they passed.

The train slowed and Claire realized that she'd heard the brakes squeal a few minutes before. They were drawing closer to another stop. "I should go back to bed," she said. "Try to get some sleep."

"Yes," the stranger said. He picked up the pack of cigarettes and returned them to his pocket. Then he picked up the matchbook Hampton had left behind on the table. He pulled a watch from his pocket and looked at it. "It's after two A.M. now." He left his cigarette burning in his mouth and leaned forward and pulled the schedule from his back pocket. He removed the cigarette and held it in his hand and unfolded the schedule. He studied it for a moment and smiled.

"What is it?" Claire asked.

"That's funny," he said. "The next stop is Lynchburg. And here we are talking about your daddy and Lee Overman." He looked up at Claire. "Lynchburg. Isn't that something?"

CHAPTER SEVEN

Richard McAdam

Saturday, May 25, 1929

Richard McAdam weaved through the crowd, shaking hands and accepting congratulations while dodging Negro waiters with trays of hors d'oeuvres and drinks held above their heads. The band had just struck up the first song of the evening, "It's a Million to One, You're in Love," and young people, most of whom had been Claire's friends since childhood, along with several more recent friends from the teachers college, streamed past Richard toward the dance floor as he tried to escape with as little notice as possible. Most of the guests had arrived already; there remained only one guest in particular that Richard was waiting to see, and that man was yet to appear.

The double doors that led to the lobby creaked when he pushed them open. He stepped into the otherwise empty foyer as Grace and Nadia Ingle, the daughters of the club's manager, sprang from their seats as if they'd been caught breaking the law by relaxing for even a moment. The two girls had spent the damp evening collecting guests' rain-soaked hats, coats, and umbrellas, and Richard did not mind finding the girls in repose. He and Katherine had known them since they were children, since their father had taken the job at the club a decade earlier. Now the girls were fourteen and nineteen. Katherine had informed him that Grace's father did not have the money to send her back to school for her sophomore year at Peace College in Raleigh, and Richard, upon seeing the girl, reminded himself to approach Ingle about offering the family a helping hand.

He smoothed the lapels on his black suit and ran his hand over the red silk tie that Katherine had presented him with that evening while he'd stood trimming his mustache before the bathroom mirror. She'd said something about Claire and Paul, about their engagement. She may have even said something about Richard and herself, perhaps something about their own engagement, but as usual Richard had not been able to slow his mind enough to listen to her, to take in her words and register their meaning. His ears had sped through Katherine's speech, and now all he could picture were her beautiful but sad brown eyes that sought his in the bathroom mirror.

He pushed the memory from his mind and smiled at the two girls in the lobby. Nadia giggled with relief. Grace rose from her seat.

"Hello," he said.

"Hello," the two sisters replied.

"Thank you for keeping our guests as dry as possible." In the ballroom on the other side of the doors, the band struck up another song. Richard tried to catch the tune over the sound of the voices inside, but he didn't recognize it. He smiled at the girls. "Of course it rains like this in Wilmington too," he said, "but you'd never know it by how my future in-laws are acting."

He slipped his hands into his pockets and walked across the lobby toward the entryway. As if by instinct, Grace and Nadia both stepped toward the door so they could open it should Mr. McAdam want to step outside, but Richard was not yet ready to step outside. Instead, he stood by the chair where Grace had just been sitting and pulled back the curtain and looked out the window at the evening.

It was near dark, the rain still falling in great smacks against the already sodden earth.

"I'm expecting a few more guests," Richard said. He let the curtain close and turned back to Grace and Nadia. "Do you know Mr. Guyon?"

"Yes," Grace said.

Richard wasn't surprised. Everyone in town—even those not in textiles—knew Hugo Guyon by now, the superintendent at Loray Mill, a northerner but still one of the most powerful men in the city, a man now mired in the politics of the strike that had unfolded over the past few months with violent speed.

"And you've heard about the strike?" he asked.

"Yes, sir," Grace said.

Nadia nodded her head *yes*. "I've heard about it too."

"Well, apparently my future in-laws heard about it as well, but it seems that hearing about it wasn't good enough. When they left the Armington this evening they asked the driver to take them by the mill so they could see the strike for themselves. The people picketing in front of the mill weren't too happy at the sight of a big black limousine cruising by for an eyeful." He pictured the scene as he'd been imagining it since first hearing of it only an hour or so earlier: the screaming, dirty faces of women and children pressed against the car's windows, fists beating against the glass, knees and feet kicking against the doors. He stifled a smile. Something about the fear he'd seen on the Lytles' faces had pleased him. "The strikers left a nice dent in the front left fender and busted out one of the headlights. Nearly scared the Lytles to death. Mrs. Lytle was still crying when they arrived." He shook his head and fought the smile again.

"Can you imagine that?" he asked. "Wanting to see something like a strike, as if it's a spectacle or a parade or a baseball game? Wanting to see the tent colony? Can you imagine it in this weather? This rain? All those haggard people, sopping wet, those smoky oil lamps. Mr. Lytle said it looked like the Allied front." He shook his head. "That man has no idea what war looks like."

It suddenly came to his mind that Claire must have told the Lytles about the group of strikers she'd encountered in Washington during the tour with Lee Overman. She'd cried when she'd told Richard about how poor and hungry they looked, about how she feared that something bad was going to happen to them after some singer had confronted the senator. Claire had to have told Paul as well, and Paul had to have told his father, and George Lytle just had to see the tragedy of humanity for himself.

Outside, the rain had ended and the silence of its not falling now filled the lobby. The music stopped and the ballroom broke into applause.

Headlights flashed across the windowpanes, followed by the sound of an automobile coming to a stop in one of the parking areas. Richard turned and looked at both Nadia and Grace. "Thank you so much for your help this evening," he said. "Tell your father I said as much when you see him. I'm sure he's tucked away in the kitchen overseeing dinner. He always does such a wonderful job for us. Tonight's no exception."

He opened the front door and stepped into the night. Water dripped from the canopy of pine boughs that shadowed the already dark lawn in front of the club. He stood beneath the portico without moving. White columns ran along the porch on either side of him. He peered into the darkness in search of the car whose headlights he'd just seen and whose tires on the wet road he'd just heard. In the distance, raindrops glimmered on the hoods of the automobiles parked beneath the pines. A door slammed shut, then another, and Richard heard footsteps approaching. He held his breath and steeled his nerves. The silhouettes grew closer and Richard recognized the Wrights, an older couple from his and Katherine's church, a man and woman with whom his parents had been close friends before they'd passed. Mr. Wright saw Richard standing on the porch and raised his hand in greeting. His other hand grasped his wife's elbow as if steering her down the wet path toward the stairs.

"Hello, Richard," Mr. Wright said, his thin face and gray mustache lit by the light coming from behind Richard. Mrs. Wright looked out at Richard from beneath a plum-colored pillbox hat, a spray of yellow flowers set into its brim. "I'm sorry we're late," Mr. Wright said. "Wanted to wait out the rain. Didn't know we'd be waiting this long."

"Oh, it's perfectly all right," Richard said, smiling, exhaling. Although no one would ever know, it embarrassed him to be so relieved at seeing the couple instead of Guyon. "Dinner hasn't started yet. It's just been music and dancing so far."

"Then we haven't missed a thing," Mr. Wright said. He laughed. "I'm not one for dancing, but I've never been one to miss a meal."

Richard offered Mrs. Wright his hand and helped her up the steps, and then he moved aside and opened the door. Mrs. Wright smiled and congratulated him, and Mr. Wright shook his hand. Richard closed the door behind the couple, then he turned and faced the night again.

He worried that he'd be unable to hide this jumpy nervousness when he confronted Guyon and asked him to cover the cost of the Lytles' damaged car. Although Guyon wasn't a mill operator *and* owner like Richard was, he had spent the past decade as superintendent at Loray, one of the largest mills in the country and easily the largest in the state.

He didn't know Guyon well. The first time he'd met him was in the fall of 1919, when several local mill owners organized a hunting trip to introduce Guyon to the community. Three carloads of men had traveled south from Gastonia through Columbia and on to Savannah before taking a ferry out to Hilton Head Island. The whole operation had been started just a few years earlier by an old man named Silling, who owned a handful of mills over in Kings Mountain. He'd rallied a group of investors from Tennessee and the Carolinas to fund the Hilton Head Agricultural Company, which sounded grand at the time, but after Richard and his group arrived on a Saturday afternoon in mid-November, all he'd found was a clapboard clubhouse; a Sears, Roebuck kit cabin where the men would bunk for the night; two old colored guides; and a cook in the form of an old colored woman who spoke Gullah and looked upon the newly arrived men as if they were idiots.

For a reason none of them could remember, perhaps both to keep up appearances and to keep their wives from worrying, it had always been tradition to invite one of the men's ministers to accompany the group on a hunting trip. They were all conservative Protestants, but when it came to the invited clergy the men tended to lean Episcopalian, since Episcopal clergymen seemed the most willing to have a drink and the least likely to look down on those who had more than one. On the year they included Guyon, someone in the group suggested they invite one of the priests from the monastery at Belmont Abbey. The men had heard that Guyon was Catholic, and it seemed an act of goodwill. They were all surprised, which is to say uncomfortable, when an older, white-headed man in a cassock joined the caravan. Father Gregory rode in the backseat of a car with Guyon. The two men barely spoke during the trip. They were strangers to one another just as they were strangers to everyone else.

Richard remembered it as a bizarre week of drinking whiskey and firing rifles. He was just back from the war and found that he had little use for either. He spent most of his time sitting on the porch of the clubhouse, staring out at the six-foot alligator a couple of the men had caught in the swamp on the first day and tethered to a palm tree in the center of camp. At night, after dinner, he'd watch the same group of daredevils drink whiskey and stumble out to the flagpole, where they'd place chicken livers in their palms and tempt the gator to eat from their hands. They'd eventually lose interest and toss the livers onto the sand. In the morning the livers would still be there, dry and shriveled, inches from the alligator's snout.

Guyon had been quiet and friendly during the trip, somewhat deferential to the men who'd all known each other for years. But after a few days, it appeared to Richard that Guyon had integrated himself better than Richard ever had, despite the fact that Richard had grown up with most of these men. Their fathers' and grand-fathers' relationships had been marked by rivalries and partnerships in the same ways rivalry and partnership marked their own relationships now.

On the first night of the trip, after they'd settled into their bunks, the men presented Guyon with a "welcome" gift: a Springfield .30-06. It was a better gun than half the rifles the men had brought with them, far better than Richard's .22, which he hadn't cleaned or fired since before the war. They'd even pooled their funds to get Father Gregory a rifle, a Winchester 270. The old man opened the box and stared at it as if it were some kind of relic whose usefulness would have to be divined after careful consultation with specialists. The entire week, no one ever saw Father Gregory load the rifle, much less fire it, but he carried it with him whenever he left his private room for a meal or drinks in the evening.

Guyon quickly joined in on the lies and teasing that took place during what came to be known as alibi hour, when the men sat around the bunkhouse before bed and ribbed one another about bad marksmanship and the inability to hold one's liquor. Three cut shirt-tails had been left pinned to the wall beside the door, each representing a man's bad aim or a missed opportunity to bring down a deer during the trip.

At night, the conversations inevitably turned to life in the mills back home. Several of the men refused to hide their pride that Gastonia had come to be known as the "City of Spindles" and would soon be the nation's combed-yarn capital. A man named Cloninger, whose grandfather had built Highland Shoals Mill on the Catawba River just in time to die in the Civil War, took particular pride in the idea that the South would soon outpace the North in textiles.

"That's what we're doing," Cloninger said. He looked at Guyon and smiled. "Luring folks like you across the Mason-Dixon just like the good man down in Atlanta suggested we do." He turned from Guyon and roundly toasted the group with a metal shot glass filled with whiskey. "Out-Yankeeing the Yankee, by God. It's just like the war never happened."

The men had all laughed at the joke, even Guyon, and they'd passed around a jug and refilled their cups. Guyon cleared his throat.

"It's true," Guyon said. "We were lured across the Mason-Dixon. It's like Bull Run all over again." The men laughed. "But I can tell you it's going to be pretty damn hard for you sons of bitches to out-Yankee the Yankee when you're trying to do it with the Yankee's dollar." He shot a look at Cloninger and then raised his glass. The room was silent for a moment, and then a fat man named Duke Jeffords, who'd been drunk for three days and who'd never liked Cloninger anyway, burst into laughter. The room erupted right along with him.

By Tuesday evening, the men had all turned their taunts toward Richard, who was the only man aside from Father Gregory who had yet to squeeze off a shot. He didn't have the heart or the will or the patience to explain that he'd done enough shooting and killing in Europe to spend the rest of his life not wanting to do either, and so the next day he separated himself from his party and blasted two rounds into the woods about a mile from camp. That night, Cloninger used a Case knife to cut Richard's shirttail before pinning it to the wall, where it remained until they caught the ferry back to Savannah on Saturday morning.

Standing on the bottom deck of the *Clivedon* where it had docked at the Jenkins Island Landing, Richard fished the cut shirt from his bag and looked inside its collar, where Katherine had asked her seamstress to sew a silken tag with his name embroidered on it in fancy cursive letters. He knew she would discover that the shirt had been damaged, and he knew she would ask why. It would be easier just to tell her that he'd left it behind by accident. He tossed it into the black water and watched it sink. He'd left the shirt buttoned, and as it filled with water it took on the shape of a man, its body expanding as if a rib cage bloomed beneath the fabric, its arms reaching up toward the surface like it was afraid of disappearing.

The club's front door opened behind him, and Richard turned and saw Katherine crane her long, elegant neck onto the porch. Her eyes found his. She smiled, but Richard knew it to be a smile that showed just how weary she'd grown of him.

"There you are," she said.

"Yes," Richard said. He dropped his cigarette and stubbed it out with the toe of his shoe. "Here I am."

"They're looking for you," Katherine said.

"Who?"

"They," she said. "The party. Claire and Paul. Our friends. Me. Everyone." She stepped onto the porch and let the door close quietly behind her. She wore a beautiful gown of pale blue sequins that made him perfectly aware that on nights like this, Katherine appeared much younger than him and could easily pass for Claire's older sister.

She looked toward the darkness over his shoulder and folded her arms across her chest as if she were cold, then she smiled again. She reached for him, and he let her take his hand.

"I was just telling Ingle's girls about the Lytles' run-in with the strikers down at Loray," he said. He shivered ironically as if the story induced real fear.

"Richard!" Katherine said. She let go of his hand and pretended to swat at it as if scolding him. "The Lytles were simply curious, that's all. They're fine people."

"Perhaps so, but no matter how fine they are, they're still going back to Wilmington with a very skewed idea of life here in Gaston County."

"Well," Katherine said. She crossed her arms again. "I say, 'Let them go, Richard.'"

"It just dawned on me that Claire must have mentioned the strikers in Washington. Paul's father's going to think this thing has made it all the way to the halls of Congress, which, apparently, it has."

"Let them think what they will, Richard. I don't understand why it bothers you."

"It bothers me because our people do not behave that way, Kate, and the Lytles are going to paint mill people with a very broad brush, and it's not fair. Keep in mind that we're mill people too, but we'd never have a problem like this. We have good people. Satisfied people. Let the Bolshevists and communists and socialists come to McAdamville. They'll all go back to New York disappointed."

"Come back to the party, Richard," she said. She moved toward him, stopped, came closer, and planted a soft kiss on his cheek. "Don't worry about the Lytles, Richard, not tonight. Please."

"I'll be in in a moment, Kate. I promise. I'll wait for Guyon for just a few more minutes, but I'll be in."

Katherine sighed. She turned and looked at the closed front door, perhaps thought of the party that was going on inside. She looked at Richard again.

"Did you talk with Ingle about Grace's schooling?" she asked.

"No," he said. "I will. I promise."

"She's a fine girl, don't you think?"

"Yes," he said. "She always has been."

"They've just hit a rough patch."

"I know," he said. "We'll help however we can." But he wanted to say, *Yes, we'll help her, just like we help everyone else. Just like I'm about to help Lytle. Just like I've helped everyone who's ever come to me.*

"Okay," she said. "She's such a wonderful girl." She looked toward the shadows on the far end of the porch. "Do you know what you're going to say?"

"To whom? Guyon?"

"No," she said. She furrowed her brow, looked down at her hands, spun her wedding ring on her finger. "Tonight, to the guests. You're the father of the bride-to-be, Richard. We talked about your saying something."

"Of course," he said. "I'm ready."

"Okay," she said. She looked up at him, smiled. "Please come inside soon. We all miss you. I miss you."

"I will," he said. "I'll be in in a moment. I promise."

She turned, her gown sweeping across the porch in a small arc. She opened the door and he watched through the windows as she walked through the lobby and disappeared into the ballroom.

Aside from the conversation with Guyon, Richard was also plagued by the speech he was expected to give. Katherine had been urging him to prepare a few comments about Claire and Paul's first meeting, their engagement, their new lives together. Richard had spent hours writing down and scratching out phrase after phrase, trite saying after trite saying. He'd arrived at the club that evening with nothing written down, only a head full of vague notions of things he wanted to say, emotions he wanted to convey, ideas he somehow wanted to condense into words.

But then this debacle with the Lytles on their trip over from the hotel. Now he was rattled and standing outside and smoking what he hoped would be his last cigarette before dinner, his mind turning over the things he could say in front of this audience that would make some kind of lasting impression on the Lytles. He wanted to give them something to think about while they traveled back to the coast, where oak trees and dew-damp magnolias awaited them at the great plantation they'd managed to cling to in the years following the War Between the States. He wanted them to part with a clear idea of who his family was, what his town was, what his role in all of it was.

He squinted his eyes as if doing so could allow him to look into his own brain for any words that might be floating past the screen of his mind.

"When one thinks of today's youth," he whispered to himself. "When one thinks of today's youth, it is easy to consider what one sees before him on the streets of a city or hears on the radio or learns of through rumor and assumption. But we must not, we cannot, confuse those youth with our own, these great young men and women who have gathered here tonight to celebrate the greatest young man and the greatest young woman I have ever known. These are the youth that a great state like ours and a great city like ours give rise to." But he stopped when he considered that Paul was not from Gastonia or Gaston County, and Richard certainly wasn't willing to invoke the grandeur of Wilmington or New Hanover County on a night like this after what the Lytles had seen.

He closed his eyes more tightly and blotted out the screen in his mind, the white light that had been thrown upon it slowly burning into a hot rage against Lytle. He opened his mouth and began again.

"When I think of today's youth, I do not think of what I see and hear. I'd be a fool to be so blind. No, I think of who and what I know, and I know the wonderful young men and women in this room tonight, so many of you from here in Gaston County, so many of you dear friends of Claire's since her birth. And it's such a pleasure for Claire's future in-laws to have the chance to witness the best of what a city like ours has to offer."

He was getting closer to what he wanted to say to the assembled crowd, what he wanted to say directly to George Lytle, a man whom Richard had seen only once before this evening. He'd met Paul a handful of times while he and Claire were courting. He'd found the young man shy, awkward, soft-spoken, and kind, somewhat provincial, but that was to be expected of any landed family from coastal North Carolina, where so much of the state's power and former glory had once been seated.

Richard's first meeting with Mr. Lytle had not come until March, when the Lytles had hosted their own engagement party for Paul and Claire at their home just east of Wilmington, on a wild expanse of land that rested between the city and a thin slip of barrier islands. It had not been a working plantation for more than sixty years, but it was immediately apparent to Richard that the Lytles' lives were defined by an all-consuming desire to resurrect and reanimate the past.

The Lytles' party had been a grand affair comparable only to the many other grand affairs that Richard quickly learned were the hallmark of the family's wealth and prominence. Although the Lytles had made their fortune in rice on the coast and tobacco farther inland, the current generation now staked the family name on their social standing and willingness to express it. What seemed like hundreds of guests attended the party and floated in droves from one high-ceilinged room to another. In the crush of men in tuxedos and Confederate gray and women in sequined gowns and antebellum dresses, Richard quickly lost track of names and associations. Claire had already slipped away from them and disappeared into the crowd with Paul and the other young people, and Richard clung to Katherine's hand while she navigated the crowd just as effortlessly as she seemed to navigate everything else in her life.

He'd always viewed Katherine this way. His earliest memories of her were rose colored with her easy nature, and he often caught himself remembering her as the fifteen-year-old girl who'd helped him and her distraught father load boxes of her dead brother's books and clothes and belongings onto the train platform in Raleigh all those years ago. Richard and Katherine's brother David had been college roommates at Chapel Hill, and Richard could still feel his throat where it had cinched tight with worry and uncertainty about what to say to David's father, a man who at that time had been no older than Richard was now. Although they'd hardly spoken to one another, Katherine's soft eyes had peered at him over boxes and stacks of her brother's books as if to assure him that his sadness at her brother's death was something that would pass, something that even so young a girl knew would not last forever.

Richard, on the other hand, had always felt constricted, confined, unsure of which way to step or how to hold his smile or where to look or what to read into the faces of the people before him. He'd been drawn to Katherine because she'd always been the one to lead him through their shared emotional territory. They'd never spoken of it, but both he and Katherine knew that he'd returned from the war even more cautious, guarded, and uncomfortable than he'd been before he left. Claire had only been seven years old at the start of the war, but she was almost eleven by the time he returned, and it had seemed that the two of them found themselves strangers to one another, as if their lives had continued in those four intervening years on separate trajectories that would never realign.

His difference upon returning wasn't simply marked by an emotional distance. A physical bulwark had been set in place as well. In bed at night, it wasn't uncommon for him to leap toward Katherine in his sleep if her toe were to graze his leg. His hands had even once found her neck before he opened his eyes and saw her terrified face in the soft predawn light coming through the curtains. Loud noises—bursts of laughter, a piece of silverware falling to the floor, music—often provoked the same terrified feeling as an invisible body touching his own in the darkness of his bedroom. The only thing he could control was his work at the mill, and his life disappeared into it. He often lost all awareness of time. Days, weeks, and months seemed to pass, their goings only marked by what kind of hat and coat he wore during his walk down the hill to the mill office. He found that the stiller he remained, the quieter the world around him became, and it wasn't long before he recognized stasis as his favorite posture, no matter whether he were standing in the carding room at the mill or sitting at his desk or lying in bed beside Katherine, willing his eyes to remain closed and his hands to stay by his sides if and when something of her body touched his in the night.

He never knew for certain what terrified him so. In the beginning he explained his outbursts in terminology she might understand: "Bombs," he'd say when she'd ask him what he was dreaming of when he screamed himself awake. But as the war receded into the distance and time lurched forward he found it more difficult to think of the war, much less talk of it, even in the smallest and shortest of terms, so he found other ways to explain his terrors. "I was dreaming that someone was in the house," he'd say. "Someone was trying to hurt you and the baby." And other times he would shrug his shoulders beneath the cloak of darkness and roll to his side and pretend to fall back asleep.

At the Lytles' party, Richard had felt hemmed in by the number of people, especially the colored help: young, dark-skinned waiters who carried trays of champagne and wore neckcloths and long blue coats festooned with brass buttons; middle-aged mammies in frocks and headscarves who served food from great silver bowls; an old, shoeless bald man Mr. Lytle had introduced as "Uncle Peter," who wore only a muslin shirt and tattered breeches stood in the parlor, a squeaky violin hoisted to his shoulder.

George Lytle had spent most of the evening with a drink in one hand, his other resting on the mantel, above which an oil portrait of his aged grandfather loomed. To anyone who would listen, Lytle told story after story of his grandfather's bravery on the battlefield, his family's stake in the history of the South, the duality of war that awards both honor and ruin to the survivors. Lytle spoke as one who'd been to war himself, but Richard had known better. The only war Lytle had ever known was the one he'd heard about and read about and talked about during dozens of parties just like this one.

Although Richard had been prepared not to like Lytle even before meeting him, he'd absolutely hated him after that evening at their plantation. Since then his heart had recoiled at the idea of handing over Claire and his future grandchildren to the family. He and Katherine had no illusions that the couple would do anything other than settle in Wilmington after the wedding in October. But "to lose a daughter is to gain a son," they always say, and, after all, wasn't a son what he had always wanted? Of course, he'd been proud to have a healthy child after what had happened earlier in their marriage, especially a child as wonderfully bright and kind as Claire had been from the moment she was born; however, memories of his own father and grandfather pulled at him, arriving with the realization that he lacked a son to carry on the family name and the family business, a business he was certain Paul would have little to no interest in inheriting and certainly no interest in managing. Even Richard's grandfather, Yancey McAdam, hadn't had that much interest in managing the very mill he'd founded. It was almost something he'd come by in the course of laying railroads across the state, beginning in Charlotte, where he'd opened a bank with local investors in 1867. He arrived in Gaston County a few years later and followed the branches of the Catawba River west, where he discovered that the river was making men rich by powering their whiskey stills and cotton mills. Yancey decided that the cotton mill had the best chance of running itself and creating passive income once he'd moved on, which he did in 1881 after the McAdam Mill was up and operating. Yancey continued to lay railroad tracks through the piedmont toward Asheville and beyond, where he literally tore down ridges and blew holes in stone to cut passages through the Blue Ridge Mountains, for Tennessee and the open country of the West waited on the other side. Richard had always pictured his grandfather as a man who only had to touch the earth for it to spring to life under the warmth of his open palm. In Richard's imagining, railroad lines poured from the old man's fingertips and snaked across the landscape. Eleven children sprang from his flesh with ease. One cotton mill and then another rose like mushrooms from the damp woods along the South Fork of the Catawba River. McAdamville grew into a fiefdom where Yancey McAdam was the too-often-absent king.

At the end of the war, the old man followed his railroads farther west, but not before handing off the mill to his son, Richard's father, who at only eighteen years old embraced both his role as the mill's president and his role as its employee. The mill only had a few dozen workers, but Richard's father designed, paid for, and assisted in the construction of small brick homes for his workers. What Richard's father lacked in his own father's frontier spirit he made up for in a nature that embraced both technology and social progress. Over time he equipped each home in the mill village with toilets and bathtubs. In 1884 he stood alongside Thomas Edison as the famous inventor installed Dynamo #31 and ushered in a new wave of production. McAdamville's two mills were the first in the state to run all night beneath bright, hot bulbs of electric light. That very dynamo was still churning out power.

This was the place and the legacy Richard had inherited when he'd assumed the presidency of the mill after graduating from Chapel Hill, and it was this past and present of fine industrialization that Richard wanted the Lytles to understand marked him and his family as being one of the most progressive and upstanding families in the state, if not one of its most wealthy and famous. While the Lytles' ancestors had sipped juleps on the veranda and overseen the work of enslaved black bodies in brackish water, Richard's father and grandfather had moved mountains, electrified production, cared for the poor, and changed the state forever.

And now Richard had inherited the mantle they'd left behind. And he'd gone to college at the state university. And he'd gotten married. And he'd had a child and served in the Great War. And he'd executed his life in a manner befitting both his talents and his station. So let the Lytles think what they would think after seeing what they'd seen at Loray that afternoon.

If George Lytle asked, Richard would tell him that there could not be two places more different than McAdamville, with its brick houses, indoor plumbing, and well-kept yards, and the Loray Mill, with its village of rotting shacks, muddy roads, and transient workers. In some ways, Richard thought, Loray deserved exactly what it was getting. He'd never admit it to anyone, including Katherine, but something about it allowed some semblance of pride to bloom inside him.

The rain had moved east toward Charlotte and the clouds had parted, revealing a quarter moon that stared down upon the pine trees and clubhouse like an eye only partly open. In its light, Richard was able to spy something moving toward him down the lane from Franklin Avenue. It was a black Packard 633, and as it drew closer he knew Hugo Guyon sat in its backseat, gazing out on the dark night, his head probably full of concerns about the strike.

Instead of parking, the Packard roared into the roundabout in front of the clubhouse, its huge engine vibrating under the rain-slicked hood. The driver left the motor running and stepped out and came around to the side of the car facing Richard, then opened the back door. Hugo Guyon swung both feet out and unfolded himself from the seat. In his early fifties, he was a large man, easily over six feet tall, with hair so short and fair as to make him appear bald. When Guyon saw Richard standing atop the porch, he nodded his head gravely as if he'd just returned from the front and there was nothing but bad news to report.

Although Richard had never met Guyon's wife and couldn't even remember if he was married or had ever been married, he was surprised when the door opened on the other side of the car and a man's face appeared. He was much shorter than Guyon, round-faced and jowly. He wore a simple black suit and a derby pushed back off his forehead. A short, damp cigar clung to his lower lip.

Guyon said something to the driver that Richard couldn't hear, and the driver got back inside the car and revved the engine before pulling the Packard out of the roundabout and disappearing around the corner, where the other automobiles were parked. The two men—Guyon and the stranger—stood in the road before the club and spoke quietly to one another, and then Guyon turned toward Richard and smiled.

"Mrs. Guyon isn't well this evening," he said, his fading Yankee accent still marking his words with precision and sharpness. "I hope it's okay that I used my and guest on this ugly son of a bitch." He clapped the other man on the shoulder. The stranger smiled and looked up at Richard, and even though it was dark and the men were more than twenty feet away, Richard could see that the man's eyes were crystal blue and vaguely unsettling.

The two men walked up the steps toward Richard, the portico momentarily tossing them into shadow until the lights from the club's windows behind Richard illuminated their faces. Guyon introduced the stranger as Percy Epps, Loray's attorney and head of security.

Guyon looked at Richard, and then he looked at the club over Richard's shoulder as if he were expecting someone else to open the door and walk outside.

"Are we that late?" he asked. "Party over?"

The question embarrassed Richard. It was a strange thing, wasn't it, to be standing out on the porch alone on the night of his daughter's engagement party, waiting for Hugo Guyon, a man he didn't know that well to ask him to quell a situation of which he wasn't part. All this so that another man he didn't know that well would think well of him and his family.

"No," Richard said, "there's still plenty of the evening left. I was just getting some air before dinner."

"You're not having second thoughts about giving your daughter away, are you?" Guyon asked. Epps smiled.

"No," Richard said. "No more tonight than I have for months." He cleared his throat and fought the urge to reach into his jacket for another cigarette. Instead he put his sweaty hands in his pockets. "I was also waiting for you," he said. "I wanted to speak with you about what's going on down at Loray. About the situation there."

Guyon sighed as if it were the last thing he wanted to think about. He raised his head and looked up at the porch's ceiling, where a single hanging lamp shone down upon them.

"Out with it," Guyon said. "I'm waiting."

"Can we have a word, just for a moment?" Richard asked. Guyon lowered his gaze, and Richard's eyes darted toward Epps and back to Guyon.

"There's nothing you'll say that I won't tell him later," Guyon said.

Richard nodded his head as if he understood; then he looked behind him, where he could see the empty foyer through the windows. They were alone out here on the porch, and there was no one inside who could see them, but the need for privacy still provoked him. He gestured for the men to follow him to the end of the porch, out of reach of the front door and the light from the lobby.

Richard stopped when they reached the far side of the porch, where three small windows looked into the hallway. He watched waiters, trays held aloft, scurry in and out of the kitchen. Unable to resist the urge any longer, he reached into his pocket for a cigarette, and when he lifted it to his lips he saw that Epps held a flame out before him. Richard leaned forward and lighted his cigarette. Epps then lifted the flame to a fresh cigar and puffed until its tip glowed orange in the semidark.

"What about the strike, Mr. McAdam?" Guyon asked.

Richard pulled on his cigarette and took a moment to ponder the best way to broach the subject about what the Lytles had seen.

"My future in-laws are from the coast," he said, hoping that by mentioning their geography it would be clear that their understanding of the world and its diverse economies was not the same as the understanding that men like he and Guyon and possibly Epps shared. "The family is from Wilmington. Has been for generations."

"I know them," Epps said. "Known the Lytles for years."

Richard was surprised, and he knew his face portrayed it.

"How do you know them?"

"Tobacco," Epps said. He puffed on the cigar and blew a plume of smoke out of the corner of his mouth. "Business. Land. The ways people know each other on the coast. The way they know each other everywhere else too." He put the cigar back into his mouth and narrowed his eyes as he took another puff.

"I see," Richard said. He stared at Epps for another moment, then turned to Guyon again.

"This afternoon, the Lytles left their rooms at the Armington to join us here at the club, and for some reason, perhaps being a curious sort and perhaps a little too cavalier, Mr. Lytle asked the driver to take them by Loray so he could see the strike firsthand." He stopped and took another drag on his cigarette. "Their car was attacked by some of your strikers, and needless to say, we're all very upset by this."

"The attack on the car or their desire to see the strike?" Guyon asked.

"Both, but for different reasons," Richard said. "I don't know why in the hell Mr. Lytle wanted to see it, but I couldn't care less about his reasons. I am concerned, however, about having to pay for the damage to the car—"

"We'll cover it," Epps said.

Richard stopped speaking and looked at Epps. Epps stared back at him without blinking. Guyon seemed either not to have heard him or was indifferent to his claim.

"Very well," Richard said. "I appreciate that, but it's not the real matter."

"What's the real matter?" Guyon asked.

"Well, it's going on two months now since the strike began," Richard said, "and—"

"We're not even at eight weeks," Epps said. "And the strike has already failed. We're operating at full power. Production is back to normal."

"That may be," Richard said, "but it *looks* like things haven't changed."

Epps sighed and shifted his weight from one foot to the other. Guyon turned toward him and put his hand on Epps's shoulder as if calming him. It was clear that the conversation had provoked Epps, and Richard realized that he might have crossed a line he hadn't been aware of. His mind cycled back through all the things he'd said since meeting Guyon and Epps after they'd stepped out of the Packard and stood before the club.

"What your in-laws saw was the bad element of outside agitation," Guyon said. "It's the work of the NTW. New York City communists, all of them. There's still a handful of them that we're rounding up so our workers' lives can get back to normal. Chief Aderholt has worked very closely with us to see that it's done as peacefully and quickly as possible."

"And I appreciate that," Richard said. "Believe me, I appreciate the difficulty you've faced with these communists. But when we have guests from out of town who travel to Gaston County, we want to make certain they leave us with a clear idea of who we are and what we stand for."

"Mr. McAdam," Guyon said, "I'm sorry that you've been embarrassed, I am. But I can't apologize on behalf of the NTW or the Communist Party, and, believe me, you won't hear an apology from them either."

"But surely something more can be done," Richard said. "Just last week my daughter was in Washington with her classmates from the women's college in Greensboro, and they were accosted by a gang of Gastonia strikers." He pointed to the club, where he knew Claire was somewhere inside. "She was devastated. She came home in tears. It ruined her trip, seeing some poor woman beg Senator Overman for help."

"We know about the D.C. trip," Guyon said. "And we know about this 'poor' woman. Her name's Wiggins. She's not one of ours, but we've kept an eye on her. Overman's office has been in contact. He's very interested in our situation here. He's sent a representative down to get to the bottom of things."

"He's very interested," Epps said. "Interested enough to send the best."

"Pinkertons?" Richard asked.

"Let's just say he's sent the best," Epps said.

The men were quiet for a moment, as if they stood on the edge of a great secret that they all knew but did not want to share.

"Again," Richard said, "I understand, but when we have guests from out of town, they're not privy to the same information you're giving me. Their impression is that Gastonia is a wild, lawless place."

"Everything is being done that can be done," Guyon said. "I

assure you." He leaned against the porch rail and put his hands in his pockets. Richard heard something jingle inside Guyon's pocket. Keys, perhaps a few coins. Guyon cleared his throat. He began to speak, but then he hesitated. He looked at Epps. Epps nodded.

"But there is an opportunity to do more," Guyon said. He furrowed his brow and looked at Richard through narrowed eyes.

Richard had the vague sense that he was about to hear something he might later regret hearing. A palpable darkness swept over him and he felt a desperate urge to return to the party and forget the Lytles and the mess they saw at Loray. But he feared he'd insulted Guyon earlier, and he didn't want to leave him with the impression that he was soft or a worrier or a man who was afraid of hard times.

"What is it?" Richard asked. "What else can be done?"

"We're not being public about it," Guyon said. "So I apologize for bringing you into something that may make you uncomfortable."

"Go ahead," Richard said. "I'm willing to help if I can."

Guyon took his hands from his pockets and ran his open palms along the wet porch rails. He shook the rain from his hands and put them back in his pockets. Behind him, the wet pine boughs glistened under the moon as if trying to catch Richard's eye.

"It's just a small committee," Guyon said. "A small committee dedicated to ridding this county of the Bolshevists and getting our lives and the lives of our people back in order."

"What's the name of the committee?" Richard asked.

"It's made up of some people you may know," Guyon replied. "Some you may not. But all of them are committed to this cause. We need to take our city back."

"Some of the most powerful men in the city have made donations," Epps said.

"Money or men or—" Guyon stopped speaking, moved his lips in silence as if searching for the best, perhaps safest, word. "Materials," he said. "They've volunteered legal expertise, exerted influence in the mayor's office, assisted with security, called on the governor."

"It's more of a civic group than anything else," Epps said. "Just concerned citizens."

"Just concerned citizens," Guyon echoed. "The best of Gaston County." He paused. "Would you be interested in joining us?"

"It would send a powerful message if the owner and operator of McAdam Mills were to contribute," Epps said. "Men in this town think an awful lot of you and your business."

"An awful lot," Guyon said.

"I suppose I could make a donation," Richard said. "If that's what you have in mind." The blood that had stagnated in his heart slowly disbursed itself.

Someone threw open one of the windows in the hallway behind Richard. He turned at the sound and saw a colored waiter trying to whisk smoke through the window with a white napkin. The smell of burned cakes floated out to the porch. The waiter looked at Richard through the open window.

"Sorry, boss," he said.

Guyon raised his brows as if the three of them had narrowly missed being caught doing something they should not have been doing. He motioned for Richard to follow him. The three men walked across the porch and down the steps into the yard. They stopped by the hawthorns that ran along the side of the club in great, wild clumps. The three of them stood in the shadows. The lighted kitchen windows above them cast glowing yellow squares onto the wet grass. The shapes of people moved back and forth through the squares. The windows were open and Richard heard loud but muddled conversations coming from the kitchen above.

Epps pulled a flask from inside his coat and unscrewed the top. He offered it to Richard, who took a pull and passed it toward Guyon, who waved it away. Richard returned the flask to Epps, watched him take a long drink, and then another.

"A donation is a fine gesture," Guyon said.

"A fine gesture," Epps repeated.

"But, McAdam, we need a little something more from men of your station, of your prominence in the community," Guyon said. "I'm not talking about anything grand or overly complicated here."

Epps took another swig from the flask and nodded in agreement. He passed it to Richard. He took a long drink and returned the flask to Epps.

"Just a few men," Epps said. "If you can spare them. Just a few men who'll lend us a hand keeping order around the village."

Guyon looked at Epps as if he'd said something he shouldn't have.

"We're not talking about violence here," Guyon said.

Epps looked incredulous. "Of course not," he said. Richard realized that his head was too foggy and warm with whiskey to know whether or not Epps's reaction was some sort of act. "Of course not," Epps said again. "No violence."

"Just a friendly presence," Guyon said. "A good show of good people—mill people—to let the Reds know they're outnumbered."

"I'll talk to my supervisors on Monday," Richard said. "I'll see if we can spare any men. Of course, it can't cut into production."

"No," Guyon said. "You can't lose money on this."

"Money's what this whole thing's about," Epps said. "No need for anyone to lose money."

"And only contribute any funds you feel comfortable contributing," Guyon said. "You may have seen a few of the ads placed in the *Transom* by the Council of Concerned Citizens of Gaston County." He smiled, raised his eyebrows. "Those don't come free, or even cheap."

"One hundred sixty dollars or fifty cents an inch," Epps said.

"The same price as anyone else," Guyon said. "It's costly, but it's important that we disseminate the truth about these Bolshevists. The thing is that half these millhands wouldn't know a damn communist from a cockroach if it weren't for people like Fred Beal."

"That's right," Epps said. "Most of them didn't know a thing about unions before Beal."

"Take this Ella May Wiggins woman, for instance," Guyon said. "The one who accosted Senator Overman."

"Claire said something about her being a singer," Richard said. Epps laughed, took a swig from the flask, and passed it to Richard. Richard took another drink.

"She's a linthead that can carry a tune," Epps said. "But she's no professional singer. That's fake news one of the papers started. She's no better than the rest of them."

"She works at American in Bessemer City," Guyon said. "It's a nigger mill, and she's trying to organize them there. She's trying to get niggers to join the union."

"And that's what the Reds want," Epps said. "They want niggers working alongside whites. Want them competing for the same jobs."

"We've got a couple of men inside the union," Guyon said. "Word is that the local strikers don't want to be integrated, but the union in New York is pushing back, sending down a colored organizer next week. Going to try to rally colored workers from other mills to join the strike."

Epps took a drink. "If he comes to Gastonia, it'll be the last trip south that nigger ever makes," he said. He passed the flask to Richard.

"But take this woman," Guyon said, "this Ella May Wiggins. She gets up there onstage during the meetings and works them up and sings hillbilly songs and colored music and all kind of filth. And the whole time you know she wouldn't have a thought in her head if it weren't for Beal. He's the brains of this whole thing. These hillbillies wouldn't be picketing or marching or striking if he hadn't shown them how to do it."

"She's got a whole brood of kids who live with niggers over in Bessemer City," Epps said. "Something like ten little kids, all of them bastards."

"She's not the virtuous kind," Guyon said. He nodded toward the clubhouse. "Not like these fine women here tonight."

"No, she ain't virtuous," Epps said. "She's loose. The kind of woman who'll let a man get away with anything. Just a nasty woman."

"That's a shame for children to live that way," Richard said.

"But she gets up onstage and talks about how her boy died because of the mills," Guyon said.

"As if the mills kill people," Richard said.

"Kid's better off dead," Epps said. "She's got too many. Wouldn't hurt if another two or three of them said good night."

"At least he's out of his misery," Richard said. "Sounds like she couldn't take care of him."

"She doesn't take care of the ones that are still living," Guyon said. "Instead she gets up onstage and sings and runs wild with communists. She might be at home with those babies if it weren't for the union. It's all Beal's doing."

"And what can you do about him?" Richard asked. He was still holding the flask, but when he turned his hands out to question Guyon, it slipped from his grasp and fell to the grass. He bent down and the world seemed to move with him. He felt around the damp earth, unsure of how many drinks he'd taken, relieved to find that the cap was still on the flask once his fingers closed around it. He stood, removed the cap, and took another drink, felt the last of the whiskey trickle into his mouth. He passed it to Epps, who gave it a shake to assure himself of its emptiness before slipping it back into his coat pocket. "You really think some newspaper articles are going to scare these communists?" Richard said. "Or change the strikers' minds?"

"We'll do what you have to do when you kill a snake," Epps said.

"And what's that?" Richard asked.

"We'll lop off its head," Guyon said.

"And what about this woman?" Richard asked. "This singer. A snake with its head cut off can still bite you."

Epps smiled. "I reckon we'll just have to cut out its tongue."

CHAPTER EIGHT

Katherine McAdam

Saturday, May 25, 1929

The band had already left the small stage and the guests had just been served their entrees when the ballroom doors were thrown open and Richard walked inside. As soon as she saw him Katherine knew that he'd been drinking. He was accompanied by Hugo Guyon and a fat, ugly man Katherine had never seen before. Guyon and the other man stopped just inside the doors and scanned the ballroom as if searching for available seats.

Richard walked toward the family's large round table, where Katherine and Claire sat with Paul Lytle and his mother and father. Richard made a grand gesture of stooping to kiss Claire on her cheek, then he moved around to where Katherine sat and kissed her on top of her head. He pulled his napkin from the back of his chair and took a seat. Katherine caught Claire's eye across the table. It looked as if her daughter was trying to blink back tears.

"Excuse me for stepping out," Richard said. He didn't seem to notice that no one had said a word since he'd appeared. The waiters had offered a choice of pheasant or steak, and Katherine had ordered Richard a steak. "This looks delicious," he said. He reached beneath the table and gave her fingers a discreet squeeze. She hoped her hand felt as lifeless and sick as her heart.

"It certainly does look delicious," Mrs. Lytle said. She, like Katherine, had ordered the pheasant, and now the woman stared down at her plate and set about picking at her dinner as if she'd never finish it.

"Where have you been?" Claire asked her father from across the table. Beside her, Paul was clearly watching Richard's plate to gauge when it would be acceptable to cut into his own steak.

"Yes, Mr. McAdam," Paul's father said. "We've missed you." He set down his silverware and passed his napkin across his mouth. He took a sip of water. "I thought you might be out there in the rain, trying to fix my car." He winked at Richard, whose eyes were locked on the table. "I was about to go search for you and show you how to use a wrench." He laughed.

"No," Richard said. "Quite the opposite. I was outside, very much hoping to be seen." He cut a hunk of steak and put it into his mouth. He chewed it slowly, glanced at Katherine, and made a grotesque face meant to show that he couldn't believe how good the meat tasted. She tried to smile at him, if for no other reason than to keep up appearances in front of the Lytles. Earlier, while Claire and Paul had orbited the ballroom, dancing and greeting guests before dinner, she'd been locked in a dry conversation with Mr. Lytle about the differences between growing rice and cotton, instead of speaking to her friends or spending time with Claire. And then this business with the burned cakes and the things she'd overheard.

"Those men there," Richard said, using his fork to point across the room to where Guyon and the fat stranger had finally found seats at a table, "those men who came in behind me are going to pay for the car that was damaged today, Mr. Lytle. So there's no need to worry about it."

"I wasn't worried about it," Lytle had said. "I didn't damage it. And I know Percy Epps. I would've had it taken care of myself."

Richard set his silverware down on either side of his plate. His mustache was shiny with the steak's blood, and Katherine saw that his face was flush with color. He turned and stared at Mr. Lytle.

"That's not my point," Richard said. "I was just telling you that it's being taken care of." He turned back to his plate and cut into his steak. "Hugo Guyon's the superintendent at Loray. A big man in this community."

"Never heard of him," Mr. Lytle said. "But I believe that if this superintendent were better at his job, his people wouldn't be rioting. The car wouldn't have been damaged in the first place."

"It's an outside element," Richard said. He smiled, popped another piece of steak into his mouth. "It'll soon be gone."

Katherine looked across the table at Mrs. Lytle.

"I love your dress," she said. "You always look so lovely."

"Thank you," Mrs. Lytle said. "You look exquisite in that gown." She looked to her right, over her son's plate, and spoke to Claire. "You both do. Do you ladies shop together?"

Claire smiled. It was the first real smile Katherine had seen her give since Richard had disappeared earlier in the evening.

"We have been, recently," Claire said. "Since I've been home."

"And we'll go more," Katherine said, smiling at Claire. "Now that you're home, we'll go more. Perhaps more than we should, I promise." Claire smiled back at her.

"Yes, quite often," Richard chimed in, attempting to join in on the joke.

"There are so many wonderful stores in Charlotte," Katherine said. "Perhaps on your drive home—"

"There are quite a few nice stores here in Gastonia, as well," Richard said.

"Of course," Katherine said. She leaned back in her seat and settled her eyes on her pheasant.

"Of course," she'd heard Mrs. Lytle say.

KATHERINE NOW SAT alone in the Essex where Richard had left it parked in the roundabout after retrieving it. He'd gone back inside the club to speak with Ingle about his daughter Grace and to tip him and the waitstaff. After the dinner was over and the cakes had been served, the burned tops cut away and discreetly covered with icing, she and Richard had watched the Lytles climb into the limousine, the dent in its hood catching the light like a black crater on a dark moon. Once Richard stepped inside the club, Claire had asked Katherine if it would be okay if she went to a party with friends. Paul would see her home afterward. Claire had promised that she would not be home too late. Although it was already past 11 P.M., Katherine knew how exciting it must be for Claire to have her friends and her fiancé all in town, and she saw no reason that Claire shouldn't go off and do as she pleased. In a few months she would be a wife. She would have to make much greater decisions than these without Katherine's blessing. Besides, she thought, I wouldn't come home either. Not until Richard was asleep and this night and the things of this night were behind them all.

Katherine found herself envying her daughter, not for her youth or her upcoming wedding or for all the life that awaited her, but for her freedom to return or not to return home as she so desired. The old house atop the hill that overlooked the McAdam Mill village would always be there if Claire were ever to want it or need it. And, unless one of them died, Katherine and Richard would always be there too. Unlike them, Claire didn't have to return at all.

Katherine had left her car door open. She sat with her foot on the running board and looked out onto the damp night, where frogs called to one another from the darkness. The air smelled of wet pine needles. She listened as a few distant automobiles rumbled down Franklin Avenue toward town. She and Richard had now been married for almost twenty-four years, and in those almost twenty-four years she had seen changes she'd never imagined. Even the land around her now had morphed into something brand-new in just the past decade. When Richard first brought her to Gaston County, the very piece of land on which she sat had been part of the Woltz family's dairy farm. A nine-hole golf course now covered the area that had once been a cow field. She thought of all the new things she'd seen in her lifetime: the record player and the radio she and Richard kept in their sitting room at home, the automobile she waited in now, the airplanes they'd seen fly over the city and touch down at the little municipal landing strip south of town. It made her tired to think of what was to come, to think of what Claire and Claire's children— her grandchildren, for God's sake—would see in the years ahead, the years she might not spend on this earth.

The car creaked on its axles and she heard Richard open the door and climb in, then close the door behind him. She kept her eyes on the darkness outside.

"Are you okay to drive?" she asked.

"Of course," he said. "Why wouldn't I be?"

She pulled her foot inside the car and closed the door.

"You're not too tight?" she asked. The engine roared to life when she spoke, and she knew that Richard could act as if he hadn't heard her.

Richard drove the Essex through the roundabout and took the dark lane out to the boulevard. The guests had all left. The parking areas were empty. The wet asphalt shined beneath the Essex's headlights. He turned east and headed toward McAdamville.

They rode in silence for a few moments. Through her window, Katherine watched the shuttered businesses as they passed them, their lights off and the windows drawn against the night.

"I just spoke to Ingle about Grace," Richard said. "He's upset of course, embarrassed really. Especially after the members took up the collection last year. He wants to pay everyone back since he says she won't be returning to school."

"That's unnecessary," Katherine said.

"That's just what I told him," Richard said. Katherine heard a lilt in his voice, as if a smile had come into it somehow, as if this small agreement boded well for the rest of the evening, perhaps for the rest of their lives together. "That's just what I told him. I told him it was unnecessary."

He slowed and made the left onto Wesleyan Road. They snaked along toward McAdamville. The sky misted rain fine enough to look like snow, and Katherine could see it only in the streetlamps and the headlights of the few automobiles they met on the road. When they followed the hill down into the mill village, she had the sensation of descending into a glass snow globe. She wondered, if she were to look up, would she be able to spy the clear, impervious dome that had come down over her life?

"And I told Ingle we'd be happy to make another contribution," Richard said. He hesitated. Waited. Katherine knew he expected her to ask if he'd promised a certain amount. They had the wedding to think of, after all. Business had slowed in the years since the war. Things were changing. The country was changing. It seemed it would continue to do so. But she wanted to help the Ingles, and she was simply too tired to play cautious with Richard. "On Monday I'm going to reach out to a few of the board members to see if we can get something together, some kind of donation, a second collection, if you want to call it that."

"Okay," Katherine said.

"Because I think it's important that we all do our part to help young people like Grace Ingle, young people who are doing everything in their power—" But his words trailed away and silence reclaimed the space where his voice had been. Katherine thought about the speech he had delivered as the doctored cakes were being served. When he'd been called to speak his face had turned slightly pink, flushed with either liquor or embarrassment, and when he stood he'd held the tips of her fingers in one hand and a flute of sparkling cider in the other. His speech had sounded like so much of what he was saying to her now—"When I think of today's youth"—but Katherine had simply watched her husband speak as if he were on the other side of the glass dome that she now imagined had closed her off from the world. She could see him, but she wasn't quite able to hear him.

It wasn't until much later in his speech that Richard had let go of her fingers and walked around to the other side of the table, where Claire and Paul were sitting.

"And Claire," he said, "you are the finest young person I've ever known. Your mother and I had only one child, and I cannot express to you how happy, proud, and thankful we are that that child is you."

As the audience broke into applause, Katherine had lifted her napkin to her eyes to hide her tears. Richard came back around the table and placed his hand on her shoulder, and then she felt his breath against her ear when he kissed the side of her face.

The rain had begun to bead on her window, and Katherine listened as Richard resumed his talk about young people.

"Not all of them will be able to afford college like we've afforded it," he said. "No, they won't all have dinners and parties and weddings like the one Claire and Paul are going to have."

It must have been his mention of her name that alerted Richard to the fact that their daughter was not with them. He turned and looked over his shoulder and saw that the backseat was empty.

"Where's Claire?"

"Out," Katherine said.

"Out where?"

"I don't know," she said. "Out. She wanted to be with Paul and her friends."

Richard sighed as if he were disappointed that it had only been

Katherine and not Claire too who'd witnessed his second impassioned speech of the evening. He clearly had much to say about "today's youth."

"You'd think she'd want a few more nights at home with us before the big day."

"Why would we think that?" Katherine asked. "Why? Her life is changing. It's already changed. Everything is changing. Why doesn't anyone understand that?"

They passed the lake in the center of the village, the fountain at its middle pulsing with life. Across the water, the mill shone in the night like an enormous ship. Katherine thought of Edison's Dynamo #31, its heart pumping mindlessly, giving life to it all.

After these many years in McAdamville, she'd tired of the legend of Edison's trip to the village, during which he'd personally installed the dynamo in the mill, and she reminded herself of all the other things Edison worked to invent: the telegraph, the lightbulb, the phonograph. She remembered reading that Edison had envisioned that his phonograph would be used to record messages, last wills and testaments, the voices of loved ones so they could speak to us for eternity.

Katherine had been seven years old the first time she heard music on a phonograph. She and her father had been standing on the porch of Tipton's Grocery back in Hickory when someone set up the player. Once the music began, a song called "Daisy Bell," a crowd of people had gathered to listen. Katherine held her father's hand, and with her other hand she held a cold bottle of limeade. A hen with several chicks scratched in the dirt just beyond the bottom of the steps. It was summer, dusty and dry. She watched the chicks and wanted to touch one of them, but she didn't want to let go of her father's hand, and she didn't want to set the limeade on the porch floor for fear of it being overturned.

Katherine closed her eyes and leaned her head against the car's window and thought of the little girl she had been and considered how much of her life she would change if she could. What message would she record and leave behind for the little girl who would grow up to be her? *Perhaps none of this will happen, Katie,* she would tell her. *Perhaps all of it will happen.*

Katherine opened her eyes, looked out at the dark, empty streets of McAdamville, saw the well-kept yards that fronted the small brick homes. Richard had always relished passing through the village at night when the streets were quiet. It allowed him to slow down and enjoy it without anyone witnessing his admiration of his own family's legacy.

"Perhaps we should've hosted tonight's party here in McAdamville so the Lytles could see how the best mills are run," he said. "And what the best mill villages look like."

They crested the hill above the village and followed the gravel driveway toward the old house, the few lights they'd left on winking at them through the wet trees. Richard pulled the Essex into the garage.

Katherine let herself into the house through the back door and followed the long hallway past the kitchen and turned left into the sitting room. She turned on the light and kneeled before the cabinet atop which the phonograph sat. She opened the cabinet's doors and thumbed through the many records they'd collected over the years. She found the one she was looking for, and she stood and took the stairs up to their bedroom. She heard the back door open and close. Richard's footsteps echoed from the hallway below her.

She leaned over the banister and called down to him.

"Will you bring the phonograph upstairs and leave it in the bedroom?" she asked.

Richard appeared at the bottom of the stairs and looked up at her. He'd removed his jacket and had folded it over his forearm.

"Why?" he asked. "We're about to go to bed."

"I want to hear music," she said. He sighed and draped his jacket over the stair rail and walked into the sitting room. Katherine crossed the hallway and went into the bathroom. She set the record on the vanity and closed the door behind her.

The rain had dampened her hair. It now lay flat against her forehead. She pushed it away from her eyes and removed the pins and allowed it to fall down around her shoulders. She ran a brush through it, and then she moved it behind her ears. She leaned toward the mirror and unscrewed the backs from her diamond earrings, all the while listening to Richard downstairs in the sitting room. He'd have to move the desk beside the cabinet to unplug the phonograph, and then he'd have to lift it. He was muttering something, but she didn't want to hear him, so she turned the faucet and ran water in the sink.

When she walked into their bedroom, she found Richard bent over and reaching behind the bureau to plug in the phonograph. He'd left it sitting atop a low dresser beneath the window. She slid the record from its sleeve and put it on. The sound of static was nearly indistinguishable from the light patter of rain against the window. The song's opening notes filled the room.

> *Here is a flower within my heart*
> *Daisy, Daisy*
> *Planted one day by a glancing dart*
> *Planted by Daisy Bell.*

Richard stood with his hands on his hips and stared at the phonograph.

"What's this?" he asked.

"It's an old song," she said.

"I know," he said. "Why are you playing it?"

"I was thinking of it tonight."

He smiled. "It was a great night, wasn't it?" he said. "Quite a party."

"Yes," she said. She lifted her right hand and unclasped the bracelet from her wrist and placed it in the jewelry box. She reached behind her head and fumbled with the clasp on her necklace. She felt Richard's eyes on her.

"Do you need help?"

"No."

"Are you feeling all right?" he asked. "You've been quiet tonight."

"I'm fine," she said. "Just tired."

"Are you sure?"

"Yes," she said.

"You seem upset," he said. "Is it Claire?"

"I don't know," Katherine said, her fingers still struggling with the necklace.

"Is it the wedding? Are you sad that our little girl is getting married in a few months?"

"Of course I am," she said. She finally unhooked the clasp. "But I'm not. I'm happy for her. For them. They're a good match. He has a fine family."

"I suppose so," Richard said.

Katherine turned away from him and reached behind her back for the dress's zipper. She felt Richard's fingers close around hers, and she dropped her hands to her sides and let him unzip her.

"Then what is it?" he asked.

"Tonight," she said, "I heard you talking with those men."

"Which men?"

"Hugo Guyon and that other man," she said. "I don't know who he was."

"He's an attorney," Richard said. "For Loray."

"I heard you."

"What do you mean? What did you hear?"

"They'd burned the cakes," Katherine said. Across the room, their closet door was open, and she stared into it. Dresses and suits hovered there in the dark. "And Ingle called me into the kitchen. He was frantic." The phonograph's needle skipped and then caught.

Daisy, Daisy, give me your answer, do
I'm half crazy all for the love of you
It won't be a stylish marriage
I can't afford the carriage

"Ingle didn't want to serve the cakes," she said, "but there wasn't any time to bake more. I couldn't find you to ask you, and I didn't want to ask Claire because I didn't want to upset her. I was trying to laugh at Ingle's fussiness, but I didn't want to do the wrong thing and ruin the night. I looked at the cakes and told him just to cut away the tops and frost them. And then I heard voices outside, and I heard your voice. You were talking about the strike."

"I'm sorry, Kate," he said. "I didn't mean for you to hear us. I was telling Guyon about what happened to the Lytles. I let him know that what's happening down at Loray has upset a lot of people, Claire included."

"I heard what you said."

Her dress slid off her shoulders and fell down around her ankles. She stepped free of it and stood in her slip with her back to him.

"What did I say?" he asked.

"They were talking about the poor woman who'd lost her baby, the woman in Bessemer City. I don't remember her name. You said that her son was better off dead, that she couldn't take care of him anyway."

"Katherine, I said no such thing. You heard wrong." His hand came down lightly on her bare shoulder. She flinched at his touch, as if his skin had become a dangerous thing. He cleared his throat, lifted his hand away from her.

"It was your voice."

"I said no such thing."

"Who said it?"

"I don't even know what you're talking about." She heard him pulling at his tie.

"And then what you said to Claire tonight, during your speech, about us having only one child."

Richard stopped moving. She could hear his breathing.

"Katherine," he said, his voice a whisper, "I didn't mean it that way. She's never known. We've never told her. What was I supposed to say?"

"It made me think," she said, but she stopped. Words tossed themselves through her mind; she picked up as many as she could and looked at them closely, then she set them back down and looked for others. "It's just when you said that about the woman at Loray—"

"I told you," Richard said, his voice rising, "I didn't say that." He squeezed past her and disappeared into the closet. The light came on inside. She listened as he yanked at his tie again as if he struggled to remove it.

"When I heard what you said about that poor woman, and then I heard what you said to Claire, it made me wonder if you thought that of me. If you thought that we lost the baby because I couldn't care for him. If he was better off."

"No, Katherine," Richard said from inside the closet. "Of course not. Of course I don't think that. This whole thing has been taken out of context. This whole evening—" But he didn't finish.

The song ended, and without looking at the phonograph, Katherine lifted the needle and the song began again.

> *Here is a flower within my heart*
> *Daisy, Daisy*
> *Planted one day by a glancing dart*
> *Planted by Daisy Bell.*

Richard reappeared from the closet wearing only his undershirt and shorts. He caught Katherine looking at him, at his body.

"You've changed, Richard."

He looked down at himself, stared at his belly beneath the shirt. "I've gotten old, Kate. Everyone changes."

"That's not what I mean," she said. "I never notice your aging, but I've watched you change. You weren't always who you are now."

"Who was I then?" he asked.

"I don't know," she said. "Now you just seem so concerned, so goddamned concerned of what other people think of you."

"Katherine!" he said. His voice arched around her name because he'd never heard her speak this way, but she didn't care. She couldn't help it. "Really, Katherine?" he said. "Really?"

"Yes, Richard," she said. "It's true. You're just so goddamned concerned. I feel like I don't know you, which is awful because the first time I ever saw you I felt that you were someone I'd always known."

"I felt the same way about you."

She didn't want to recount the story because she knew it would hurt to do so, but she hoped it would hurt Richard too, this memory of who he'd been, of who she'd been, of who they both were before they were a couple.

"David had told us about you in his letters, talked about you over Christmas, the last time he was home," Katherine said. "And when we arrived at the university you'd already packed up all of his belongings."

"They asked me to do it because they wanted to move another boy into our room," Richard said. "There was a wait list, but I kept the door locked when I wasn't there. I didn't want anyone else to touch his things."

Tears came into her eyes, and she wiped them away. She looked down at her hands, spun her wedding ring on her finger.

"And you'd had all the boys sign his yearbook for us. And then you helped Father carry everything out to the carriage, and then you went inside for your coat and rode with us to the station."

"It was April," Richard said. "And it had turned cold. I remember that the dogwoods had blossomed, and you were worried about them dying during the night."

"And at the station, you went out onto the train platform to see us off. I remember my father crying and you put your hand on his shoulder and said—"

"'The valiant never taste of death but once.'"

"I thought it was so beautiful," she said. "And so fitting, for David. All these years, I've never forgotten it."

"It was Shakespeare," Richard said, "from *Julius Caesar*. I'd just heard it that morning in Professor Hume's class. I'd memorized it because it made me think of David. I wanted to tell it to your father if I met him. I didn't expect you. But I'd seen you in a photograph David had. I was so nervous in front of you. I'd rehearsed how to act in front of your father, but I didn't know how to act when I saw you."

"You didn't seem nervous," she said.

"I was."

"You seemed kind and generous and honest."

"Do I no longer seem that way to you?"

"I don't know," she said. "I don't know what you seem like now."

She had turned to face the window. She stood there looking into her own reflection. They were both silent, although Katherine knew that one of them needed to say something to the other; but she could not think of what it would be. Richard stood by the closet. He walked across the room. She heard him step into the hall and go into the bathroom. He closed the door.

"Daisy Bell" had ended and a new song, one she didn't recognize, had begun. She lifted the arm on the player. The record continued to spin in near silence beneath her. She listened for Richard's movements, but the only thing she could hear was the humming silence of the house, the soft patter of the rain. She imagined him inside the bathroom, standing with both hands on the vanity, his eyes looking at everything around him except his own face in the mirror. Was he listening for her as she listened for him?

Katherine unmade the bed and picked up Richard's pillow; then she opened the trunk that rested at the footboard and found a blanket. She set the pillow and the blanket on the floor in the hallway and closed the bedroom door.

She crossed the room and stood before the window again, reached out, and turned off the lamp on the dresser. Her face in the window disappeared, although the hallway light from beneath the closed door threw a faint, ghostly outline of her body on the glass. She peered into the darkness, the record still spinning. There had been a time, when they were first married, that she could stand here and see all the way down into the village to the lake and to the mill beyond it. But now the trees were too tall and dense. It was late May, and had it been day she would have seen the bright green leaves and tiny red buds that clung to the limbs.

But she was trying to see through the trees, past the limbs and leaves and buds, and into the mill village, where she knew a few last lights still burned in bedrooms and kitchens. She imagined a woman inside one of the millhouses peering through the rain toward the big house on the hill on the other side of the trees. A woman who was a mother just like Katherine—younger, perhaps, but a mother just the same. The woman stood, her fingers intertwined over her stomach just as Katherine had intertwined hers, her arms empty of the child or the children she birthed and raised and let go into the world, her womb empty of those children as well, but empty of something else too, something now lost and far away, something that felt forgotten by everyone but her and the other women who stood at windows on nights like these.

Then Katherine remembered the woman's name, the name she'd heard the men say that night while they stood in the dark beneath the window.

Ella May Wiggins.

GASTON TRANSOM-TIMES

MAY 26, 1929

Do the people of Gaston County know what they are subscribing to when they believe the preachments of men like Beal and Reed? They advocate racial equality, intermarriage of whites and blacks, abolition of all laws discriminating between whites and blacks. Here is their platform:

"1. A federal law against lynching and the protection of negro masses in their right of self defense.

"2. Abolition of the whole system of race discrimination. Full racial, political and social equality for the negro race.

"3. Abolition of all laws which result in segregation of the negroes. Abolition of all Jim Crow laws. The law shall forbid all discrimination against negroes in selling or renting houses.

"4. Abolition of all laws which disenfranchise the negroes.

"5. Abolition of laws forbidding intermarriage of persons of different races.

"6. Abolition of all laws and public administration measures which prohibit, or in practice prevent, negro children or youth from attending general public schools or universities.

"7. Full and equal admittance of negroes to all railway station waiting rooms, trains, restaurants, hotels and the theatres."

What will it take for us to stand up and rid this city and this state of the threat of bloody red Bolshevism? Violence? We've witnessed violence. Protests? We've experienced protests. Anger? There is plenty of anger on all sides.

Will we wait to act until our Constitution has been destroyed, our churches pulled down upon us, our classrooms and courtrooms taken over by self-professed godless men like Fred Beal? Will we wait to act until our children learn and eat and play and sleep alongside the Negro? Will we wait to act until our very voices cry out for mercy in a Russian tongue?

The good people of this community are getting tired of these wops from the east side of New York telling our folks what to do and how to do it. It is time we are being rid of them. We can settle the strike without their aid and suggestions. Get them out of town, and the strike will be settled and in a way that will be satisfactory to all. As long as the union stays here, we shall have trouble, and more serious trouble than any that has yet happened.

Advertisement Paid for by the Council of Concerned Citizens of Gaston County

CHAPTER NINE

Ella May

Sunday, May 26, 1929

The brief burst of rain that closed the night's meeting had ended, and Ella and Sophia shuffled and slipped their way along the muddy road away from the headquarters. To their right, dozens of wet canvas tents gleamed against the light of hanging lamps. Out in the dark field, strikers stoked soggy campfires and prepared late dinners.

Ahead of them, thirty or so Bessemer City workers in small groups of twos and threes walked over the railroad tracks, their bodies thrown into momentary silhouette by the lights from Loray, which blazed farther south.

"Well, looky there," Sophia said. She pointed into the damp woods that ran along the north side of the railroad tracks. An automobile sat parked deep in the trees.

"Looks like a police car," Ella said.

As they passed, the driver drew on his cigarette, and the faint light was enough for Ella to recognize Officer Tom Gibson behind the wheel. She assumed that the large, round head in the passenger's seat belonged to Officer Albert Roach. Two others sat in the backseat, but it was too dark and they were too far away for Ella to see them clearly.

"That's Gibson for sure," Ella said. "Looks like Roach too. Got a mind to knock on the window, ask Gibson for a cigarette."

"You don't smoke," Sophia said.

"And you quit."

"I reckon we'll leave them alone then," Sophia said, but as if unable to resist, she raised her hand and waved. "Hey, boys!" she called. She blew a kiss. Ella laughed.

Ella and Sophia clambered up the rise toward the tracks. Beneath them the strikers' dark figures had already made their way down the other side of the embankment. "Police are just watching us," Sophia said. "Just waiting to see if Hampton's here yet."

Ella turned back and looked at the police car, saw that it hadn't moved.

"You think they know he's coming?"

"Oh, I'm sure of it," Sophia said.

"Beal doesn't even know," Ella said. "What makes you think they know?"

"You saw what the Council put in the paper this morning, and now they're sitting out here in the dark like a lynching party," Sophia said. "They know. Somebody's tipped them off."

"Police are always out here," Ella said. "If it ain't Gibson and Roach it's somebody else. Tonight's no different."

"Well, it feels different," Sophia said. "Things have changed."

Ella knew that was true: things had changed. In the twenty-one days since she'd attended her first rally in Gastonia, word of the strike had spread to Bessemer City and other mill towns where workers had grown desperate enough to be curious about the union. The rallies had gotten larger as people from outside Gastonia came to view the crisp tents that housed the evicted Loray strikers, to listen to music, to hear speakers, and, sometimes, to eat free food until the food ran out.

The one truck owned by the union soon proved insufficient, and a Gastonia striker named Anderson Chesley had lent his truck to the cause. They could shuttle more people now, and it was safer to have two trucks on the highway at night.

Ella had changed too. It had only been three weeks since she walked off her job at American and joined the union, but she'd traveled by car to Washington, D.C. She'd given a United States senator a piece of her mind. She'd heard rumors that record companies in Charlotte and Nashville were planning to send music producers to the rallies to record her songs, although none of them had shown up yet. She was beginning to understand the ebb and flow of the strike, the inner workings of the union, and, once she'd gotten Loray's attention and made a name for herself among the strikers, mill owners, newspapermen, and politicians, she was beginning to understand her role in it all too.

She'd written more songs, sung them at the meetings here in Gastonia and at impromptu rallies elsewhere when she'd been invited. Everywhere she went people asked her to sing the "mill mother song," the song she'd sung her first night in Gastonia, and "The Mill Mother's Song" was what she'd begun to call it as well. She'd written it as a love letter to her children, but her heart had turned toward angry protest, and she'd told Sophia that "The Mill Mother's Song" might be the last ballad she'd ever sing. The songs she sang now were still based on popular melodies, but the lyrics had grown more political: "Two Little Strikers," "On Top of Ol' Loray," "All Around the Jailhouse."

She spent every day organizing workers in Bessemer City, waiting outside gates during shift changes, handing out leaflets on paydays downtown. Beal had done his best to keep his word about Ella's pay, and Sophia had done her best to make sure of it. Ella's pockets and her children's bellies had been full more often than not, and although the union relief funds were not consistent, the food she'd been able to come by was at least reliable.

And now she'd told Charlie about the baby. He'd mostly disappeared, but not before accusing her of being unfaithful and threatening her if she didn't stay away from Gastonia. She wasn't any more scared of him now than she'd been before sharing the news, and his selling his guitar and buying a rifle hadn't changed her feelings. She'd already risked her life by joining the union. After that, Charlie Shope with a gun in his hand didn't seem so scary.

But Ella was about to risk the union itself because she wanted Violet, her friends from Stumptown, and her former coworkers at American to be welcome beside her at rallies and alongside her on the trucks that drove strikers to and from Bessemer City each evening. Ella knew they were as hungry as she had been, just as overworked and underpaid. The only advantage she had over them was the color of her skin, and she knew that was the only reason she was here now while Violet and all the people who looked like her were stuck in lives they didn't deserve. It wasn't right. She wanted to open the union to them because they'd opened their homes and lives to her. They'd given her food and clothes without her asking. Violet and Violet's mother had watched her children—were watching them right now, as a matter of fact—and never asked for anything in return. They hadn't asked for the union either, but they deserved it. Everyone deserved it. They just needed to feel welcome, to see someone who looked like them among the union ranks. Maybe then they'd believe that the Local could be integrated. Maybe then the Local would believe it too.

Ella and Sophia had been working—without Beal's or the Local's knowledge—to arrange for the national office to have a colored organizer, an old friend of Sophia's named Hampton Haywood, sent south. He was scheduled to arrive on the train in Charlotte a week from tomorrow. They'd do everything they could to keep it quiet until then. Ella knew that if they were going to integrate the union they'd need secrecy right up to the moment when everyone's hands were raised and the votes were tallied.

Water squished inside Ella's shoes, soaked her stockings. When she reached the bottom of the embankment she slipped off both of her shoes, turned them up, and watched water trickle out. She tried to wipe the water from her stockings, but they were sopping wet, and she saw no solution but to step out of them one leg at a time. Sophia stood beside her and waited for Ella to step back into her shoes with her bare feet. The strikers began to load up into trucks, which sat parked on the side of the road as it curved to the east and ran parallel to the railroad tracks. Men in overalls and women in dresses kicked mud from their shoes and helped one another climb over the open tailgates into the truck beds. Ella buckled her shoes, raised her head, and saw Sophia watching the strikers as if appraising them somehow.

"We're going to bring fifty more on Friday night," Sophia said. "Maybe more. Who knows? Could be a hundred colored workers."

Ella stood, nodded toward the men and women in the trucks. "As long as they don't run them off."

"They won't," Sophia said. "They won't even see us coming until we're here."

"Hopefully nobody gets hurt," Ella said. "Or killed."

"I already told you, Ella May. Ain't nobody getting killed."

They walked without speaking for a moment, as if practicing the silence of the secret they shared. Ella cleared her throat. "Will you do me a favor, Miss Blevin."

"What's that, Miss May?"

"When your friend gets here, you tell him to let me do the talking," Ella said. "Colored folks I know ain't going to listen to him just because he looks like them. And you need to make sure he don't put on northern airs or wear fancy clothes. It's not going to impress them. But if they see that he's humble like them, maybe even poor like me, then they'll listen."

Ahead, Anderson Chesley stood on the running board of his truck. He was in his early twenties, certainly older than Sophia, probably not too much younger than Ella. She'd heard that, like her, he was from somewhere up in the mountains too, but she'd never found out exactly where, and she didn't want to ask him. She didn't want to think about the mistake she'd made in leaving those mountains behind. She figured Anderson Chesley didn't want to think about it either. As Ella and Sophia drew closer to the trucks, Ella could see that Chesley stood with a rifle slung over his shoulder. Sophia saw it too. She clucked her tongue in disappointment.

"No weapons in view, Mr. Chesley," Sophia said. "Not this far from headquarters anyway."

Chesley looked down at his boots where they stood on the running board as if he were thinking of how to respond, and then he looked up at Sophia.

"I seen that car back there," he said. "That's Gibson and Roach, Miss Blevin: police officers. A few nights back, somebody followed us all the way to Bessemer City. Got right up on my tail when I turned off the highway. Nearly hit me. There were four men inside. Might have been them."

One of the men standing by Chesley's truck spoke up. He was a tall, red-faced man named Will Mason. He was a machinist at Ragan Spinning Company.

"He's right," Mason said. "Came right up on the back of us, liked to hit us almost. There were four men inside, but it was too dark to see any faces."

"Could have been a bad driver," Sophia said. "No reason to go shooting at people for being bad drivers."

"I ain't about to go shooting at people," Chesley said. "Not yet, but I will. Last night, after I went to bed, another car sat out in front of my house. I looked out the window and seen it. Whoever it was wouldn't leave until I went out there on the porch and showed them this here rifle."

"Beal doesn't want anybody to be seen carrying weapons off the premises. Weapons are only to protect headquarters and the commissary," Sophia said. She looked at the faces around her. "You all know better: no guns."

Chesley slipped his thumb beneath the rifle's strap as if he were going to slide it off his shoulder, but he stopped, changed his mind.

"Well, Beal can go to hell," Chesley said. He sat down in his truck and laid the rifle across his lap. He slammed the truck's door, poked his face out its open window. "Let Beal drive out here by hisself one night," he said. "He'll be begging for a rifle after that. It's easy to say 'no weapons' when you got guards protecting you up there." He nodded in the direction of the headquarters, on the other side of the tracks. "But it's a different thing when you're out here, surrounded by strangers."

When he said the word *strangers* his eyes fell on a woman Ella had not yet noticed. She stood in the middle of the road, several feet away from the group of workers who were still climbing up into the trucks' beds. The woman must've felt the group's eyes upon her, because she coughed, ran her gloved hands across the front of her thin jacket as if smoothing away wrinkles that she knew were not there. The jacket had a matching belt that she'd cinched tight at her waist. A fine hat sat tipped toward her eyes. She wore boots with a thin heel. Ella didn't know who she was, but she knew that she wasn't a striker. It scared her, the thought of someone she didn't know being so close by without her sensing it.

"There's just too many strangers," Chesley said. He cranked the engine. It sputtered, caught, then fired. Sparks shot from somewhere beneath the truck. The woman in the road jumped at the sound. A few of the workers laughed.

The woman turned, looked at Ella. Her face was pretty, her cheeks brushed lightly with rouge, her mouth red with lipstick. Ella figured her for an out-of-town reporter who'd suddenly found herself surrounded by a rough bunch of millhands.

"You're Ella May," the woman said, her voice lilting in a way that made clear that she was asking a question but was afraid to do so outright.

For Ella to hear her name in the mouth of a stranger was akin to someone standing on her chest and forcing the air from her lungs. It had been happening more and more often, ever since the first night she'd spoken at the rally, but she had yet to grow used to it, and each time it happened it was accompanied by the dizzying realization that people she did not know somehow knew her. Ella looked over at Sophia, who didn't seem bothered by the woman's presence. She must have figured her for a reporter as well, and Ella knew how much reporters and newspapers excited Sophia. Sophia nodded at Ella and flicked her eyes toward the stranger, clearly encouraging her to answer.

"Yes," Ella said. "I'm Ella."

"Are you a reporter?" Sophia asked.

"No," the woman said. "I'm not a reporter. I'm . . . I . . . I don't know what I am, actually."

Sophia smiled, nodded toward Ella. "You a fan?" she asked the woman.

"I . . . I don't know," she said. She looked at Ella. "I just wanted to meet you."

Sophia whistled as if in disbelief. She shook her head, turned away from the woman, and walked back toward the truck.

"Why?" Ella asked. "Why'd you want to meet me?"

The woman took a step toward Ella, stopped, took another. She interlaced her fingers, held her gloved hands before her as if they offered something either invisible or too small to be seen.

"I've heard about you," the woman said, "and I heard you sing tonight. It was just lovely, wonderful. I wanted to talk to you."

"About what?" Ella asked.

"I don't know," the woman said. "I just—"

She opened her mouth to say something else, but instead she

looked past Ella to the two trucks that sat on the side of the road behind her. The woman's gaze moved from one truck to the other. Ella turned and saw that the workers had all been watching and listening.

It began to rain. The woman coughed, put her hands in her pockets. Ella wondered if the woman would leave now. The woman shifted her feet, coughed again. Otherwise, she didn't move.

Sophia opened the driver's-side door of her truck and climbed inside. An older woman named Maize Creedmore was already sitting on the passenger's side. Sophia cranked the engine. It was too dark and rainy to witness the black smoke that Ella knew belched from the tailpipe.

The trucks were all loaded. Ella and the woman were the only ones left standing in the road.

"Good night," Ella said.

She walked to the back of the truck. It began to rain harder. The people in the truck had huddled together. A few men opened small umbrellas and held them overhead. Others crowded beneath. Ella sighed, grasped the tailgate, put her foot on the step up. Her toes squished together inside her wet shoe.

"Wait, Ella," the woman said. "I can drive you. I have a car." She took a step forward. Dropped her hands at her sides. "It's no trouble."

Ella kept her hand on the tailgate and her foot on the step. She looked up at the faces inside the truck, most of them downcast or darkened by shadow. There suddenly didn't seem to be room enough for her, and she pictured the long, wet ride squeezed up against her fellow passengers, all of them smelling of mud and rain and damp clothes. Someone would have a flask, but it wouldn't be enough to keep the drive from being miserable.

Ella looked over at the woman again and reacquainted herself with the nice jacket, the perfectly perched hat, and the woman's made-up face, and she imagined the dry, comfortable interior of an expensive automobile. She dropped her hand and lowered her foot to the road.

She walked alongside the truck to Sophia's window. Sophia was watching the woman where she stood out in the road.

"She wants to drive me," Ella said.

"I heard," Sophia said. She stared at the woman. Rain fell into Ella's eyes. She wiped it away. "Do you think she wants to be president of your fan club? Do you think Gastonia's ready for a female president?"

"She said she wanted to meet me," Ella said. "I don't know why."

"You're famous now, you know," Sophia said. She smiled. "I guess Beal was right in wanting there to be music, wanting you to sing it."

"You think it's safe?" Ella asked.

"No woman dressed like that on a night like this is up to any devilment," Sophia said.

"You'd go?" Ella asked. "If you were me?"

"Sure," Sophia said. She dropped the truck into gear. "Why not? It could be interesting."

Sophia turned her truck around in the road so that it could head back down South Loray Street to Franklin. Chesley's truck followed. When Sophia passed Ella and the woman, she called out, "You girls have fun!"

The sounds of the trucks on the wet road faded away, and then it was just Ella and the woman alone on the dark street.

"Well," the woman said. Her breathy voice sounded nervous, uncertain. Even through the heavy rain Ella could see the hesitation on her face. "Shall we go?"

"Yes, ma'am," Ella said. Then, "Thank you for the offer."

"Please," the woman said. She reached out her hand. Ella took it. "Please call me Kate."

"Okay," Ella said.

"Okay," Kate said.

They walked east down South Loray Street in the opposite direction. Ahead of them, a large green sedan sat parked along the road.

As they drew closer, Kate reached into the pocket of her jacket for a set of keys.

"Is this your car?" Ella asked. She stood on the driver's side, her eyes taking in the length of the automobile. Its shiny chassis gleamed in the rain.

"Yes, well, kind of," Kate said. "It's my husband's car."

Once inside, Kate inserted the keys and popped the clutch. She turned the ignition. The engine fired immediately. Ella felt the automobile hum beneath her, and she thought of the way the floor vibrated with the power of the machines in the spinning room at the mill.

Rain beaded the windshield. Kate stared down at the knobs and buttons on the dash. She lifted her hand, her finger hovering for a moment, and then she pushed one of the buttons. Wipers came up from beneath the windshield and cleared the rain from the glass. Kate pulled the car onto the road.

"What kind of car is this?" Ella asked.

"An Essex," Kate said. "My husband says it's more properly called the Super Six, but it's an Essex."

"It's beautiful," Ella said.

"Thank you," Kate said.

"I don't know a whole lot of husbands who'll let their wives drive."

"Right now, my husband's in no position to have an opinion of what I do," Kate said.

"Well, it's a nice car, anyway," Ella said.

"Where am I going?" Kate asked.

"Head back out to Franklin," Ella said. "Then take a right. Just keep driving west until we get to Bessemer City."

THEY WERE ON the open road outside Gastonia within a few minutes, the lights of the city behind them. The Essex cruised along, its headlights shining on the wet road. Another automobile appeared in the distance, and Ella saw that it was the back of Chesley's truck.

Kate veered around it without slowing, without showing any sign that she'd noticed it. As she flew past Chesley's truck and then Sophia's, Ella turned her face away from the window so that she wouldn't be seen.

"My husband always had an opinion about what I was doing," Ella said.

"What makes you say that?" Kate asked.

"Because of what you said earlier," Ella said. "You said your husband didn't have no opinion about you right now."

"Oh," Kate said. She laughed. "I don't think that's true. I'm sure he has opinions about me. I just don't care to hear them."

Ella looked around the inside of the car. It was the nicest automobile she'd ever seen. She fingered the leather seats, closed her hand around the metal crank that would lower the window if she were to turn it.

"What kind of work does your husband do?"

"He runs a family business," Kate said. "Nothing interesting."

"In town?"

"No," Kate said. "Not in Gastonia, but close by over in McAdamville. Do you know it?"

"I've heard of it," Ella said. "Is it nice there?"

Kate grew quiet, and Ella wondered if she'd done something wrong by asking the question.

"It should be nice," Kate finally said. "But, no, I don't find it that way. Others do. My husband does."

"Husbands," Ella said.

Kate smiled.

"It sounds like you understand," Kate said.

"I do," Ella said, "but my husband's gone, so I don't have to understand him as much as I used to."

"I'm sorry," Kate said.

"Oh, he's not dead," Ella said. "He's just gone. I don't know where to. He's better off wherever he is. So am I."

"How long were you married?"

"Since I turned sixteen," Ella said. "My mother and father both passed away real close together. I got married because I didn't know what else to do."

"It must have been awful to lose your parents so young," Kate said.

"It was," Ella said. "My older brother ran off as soon as he was old enough."

"Where to?"

"Detroit," Ella said. "I've never seen him since. I was little when he left, probably ten or twelve. I think he went up there to build cars." She wrapped her knuckles on her window. "He could've built this one here." She looked over at Kate. "Wouldn't that be something? Me just sitting here riding along in a fine automobile that my brother Wesley built, not having any idea that he's the one that built it. It's a nice thing to think, isn't it?"

"Yes," Kate said. "It is nice."

"After my daddy died, the lumber camp doled out my widow's pay. I had nowhere to go. All I could think to do was find one of them old letters that Wesley had wrote us from up north, and then go down to the train station and buy a ticket to wherever he was."

"Is that what you did?"

Ella thought about not saying another word about herself, about not telling Kate, this stranger she'd never met before, any more of her story. But something about the silence of the car and the feel of the night made her want to keep talking.

"It's what I would've done," Ella said. "It's what I would've done if John Wiggins hadn't been sitting on a bench in that train station waiting for a girl just like me.

"He was good-looking too, dressed in a fine suit of clothes, probably the only thing he owned at the time. He asked me where I was heading, and when I didn't have my answer ready I figure he probably knew I was the one he'd been waiting for.

"We spent our first night in a boardinghouse right there in Bryson City. That night I laid in bed in a strange room beside a strange man and listened to the train whistle out there in the mountains. And each time I heard it whistle I wondered if that was the train that was supposed to be taking me to Detroit. But instead, here I was laid up in bed with a fine-talking stranger, our bellies full of steak and champagne. A whole lot of my money already gone. It was just about the loneliest I've ever felt in my life."

She'd said too much, revealed too many things about herself, about who she'd been. Ella could almost feel Kate tossing around images of her in her mind: the sight of her in bed with John, the feeling of champagne slipping past her lips, the echo of the train whistle in the night. She wanted to open her mouth and suck the words back into it, but instead she kept talking, kept throwing words after the ones she'd already said as if they could reconstruct instead of underpin the idea Kate already had of her.

"I'd never done anything like that before, you know, *spent the night with a man,* and I said to him, I said, 'You reckon we better get married now?' And he said, 'No, no, no. We don't got time for that kind of thing.' Well, I couldn't figure out what time had to do with it, but looking back on it now, I know he said that because he was planning to cut out just as soon as we ran dry of my widow's pay. And then a few weeks later I told him I thought I was pregnant, which I was. And I asked about us getting married then, and he said, 'Well, I reckon we ought to now,' and that's about as romantic as he ever got. *'I reckon we ought to.'*"

"How long ago did he leave?"

"About two years ago," Ella said. "Right after I got pregnant with my youngest. I reckon it took John Wiggins that many years to do what he'd wanted to do the first morning he woke up beside me." Ella looked over at Kate. Her face grew hot. She'd said too much again. She turned toward Kate, nearly felt herself throw the onus of speaking into Kate's lap. "Where'd you meet your husband?"

"In Chapel Hill, at the university," Kate said.

"You went to college?" Ella asked.

"No," Kate said. "I wish I'd gone. I begged my daughter to go to college because I didn't, and I grew up wishing I had. But, no, my older brother went to college in Chapel Hill. My husband was his roommate until my brother passed away. He died young. He was eighteen."

"I'm sorry," Ella said.

"Thank you," Kate said. "It was a long time ago."

"It don't get no easier to lose somebody you love," Ella said. "No matter how long it's been."

"That's true," Kate said.

Silence hung between them for a few minutes after that. The quiet nearly blotted out the sound of the air as they cut through it and the noise of the car's tires on the wet road.

"This is a fine car," Ella said, certain that she'd already said something to that effect earlier. Then, "Nobody'd think to follow a fine car like this one."

"What do you mean *follow*?" Kate asked.

"The mill's people have been following us when we head home after meetings," Ella said. "They'll run you off the road. Come up on you and hit your bumper, try to crash you. They'll shoot at you too, least that's what I've heard. I hadn't ever been shot at though."

"Who are the 'mill's people'?" Kate asked. "Employees?"

"I don't know," Ella said. "Nobody knows. I reckon you've seen the ads in the newspaper run by the Council. We figure that's who it is. Each time it happens we say, 'Well, the Council was out last night.' Back in April, a mob tore down the first headquarters and broke into the commissary. People said it was the Council that did that too."

"It sounds terrifying," Kate said.

"Aw, we're fine in a nice car like this one," Ella said. She ran her hand along the dash. "This is the nicest car I've ever rode in."

Kate smiled, looked over at Ella, looked back at the road.

"Would you like to drive it?" Kate asked.

Ella laughed.

"I can't drive a car like this," she said.

Kate laughed too.

"Believe me," she said. "If I can, you can."

"I don't know about that."

"Let's find out," Kate said. She looked over her right shoulder, then she slowed and pulled to the side of the road. She parked the car, put on the brake.

"What are you doing?" Ella asked.

"Let's switch," Kate said. "You drive."

"I don't know."

"Come on," Kate said. "You'll never know unless you try. To-night's the first time I've driven the damn thing."

Ella looked from Kate to the road in front of them. It had stopped raining, but the wipers were squeaking across the glass. Kate turned them off. It was quiet.

"Let's switch," she said again. She raised her eyebrows.

Ella smiled, nodded her head. The women laughed awkwardly as they climbed around one another in the front seat. Ella caught scents of powder and faint perfume as Kate moved over and around her. She found herself sitting in the driver's seat, the powder and perfume floating in the air. She lifted her hands, closed her fingers around the steering wheel.

"All right," Kate said. She pointed to the floorboard at Ella's feet. "Put your left foot there. That's the clutch. And your right foot goes there for the gas and right there for the brake. Go ahead, press the clutch."

Ella did. Kate moved Ella's hand from the steering wheel to a lever beside it.

"This is the gearshift," she said. "Let's put it in first, and then lift your foot off the clutch and give it some gas."

Ella did as she was told. The car rolled forward.

"That's it," Kate said. "Give it more gas. Ease it back onto the road."

Soon Ella had the car cruising along. Darkness and intermittent flashes of light flew past her window and streaked across her eyes, but Ella didn't see anything aside from the road directly in front of her.

"You're moving at a good clip now," Kate said. "I can't believe you didn't think you could drive this car."

"That's just because I ain't driven one before," Ella said.

"What?!" Kate said, laughing. "Never?"

"Never," Ella said. "Never until now."

She pressed her foot more firmly on the gas pedal. The car picked up speed. With each second that passed, Ella felt as if another layer of time, another layer of herself were peeling away. It thrilled her. She thought of a book she'd read when she was a girl, *The Time Machine,* one of the few books her mother had had in the string-house at the lumber camp. She remembered how the machine had allowed the Time Traveler to go back millions of years, and she imagined herself doing that now as she rocketed through space in what felt like the middle of the night. She did not know about fuel or mileage or any of the particulars of automobile travel, but she felt that if she could just keep driving in the straight line in which she was driving now, she could pass Bessemer City by, go through Shelby and Forest City, past Hendersonville and Asheville and into the Smoky Mountains. She didn't want to go back millions of years. She just wanted to go back far enough to find herself as the young girl who'd never left home, whose mother and father were both still alive, whose children somehow existed in the world as well and would be waiting for her on the porch at the lumber camp.

ELLA WANTED TO drive past American Mill No. 2. She wanted to slow down, pull into the gravel lot in front of it, lean her elbows on the horn until the night shift came outside. She wanted to stand up on the hood and organize them all right there. Mostly, though she didn't want to admit it, she wanted them to see her inside this fancy car with a woman dressed as fine as Kate. She wanted Goldberg's brother and Dobbins to come out and get an eyeful of Ella May behind the wheel of an Essex Super Six.

But instead, she kept driving as she drew closer to the mill, and then she drove past the turn she would have taken that led right to it. She reached the crossroads, the same crossroads where she'd been standing and waiting when Sophia and Velma appeared on the horizon. She turned left on the Kings Mountain Highway and headed for Stumptown. Her foot found the brake, and she slowed when they got closer to the road that would take them down into the cluster of cabins and trees.

"I don't think I should drive down in there," Ella said. "We might get stuck. Water runs off the highway and swamps the road."

"Oh," Kate said. "Of course. Maybe pull off here. We can leave the car and walk."

"You don't have to do that," Ella said. "I'm fine to go on my own. It's what I'm used to."

"I want to see you home," Kate said, "and I want to see where you live."

"You don't want to see it," Ella said. "There's nothing to see. You probably live in a big, fine home. I'd be embarrassed for you to see mine."

"Don't be silly," Kate said. "I'm sure it's lovely."

Ella parked the car and took the keys from the ignition. She closed her hand around them for just a moment before giving them to Kate. The two women crossed the road and walked down into Stumptown. It had stopped raining, but it was cloudy, and there wasn't much light.

"Watch where you walk now," Ella said. "There's holes that'll get your shoes good and wet. Just walk along behind me. I could do this with my eyes closed."

A few lights burned in the cabins they passed, and a few people recognized Ella's shape as she moved down the road toward home. They called out to her, and she said hello, said, "I've got a friend here with me," and they said, "Okay, well, y'all have a good night," and Ella said, "You too."

"How did you come to live here?" Kate asked.

"You mean how'd I come to live with colored folks?"

"Well, I didn't mean—"

"Because I'm poor," Ella said. "And they're poor too." She turned around, faced Kate, and walked backward for a moment. She lifted her arms as if showcasing everything around her. "And here we all are."

Lilly had an oil lamp burning inside the cabin, and she and Rose were sitting on the floor, playing a game. Their fingers were threaded with yarn, and they moved their hands in a way that weaved some kind of pattern. Wink was asleep on one of the skids, his face turned away from the light.

"Otis is still out somewhere," Lilly said. "I told him to be home before it got dark, but he don't care a lick about nothing I tell him."

"I'll get after him," Ella said. She smoothed down Lilly's hair, bent and kissed Rose. She saw that Lilly stared up at Kate. Rose noted her sister's interest in something, and she lifted her face and looked up at Kate too.

"This is my friend," Ella said. "This is Miss Kate."

Kate held her hands behind her back, but she lifted one of them and gave the girls a small wave. She looked over to where the baby slept.

"Hello," she whispered.

Lilly raised her hand and waved back, but neither she nor Rose said anything.

"These are my babies," Ella said. She put her hand back on Lilly's head. "This here's Lilly, my oldest. And this is Rose, and that's Joseph over there. We all call him Wink."

"It's 'cause he winks instead of blinks," Rose said. She pointed to her eyes and did her best to wink one and then the other at Kate.

"That's right," Ella said. "He winks when he blinks."

Rose laughed, looked back at her sister. The girls returned to their game.

"Did you eat?" Ella asked.

"Yes, ma'am," Lilly said. "We ate what you left out."

"Good," Ella said.

"Did Otis eat?"

"Yes, ma'am," Lilly said.

Ella walked to the stove, found a biscuit that Lilly had left behind for her. A small cut of salt meat had hardened in the pan. Ella looked up at Kate, who was standing just inside the door. She hadn't moved.

"You hungry?" Ella asked.

"No," Kate said. "I'm fine. Really. I couldn't eat a thing."

OTIS HAD COME in a few minutes after Ella and Kate had arrived. Ella had made him introduce himself to Kate, made him take her hand "like a grown man should do when he meets a lady." Otis was shy; he always had been. He stood barefoot, the bottoms of his pant legs damp.

"I don't like you being out there after it gets dark," Ella had said. "What would you do if some booger came along and tried to snatch you up and run off with you?"

"I'd punch him right in his nose," Otis said.

"Some boogers don't got noses," Ella said. "So you'd be in real trouble if you met up with one of them, wouldn't you."

Kate had stood by while Ella put each of the children to bed, Rose first, then Otis, and Lilly last. She kissed each one of them, pulled a thin sheet up around each of their shoulders even though the night was warm. Lilly curled up beside the baby like she always did. He'd begun to snore.

"Y'all want a song?" Ella had asked.

Lilly and Rose had nodded their heads *yes,* but Otis hadn't responded. He always wanted Ella to sing them to sleep whenever she was home for their bedtime, but Ella knew that now he was trying to look tough in front of Kate.

"What do y'all want to hear?" Ella asked.

Lilly turned and looked toward Kate, who'd taken off her jacket and sat down on the floor. Her legs were curled beneath her. She propped herself up with her right hand.

"Do you know any songs?" Lilly asked her.

Kate seemed surprised. She picked up her hand, dusted her palms against one another, and leaned toward Lilly, readjusting herself so she could get closer.

"I do," she said. "I know some songs. My daughter used to be your age, and I used to sing to her just like your mother sings to you. But my little girl's old now. She's getting married soon."

"What's her name?" Lilly asked.

"Claire," Kate said. "Her name's Claire. And she's marrying a nice man named Paul."

"What songs do you know?" Lilly asked.

"'Two Little Blackbirds' is my favorite," Rose said.

"That's a good one," Kate said. "Does everybody like that one?" Ella watched as Kate looked toward Otis. He nodded his head *yes.* Kate looked over at Ella, smiled. "I'd be embarrassed to sing in front of you," she said.

"You shouldn't be," Ella said. "I bet you've got a fine singing voice."

Kate cleared her throat, took a moment as if she were trying to recall the words. Then she began:

> *Two little blackbirds sitting on a hill.*
> *One named Jack, one named Jill.*

Her voice was soft and high, much higher-pitched than Ella knew her own to be. Ella joined in after the first stanza, listened as her deep tone merged with Kate's.

> *Fly away, Jack. Fly away, Jill.*
> *Come back, Jack. Come back, Jill.*

A few more stanzas and, one by one, the children had all closed their eyes.

Now Ella and Kate sat in silence side by side on the cabin's steps. They both stared into the darkness of the road that led up out of Stumptown. Ella hadn't known what to do with her new friend after she'd put the children to bed. But then she'd remembered a near-empty Mason jar of whiskey that Charlie had hidden beneath the house. She'd found the jar and poured what was left of the liquor, which was barely enough to cover the bottoms of two jars, and she'd given one of them to Kate. She suggested they sit on the steps while the children settled themselves into sleep.

"It turned out to be a beautiful night, didn't it," Kate said.

It was true. Once the rain stopped for good and the clouds drifted away, a quarter moon had revealed itself. The night was full of night sounds: the chirps of crickets, the occasional frog, the gurgle of the creek off in the woods where it was fed by the spring. Ella could hear a woman's voice somewhere up the road, but it was too far away to know who it was or what she was saying. The smell of cigarette smoke drifted past Ella's nose before vanishing. Ella cupped her free hand around her stomach, fixed her mind on the small life that stirred there.

"You said your daughter's about to get married," she said. "How old is she?"

"She's twenty-two," Kate said. "And she's home for the summer. It's nice to have a child in the house again, no matter how old she is."

The question burst from Ella's chest before she fully understood that she had spent all night preparing to ask it.

"Why'd you want to meet me?" She looked down at the jar in her hand, turned it back and forth. "Why would somebody like you want to meet somebody like me? Let me drive your car? Follow me home? Meet my children?" She looked over at Kate. "Why?"

Kate tipped her jar up, drank what was left. She set it on the steps beside her.

"Tonight, before you sang, you told the story of how your little boy died. Isn't it difficult to tell people something so private?"

"It's hard for me to say why I tell that story," Ella said. "I didn't used to talk about it. It used to be that I didn't want to think about it. But I think about it now. I think about it all the time: his face, how his body felt when I held him, how his breath smelled sweet after he nursed." Something caught in her throat, and she feared that she might find herself in tears, something that hadn't happened in a long time.

"We don't have to talk about it," Kate said. Ella felt Kate's hand on her shoulder. "I'm sorry."

"No," Ella said, "I don't mind talking about it. I just hadn't thought of that sweet breath in a while." She looked at Claire. "You know what I'm talking about? The way a baby's breath smells sweet and sugary after it nurses, after it's fallen asleep with your nipple in its mouth, and you take it off and hold its face up against yours, and you can smell its lips, smell its breath when it breathes?"

"Yes," Kate said. Her eyes glistened. "I know. I remember it."

Ella turned away from Kate, looked out into the darkness before her.

"I don't know if you were raised in the church," she said, "but I was. I was raised Baptist. We always hopped around from church to church depending on where my daddy was working, but my mother was a fiery believer. My daddy wanted to stay on her good side." She smiled, allowed herself a small laugh that cut through her sadness;

with it came a quick memory of her mother and father's faces, and then they were gone. "So that meant Daddy was a fiery one too.

"In a church like the ones I was raised in, it was normal for folks to get up and talk about how the Lord had moved in their lives. When you're holy, when you're filled up with the spirit, you want people to know you've earned it, and you want to tell about it. People want to know that you've earned it too. Speaking at these rallies is something like that for me. Being poor, losing my baby, fighting for what I'm fighting for: it's the same thing as getting up in front of that church and telling those people how the Lord's moved in your life. You've earned that story. I've earned mine. I've earned this being sad, this loss, this being angry. I want to tell it to people so they'll know what it means to earn it. Plenty of the women who've heard me, probably a good bit of the men too, have lived the same kind of life I've lived. They need to know they're not alone."

She stopped speaking, considered saying nothing else, but she couldn't help it. She had to know.

"But you didn't answer what I asked you," Ella said. "Why'd you want to meet me?"

Kate dropped her hands into her lap, parted her knees, looked down at her feet. "I was seventeen when I married Richard," she said. "Not much older than you were when you married your husband. After he finished school we were married in my parents' church in Hickory, and then we moved to McAdamville so he could start working for his father." She sighed, laughed quietly just once. "I was young. I didn't know anything about my body, I certainly didn't know anything about his. I was probably three months pregnant before I realized it."

Kate raised her head, folded her arms over her knees.

"Richard was overjoyed. We both were, really. I thought that's what it meant to be a wife, to support your husband. You saw him off to work in the morning and saw him home in the evening and you gave him a baby as soon as you could.

"Richard took me to the doctor, and the doctor felt around on my belly. Oh, you know how they poke at you. And he put something to my stomach and tried to hear the baby. He said if I was right about how long I'd been pregnant, then the baby should be big enough to hear it inside there. But he didn't hear anything, and I couldn't feel anything either, and it made me wonder if I'd been mistaken. I was afraid that I'd made the whole thing up.

"And then my belly got bigger and bigger, and I knew a baby was growing inside me, and I could feel it inside there too. And when I went back to the doctor he felt around and poked at me some more and said the baby was too small. He listened and said the baby's heart was too small. He said things might not be okay, but I didn't believe him. At least I didn't want to. I thought, Here you were thinking you might not be pregnant, but you are. Anything's possible. Things could turn out fine.

"But they didn't. When he was born he was so small, Ella." She cupped her hands before her. "I remember him fitting right in the palm of one of my hands, but I know that can't be true. Surely he wasn't that small, but that's how I remember him. He was beautiful, but he was so little. And he wouldn't nurse, wouldn't hardly open his eyes. The doctor said he was sick. He didn't know what with, but he never got better. And then we lost him a few days later."

She held her hands to her mouth as if trying to keep the words inside. She sighed, looked over at Ella.

"I'm sorry to come all the way out here and tell you a story like this," Kate said. "I've just never told anyone before. Richard won't talk about it. I got pregnant with Claire a few years later, and I was scared to death. When she was born it was such a relief. I was so afraid to let go of her, terrified of her not being at my breast where I could see her, see all of her, and make sure she was okay. I wondered if I worried over her so much because I was trying to forget what happened. We never talked about it. We never told Claire, we still haven't. But now I know that I worried over her because I still worried over our son. I still thought of his face every time I saw hers, still felt his body in my hands each time I lifted her to me. I still think of him every day."

She put her hands to her eyes and held them there for a moment, and then she wiped at her nose and folded her arms back across her knees. She looked at Ella. Ella saw that her eyes had grown wet again.

"It's like what you said earlier," Kate said. "What you said after I told you about my brother. You said it doesn't get easier when you lose someone you love."

"It doesn't," Ella said. She lifted her right hand and put it on Kate's shoulder, and then she put her arm all the way around her. Kate scooted closer. Ella felt her lean toward her.

"It's brave of you to tell your story," Kate said. "I don't know how you do it."

"Living through it is the brave part," Ella said. "You don't know it when it's happening, but living through it's the hardest. After that the telling about it's easy."

The two women sat that way a little while longer, Ella with her arm around Kate, Kate with her head on Ella's shoulder. Ella had a sense of the night growing darker, quieter. She no longer heard people's voices. She didn't see light from any cabins coming through the trees. She wondered if Kate had fallen asleep, but then Kate sighed, spoke.

"It's getting late," Kate said. She stirred. Ella lifted her arm, and Kate sat up, moved away from her. She looked at Ella as if she were embarrassed by something she'd said or done. She took a deep breath, held it for a moment, and then released a long sigh. "I'm sorry to have put all this on you," she said. "I didn't plan to tell you that story."

"No," Ella said. "I'm glad you told it to me."

"It's just that I don't have very many friends," Kate said. "It's hard. It's hard to find friends sometimes."

"I'll be your friend," Ella said.

"Okay," Kate said. She smiled. "I'll be your friend too."

Movement in the road in front of her cabin caught Ella's eye. Both women looked up at the same time. A figure came toward them in the darkness. As it grew closer Ella could tell that it was a man, and by the time he reached her yard she could tell that it was Charlie. He held a rifle. He smiled. Ella could tell he was drunk.

"There you are," he said.

"Here I am," she said.

He looked at the jars sitting on the steps beside Ella and Kate. "Y'all having a party?"

"No," Ella said.

"It sure looks like a party," he said. He reached toward Ella and picked up her glass. He downed the whiskey in one swallow. He stumbled, dropped the rifle at his feet, bent to pick it up. Kate moved up one step so that she sat on the porch. Ella could feel her new friend's fear.

"What do you want, Charlie?" Ella asked.

He looked at Kate. "Who are you?"

"She's my friend," Ella said. "What do you want?"

He laughed. "No, all your friends are niggers," he said. Kate gasped at the word.

"Go home, Charlie," Ella said. "Sleep it off."

"You can't tell me what to do," he said. "Not when you say you got my baby inside you. You can't tell me nothing." He lifted the rifle, held it with two hands, kept it pointed toward the woods alongside the cabin. "And I don't believe you anyway," Charlie said. "That ain't my baby. It's probably some nigger baby."

"It won't be your baby," Ella said. "It'll be mine."

Charlie turned the rifle so that it pointed at Ella's chest. She could hear him breathing, could hear the gurgle of the spring behind the cabin, could hear Kate's struggle to keep from crying.

"Charlie, if you're going to shoot me, then at least let me go inside and make sure my babies got something for breakfast," she said. "Ain't no use in them finding me dead and being hungry too."

Kate scooted away from them toward the cabin's door, and when Charlie looked toward the sound, Ella reached out and snatched the rifle from his hands. She turned it on him, pointed it at his chest exactly where he'd just pointed it at hers.

"Go home, Charlie," she said. "I ain't got no use for this rifle, so you can have it back tomorrow, but I can't let you keep it tonight."

"You bitch," he said. He looked at Kate. "That's what y'all are: a couple of bitches."

"Don't talk nasty, Charlie," Ella said. "Like you said, she's my only white friend. Don't go and run her off."

Charlie spit at the ground by the porch steps. "I'm coming back for my gun," he said.

"Not tonight you ain't," Ella said. She held the gun on him as he backed out of the yard and turned and walked up the road toward the Kings Mountain Highway. Ella watched him until he disappeared, and then she lowered the butt of the rifle to the ground and leaned it against the porch steps. She looked back at Kate where she sat, saw that her eyes were closed, her hand covering her heart.

"He's gone," Ella said.

Kate opened her eyes; a tear slid down her cheek. "Who was that?" she asked.

"That was nobody," Ella said, "but damn it if he don't want to be somebody."

"Is he really—" She stopped, as if trying to find the right words. "Are you—"

"Yes," Ella said.

Ella turned away, looked down the porch steps and out into the dark yard toward the empty road. She felt Kate's eyes on her.

"How far along are you?"

"Not far," Ella said.

"Has he threatened you before?" Kate asked.

"Oh, yes," Ella said. She wanted to laugh, but she knew it would be inappropriate and that someone like Kate would not understand.

"He talks a game, but he's a coward. He sold his guitar for this rifle. He likes to show it to me like it means something."

"Do you think he'd use it?" Kate asked.

"No," Ella said. "He talks a game, though."

"Do you feel safe?" Kate asked. "Are you and your children safe here?"

"Yes," Ella said. "We're as safe here as we would be anywhere else. I'm not scared of Charlie, I just feel stupid. I should've known better."

Kate's jacket was folded and sitting on the other side of her. She reached for it, brought it to her, unfolded it across her lap. She reached into one of the pockets and removed an envelope. She stared at it for a moment, and then she held it out to Ella.

"What's this?" Ella asked.

"It's for you," Kate said. "I'm sorry. I'm embarrassed to give it to you. I know you'll be too proud to take it, but I want you to have it."

Ella took the envelope and opened it. It was too dark to see what was inside without removing it, and once she did she found money, at least five twenty-dollar bills, maybe more. She slid the money back into the envelope, closed it, held it out to Kate.

"Thank you," Ella said. "It's real kind of you, but I can't accept it. I can't raise my children to be too proud to accept charity and then accept yours. I can't face them with somebody else's money in my hand."

"It was in my hands before it was in yours," Kate said. "But it didn't belong to me. It passed through my husband's hands, but it didn't belong to him either."

"Who's it belong to then?" Ella asked.

"Whoever earned it," Kate said. "Probably somebody just like you. If we're friends, like you said we are, then you'll take it."

Ella looked at the envelope. Inside was at least ten weeks of what her pay had been at the American Mill.

"Please," Kate said. She pushed Ella's hand until the envelope it held rested on Ella's lap. "Please accept it." She reached into another pocket on her jacket and pulled out a small tablet and pencil. She wrote something down, tore the paper free. "And if we're friends then you'll remember me," she said, "and you'll come find me if you ever need anything." She folded the paper and slid it into the envelope beside the money.

"Thank you," Ella said. "I won't forget this. And I'll pay you back as soon as I can."

"Please don't," Kate said. "And please don't even think of it." She stared at Ella for a moment, reached out, closed her hand over both of Ella's where they rested on her lap. "It's late," she said, smiling. "I may not care about my husband's opinions of me, but I also don't want him to contact the police and report me missing."

"I'll walk you up," Ella said. She picked up Charlie's rifle. "Make sure you feel safe."

"No," Kate said. "I'll be fine." She stood up and stepped off the bottom step. She turned, looked down at Ella. "I know the way."

"You sure?" Ella asked. "Charlie's harmless, especially to someone like you. He's probably passed out somewhere by now anyway."

"I'll be okay," Kate said. "I'll yell for you if I need you. You can come save me." She put on her jacket and cinched its belt around her waist. "It was wonderful to meet you, Ella." She reached down, took Ella's hand. "I hope I see you again."

"I hope so too," Ella said.

Kate squeezed Ella's hand, then turned and walked up the road. Ella watched her go, watched until the darkness swallowed her. Her first thought was to gather the jars, go inside, and hide the money. Put it out of her mind and fall asleep quickly. She'd get up in the morning and tend to the children, spend the day canvassing the mills.

But right now, she didn't have to move, did she? She could sit on the cabin's steps and let the warm, humid night fold itself around her. She'd go inside soon enough. She'd hide the money. She'd lie in bed and allow herself to go over each step of the evening, to recall each thing she'd said and heard, everything she'd seen. She'd sleep well and wake in the morning and see her children. She closed her fingers around the envelope, remembered that Kate had written down the address of her home in McAdamville. Ella's life, which had already changed so much in such little time, had changed again.

The sound of music drifted toward her where she sat. She raised her head and listened, wondered if it was Fox Denton's phonograph, something she'd never heard this far down the road. She closed her eyes, listened closely, and then she heard the music for what it was: the faraway sound of Kate singing "Two Little Blackbirds" as she walked up the road alone.

CHAPTER TEN

Hampton Haywood

Monday, June 3, 1929

His father had shot and killed a white man in Mississippi in 1910. Hampton had been six years old at the time and had slept through the sound of the man yelling and beating on one side of the cabin's door while his mother and father whispered and prayed on the other. But what he hadn't slept through was the sound of the shotgun blast. It had jarred him awake. He opened his eyes, moved his body just enough to look at his two-year-old sister Summer where she lay in bed looking back at him, her open eyes portraying the same measure of fear and surprise that she must have seen in his own.

His mother threw open the bedroom door and struggled to lift Hampton and Summer from the bed at the same time. Hampton had a clear memory of clawing through the blankets as he and his mother fumbled their way toward one another, while Summer cried at the fear of seeing their mother move with such silent fury. Hampton's mother carried him and Summer into the cabin's other room. She sat him down, and he watched while she balanced Summer on her hip and gathered what food they had: biscuits, a jar of preserves, dried beans.

Hampton watched his father lean the shotgun in the corner, watched him reach for the framed picture of a praying Jesus that hung on the wall. He removed the small photograph that had, for as long as Hampton could remember, sat in the corner of the frame. His father looked at the photograph for a moment. It was a picture some-one had taken of him and Hampton's mother not long after they'd been married, when she was sixteen and he only two years older. He slid the photograph into the front pocket of his overalls, bent to the mattress he shared with Hampton's mother, and slipped his hands beneath it and ran them along the floor. He gathered folded dollar bills and a few loose coins and slid them into the same front pocket. Hampton's father stood and took in the room as if he already knew for certain it would be the last time he'd see it. He found a sack, began to stuff the family's clothes inside.

His father hurried out of the bedroom, the sack of clothes in one hand, the shotgun in the other. No one had spoken yet.

Hampton's father cradled the shotgun in the crook of his right arm, knelt and scooped up Hampton. He felt the shotgun press against his back. He turned his head, saw the barrel inches from his face, smelled the bitter residue of its blast.

"Lydia," his father said. "Let's go." Hampton's mother did not re-spond, and she did not turn around. She adjusted Summer on her hip, continued the search for food. "Lydia," he said again.

She stopped moving. Tears streaked her cheeks. She wiped them away with her free hand and then picked up the sack of food she'd gathered.

The cabin's interior had been whitewashed years earlier. Hampton saw that the buckshot had left a hole and what appeared to be dozens of black fingerprints on the door where the dark night seeped into their home. Hampton had never been awake this late at night, and that, combined with the sound of the shotgun, told him that he should be terrified of what could be waiting for them outside.

He was never able to recall whether there had been much of a moon in the sky that night, so perhaps it was the light coming from inside the cabin that allowed Hampton to see the body of the white man where it lay at the bottom of the steps.

"Don't look," his father had whispered. He'd hugged Hampton tight to his chest. "Don't look," his father had said again, but Hampton had looked anyway.

His father had given the body a wide berth as he'd stepped into the yard. The man's face was turned and shadowed in a way that Hampton could not see it. But he could see that the man wore a dark suit, that his dark tie had fallen over his right cheek, that his white shirt had been blown open and soaked through with blood. The fingers of his right hand remained closed around a small silver gun. Hampton looked beyond the body and noticed something white resting at the edge of the darkness. At first he thought that the white object must have been a chicken, and he wondered why his father did not stop and grab it and take it with them. But soon Hampton saw that what he'd mistaken for a chicken was the white man's hat.

His father did not begin running until they reached the edge of the field.

Behind them, his mother ran with Summer in her arms, the sack of food swinging against her thigh. Of all the things Hampton remembered, what he remembered most clearly was the way his father smelled on the night the family escaped, his face buried in his father's neck, the shotgun barrel bumping against his back with each step his father took. The scent he recalled was something he had not smelled since, yet he often found himself longing for it: the earthiness of his father's skin, the damp delta soil, and the perfume of the humid Mississippi night.

"That white man wanted blood for his daddy's honor," Hampton's mother would say many times in the years that followed. His parents had been sharecroppers, both of them born to former slaves. Hampton grew up hearing his mother tell the story. "Old Newcomb was holding out on us, and your daddy knew it. But every year, he'd put his specs on and thumb through his books and say, 'Sorry, Glen, you just barely broke even.' But your daddy knew it was a lie, and he finally called him on it. Said, 'No, sir. Not this year, Mr. Newcomb. I need my money.' And that was it. Newcomb's son came around that night, drunk, banging on the door, screaming for your daddy to come out. People killed over honor back then. They still do. Well, your daddy had his honor too.

"Of course we had to leave. You can't kill a white man down south, especially not in Mississippi, and expect to live." And leaving was what they had been doing that night as they fled across the cotton field.

They had run to Hampton's grandfather's house. The old man lived five miles away on a different plantation. He couldn't have been much older than sixty, but his stooped and arthritic body had been broken by field work and former masters long before it had been freed. Hampton's mother went inside and roused her father. The old man lit a lantern and led them through the woods to a neighbor's cabin that sat tucked back in the trees, where the family hid in a crawl space beneath the floorboards. The earth there was musky, and even now Hampton's nose remembered it, just like his ears remembered his mother's whispered prayers and his bones still felt the thundering heartbeat where he leaned against his father's chest and waited.

At dawn came the sound of a horse-drawn wagon creaking to a stop out front. A door opened and someone lifted Hampton and then Summer into the weak light of the early morning and carried them outside, where their grandfather waited by the wagon. Hampton's father helped Hampton climb into the back, set Summer on his lap. The sound of brief goodbyes, his grandfather's voice, his mother's crying, his father saying, "Come on, now. Time to go." His parents climbed into the wagon. The driver, a man whose face he could not remember, snapped the reins. Hampton's last memory of the land from which he'd sprung was the image of his grandfather standing with the shotgun in his hand. He lifted it over his head in goodbye. Then he turned back toward the forest and the path that would lead him home. They never saw the old man again.

Whoever had driven the wagon dropped them at the train station in Vicksburg. In the brief hours they'd spent beneath the floorboards of the house, a collection had been taken up, and the money was now used to purchase the family's tickets. Hampton had clear memories of the colored car because the colored cars had not changed since that day. He could still smell the train and hear the great hiss of the engine because, as a Pullman porter, he would smell and hear those things for the rest of his life.

It was not until the train had left the station that Hampton's father allowed himself a sigh and his mother allowed herself to shed any tears of fear she'd kept behind her eyes since fleeing only hours before. Hampton knew they must have been a sight, this family of four covered in mud and brambles, nothing with them but two ill-stuffed sacks and the dirty clothes they wore. He would laugh at the sight of these country folks if he had not been one of them.

It was at the next stop, Yazoo City, that the porter came to them and bent to his father's ear and whispered something that Hampton could not hear. Hampton's father turned to his mother, took her hands and kissed them, bent his head, and held her palms to his forehead. He picked up Summer where she lay sleeping on the seat and placed her in his lap, buried his face in her hair, and closed his eyes. Hampton listened as his father took deep breaths.

The porter said, "They're going to come on," and Hampton's mother began to cry. His father put his arm around her, pulled her toward him, kissed her on the mouth. He lowered Summer onto her lap. He reached for Hampton, pulled him close so that he stood before his father, nearly eye-level. "You be a man for her," his father said. He spread his heavy hand across Hampton's chest, ran his palm along his face and over his head, the work-worn calluses catching in Hampton's hair. He reached into the front pocket of his overalls and removed the folded bills and slipped them into Hampton's hand.

People in the car understood what was happening and what was about to happen. They began to move away from the family. Hampton looked up and saw two police officers standing above him. They reached down, took Hampton's father by his shoulders, raised him to his feet. Hampton watched them escort his father through the car and off the train. His mother sobbed, pulled Summer to her chest, reached a hand toward Hampton. "They just going to talk to him," she said. "They just going to talk to him."

She was still saying that as the brakes released, the cars moved forward, and the train left the station. She was still saying it as the train pulled farther away, gathered speed, and rocketed north.

Hampton sat down beside his mother, felt her hand on his shoulder, leaned toward her as she pulled him close. She'd buried her face in Summer's hair, but he could feel her body heaving in sobs. Summer tapped her mother's arm, said, "Mama, Mama." Hampton looked down at the money his father had given him. He unfolded the bills, saw that they'd been wrapped around the old photograph of his mother and father on their wedding day. He stared down at their young, unsmiling faces as they stared back at him.

He kept the photograph in his wallet after that, and for years he teased his mother about not smiling in what she referred to her as her wedding picture.

"Why ain't you and Daddy smiling if y'all were so happy?"

"People didn't smile in photographs back in those days," she always said. "Aside from us getting married, there wasn't nothing to smile about."

The entire course of events of their lives and the events' telling and retelling over the years had conditioned Hampton both to fear and hate white people, especially white southerners and the land they inhabited, in ways he found impossible to explain. Unlike his father, he had not shot and killed a white man to keep that white man from shooting and killing him, but he had witnessed it, and in the witnessing he retained the memory of the shotgun's heft, the kick of its blast. He had not been plucked from a train and made to disappear like his father, the way so many black bodies had been made to disappear in the years before and after, but the simple fact of his continued existence made the possibility of his own disappearance all the more probable.

Growing up, Hampton had struggled to bypass the fear for his own life in favor of the pride he took in his father's, but now, returning to the South all alone for the very first time in his life at the age of twenty-five, the fear that sat in his belly like a stone was the only thing left of that night in Mississippi. Now that same fear crept up in his throat and left a metallic taste in his mouth. The South had taken itself from him when it took his father. He knew he couldn't get his father back, but perhaps in returning to the South and inhabiting the same world his father had inhabited, he'd be able to find something of him there. Maybe he'd even be able to change something about that world. This was his chance, but the cost of this chance was a paralyzing, unmitigated terror.

He'd boarded in New York before the sun had fully risen, then changed trains in Washington in midmorning. His final stop would be Charlotte, North Carolina, in the hours before midnight. He'd been promised that Fred Beal did not know about his trip south, had been promised that someone hand-chosen by Sophia Blevin, perhaps even Sophia herself, would meet him upon his arrival, although this was the South in 1929, and Hampton knew better than to believe his meeting a white woman at a train station would go unnoticed. After departing the train, he'd been instructed to head north on

Tryon and not to stop walking until someone approached him and said the secret word: *spindle.* That person would assure his safe passage to Gastonia and the strike at Loray.

Hampton looked out the train's window and watched fields of Virginia tobacco flash by in bright green blurs. The sun was setting, the edges of the tobacco leaves rimmed with golden light. He knew that, if he wanted to, he could remain seated when he arrived in Charlotte, then switch trains in Atlanta and again in Montgomery. He'd end up in New Orleans. He thought of spending the month of June in the Crescent City among Creole girls with soft drawls. They'd drink beer and eat fresh shrimp in the early summer heat. He'd love all the girls he'd meet, but he'd fall in love with one in particular, and he'd tell her the story of his father, who'd killed the white man who had tried to break down the family's front door.

On a Saturday morning, they'd jump a train to Vicksburg and find the piece of land where his parents' cabin still sat on the edge of the cotton field. Hampton would take the girl's hand and lead her down the rows of black earth, the white wisps of cotton—something he'd never seen up close before—gathering like snow around their feet. By now, all these years later, the cabin would have begun to lean one way or the other, and he'd tell the girl that it wasn't safe, to stay right there in the yard in front of the cabin with the hot sun on her back. He'd take the first tentative step, as if the stairs might collapse under his weight, but sensing their stability he'd go up onto the gallery—for that's what they called a porch down there—and find that the door had been left open, the sunlight filling the room like a houseguest. He'd creep a little farther, shuffle his feet so as not to upset the fragile state of the settled cabin or its equally fragile place in his family's history. He'd find the old wooden door where it had been left open against the wall, a spray of buckshot blown right through its middle. He'd step inside, close the door, witness the yellow sunlight blast itself through the myriad holes the shotgun's work had left behind.

The porch would creak under the weight of a footstep on the other side of the closed door. He would picture Newcomb's son, the pistol in his hand. His heartbeat would quicken. There was no shotgun for him to reach for. He did not own a gun, had never even fired one. And then he would hear the voice.

"Hampton, baby, you okay in there?"

It was Josephine. That would be her name.

Sitting there, in the colored car of the No. 33 train, Hampton tried to remember that this was not his *first* trip south. He'd been all the way down to New Orleans dozens and dozens of times. He'd been to St. Louis, Atlanta, Mobile, as far west as Houston. But as a Pullman porter he'd almost always stayed on the train. They'd never stop in a city for very long anyway. Just long enough to restock, take in the sights from the train platform while the passengers swirled around him before the whistle wail meant they were heading north again.

Regardless of whether that old cabin still sat on the edge of the field outside Vicksburg, Hampton's father's bravery in standing up to a white man cemented him as someone important in the collective mind of his family. Hampton's mother had always proclaimed that she was someone too, and she'd always made Hampton and his sister proclaim that they were someone as well.

"You're somebody, just as good as anybody," she would say, especially when it appeared that they were as close to being nobodies as anybody could ever be. When the white policeman knocked on the door and told Hampton's mother that he'd been caught stealing pies from a vendor, stood clenched with his fingers around Hampton's forearm, saw three-year-old Summer standing behind her, said, "It's a shame for a boy to grow up without a father," his mother had watched the policeman walk down the hallway; then she had turned to Hampton and said, "You're somebody, just as good as anybody." When Hampton had to feed Summer and wash her and put her to bed while his mother worked in a factory making gloves and his friends all called him a mama's boy because he no longer roamed the streets, his mother came home from work and kicked off her shoes and sat down and rubbed her feet and said, "You're somebody, just as good as anybody." When she began working as a housekeeper for Robert Binkerd, the assistant to the chairman for the Association of Railway Executives, and came home on the evening of her first day to find Hampton still in the sweaty overalls he wore at the loading docks, Summer still damp from her work at the laundry, she kicked off her shoes and sat down and rubbed her feet like she always did and said, "Mr. Binkerd told me it ain't unusual to have a Pullman porter young as you. He could put in a word. He offered." And once that offered word had been put in and a nice yet slightly too-small suit had been loaned and a meeting—which Hampton learned upon arrival was more of an audition—had been set up at the association's office, he stood in their tiny tenement room while his mother smoothed the lapels on the suit jacket and said, "You're somebody, just as good as anybody, and don't you forget it." And Hampton never once forgot.

He'd always known, felt, that he was somebody, and that's why, three years later, he'd joined the Brotherhood of Sleeping Car Porters after listening to A. Philip Randolph at a meeting of the Porters Athletic Association in Harlem. Everything about the forty-year-old Randolph had seemed deliberate to Hampton, and when Randolph spoke of the need for unionization in the face of increased work and stagnant wages, Hampton had been interested. But it wasn't until Randolph made clear that no other union would represent the black porters, that other unions had, in fact, treated them like a bunch of nobodies, that Hampton knew for certain that he wanted to become a union man.

And that was how it had all started.

From the night he first heard Randolph speak about worker solidarity, Hampton followed in his footsteps and joined the Socialist Party. It was on the sidewalk after a party meeting one night two years later that Hampton met a pretty white girl named Sophia

Blevin. It was mid-August of 1927. Humidity smothered the city like a wet blanket.

"Hey, brother," she said. She stood before him, her hip cocked to one side as if it alone could keep him from passing. She held a bucket in one hand, dozens of leaflets in the other. "Help your brothers and sisters on the Passaic picket line?" She rattled the bucket. Coins jingled inside. Hampton had never heard a white person address him as "brother." He smiled at the girl, dug into his pocket for a dime, and tossed it into the bucket.

"How old are you, *sister*?"

The girl looked down into the bucket, turned it so that the light from the streetlamp overhead caught the glint of the copper and silver inside. She studied the coins, puckered her lower lip as if satisfied with Hampton's contribution. She looked up at him, shook the dark curls away from her eyes, smiled, handed him a flyer.

"I'm seventeen," she said. "How old are you?"

She was the first white friend he'd ever had, and she introduced him to her other white friends, and then he had more. She was a communist. Her friends were communists.

"If you care about workers," Sophia said, "you'd better hook your wagon to the Communist Party. Socialism is acclimation through accommodation. It takes too long." She spoke in slogans, snatches of passages she'd read in books, heard from speeches, taglines party leaders had taught her to remember. Hampton didn't mind. He found her interesting, this young white girl from Pittsburgh with foreign parents and a heart for justice. "What this country needs is radical transformation," she said. "Workers' rights. Gender equality. Integration." The more he listened to her, the more Hampton agreed, and the more he saw it all as completely possible.

Sophia introduced Hampton to party leaders: Secretary Alec Weisbord, one of the organizers of the Passaic strike and the only one among them who'd traveled outside the country after the party had sent him to Mexico and Moscow; Velma Burch, a fellow orga-

nizer; and eventually Fred Beal, who was from Lawrence, Massa-
chusetts, and who, by the autumn of 1928, had organized the textile
strike in New Bedford, which everyone except Beal viewed as an
embarrassing failure.

"What the party needs is diversity," Sophia said. "What it needs
are more people like you, Hampton."

So, in the fall of 1928 Hampton set out to recruit his fellow Pullman porters into the Communist Party. A few of the men he worked
with, most of them much older than Hampton and with wives and
children to support back home, would attend the occasional meeting with him, nod their heads, even speak if they felt led to speak,
but they slowly drifted away, begged off when he invited them to
more meetings or organized rallies. One night, after a meeting of the
Brotherhood of Sleeping Car Porters, Hampton understood what
was happening.

At the conclusion of the evening, Randolph called Hampton's
name and asked him to come down to the speaker's stand at the front
of the room. Then, as the hall emptied out, Hampton watched Randolph gather his papers and file them into a suitcase before reaching
for his hat. He turned and looked at Hampton.

"Mr. Haywood," he said, "would you walk with me?"

They left the hall and turned west on 139th Street, walked toward
the river. It was January 1929. Mounds of dirty snow were piled beneath the streetlamps. Christmas decorations still hung in shop
windows. Hampton tipped his hat toward his eyes and pulled up
his coat's collar. He put his hands into its pockets. Randolph walked
beside him.

"What are you doing, Mr. Haywood?" he asked.

"I'm not sure what you mean, sir," Hampton said.

They kept walking, their shoes stepping alternately on cement,
ice, compacted snow.

"This girl," Randolph said, "this Blevin; how long have you
known her?"

"A year," Hampton said, caught off guard at the mention of Sophia's name. "A year and a half, maybe."

"How long have you known of her affiliations with the Communist Party?"

"For as long as I've known her."

"I see," Randolph said.

They stopped on the corner of Broadway. The night sky had begun to release tiny ribbons of snow. A diner sat on the corner. Inside, a young black boy and a man who could have been his father, a man about Hampton's age, were drinking something hot from the same mug. They passed it back and forth across the table. The boy said something, the man laughed. Hampton recalled his father's face, the sound of his laugh, the feel of his father's hand spread across his chest that morning on the train, his fingers passing over Hampton's head before he disappeared forever.

"You could have a future in the Brotherhood, Mr. Haywood," Randolph said. "You're young, hungry, smart. Don't ruin it. Don't encourage your brothers to ruin it."

"What are you saying?" Hampton asked.

"I'm suggesting that you stick with whom and what you know."

"You're telling me not to mix with white people," Hampton said.

"Not the ones who will get you killed. And, Mr. Haywood, there are many kinds of death."

With that, Randolph turned the corner and headed north on Broadway. Hampton watched him go; then he looked at the table inside the diner where the boy and the man had been sitting. They now stood by the cash register. The man let go of the boy's hand, reached for his wallet. The boy turned, saw Hampton staring at him through the window. He waved. Hampton waved back.

Hampton decided to leave the Brotherhood and threw himself into the Communist Party. He wanted to be bold, heroic. He wanted to lift all workers, not just himself and those who looked like him. He knew a story would be concocted about him somewhere along the way, a story that would take the form of some kind of official grievance against him. He'd be dismissed from his job as a Pullman porter. His coworkers would raise their eyebrows and shrug their shoulders as if in disbelief, but everyone knew that when you left the Brotherhood you left your job as well.

It had been more than five months since his walk with Randolph, and he'd stayed on the job as a Pullman porter so far, but he was certain the job wouldn't be there for him once he returned north after this trip to Gastonia.

Hampton had asked for an extended leave. He'd tried to keep his reason quiet from his supervisor, but it wouldn't be long before his coworkers knew what it was about, especially with his traveling by train, which is how the union decided he should travel. Randolph had already found out that Hampton knew Sophia Blevin, had found out that he'd joined the Communist Party. Surely he'd find out that Hampton was traveling south to organize black workers at the behest of Weisbord, who'd become secretary of the National Textile Workers Union. It was a secret too big, too political, too incendiary to keep.

The sunset burned outside the train's window. He'd reached North Carolina. The train had already passed through Greensboro, stopped in High Point. He'd traveled this route as a porter too many times to count, and he ticked off the stations as the train slowed down and passed through them: Thomasville, Lexington, Linwood. Spencer was next, then Salisbury.

A week ago he'd received a telegram from Sophia. "Sec. Weisbord says integrate," it read. "Beal says no. If Sec. asks please come."

A few days later, a note from Secretary Weisbord was delivered, and Hampton met with him the next day. Hampton found Weisbord at a park off West 124th Street. It was the last Friday in May. The city had returned to life after the long winter and the chilly spring. Weisbord sat on a bench that overlooked a pond. A fountain pulsed at its center, tossing sprays of water that were misted by the breeze.

Weisbord was a short, dark-haired man who wore spectacles, but the measured way in which he spoke made him seem more commanding. Hampton sat down beside him.

"Thank you for coming," Weisbord said. He finished eating a sandwich of some kind and crumpled the paper that had been wrapped around it. He slipped the paper into his pocket. "I know it's sudden."

"I was glad to hear from you," Hampton said. "Sophia mentioned that I might."

"Good," Weisbord said. He reached into his coat pocket for a packet of cigarettes. He offered the cigarettes to Hampton, but he shook his head. Weisbord lit a cigarette and settled his back against the bench. "So you might know that I'm concerned about the situation in North Carolina. Like you, I've been in communication with Miss Blevin. Loray is back at full production." He took a drag on his cigarette, picked a piece of tobacco from his tongue. "The strikers are leaving the picket line and going back to work until payday, and then they're walking out again. As you can imagine, Mr. Haywood, a cycle like this will not keep a strike alive. Loray has no incentive to respect us if profit is not affected. Creating a nuisance isn't enough, but a nuisance is all we are. Beal isn't being honest with himself, or us."

"It seems that Mr. Beal has a history of not being honest with himself, sir," Hampton said.

"I would agree," Weisbord said. "His new plan is to hold a rally on the night of June seventh, which is a payday, the day workers are most willing to walk off the job. Beal wants to gather a mass of strikers to march down to the gates of Loray and demand that the night shift walks out." He smoked, uncrossed his legs, leaned forward so that Hampton couldn't see his eyes.

"It's a fine plan, not unlike other plans Beal has had, but the party has a plan as well." Weisbord stopped speaking and looked at Hampton for a moment, then he looked back toward the pond. He took a final drag on his cigarette and dropped it at his feet, crushing it with the toe of his shoe. "The Comintern wants to integrate all branches of the National Textile Workers Union, even our Gastonia Local," he said. "They believe it's time. So do I, but Beal doesn't agree. His argument is that white strikers are not prepared to work alongside blacks. He worries that it could make trouble."

Hampton's mind exploded with images he'd seen on postcards and in the newspapers: black bodies, some of them burned, hanging from trees or lying in roadside ditches, riddled with bullet holes. He thought of the cabin in Mississippi, the flight through the cotton field, the long, dark night beneath the floorboards of the strange house.

As if he'd been able to see the thoughts as they roiled across Hampton's mind, Weisbord said, "We can't let fear and oppression win, Mr. Haywood." He put his hand on Hampton's shoulder. "Especially when fear and oppression are propagated by our brothers and sisters in this struggle," he said. "Imagine if, on June seventh, the Loray bosses look out their windows and find hundreds, maybe thousands, of black and white workers walking the picket line, side by side. What kind of message would that send to the bosses? What kind of message would that send to other mills, other workers, white and black? The Loray strike could become a general strike all across the South. We could turn the tide for labor."

He leaned back against the bench.

"Mr. Haywood, I do not know you well, but I know your story well enough to know that you are a son of the South. Regardless of what brought you here, to the North, the South is your homeland, and the black men and women there are your people. They need a leader. Could it be you?"

Hampton looked at the pond at the center of the park. Two white children, brothers perhaps, in blue sailor suits pushed small sailboats out into the water. Hampton watched the boys and thought of Weisbord's proposal. He dropped his gaze from the pond and took a breath, nodded his head *yes*.

"Wonderful," said Weisbord. "Wonderful."

"When?" asked Hampton.

"Monday," Weisbord said. "Your ticket will be ready."

THE TRAIN'S BRAKES squealed, and Hampton felt the cars slow as they drew closer to the Salisbury station. It was almost 9 P.M. He'd be in Charlotte in a few hours. After that, he didn't know what would happen.

The train stopped. Outside, the night was dark but for the few lights that lit the station. Hampton could see the shapes of people milling about the platform. He kept his seat and watched as a few people around him gathered their things and exited the colored car. Some of them had been traveling with him since New York, but he hadn't spoken to anyone aside from the few porters he knew. He looked up to see one of the porters, a middle-aged man named Gerald, walking toward him. He'd spoken to him when he'd first boarded. Hampton had brought a sandwich with him and had asked for nothing during the trip, although Gerald had brought him a cup of coffee that afternoon.

Gerald looked around as if waiting for more people to exit the train, or perhaps he was looking to see who would enter the car.

"Hampton," Gerald whispered, "there's some white men on the platform. They're asking for you."

It felt as if the ceiling had come down around Hampton and the sky on top of it. Gerald said something else, but Hampton either could not hear him or his mind was panicked, unable to register the words he heard. He turned his head one way and then the other, hoping that one of his ears could pick up the sounds and understand what they meant, but neither ear seemed to be working.

"What?" Hampton asked. The words crossed his lips like a whisper. He considered placing his hand over his heart to keep it inside his chest.

Gerald looked from Hampton to the windows on the other side of the car. He lowered his head as if searching for a specific face out on the dark platform.

"White men," Gerald said, looking from the window back to Hampton, "out there. They told me to get you off the train."

Hampton looked out the window beside him. He didn't see anyone, but he was afraid of standing and trying to get a better look. He remembered the two policemen who took his father off a train not much different than this one. "Is it the police?"

"No," Gerald said, and in that answer Hampton understood that perhaps a fate worse than his father's awaited him.

"What do they want?" Hampton asked.

"I don't know," Gerald said. The man's forehead glistened. He was nervous, perhaps just as scared as Hampton. "I don't want any trouble, Hamp."

A few people sitting close to Hampton seemed to understand what was happening. They turned their faces away from Hampton as if not witnessing what could happen would keep it from happening.

"What do they want, Gerry?" he asked. "Please, ask them. Please."

Gerald looked to the window again, nodded his head, left the car.

Hampton sat and watched him go. His mind ran through the possibilities of who could be asking for him out on the platform. Had the Loray Mill sent men to Salisbury to pull him off the train? Had they heard that it was Sophia, a white woman, who'd invited him down?

And then he remembered the white girl on the train from D.C. just a few weeks ago: What was her name? Donna. She was from Salisbury. There'd been a man with her that night in the dining car. Perhaps it had been her father. Perhaps she'd told her father about him. Even then, even before he'd spoken to her, something had told Hampton that it would be stupid and careless of him to do so, to think for one moment that she'd want him to talk to her. He'd even told her his name. She must have told someone back home that Hampton had harassed her, been inappropriate, too familiar. He should have remembered that this wasn't Harlem, where a girl like Sophia could speak to you on the street, invite you to meetings, address you by your first name, call you *brother*. This was the South, after all, where buckshot blew through doors and lives were abandoned in the night and lost forever.

Gerald walked back into the colored car. Hampton saw that his face hadn't changed. Everyone in the car watched him, waited. They all leaned closer when he spoke.

"They say they know you," Gerald said. "They want you to get off the train, or they're coming on." The train had already been at the station for a few minutes. Hampton knew the platform was emptying. The train would leave soon. Would they really come aboard after him?

"Who are they?" Hampton asked.

"I don't know," Gerald said. "They said they know you. Said some girl sent them."

Terror closed around Hampton's heart like a fist.

"Who?" he asked. "What girl? I don't know any girls down here."

"Sophia," Gerald said. "They say you know some girl named Sophia."

The fist around his heart loosened its grip. Hampton found himself cupping his hands around the glass, peering out onto the darkened platform. A cluster of bodies waited beneath one of the lamps at the far end. A man turned toward the train as if looking for something, pushed the hair away from his eyes.

It was Fred Beal.

HAMPTON PULLED HIS duffel bag free of the overhead compartment and exited the train just as the whistle blew and steam rolled down the platform. Beal and a man Hampton had never seen before remained at the far end of the platform, beneath one of the lights.

Beal looked up and saw Hampton. His face registered a moment of recognition. He nodded, said something to the man standing with him. They both turned, and Hampton watched as they walked into the station. Hampton put on his hat and hurried to catch them.

The empty station hummed with silence. Hampton scanned the brightly lit room, but didn't see them. He walked to a window and looked out into the night. The two men walked across the parking lot. Hampton opened the door and stepped outside, called Beal's name. The other man stopped walking, looked back at Hampton where he stood just outside the station's door. Beal continued on toward a Model A coupe that waited in the shadows on the far side of the gravel lot.

Hampton called Beal's name again, and then he threw the strap on his duffel over his shoulder and ran down the stairs. He wondered if Beal planned to leave him behind here in Salisbury. He didn't know what to think.

The man Hampton didn't know stopped at the driver's side and pulled a set of keys from his pocket. Beal faced Hampton as he grew closer to the automobile.

"Beal," Hampton said.

Beal looked around as if trying to decide whether anyone else had heard his name, whether anyone else had seen the three men in the parking lot together. He looked back at Hampton.

"What the hell?" Hampton said.

"Stop it!" Beal said. His voice was a hoarse whisper.

Hampton froze in midstride. He stared at Beal.

"Goddammit, Haywood," Beal said, "stop screaming my name."

Hampton was unsure of what to do next. His duffel bag slipped from his shoulder and landed in the gravel. He did not move to pick it up. Beal looked down at the bag where it had fallen, then he looked at Hampton. He rolled his eyes.

"Well, come on," he said. He motioned for Hampton to move

quickly. "Come on, come on," he said again. "We're sitting ducks out here."

Hampton picked up his duffel, slung the strap over his shoulder, and started toward the car. The man opened the driver's-side door and climbed inside. As Hampton approached, Beal unfastened the compartment that housed the Model A's rumble seat. He reached out his hand toward Hampton. At first, Hampton thought Beal had done it in greeting, but then he realized Beal was reaching for his luggage. Hampton handed the duffel to Beal. Beal tossed it into the darkness at the bottom of the rumble seat.

"Climb in," Beal said. "All the way in. We need to get out of here."

ALTHOUGH THE GRAVEL parking lot had been dark, the rumble seat's interior was what Hampton expected to find at the bottom of the grave. It was hot, nearly stifling. He could smell the automobile's exhaust, its burned oil, hear its creaking and rocking as they careened down the road.

Hampton drifted into sleep. Something in his mind screamed at him to stay awake. He panicked at the thought that he could run out of air or succumb to the car's fumes. The panic was fleeting, and soon the blackness into which he stared dematerialized. He settled into a dream in which he was still sitting on the No. 33 train as it barreled south toward Charlotte.

He did not know how long he'd been sleeping when he felt the car slow and roll to a halt. Beal's muffled voice, and then the stranger's, came from inside. A door opened and closed, and then another. He heard footsteps in the gravel, then the sound of water.

He arched his back until it touched the lid of the rumble seat. He pushed against it. It didn't move. He pushed again, harder this time. Again. He felt the car rock on its axles. Another push and he heard a click as the latch released itself. Hampton unfolded his body from the compartment. The first thing he noticed was the intense smell of the air: manure, hay, a fire burning somewhere far off in the warm night. The car sat parked along a dirt road on the edge of a pasture. Nearby, a cluster of milk cows grazed silently on the other side of a low fence, their tails swishing in the shadows. Hampton turned, looked behind him, saw Beal and the other man urinating on the side of the road with their backs to him.

Hampton climbed out of the rumble seat and walked to the edge of the road and unzipped his fly. He stood there, wetting the dark ground at his feet. He stared at the cows. A few of them raised their heads and considered him; then they looked back down at the earth and continued tearing at the grass.

When he finished he turned and saw that Beal and the man now leaned against the driver's side of the car. Both men stared at him. Beal had his arms folded over his chest, his ankles crossed before him. The other man lit a cigarette.

"This is a bad idea," Beal said.

"What's a bad idea?" Hampton asked. "Stopping out here? Taking a piss on the side of the road? Or are you talking about squeezing me into a rumble seat? Shit, Beal, I could've suffocated."

"No," Beal said. "I'm not talking about that." He spread his arms, and turned his body as if to take in the entire scene around him. "I'm talking about this," he said. "All of it, especially you. You coming down here was a bad idea. It changes everything."

"Yeah, well maybe you need my help."

"I don't," Beal said.

"The party thinks you do," Hampton said.

"This is the South, Haywood," Beal said. "This isn't New York City. You don't know the South, not like I do."

But the darkened field that surrounded them made Hampton disagree with Beal, as did the humid air and the smells of animals and turned earth. The terror that had lived in his heart since that Mississippi night back in 1906 burst free and he threw himself at

Beal, crossing the ground between them in just a few strides. He threw a right hook and caught Beal on the jaw. Hampton staggered with his own momentum and struggled to regain his footing in the damp grass. Beal covered his face and crumpled against the side of the automobile; then he sprung at Hampton, grabbed him by the collar, and pulled him to the ground. They rolled through the grass. Hampton heard Beal cussing, heard himself screaming, "Don't tell me what I know, you son of a bitch! Don't tell me what I know!" They stopped rolling. Hampton found himself on top of Beal, straddling his body. Beal covered his face, and just as Hampton raised his fist to strike him, he heard a gunshot. The cows flushed at the noise, galloped into the darkness, and disappeared. Hampton turned, his fist still clenched and held above his head. The stranger pointed a small revolver at him. The man cocked the hammer.

"Don't be stupid," he said.

Hampton lowered his arm, unclenched his fist, felt Beal's chest heaving beneath him. He climbed off Beal and sat on the ground beside him. Beal propped himself up with his elbows. On the other side of the field, a light winked on at a small, white farmhouse. Beal and Hampton both saw it. They got to their feet. The man kept the revolver on Hampton. A dog began barking somewhere out in the dark near the farmhouse. The man looked behind him, saw the light, looked back at Hampton.

"Don't be stupid," he said again.

"Who are you?" Hampton asked.

"This is Carlton Reed," Beal said. "And Carlton Reed should've shot you."

"No one needs to get shot, Fred," Reed said. "But, Haywood, he's right about one thing: your coming down here is a bad idea. Punching a white man in the South is an even worse idea. We're on the same side, and we're your brothers in the struggle. You should trust us, because if we weren't we'd be looking for a place to bury you."

IT WAS WELL past midnight now, the streets deep with shadows and the shapes of rickety houses leaning away from one another at wild angles. Hampton climbed down from the rumble seat. Reed had killed the engine, but he still sat behind the wheel, smoking. The motor popped and hissed. Beal, his hands in his pockets, stood beside Hampton. Beal turned, looked up the street behind him as if expecting someone to appear. He stared for a moment, consulted his wristwatch. Beal nodded south where a dull light hovered in the sky. "That's Loray," he said.

Hampton stared at the light, then his eyes took in the houses around him, most of them small, a few of them two stories or more. Beal nodded toward a house several doors down the street. It was three stories high with gables along the roof.

"You'll be staying there," Beal said. "Miss Adeline takes Negroes in the attic rooms. She thinks you're visiting family. Don't give her a reason to think any different. Use the back staircase. Use the back door. Don't go in the common areas. Don't talk to the white boarders. Don't look at white women." He sighed, lit a cigarette. "Welcome to Gastonia."

Something over Beal's shoulder caught Hampton's eye. A figure made its way down the street toward them. Beal turned and watched it too. As it came closer Hampton saw that it was a woman. It was Sophia. She waved. Hampton could see that she was smiling.

"Late, as usual," Beal said.

"Fancy seeing you here, city boy," she said when she was close enough to be heard. Her voice was bright and clear. Hampton almost smiled for the relief of seeing someone who cared about him, but the events of the night weighed too heavily on him, and now that he was free of the rumble seat, he was aware of the aches in his body. The left side of his face throbbed too, and he wondered if Beal had hit him, although he had no memory of it.

"Your package has arrived," Beal said.

Sophia stopped and stood before Hampton and Beal. She reached out, touched Hampton's shoulder, which seemed the only manner of greeting she was comfortable expressing. He kept his arms by his sides, his duffel bag at his feet.

"How was your trip?" she asked.

"I'm here," Hampton said. He kept his voice cool, flat. "I survived."

"We already gave him the speech," Reed said from the driver's seat.

Sophia looked toward the car as if she just realized someone had been sitting inside it.

"What speech was that?" she asked.

"The 'don't get lynched' speech," Reed said. He cranked the engine. He leaned forward, looked out the passenger's window where Beal stood. "It was a good speech, wasn't it, Fred?"

"It was," Beal said. He opened the car door and put one foot inside, but then he stopped. "This is serious, Sophia," he said. "I'd hoped we trusted one another more than this."

"This has nothing to do with trust," Sophia said. "It's about taking action."

Beal looked from her to Hampton.

"Whether or not we need action," he said, "it's what we're going to get. You've both made sure of that." He climbed inside the car and closed the door. The automobile rattled off down the dark street and turned left at the corner. Sophia watched until it disappeared.

"Cowards," she said. She looked at Hampton, who stared back at her. She lifted her hand, touched his shirt collar. He felt it lift away from his neck. She let it go, and it flopped back into place. "Why is your shirt torn?" She stepped away from him as if appraising him. She must have noticed the grass stains on his pants, the sodden knees where he had kneeled over Beal in the mud. "What happened?"

"What happened?" Hampton asked. "When? When I was yanked off the train in Salisbury? When I was suffocating in the rumble seat? Or are you asking about when Reed pulled a gun on me?"

"Reed pulled a gun on you?" Sophia asked. "Why?"

"It's a long story. It's all been one long story."

"I wanted to meet you in Charlotte," Sophia said. "But they found out, and once they found out, it wasn't safe."

"Who found out?" Hampton asked. "Beal?"

"Yes, Fred, Reed, everyone. Probably Loray too."

"How'd they find out, Sophia? This was supposed to be quiet."

"And I tried to keep it quiet," she said. "I did. But this place is a hornet's nest, Hampton. I've never seen anything like it. It's loud and busy, and sometimes you can't hear over the noise and you can't find your friends, and if you shout you don't know who's listening."

"Well, no more shouting, then," Hampton said.

"We won't have to," she said. "You're here."

She looked down the street at the house with the gables. Hampton turned and looked at it as well. Faint light burned in a few of the windows.

"That's your boardinghouse," Sophia said. "Miss Adeline takes Negroes."

"I know," Hampton said. "Use the back door and the back staircase. I'm here visiting family. Don't talk to white folks. Don't look at white girls."

"Very impressive," Sophia said, trying to smile.

"You can take the boy out of Mississippi."

"There are so many people I want you to meet," she said. "I told you about Ella May, but there are so many wonderful people here."

"I hope they're all just as wonderful as Beal and Reed," Hampton said.

"I'm sorry," Sophia said. "I didn't know that any of that was going to happen. But you made it, and we'll start organizing tomorrow. I'll pick you up at eight A.M. and we'll head to Bessemer City and meet up with Ella. She's got a list of workers to visit."

"Eight A.M.," said Hampton. He had no idea what time it was, but 8 A.M. did not seem very far away.

"Get some sleep," Sophia said. She turned and walked up the street in the direction from which she'd come. Hampton bent to pick up his duffel and then he heard Sophia call his name. He looked up, saw her a block away, a shadowy figure on the sidewalk.

"Spindle," she said.

Hampton stood, threw the strap of his duffel bag over his shoulder, looked in the direction of the boardinghouse, looked back at Sophia. "Spindle," he said.

THE NEXT MORNING, Hampton found himself the lone passenger in a rickety truck en route to a town called Bessemer City with Sophia at the wheel. He'd slept poorly in his hot attic room, opening his eyes at every sound: each pop or crack of the house during the night, the rumble of every passing automobile, and, at dawn when workers left their shift at Loray and headed home, the cacophony of footsteps and voices on the street three floors below.

Hampton woke to a hot morning that had grown hotter in the hour since, and now he sat looking out the passenger's-side window, long periods of silence passing between him and Sophia. The brick and glass storefronts on Franklin Avenue in downtown Gastonia quickly gave way to long expanses of forests, broken by farms where men in distant fields guided plows behind mules. Gulches ran alongside the road, rimmed with red gashes of dirt that made it seem that skin had been torn away from a body. On the other side of barbed-wire fences, cotton grew in great green and brown clusters, the bolls bulging as if they would burst open in relief.

Sophia turned off the main road and the truck snaked along the hills and curves that took them past more farms and small houses that sat in the midst of cleared fields. They entered a small downtown that looked like a miniature version of Gastonia. The streets were alive with automobiles and well-dressed white men and women on foot passing in and out of stores, a market, a bank, a post office.

"Is this it?" Hampton asked.

"This is Bessemer City," Sophia said, "but this ain't *it*."

The *it* was a settlement Hampton later learned was called Stumptown. He sensed the place even before they pulled off the main road and followed the gravel-strewn dirt lane that led down into it. The land had grown wild once they'd left downtown and the flat farmland rolled into hills. He saw whitewashed, crumbling cabins, churches, and other structures that seemed to be abandoned.

As he and Sophia entered Stumptown, Hampton remembered rural Mississippi: small, rambling shacks, barefoot children kicking up dust as they ran across smooth-swept yards, old women with hard-set eyes wearing bandanas and long cotton shifts walking beside the road. Stumptown felt like a place he'd known before.

The lane was so narrow that trees and bushes enclosed the truck as they descended into the settlement. In the road before them, flakes of mica and pieces of quartz sparkled beneath the bright morning sun. The yellow light that poured through the trees was tinged with a green otherworldliness that made Hampton feel as if the glass in the truck's windows had been tinted.

Sophia eased the truck down the lane, passing cabin after cabin that seemed too dilapidated to inhabit. Exterior walls were unpainted and left exposed to the elements, tarpaper flapped over windows, collapsed roofs were covered with tarpaulins. Sophia parked at the end of the road, in front of a cabin shadowed by tall trees. She turned off the engine, and they sat there for a moment, looking at the scene before them. "This is where Ella lives," she said.

"I thought she was white," Hampton said.

"She is."

The cabin's door burst open, and a tribe of dirty children poured onto the porch and stumbled down the stairs. Sophia climbed down from the truck. One of Ella's children, an older girl, was waiting for her, and the two hugged. Hampton got out of the truck and walked over to where Sophia and the girl stood by the front bumper. The girl held the hand of a much younger girl who must have been her little sister. A boy stood by the porch steps as if waiting to discover the reason for their visit before deciding whether or not to welcome them.

The three children were frighteningly thin, all angles and sharp edges and quick, cutting eyes and bare feet with thick, yellow calluses. The girls, whose names were Lilly and Rose, wore long cotton dresses that once upon a time must have been white but were now an earth-tinged tan that nearly matched the color of the girls' skin. The boy, whose name was Otis, wore tattered knee-length breeches and a cotton shirt that seemed to have been made at the same time and of the same material as the girls' dresses. The sight of the children and the cabin in which they lived made Hampton ashamed of his bleach-white shirt, the pressed pants, his leather wingtips.

"Is that him?"

Hampton looked toward the voice and saw a small white woman with dark hair standing in the cabin's doorway. She wore a collared dress and loose stockings, and she was as thin as the children. She had a young baby in her arms. The baby held what looked like a stuffed sock in its hands and gnawed its tip.

"This is Hampton Haywood," Sophia said. She touched Hampton's elbow as if to prompt him. "And this is Ella."

"Hello," Hampton said.

Ella nodded, adjusted the baby on her hip. "Welcome to Stumptown," she said.

Hampton was shocked by the poverty before him, but the source of his horror was the only thing that surprised him. He'd actually expected to come south and find poor Negroes living hand to mouth, barely getting by on what they could earn, save, or grow, but he hadn't expected to find white people living this way.

He followed Sophia through the yard and up the rickety porch steps. The three older children opened the truck's doors and climbed inside. The horn honked. Hampton turned and saw Lilly behind the wheel. She raised her hands as if asking Sophia a question. Sophia held up the set of keys so the girl could see them. "Learned my lesson last time," she said. The girl frowned.

They stepped up onto the porch. Ella kissed the baby's head and handed him to Sophia.

Ella stepped back and looked at Hampton. She narrowed her eyes and crossed her arms as if appraising him. She looked at Sophia. "I thought you might've mentioned something to him about dressing fancy."

Hampton looked down at his clothes. He thought she might be joking, but it became clear that she wasn't. He'd never felt fancily dressed before. In the city he spent more time wondering whether his clothes were fashionable enough. It had never occurred to him that he would ever feel overdressed and out of place.

"I guess I forgot," Sophia said.

Ella stepped toward Hampton. She opened the buttons on his cuffs and folded the sleeves up each forearm; then she unbuttoned the top button on his shirt. Hampton didn't move, not because he was scared, but because he was surprised. He'd never had a woman he didn't know, much less a white woman, touch him with such abandon. He'd never been so aware of someone's skin as it brushed against his own, her thin fingers as they grazed his arms.

"Put this in your pocket," Ella said. She held up his wristwatch. She'd removed it without his knowing. Hampton looked at Sophia and raised his eyebrows, gave her the first real smile he'd given her since arriving the night before. Sophia kissed the baby's cheek and stifled a laugh. Ella stepped back and stared at him. She crossed her arms again.

"Wait right here," she said. She disappeared into the dark cabin.

"I didn't know about the dress code," Hampton said. He slipped his watch into his pocket. "Anything else you need to tell me?"

"Nothing comes to mind," Sophia said.

Ella reappeared holding a dipper full of water. She tossed the water at Hampton's shoes, as if she were putting out a fire. The water landed between his feet and splashed onto his wingtips. He made to jump away from it, but it was too late; they were soaked, the leather already turning dark.

"What the hell?" he said.

"Go on out in the yard while they're wet," Ella said. "Stomp around, get them good and dusty. We'll be ready to go after that."

THEY LEFT THE truck parked at Ella's and set off up the road. Ella's children stayed behind and played in the truck. Hampton overheard Lilly arguing with Otis about whose turn it was to "drive."

Sophia and Ella walked ahead of Hampton, and he wondered what someone might think if they were to lift a tarpaper flap and look out their window to see a finely dressed black man following close behind two white women in an all-black town. The sun was hot on his face, and he assumed it was nearing 10 A.M., but he hesitated to consult his hidden wristwatch for fear of drawing Ella's attention.

"You think she'll come?" Sophia asked.

"I hope so," Ella said. "I'd feel a whole lot better if she did."

Ella and Sophia turned off the road and followed a path toward a cabin that looked just as pathetic as the one in which Ella and her children lived. But there was a domesticity about this place that Ella's lacked. The path was lined with flowers and short shrubs. Colored bottles hung from one of the trees and clinked together almost soundlessly in the breeze. Clothes hung drying from a line on the porch.

As the three of them drew closer to the cabin, a woman of imperceptible age came around from the backyard. She wore a head kerchief and a long dark dress and held a hoe in her hand. She smiled when she saw them and leaned the hoe against the side of the cabin, wiping her hands on the seat of her dress.

"Morning, Miss May," the woman said.

"Good morning," Ella said. "How's it going back there?"

The woman smiled. "We might not starve come fall," she said.

Ella nodded toward the cabin. "She up?"

"Will be soon if she's not already," the woman said. "I'll go check." The woman walked up the porch steps, opened a screen door, let it close silently behind her. A young girl stood in the doorway and looked out at them. Ella waved.

"Hey, Iva," she said.

The girl opened the screen door. She wore a dress the color of an old potato. Her hair was pulled back in a single braid that brushed the nape of her neck. Hampton saw that, just like Ella's children, the girl wasn't wearing shoes. She looked at Sophia.

"Y'all leave the truck down there?" she asked.

"I did," Sophia said. The girl leaned her head back inside. Hampton heard her say, "I'm going to go down to Lilly's."

"You bring them back up here if they hungry," the woman's voice said. Hampton saw that Ella stared at the ground as if she hadn't overheard the conversation.

The girl leapt off the porch and tore across the yard at a sprint.

Sophia called after her. "I told Lilly I've got the keys with me."

The girl kept running and said, "Otis'll get it started."

"He better not!" Ella hollered.

The screen door slammed shut, and Hampton looked up to the porch to find a young woman about his age blinking her eyes against the midmorning light. Her hair was plaited into two thick braids that grazed her shoulders. She wore a dress that buttoned down the middle, and it was open at the collar so that he could see the shadows that pooled in the hollowed spaces her clavicles made. She had big brown eyes and a gentle, frowning face that was at once innocent and world-weary. Hampton thought she was the most beautiful woman he'd ever seen. She stood on the porch, her hip cocked, and stared down at Ella. She crossed her arms, shook her head. "I done told you," she said.

"Well, you going to have to tell me again," Ella said.

"I can't do it," the woman said. "I just can't."

Ella stepped in between Sophia and Hampton, grabbed hold of his hand, and pulled him toward the porch steps. "This man here came all the way down from New York City to knock on doors," she said. "You mean to tell me you can't walk up and down the street?"

"This ain't New York City," the woman said. "Ain't none of your white friends want to see a colored girl join your union."

Ella pointed to Sophia. "This one does," she said.

"She's right, Violet," Sophia said. "We need you, and we need your help."

The woman named Violet sighed and shook her head again. She looked at Hampton as if seeing him for the first time. Hampton slipped his hands into his pockets, fingered his watch.

"Violet, you've given American Mill Number Two every night of your life for as long as I've known you," Ella said. "Give us the afternoon."

"Just the afternoon," Violet said. "And it don't mean nothing."

Ella smiled. "It means something to me," she said.

THE FOUR OF them spent the rest of the morning knocking on doors in Stumptown, approaching people bent to their work in small patches of gardens, sitting down on porch steps, and standing in open doorways. Although Ella and Violet knew them all, the men and women of Stumptown looked at Sophia and Hampton with stone faces and reticent eyes. Hampton studied the men he met, regardless of their age, and tried to mirror their country formality, tried to stand with the same rigidity, to measure his words with the same deliberateness.

After a lunch of chicken and dumplings at Violet's mother's house, they loaded themselves into the truck and drove to a tiny town called Waco, where Ella knew of a few workers who might be interested in the union. Waco, which was near Cherryville's few mills, was almost an hour's drive away. When they arrived Hampton saw that it was hardly more than a crossroads of shanties, shotgun houses, and lean-tos set in the midst of rows of cotton fields owned by white people but worked solely by blacks.

Hampton took the lead in Waco, and while he spoke to strangers in hot, crowded rooms with low ceilings, he felt the eyes of his three companions upon him. He did his best to explain the inalienable rights of the worker, how those rights extended to whites and Negroes alike, how disagreement about these rights had caused a major struggle just a few miles away, in Gastonia, in the shadow of the Loray Mill.

But no matter what Hampton said, talk always turned to the weekend-long jamboree to honor Confederate veterans that was scheduled to take place just a few miles away in Charlotte beginning on Friday morning. It was the first news Hampton heard of the Confederate gathering, and although he was from the North, the side that had actually won the war, he'd never seen or heard of any celebrations like this. It seemed to him that the South now reveled in its loss as if it had been a victory.

On the drive to Waco, Hampton had ridden alone in the back of Sophia's truck while the three women had squeezed into the cab, but the day had turned blisteringly hot, and on the return trip to Stumptown, Violet opted to ride in the open air with him. They sat with their backs against the cab, Hampton's feet crossed at the ankles, Violet's legs pulled up beneath her dress. The sun was behind them now, and the cab offered a little shade. Violet looked over at Hampton.

"What about your accent?" she said. The truck must have changed direction because the sunlight hit her eyes. Hampton noticed they were a lighter shade of brown than he'd assumed. Violet lifted her hand and cupped it over her eyes, dropping them back into shadow.

"What about it?" Hampton said.

"Half the time you talk, you sound like you're from down here," Violet said. She lowered her hand but didn't look away from him.

"I am from down here," he said. "Was, anyway. Went up north when I was six."

"You got free of it."

"More like 'got gone of it,'" he said.

"Where?" she asked.

"Mississippi." He pulled his legs up to his chest and rested his elbows on his knees. Hampton opened his mouth to speak, but he stopped. He tried again. "My daddy shot a white man. The plantation owner's son. He killed him before he could get killed."

"What happened?" Violet asked.

"They yanked him off a train the next morning," he said. "Never saw him again."

Violet put her hand on his arm. "I'm sorry," she said.

Hampton shrugged. "I try not to think about what might've happened to him. Just imagine that the South took him. Makes it easier," he said. "Makes it easier just to say that the South killed my daddy."

"My daddy keeled over dead in a white man's field while Mama was pregnant with Iva," Violet said. "I reckon you could say the South killed him too. Maybe we should have jumped on a train north."

"Still can," Hampton said. "Plenty of trains going north."

"Shoot," Violet said. She smiled. "You got an extra ticket?"

"Might could find one."

"Shoot," she said again, still smiling.

Bessemer City began to make itself apparent around them. A few cars passed going in the opposite direction. The homes were suddenly larger, set closer together. The truck skirted the edge of downtown on its way back to Stumptown.

"So," Hampton said, "you going back to the mill tonight?"

Violet stared down at her lap as if looking for an answer. "I hadn't decided yet," she said.

Hampton reached into his pocket and removed his wristwatch, saw that it was almost 4:30 P.M. "You got an hour and a half," he said.

Violet looked surprised to see him holding the watch. "Let me see that," she said. He passed it to her. She looked at it for a long time, draped it over her wrist, held it so that the sunlight caught it.

Hampton wondered if she'd ever held a piece of jewelry as fine as his watch. He'd saved up for the watch for more than a year, and he'd owned it for less than that, but something urged him to give it to her. He could not tell if he wished to impress her or to prove to himself that he was capable of such giving. "You can have it," he finally said.

She stopped playing with the watch and looked up at him. She smiled, shook her head.

"It's yours," he said, "if you want it."

She laughed, handed it back to him. "What do I need a fancy watch for?" she said. "I only care about four times: waking up time, going to work time, getting off time, and going to sleep time. I know when to do what."

Hampton held the watch for a moment, shame creeping over him as he realized that he'd offered the watch knowing that Violet wouldn't accept it. He draped it over his wrist and began to fasten it. Violet put her hand over his.

"Put that back in your pocket," she said. "You already sound like a city boy half the time. No use looking like one too."

VIOLET DID NOT return for the night shift at American Mill No. 2 that evening, and over the next four days the four of them canvassed Gaston County in advance of Fred Beal's Loray rally on Friday night. Four days of heat and rain and Hampton's ruined shoes traipsing from shack to shack, from lunch counter back rooms in the stark daylight to darkened juke joints set off in the dense woods at night. Hampton's head buzzed with the names of people he'd met and the names of the communities he'd visited: Ranlo, Booger Mountain, Shuffletown. He'd sat through a Wednesday night church service, smacked mosquitos against his skin that were so fat and full of blood that it looked like he'd been shot, and witnessed a baptism at a muddy creek near a place called Cramerton. He'd eaten things he'd never considered eating before, seen more guns than he'd ever seen in his life. More than once he'd been pulled aside by an older gentleman and asked how he'd come to be wandering through town with three women—two of them white—in tow.

Late Friday afternoon, Hampton found himself holding Violet's hand while standing shoeless and calf-deep in cold spring water. Along with Ella and Sophia, they'd spent the morning in Bessemer City handing out leaflets outside the gates of American Mill No. 2 and telling black workers about that night's *integrated* rally in Gastonia. Then they'd visited the back room of a diner where a group of Negro railroad men hunched silently over their cooling lunches while Ella talked about the union. The afternoon had been devoted to sitting on porches and porch steps in and around Stumptown, until Violet's mother finally invited them all over for supper. After that they planned to gather as many black workers as they could and head for Gastonia at dusk.

While Violet's mother made dinner, Hampton stood out in the dirt road that ran through the middle of Stumptown and tossed a baseball back and forth with Ella's son Otis. Neither of them wore mitts. The boy's arm was surprisingly strong and accurate given his slight frame. He was nine, but, to Hampton, he looked no older than six. He'd learned that Hampton was from New York, and he'd asked him all about the Yankees.

"Babe Ruth's my favorite," the boy said. He threw the ball to Hampton. Each time he caught the baseball, Hampton's hand wanted to recoil at the feel of it. It was sodden and near rotted, the frayed stitching coming loose. Sweat poured off his forehead.

"Babe's pretty good," Hampton said.

Otis caught the ball, stared at Hampton, his mouth hanging open as if portraying shock. "Pretty good?" he said. "Pretty good?"

They tossed the ball back and forth. Ella and Sophia and Violet sat talking on the porch. Ella's daughter Rose was sitting on her mother's lap, and Hampton could hear her raspy cough. Violet cradled Ella's baby boy in her arms. Occasionally Hampton could feel Violet's eyes on him, but he did not raise his head to look at her. Hampton watched the boy toss and catch the ball and caught himself wondering what it would be like to have a son.

"Yankees played a spring training game over in Charlotte just a few months ago," the boy said.

"Oh, yeah," Hampton said. "You go see them?"

"No," the boy said. "I didn't get to."

"We'll go see a Yankees game if you ever visit New York," Hampton said.

The boy's face exploded in a grin. Hampton did not have the heart to tell the boy that he would never visit New York, that he might never leave North Carolina or even Gaston County. He did not have the heart to tell the boy that he'd never even been to a Yankees game himself, could not afford both the ticket and the time off work, and even if he could, he could not imagine taking this white child along with him.

Hampton looked toward the porch, saw Violet hand the baby over to Sophia. She stood, walked down the few porch steps, and continued out into the yard. Hampton turned his eyes back to Otis and their game of toss. He was aware of Violet coming to a stop only a few feet away, aware of her watching him as he caught and threw the ball. He fought the urge to look at her, her dark skin against her pale blue dress, her hair now unbraided and pulled up and tied back with a white sash. She was beautiful, the kind of woman he believed he would have fallen in love with had he never left Mississippi, the kind of strong, country-hewn woman his mother may have been before she left, the kind of woman his younger sister Summer could have become had she grown up in the South.

"Hot, huh?" Violet said. She passed her hand across her forehead, shifted her weight to the other leg, put her hands on her hips.

"Yes, ma'am," he says. "It is."

"You got heat like this up where you're from?"

"Sometimes," he said. "Sometimes we got heat like this." He looked at her and smiled.

Violet raised her eyebrows, smirked as if she doubted everything he'd ever said.

"Is it too hot for a stroll?" he asked.

They walked side by side to the end of the dirt road and followed a path behind Ella's cabin that led to a spring nearly hidden by willows. Hampton's body welcomed the shade. The heat stripped itself from his skin as if being peeled away. He bent to the clear, cool water, cupped a handful to his mouth, took a drink. It ran down his chin. Violet laughed. He looked up at her, flicked his damp fingers at her legs.

"You not supposed to drink it?" he asked.

"No, you can drink all you want," she said. "It's just funny to see those nice shoes with mud on them."

Hampton stood and looked down at his shoes. He saw that mud had crept up over the soles, that dust from the road had frosted the leather. He lifted his left foot, unlaced his shoe, and removed his sock. He tossed them behind him. The mud squished between his toes. He lifted his right foot, did the same. He rolled his pants up to his knees, stepped into the cold water, watched as the minnows fled. He looked back at Violet, gestured toward her feet. "Come on, country girl." She laughed, slipped off her shoes, and stepped into the water beside him.

"Speaking of country," she said, "I bet you never thought you'd be out in the woods like this." She stepped forward. Her foot slipped. Hampton took her hand until she steadied herself.

"I didn't know where I'd be," he said. "But I'm glad to be here."

"I heard you talking about New York. What's it like?"

"Come visit and find out," he said. He smiled, reached for her hand again. She let him hold it, let him intertwine his fingers with hers.

"Why'd you come down here?" she asked.

"Because I believe in the party," Hampton said. "I believe in integration."

She shook her hand free of his and reached up, closed her fingers around the thin branch of a willow tree, and stripped it of its leaves. She cupped them in her hand. "That's an answer," she said, "but that ain't no *reason*."

"I guess I wanted to see the South," he said. "Really see it, not just from a train window or through somebody else's stories. I wanted to find out if it's what I imagined."

Violet tossed the willow leaves, one by one, onto the face of the water. Hampton watched her. "What did you imagine?" she asked.

"I don't know." He laughed. "Banjos. Rednecks. Oak trees. Singing darkies, pickaninnies." He smiled, looked at her, and saw that she was smiling as well. "Pretty girls."

"You find all that?" she asked.

"I found you."

"Shoot," she said. "I bet you got a girl back home, don't you?"

"You got a man down here?"

"I asked you first," she said.

"No," he said. "I don't have a girl back home. I travel too much."

Violet smiled, raised her eyebrows. "You got girls everywhere else then? Philly? Detroit? Atlanta?"

"No," he said. "No, I never even get off the train. I never get to meet nice girls like you."

He looked over at her just as she lifted her eyes to his. He reached for her hand again and pulled her toward him. The few willow leaves still in her hands spilled onto the water. He touched her chin, brought her lips to his, felt her mouth open.

After a moment, she pulled away and looked into his eyes. "I don't even know you," she said.

"I don't know you either," he said. He pulled her to him again, but she shook free of him. She wiped his kiss from her lips.

"You taste like you been kissing on white girls," she said.

He frowned, stepped away from her. She was teasing him, but it still bothered him. Sophia had told him that Ella was trying to free herself of a rough character named Charlie Shope, and Hampton didn't want any rumors circulating that would tie him and Ella to one another. He didn't want trouble that he didn't deserve. "I haven't been kissing on nobody," he said.

"You sure?" she said. "I never met a colored boy who spends so much time running around with white girls."

"I been running around with you too," he said. "And I thought Ella was your best friend."

Violet stepped out of the water, reached for her shoes. "Well, I ain't hers," she said. She kicked the water from her feet, stepped into her shoes, and fastened them. "She's got white friends now. Rich white friends."

"Sophia?" he said. "Hell, Sophia ain't rich. I can promise you that."

"I ain't talking about her," Violet said. "I'm talking about some rich white lady over in McAdamville."

Hampton followed her out of the water, stepped into his shoes, tucked his socks into his back pocket. "Come on," he said. "You afraid somebody's taking her away from you?"

"Yes," Violet said. "That's exactly what I'm afraid of."

"She's meeting new people because she's working for you, even if you don't see it that way," Hampton said.

"That's not what I'm talking about," Violet said. "I'm afraid of something happening to her." She walked up the path away from the spring.

"She's working to open the union to you, Violet. What was it Jesus said? 'I've gone ahead to prepare a place for you'? That's what Ella's doing. That's what I'm doing too."

Violet stopped and turned to face him. "Jesus said that after he was crucified," she said. "That don't make me feel no better."

"You don't have to feel anything but hope," he said.

BUT THE HOPE of which Hampton spoke turned to frustration as he and Violet and a handful of other black workers loaded up into the back of Sophia's truck for the trip to Gastonia and that night's rally.

Once the tailgate was slammed shut there was just enough room to accommodate them all if they stood, and when the truck lurched forward a few of the older workers nearly lost their footing. Hampton surveyed the group of a dozen or so men and women: he and Violet were by far the youngest. Most of them worked at American Mill as spinners or openers or in some other low-skill, low-pay positions. A few of them came from other mills in the surrounding countryside. Hampton felt that none of them—himself included—quite knew what they were doing in the back of this truck helmed by two white women en route to an all-white rally. It hurt him to think of it, but he couldn't help but picture the hundreds, maybe thousands, of train cars full of cattle he'd seen during his years with the railroad. He pictured those cows standing just as close to one another as he stood to these strangers now, the only difference between him and the cows being that the cows were always dumb about the end that awaited them, while he was all too aware of the potential fate that lie ahead.

He was the only union man among them, certainly the only member of the Communist Party, and he knew it was his duty to inspire them. He suggested they sing together, and while he tried to lead them in a couple of well-known protest songs, they stumbled over the words. The only songs they all seemed to have in common were hymns, so that's what they sung: "Amazing Grace," "Let Us Break Bread Together," "Onward, Christian Soldier."

As they barreled down the highway in the gathering dusk, Hampton pictured the sight they must be. He imagined a farmer walking along the edge of his field and looking up at the sound of a truck passing, the music of their voices lifted in song.

Once they reached Gastonia, Sophia parked the truck on the south side of the train tracks. Hampton opened the tailgate and helped a few of the older members of the group as they climbed down from the bed. Sophia and Ella walked around back and waited for everyone to gather around them. Hampton looked up the road, where the field was lit with lanterns. A dark mass of people stood in front of the stage. He could hear the voice of the person leading the rally, but he could not make out what the voice said.

Ella cleared her throat, and Hampton turned his gaze to her where she stood in front of the group of Bessemer City workers.

"I want to thank all of you for coming tonight," Ella said. "I really mean it. I think something good's going to come of this. I really do." She stared down at the ground as if looking for words. "We're going to walk up the road here to the rally, and I want you all to follow me, and I want us all to stay together. No matter what, let's all stay together.

"There's going to be a whole bunch of strikers up there, and keep in mind that they ain't no different from you. They work in mills just like you do. They're poor just like you are, just like I am. Now, there's going to be some police up there because there's always police up there. Tonight ain't no different. And there's going to be some newspapermen and some cameramen too. There ain't no reason for any of them to say a word to us, so let's not say a word to them. Let's mind our business. The goal tonight is to force a vote that'll open this union to anybody who needs it, and I believe all of you need it as much as I do."

Ella stopped speaking, looked at Sophia. "You want to add anything?" she asked.

"No, ma'am," Sophia said. "Not a thing."

Ella looked at Hampton. "Mr. Haywood?" she said.

Hampton felt Violet's shoulder brush against him, felt her hand take his. Hampton looked around the group. "Let's all stay together," he said. "Just like she said."

They set off up the road toward the headquarters and the field that sat across from it. A couple hundred people stood out in the open field, the white tents of the strikers' colony off in the distance near the woods. Onlookers from town, reporters, and a few uniformed police officers milled about. Violet squeezed his hand.

"I don't like this," she said.

He looked at her, saw that she seemed uncertain for the first time since he'd met her.

"It's okay," he said.

The group followed Ella, who led them through the crowd and toward the stage. Carlton Reed stood behind the podium, giving an update on the strike. The crowd cheered when he mentioned that a relief dinner would be served later that night. The group of workers waited, unsure of what to do next. A few minutes passed, and Hampton felt the crowd as it began to take notice of them, as word of their presence spread. He became aware of his physical body in a way he'd never been aware of it before, and he let go of Violet's hand for fear that she might feel the trembling that was taking hold of him. A man stepped in front of Hampton and lifted a camera before his face. The flash of the bulb blinded him for a moment, and Hampton stepped away from the light and bumped into someone behind him.

"Get off me, nigger," a voice said.

Hampton looked toward the voice and tried to blink the white light from his eyes. Before him stood a scarecrow version of a young man in overalls that clung to his shoulders. He didn't seem old enough to be a millworker, and Hampton couldn't understand how the voice he'd heard belonged to this boy.

"Go on, nigger," the boy said. He looked around at the group from Bessemer City. "Go on," the boy said. "All of you." He spit at Hampton's shoes. Hampton was more confused than he was angry or offended, and he turned away and pushed through the group toward Ella.

"Hampton," Violet said. He felt her hand on his arm, but he pulled free of her. Ella stood facing the stage, and Hampton stooped to speak into her ear.

"What are we doing?" he asked. "What's the plan?" He waited, but Ella didn't say a word, didn't even look at him. "Ella," he said, "what are we doing?" People around them stared and pointed, some of them whispering loud enough for Hampton to hear the things they said: Bessemer City. Ella May. Nigger lover. The crowd began to move away from them.

Hampton didn't realize it, but he was moving too, following Ella closer and closer to the stage. As the crowd dispersed and formed an encircling wall of white faces, most of whom now watched the Bessemer City workers instead of listening to Reed, their retreat left behind open expanses of grass that Ella and Hampton and the members of their group stepped in to fill. In this way they gained proximity to the stage, making it more and more difficult for Reed to ignore the disruption they caused.

Sophia came around from the back of the group and stood beside Ella. "What next?" she asked.

Ella smiled. "Let's wait until old Fred takes the stage."

Hampton saw Fred Beal standing at the front of the crowd as if he were about to speak. The two men locked eyes, and Beal shook his head as if this display of disappointment were something he'd spent time rehearsing. Hampton smiled at him. Beal waved two men over to where he stood. One of the men, who Hampton later learned was named Anderson Chesley, carried a rifle slung over his shoulder. The men both nodded as Beal spoke, and then they disappeared behind the stage.

Chesley reappeared with a coil of rope that the other man tied to the stage. Chesley took up the slack end, walked through the crowd, and shouldered his way between Hampton and Ella.

"What the hell, Chesley?" Sophia said, but he didn't acknowledge them. Instead he walked farther away from the stage, stopping only when he ran out of rope. He leaned back and pulled the rope taut and held it waist-high with both hands. Hampton saw that Chesley had cordoned off the black workers from the rest of the audience, as if they were corralled in a pen. People cheered and laughed. An empty bottle landed at Hampton's feet. A rock struck his shoulder and fell to the grass. He spun around to discover who had hurled the objects, but all the laughing faces looked the same. He didn't feel fear or uncertainty. He felt anger.

The crowd burst into cheers. Hampton looked up to see Beal walking across the stage. He and Reed shook hands. While the audience settled itself, Ella and Sophia remained on the white side of the rope, but as soon as Beal began speaking about that night's march down to Loray, Ella lifted the rope over her head, stepped beneath it, and stood beside Hampton and Violet. The rope slipped from Chesley's hands and fell to the grass. He picked it up and cracked it like a bullwhip. It caught Hampton's shoulder, and he stumbled into Violet. Chesley laughed. Hampton turned, stared at his white brother in the struggle. Chesley gave him a wink, lifted the rope, and coiled it around his own neck. He closed his eyes and let his chin loll to his chest, allowed his tongue to spill from his mouth. Ella called out.

"We want a vote, Fred!" she yelled.

The crowd booed. Another glass bottle, this one half-full of what looked like liquor, landed in the grass in front of Hampton and Violet. A rotten tomato struck the back of the white man in front of him. The man stumbled forward, whipped his body around, and searched the crowd. Hampton refused to meet his eye.

"Hold on," Beal said from the stage. "Everyone hold on, stay calm."

"We want a vote, Fred!" Ella said again. "We want a vote!"

"Membership's closed!" a man's voice screamed from the middle of the field.

"Take those niggers home!" another yelled.

Ella acted as if she hadn't heard the men's voices. She kept her eyes locked on Beal where he stood on the stage. Sophia lifted the rope and stepped under it. She cleared her throat, then she started shouting.

"In the founding documents of the National Textile Workers Union, as well as in the charter of the party that supports it, it is outlined that all workers, regardless of gender, race, or class, shall be offered membership if they embrace the tenets of the union," she said. "And, Mr. Beal, I can assure you that the brothers and sisters I have brought with me this evening embrace the tenets of this union."

"We're calling for a vote!" Ella said.

"Give them their damned vote if that's what they want," a woman's voice said.

"A vote is all we're asking for," Sophia said.

Beal's eyes scanned the crowd. He pushed his hair off his forehead. His skin glistened with sweat.

"Okay," he said. "Okay." He looked to Carlton Reed, who stood beside him. Beal leaned toward Reed. They spoke quietly. Reed nodded his head. "Okay. Let's take a vote," Beal said. "All those in favor of accepting the contingent from Bessemer City, please raise your hand."

In unison, Sophia's and Ella's hands shot up over their heads. Hampton raised his as well. Boos rained down on them.

"Put your hand down, nigger!" Chesley yelled. He dropped the rope and walked toward Hampton, who kept his hand raised. "Put your hand down, nigger. This vote's open to union members only."

"I am a representative of the American Communist Party," Hampton said. He removed his wallet from his back pocket and opened it to search for his membership card. "Which is the governing body of this union."

Chesley smacked the wallet out of Hampton's hand. It landed between his feet. He looked down, saw that the photograph of his mother and father on their wedding day had slipped from his wallet. He bent to retrieve it.

"Bow, nigger," Chesley said. He reared back and kicked Hampton in the ribs.

Hampton sprawled in the grass, sucked down two huge gulps of air. The crowd opened up and formed a ring around them. He gathered his wallet and the photo and stuffed them into his back pocket. And then he was on his feet. He lunged at Chesley and threw his arms around his body, lifted him off the ground, and slammed him onto his back. Chesley still wore the rifle on a strap over his shoulder, and he rolled to his feet, the rifle in his hands. He held it pointed at Hampton's chest. Violet screamed.

Then Hampton heard the sound of people gasping around him. He realized his eyes had been closed, and he opened them and saw that Chesley held the rifle with one hand and the other hand was at his throat, pulling at something wrapped around his neck.

Chesley tried to look behind him but couldn't, and Hampton saw that Ella held a small knife beneath Chesley's chin. She'd wrapped her other arm around his neck, used it to pull him backward, to expose his throat to the blade. She spoke into his ear.

"I'm from the same mountains you're from, Mr. Chesley, and nobody ever taught me to talk like that," she said. "Where'd you learn to talk like that?" She tightened her arm around his neck with a jolt that caused Chesley to flinch. He opened his mouth to speak, found that he didn't have the air. "Now, I need you to just let go of that rifle, and then I won't have to stick this blade into your neck." He held the rifle out in front of him as if waiting for someone to take it. "Just go ahead and turn it loose," Ella said. "That's it."

Chesley let go of the rifle. It fell to the grass. Hampton bent and picked it up.

"We cannot fight one another!" Beal said from the stage. "That's what they want, and we can't let it happen." He waited, but Ella did not let Chesley go. "Ella!" Beal screamed. "Ella May!"

Ella finally turned loose of Chesley and stepped away from him. He coughed, touched the place on his neck where the knife had pressed against his skin. Hampton grabbed Violet's hand, reached for Ella, took her arm. "Come on," he said. "Let's go."

"This is all bullshit," Sophia said.

Hampton looked at her, nodded toward the group of black workers, all of whose faces wore looks of terror. "Let's go," he said again.

At first the crowd was silent as they passed through it. Hampton let go of Ella but held tight to Violet's hand. He felt the weight of Chesley's rifle where he'd slung the strap over his shoulder. The applause began near the stage, and by the time they'd reached the edge of the crowd on their way to the road, the audience had begun to chant, "Niggers go home!" over and over.

One of the older women in their group had begun to cry, and her crying was the only sound they made as they walked back to the place where they'd left the truck. Sophia ran and caught up with them. Hampton clutched Violet's hand and pulled her along. They were far ahead of the rest of the group, and he didn't care if they were moving too fast for some of the stragglers to catch up.

"We're not giving up," Sophia said. She spoke as if she were running out of breath. "This ain't the final word."

"I ain't giving up," Ella said. Her voice came from behind Hampton. He did not turn to look at her.

"This is over," Hampton said. "This was over before it started."

Ella ran around in front of him and walked backward so she could look him in the eye. "It ain't over for me," she said. She nodded at Violet, who now walked in-step with Hampton. "And not for her." She looked over his shoulder at the Bessemer City workers behind him. "And not for them neither."

"It's over," he said.

They reached the side street where they'd left the truck parked. Hampton kept walking, but Violet stopped, shook her hand free of his. He looked back at her. "Come with me," he said.

"Where? Your room?" Violet said. "And what then?"

"Come home with me," Hampton said. "To New York."

"Are you serious, Hampton?" she said. "I can't just leave. Not like you can."

"No one's leaving," Sophia said. "Let's all just talk about this. Let's talk about what we do next."

Hampton turned and walked away from them.

Violet called his name.

"Let him go," Ella said.

The boardinghouse was only a few blocks away, and Hampton's fury pushed him toward the solitude it offered. All he wanted was to be alone in his attic room so he could pack his things for the trip home. He was as angry as he'd ever been in his life, but more than that he was embarrassed and sad. He'd walked a hundred yards or so when he turned and saw that he could see the lit field where the rally continued. The dark shapes of bodies moved in silhouette in front of the stage.

Hampton slipped the rifle strap from his shoulder and raised the gun, pointed it at the bodies in the field, felt the weight of his finger on the trigger. He had never fired a gun before. He had no idea how far a bullet would go or what damage it would do if it arrived, but he felt a near-overwhelming urge to shoot indiscriminately into the crowd of white people, to hurt and humiliate them the way he'd been hurt and humiliated. Neither he nor his father had invited violence, but it had found them. His father had met it, and Hampton wondered if he would meet it too.

But he could not squeeze the trigger. He lowered the gun, tossed it into the trees by the road, listened as it crashed through the branches. Throwing the gun caused the pain in his side to flair, and he touched his ribs, wondering what he would feel if one or more of them were broken.

He continued walking south toward Franklin Avenue and the boardinghouse. He crossed over and saw the huge, glowing form of Loray. He thought he heard the sound of footsteps behind him, but there was no one there. His eyes searched the long shadows cast by tall trees and the unlit places in between houses. He found himself desperate to discover the shape of a man rushing toward him. Maybe his imagination had created the sound; maybe he wanted the violence of another confrontation, wanted to exercise the hate that had laid its hand upon his soul.

He reached the house and climbed the three flights of the back staircase to his room in the attic. He turned on the lamp and sat down on the bed. Tomorrow he would send a cable to Weisbord and demand a return ticket to New York.

He reached into his back pocket, found the photograph of his mother and father. He stared at it for a moment, and then he propped the photo against the lamp. He lay down and stared at the ceiling and pictured his parents back in Mississippi, tried in vain to envision his father's face, but a memory of a time before that night did not seem to exist. He realized that the only memories he had of life with his father spanned the course of the few hours during which they'd fled for their lives.

Hampton closed his eyes. He knew he was waiting for something, but he did not know what it could be.

CHAPTER ELEVEN

Albert Roach

Friday, June 7, 1929

Jealousy nearly split Albert's heart in two that sunny afternoon as he and Tom Gibson stood on the sidewalk and watched hundreds of old boys march by in their Confederate battle grays. The crowd of bodies swelled around the two men, nearly pushing them off the curb and onto the street, where the veterans—most on foot with canes in their hands, some seated on the backs of convertible automobiles, the rest standing atop garlanded flatbed trailers—paraded down Trade Street beneath an early summer sun, the bodies of the marchers and the shapes of the cars and floats hardly registering shadows on the blacktop below.

Estimates were that 150,000 people had flocked to Charlotte for this four-day celebration of Confederate valor, and Albert believed that every single one of them stood alongside him. Aside from the smell of the asphalt where it radiated beneath the veterans' boots and the vehicles' tires, Albert's nose caught the smoky-sweet scents of cigars, the reek of sweaty bodies pressed too close together, the whiffs of hot dogs and chili, homebrew, and popcorn.

"There he is," Tom said. He raised a hand and pointed across the street. Albert looked and saw O. Max Gardener in a suit and tie and black stovepipe hat standing on the other side of a battle-flag-swathed barrier. Dozens of official-looking people surrounded him. "It's a pretty important day when the governor comes calling, ain't it?"

"I reckon it is," Albert said, but seeing the governor only made him feel worse. He'd never fought in a war, had never done anything that anyone could view as heroic. Albert Roach knew he was the last person who would warrant a visit from the governor.

It didn't help things that Chief Aderholt had suspended him again—this time for drinking on the job—and try as he might, Tom's little speech en route to Charlotte hadn't helped either.

"Let's just have us a nice time," Tom had said from behind the wheel. "Do a little drinking, get away from Loray and that god-damned strike."

Tom had been drinking when he'd said it, had been drinking since the moment he'd left home and picked up Albert. He'd driven with a Mason jar of white lightning tucked between his legs, and he and Albert had passed it back and forth until it was empty. Albert may have been sad standing there on the sidewalk as these heroes passed him by, but at least he was drunk, and that was better than just being sad.

Although Albert still had another week left in his suspension, he carried a pistol holstered beneath his jacket. Watching the soldiers march and hearing the bands play and seeing the red, white, and blue crepe paper strung from cables above the street made him want to retrieve his gun and fire it into the air in celebration. But he knew that Tom, who'd had even more to drink than Albert had, would be irritated by the attention.

It had been nice at first. The day was bright and warm, not yet hot on this first Friday in June. When they'd arrived the streets had been busy, but not quite as full as they were now, and they'd strolled along the sidewalk taking discreet sips from the Mason jar.

But as the streets had filled and the parade began, Albert found himself forlorn, as if his own disappointment would suffocate him if he didn't do something. He ate two hot dogs all-the-way and a candied apple covered in peanuts, but none of it made him feel any better.

"You didn't miss a damn thing not going to the war," Tom said during the ride back to Gastonia after the parade. The setting sun bronzed the waters of the Catawba River as they crossed the bridge into Gaston County. "All I did in France was drink and whore, and hell, you can do that here in Gastonia." He laughed, looked over at Albert, slapped him on the leg. "Shit, Roach," he said. "Come on. You need to liven up. Let's find you a drink or a girl, one."

Albert turned and looked at Tom. Tom had his window rolled down and the sunlight poured across his face. At forty-four he was two years older than Albert, but he was also taller, thinner, and had all of his hair, and his wife was pretty and petite, with a sweet voice. Although Albert had only met the woman on a handful of occasions, she did not seem like the kind of woman who would yell or hold a grudge. Albert pictured his own wife, Eugenia, at home, sitting at the small, greasy table in the too-warm kitchen, an apron tied tight around her neck and waist, her breasts and stomach pushing against it. In the next room, little Cicely screamed from her crib. He wasn't ready to go back there after having what should have been a grand afternoon.

"Let's get that drink," Albert said. Tom looked over at him and smiled. "Maybe find a woman too."

"Now you're talking," Tom said.

MISS GRADY MOORE'S TAVERN was just a few miles south of the bridge over the Catawba, an old house in a thicket of woods that could not be seen from the road, but everyone knew it was there, the law included. That's how Albert and Tom knew how to find it. They were welcomed not as officers of the Gastonia Police Department, but as mere citizens who needed to unwind.

Albert followed Tom through the front door and into a room off the kitchen whose windows had been covered over on the outside with pine boards. It was dark and musty; an old Edison phonograph in the corner spun a tinny, whiny song. They took a table by the dusty fireplace. Several other tables sat scattered around the room, mismatched and broken chairs pushed up under them. Naked bulbs hung overhead. A man and a woman drank and talked quietly at a table in the corner. The man had pulled his bowler hat low over his eyes. The couple didn't look up when Albert and Tom entered, so Albert didn't look their way after he'd taken a seat.

But Tom looked around as if he'd just walked into his own home. He nodded at the man and woman who sat and whispered to one another. Neither of them seemed to notice him.

"Turn that music up," Tom said to no one in particular. He leaned back in his chair and rapped his knuckles on the tabletop. "Where's my mistress?" he called. "Is she here? Is she near?"

Albert slipped his hands into his pockets, felt the holstered pistol jostle beneath his jacket. He watched Tom, waited to see what he'd do next. A rusty tin plate half-full of unshelled peanuts sat in the middle of the table. Albert grabbed a handful.

Lights burned in the kitchen. Albert could hear the sound of feet moving across the gritty floorboards. A woman appeared, her long brown hair pulled into a nest atop her head. She wore a long, dark shift that fell past her ankles and a dirty white apron that covered the front of her dress. She wasn't old, but when she smiled at Tom her smile revealed wrinkles and missing teeth.

She carried a tray with a jug and two glasses sitting atop it. She sat the tray on the table and divvied out the glasses and placed the jug in between them. Tom put his arm around the woman's waist and pulled her to him so that she half-sat on his lap. He nuzzled his head against her breasts.

"What do we have here?" he asked.

The woman let the tray dangle at her side. She put her free arm around Tom's shoulder.

"Cherry wine," she said. "Sweet and strong, like me." Her laugh was more of a cackle. Tom laughed too, squeezed her around the waist, rubbed his face against her breasts again.

"Speaking of cherries," he said. He nodded across the table at Albert. "My pal here's looking for a girl. You know any that might be free tonight?"

"If you looking for cherries you done come to the wrong place." She cackled again, coughed into the crook of her arm. "Ain't none free neither."

"You know what I mean," Tom said. "Any girls?"

The woman leaned back and craned her neck and looked toward the kitchen.

"Ain't nobody here but me," she said. "Me and James, and I got him out in the woodpile. Might be some girls here later tonight, but right now it's just me."

Tom uncorked the jug and poured a drink for Albert and then himself. Albert watched him pick up his glass and knock it back in one big swallow. He coughed.

"That's sweet," Tom said.

Tom looked toward the kitchen, then turned his face up to the woman who still sat on his lap.

"I probably need to get into that kitchen while it's empty," he said. "As an officer of the law I need to inspect it for sanitary purposes. Make sure the pipes work, make sure anything that might be wet is supposed to be wet."

"Are you qualified for that kind of work?" she asked. Albert was drunk, but not too drunk to know that most women would blush under that kind of talk; yet this girl didn't seem the least bit bothered.

"More qualified than you could ever imagine," Tom said.

The woman slid off Tom's lap and took his hand and pulled him to his feet. She turned to the couple at the table behind her.

"Y'all need anything right now?"

The man didn't look up, but the woman with him whispered something that must have meant *no*. Albert watched as Tom followed the woman into the kitchen. He listened as their feet moved across the floor. Then he heard something else: the rhythmic sound of someone chopping wood outside.

He filled his glass again, knocked it back. He fished a cigarette from a crumpled pack and lit it. He smoked, tapped his ashes into the plate of peanuts. It was nice to be drunk like this, so much of the night still left. He wanted to talk to someone about something, anything.

He resolved that when Tom came back, he'd tell him what was on his mind. He'd tell him that he'd been feeling blue about not ever doing anything great with his life. Sure, Tom may have drunk and whored his way across France the same way he'd done it across Gaston County, but at least he could say he'd been to war, and by God, that meant something. Albert wanted to do something great, wanted to believe that greatness awaited him, but he couldn't imagine what it would be or where he would find it.

But he was a patriot. He knew that for certain. He would have gone to war if he could have afforded it, but his father had needed him on the farm and his mother had been sick and his older brother had gone to the war and died somewhere in Europe and no one had wanted him to go after that. Still, he loved his country, was willing to die for it if necessary. He had always been willing to stomp out communism, totalitarianism, and fascism if anyone would have given him the chance.

And then this strike at Loray came along and he thought his prayers had been answered. He would prove the gallantry on the streets of Gastonia that he hadn't had the opportunity to prove in the trenches of Europe. If he couldn't fight communism abroad he might as well fight it at home. The enemy was the enemy no matter how far you had to travel to meet him.

He didn't know how long he'd been sitting there when Tom came barreling back into the room from the kitchen, hitching his pants up around his waist. He was smiling.

"Roach," he said, "you ain't going to believe what she just told me." He gestured toward the back of the house.

"Come on," he said, "we got to talk to this nigger."

He walked toward the kitchen, and then he stopped and looked back at Albert, who hadn't moved at all.

"Come on," he said.

Albert reached for the jug, but it was empty. He stood from the table, and the ceiling rushed toward him too quickly and the floor fell away from him and the chair in which he'd just been sitting seemed very small and very far from where he stood. He put his hands on the table and sidestepped around it and then he followed Tom into the kitchen and toward a door on the back wall. Tom opened the door and Albert discovered that it had grown dark outside. He'd lost track of time.

A light beyond the kitchen caught his attention, so he turned to his right and saw a doorway to another room. The door was nearly closed, but the crack it left was large enough to spy a nude woman lying on a bare mattress on the floor. Tom took hold of Albert's arm and pulled him outside. He was already walking through the yard before he realized that the naked woman he'd just seen was the same woman he'd seen earlier.

A greasy, smoky lamp burned out in the dark yard behind the house. The little bit of yellow light it gave off illuminated the body of a colored man surrounded by cords of firewood. He hadn't halted in his work when they'd come outside, and now he finished off two more pieces as Tom and Albert made their way toward him across the night-damp grass. Crickets and frogs called from the dark.

Tom was the first to speak.

"You James?" he asked.

The colored man froze in mid-swing, left the axe hanging just above his head. He remained there for a moment, as if deciding whether or not to turn to see who'd spoken his name. He lowered the axe and looked at Tom and Albert.

"Yeah," he said. "I'm James."

He rested the axe on a stump and crossed his hands over the end of the handle. He stood there, breathing heavy, like he was proud. There was nothing Albert hated more than a proud nigger, especially when you had questions for him. The man who stood there sweating and breathing heavily before them could have been thirty or fifty. It was hard for Albert to tell with niggers. He'd slapped one in the face a few months ago for not getting off the sidewalk when a lady passed, and the chief had dressed him down for it. It turned out that he'd slapped a twelve-year-old boy, but Albert could have sworn he'd slapped a man.

Although Albert couldn't see Tom's eyes, he knew Tom was probably staring at the axe just as Albert was staring at it. James must have felt their eyes resting on the axe because he lowered it to the ground and gave it a little toss so that it would remain out of his reach. He stared at the ground just in front of the places where Tom and Albert stood.

"Your lady inside here said you know something about a nigger and two white girls who've been coming around," Tom said. "She said they came talking about the union."

"Yes, sir," James said. "I might've heard something about it."

"About the union or the nigger and the two girls?"

"About both, sir."

"About both?" Tom asked.

"Yes, sir, about both."

"Well, what did you think about it?" Tom asked.

"About what, sir?"

"About the union."

"I don't got no need for it," James said. "They take good care of me here. Ain't no need to join no union just to cut firewood and make whiskey."

"I'd say," Tom said. He laughed, looked over at Albert. Although James did not raise his eyes from their feet, he allowed himself a brief smile.

"What the hell you laughing at?" Albert asked. The words shot from his chest but got caught up in his mouth. He seemed to have spoken a little more slowly than he'd intended.

"I ain't laughing, sir," James said. "Ain't nothing funny."

"Why you smiling then?"

"I didn't mean to, sir. It's just—"

"You ain't thinking about them two white girls, are you?" Albert asked. He took a step forward, wavered a little, stepped back, and put his hands on his hips. His thumb rested against the holster on his belt.

"No, sir," James said. "I ain't thinking about nothing."

"You better be thinking about something," Albert said. "We're asking you some goddamned questions, so you better be thinking about something."

"Yes, sir," James said. "Yes, sir."

"What are you thinking about then?" Albert asked.

James didn't seem to know how to answer, and now Albert was the one who was laughing. He looked over at Tom, but Tom just stared at the man in front of them.

"That nigger and those two white girls come around here?" Tom asked.

"No, sir," James said. "Came over to the AME in Shuffletown."

"They held a meeting there?"

"Yes, sir."

"Damn," Tom said. "You niggers'll let anybody speak, won't you?"

James didn't say anything, just kept his eyes on the ground.

"What did they look like?" Tom asked.

James seemed to think the question over for a few seconds. He opened his mouth to speak, then he stopped as if reconsidering.

"A Yankee boy," James finally said. "Seemed kind of sweet if you ask me. Fancy shoes. Nice hat."

"What about them white girls?" Albert asked. "They seem sweet to you?"

"No, sir," James said.

"What were their names?" Tom asked.

"I can't say I remember," James said.

Albert saw Tom reach into his pants pocket, and he heard the sound of coins clinking together.

"Would a quarter dollar help your memory?" Tom asked. He waited. James didn't move, didn't speak. "I'm serious," Tom said. "Would a quarter dollar help?"

"It might, sir," James said.

If Albert had had time to realize anything, he would have realized that he could not control himself. He was on top of James before the man had a chance to lift his hand toward Tom's open palm, where the quarter dollar awaited him. Albert knocked James over instead, clutched his hands around the man's throat, and said something along the lines of "This damned nigger thinks we're playing."

He didn't realize that he might have made a mistake until he felt James's fingers close around his wrists and all but pry his hands from around his neck. Albert straddled James's chest, and as he watched he saw his own hands be lifted as if they were doll's hands. The axe lay only a few feet to Albert's left, and he considered struggling free of James's grasp and lunging toward the axe. Then he remembered his pistol.

Albert freed one of his hands and unholstered his gun and pointed it at James's face. Both of them were panting now, staring one another in the eyes. Albert suddenly found himself stone-cold sober, as if he'd awakened from a drunken stupor unable to remember how he'd come to be sitting atop a colored man's chest with a gun in his hand.

Tom crouched down beside them and lay the quarter over James's left eye. The right eye watched Albert and Tom, and as it shifted from Albert's face to Tom's, Albert watched the quarter jump with each flick of the eye. Tom held a second quarter in his hand and raised it so that James could see it.

"Now, I'd hate to have to use this quarter for your other eye," he said, "because that would mean that you wouldn't be getting to spend it. You understand?"

James nodded his head, looked from the quarter to the barrel of Albert's gun.

"A little bit ago I asked you for names," Tom said, "and you don't want me to have to ask you something I've already asked you."

"Ella," James said. He swallowed hard, looked over at Tom. The quarter over his left eye trembled slightly. "That's all I remember. One of the white ladies was named Ella."

"That's all you remember?" Tom asked.

"Yes, sir," James said.

Tom sighed. He looked over at Albert.

"I don't think that's going to be good enough," he said. "I reckon you're going to have to shoot him."

Tom made to stand, and when he did James all but lifted his hand and reached for him.

"Tonight," James said.

"What about tonight?"

"They going to vote," James said. "They going to vote to let colored in the union. Tonight."

"Tonight?" Tom asked.

James nodded his head. His breathing slowed.

Tom stood, tossed the quarter onto James's chest. It bounced off and disappeared into the dark grass. James lay there without moving, the first quarter still covering his left eye. Albert climbed off him, stood, holstered his pistol. He looked down at the man, wondered how long he'd lay there without moving once they left.

"You can go on and get up," Tom said. "Get back to your wood chopping." He looked at Albert, smiled. "We've got to settle up inside, Roach, get down to Loray in time to cast our vote."

ALBERT AND TOM didn't even make it to Loray Street before they encountered a crowd of strikers marching on a picket line in front of the mill. The people hoisted signs and placards over their heads, and Albert could hear them chanting slogans. Lights burned inside the mill, casting a greenish glow on the street in front of it, and Albert saw men and women leaning from windows inside Loray to get a better look at the crowd in front of the mill.

Adrenaline coursed through his body. He felt his heart pound against his ribs and he almost forgot that he'd been drunk all night. He looked at the hand that had pulled his pistol and held it to the colored man's face just minutes earlier. The weight of the gun was still there.

"Pull over," Albert said. He pointed to the curb opposite the mill. "Pull over," he said again, but Tom kept driving.

"We can't park near that shit," Tom said. "Last thing we need is somebody spotting my auto."

"It don't matter," Albert said. "This is police business. Some nigger from New York running around with white women."

Tom pulled a U-turn and parked along the curb a few blocks west of the mill. He killed the engine, looked at Albert.

"You ain't the police," he said. "Not until Chief takes you off suspension." His eyes fell to Albert's waist. "Give me that gun."

Albert laughed. "You ain't serious."

"I am," Tom said. "Hand it over. I ain't taking the rap if you go out there and shoot somebody, drinking like you've been."

"You've been drinking too," Albert said.

"But I ain't on the outs with the chief. You are. So hand it over."

Albert removed his pistol from the holster and handed it to Tom. Tom leaned his chest against the steering wheel and tucked the pistol into the back of his pants waist.

"I thought we were friends," Albert said.

"We are," Tom said. "That's why I'm taking your gun."

Being there on the sidewalk on this warm night while something like a parade raged up the street before him reminded Albert of the afternoon they'd just spent in Charlotte, how he'd stood on a sidewalk just like this one and wished he were a better man than he was. He was drunk then and he was drunk now, but in Charlotte at least he'd had his pistol.

The chanting and cheers grew louder as they approached the crowd. Automobiles headed east and west rolled past on Franklin Avenue, honking their horns and flashing their lights, people leaning from the windows and taunting the strikers as they passed. Albert saw mostly women of varying ages, but there were a few men, boys really, walking alongside the women. He looked for weapons, but he knew that most of the men were cowards and refused to picket without their rifles, choosing instead to stay close to the headquarters where Fred Beal allowed them to stay armed.

"Let's split up," Tom said. "I'll start at the mill and head north. You start up north on Loray Street, and we'll meet in the middle. You see any niggers, you tell them you're police, and you hold them there. There hasn't been any coloreds at a one of these rallies, so there shouldn't be any here tonight."

Albert didn't say anything. He just stared out at the crowd, some of whom had started to look their way. He and Tom didn't look like police officers, but it was clear they didn't belong here with this ragtag group.

"You hear me?" Tom said. "Split up."

"I'd feel better about this if I had my pistol," Albert said.

"You'll get it back when we're done," Tom said. "Ain't no reason to worry about it until then. You ain't going to miss it." He walked off down the sidewalk and disappeared into the crowd. Albert saw a few of the strikers note Tom's arrival among them.

Albert crossed to the other side of Franklin and walked along the storefronts toward Loray Street, where the edge of the crowd gave way to the open road that led to the train tracks and the tent colony and strikers' headquarters just beyond it. He felt small and lost among this mass of people, all of them shouting and marching. He felt like he didn't belong to anything.

"Pig!" someone yelled. "Get out of here, pig!"

Albert looked in the direction of the voice and saw a young woman holding a sign, her face pinched in anger. She spit at him, but he was too far away for it to touch him.

"Get out of here, pig!" she said again.

Her appearance shocked Albert as much as what she said. She couldn't have been any older than sixteen, tall and thin with black hair and a face that looked as if it had been laid over her skull and pulled tight. The girl elbowed a woman standing beside her and said something to her that Albert couldn't hear. The other woman turned and looked at Albert. She spit at him too.

Soon ten or fifteen people were taunting him, calling him "pig" and "fat boy." A few of them even knew his name. A young man pushed his way through the crowd, his hands clenching a wooden placard on a stick. The sign read SOLIDARITY FOREVER.

"Get out of here, Roach," the man said. Albert didn't recognize him, and it was strange to hear his name spoken by someone he'd never seen before. It thrilled him. "You ain't the police no more, Roach. We know you. Get on out of here."

Albert thought the man would stop marching toward him, but he kept coming, and as he got closer Albert prepared himself without fully realizing what his body was doing. By the time the man was within arm's length, Albert had swiped the stake from his hands. The man stepped back, shocked, but not shocked enough. He charged toward Albert, and that was when Albert swung the stake, the placard's slim edge catching the man's face like a knife blade. His cheek fell open against his jaw, and blood covered his face, poured onto his shirt. It looked as if his throat had been cut, and Albert half-expected him to fall to his knees and die right there.

A woman's scream rose up from the crowd, but Albert didn't have time to see to whom it belonged. They were on him almost immediately, and he was suddenly aware that he and Tom should not have come to the mill tonight.

He swung the sign, and it was enough to keep the crowd at bay, but it moved slowly as it cut through the air like a giant fan. Albert tore the placard free so that all that remained was the stake, and he swung it like a billy club, aiming for heads and shoulders and knees. It was the first time in a long time that he felt as if he were accomplishing something, as if he were getting something done, making a difference.

In a drunkenness that quickly gave way to rage once his mind computed what the women had called him and what the boy did in disrespecting him, it did not matter to Albert that the people he struck were primarily women, some of them young and some of them very old. They were all part of the same enemy. As he swung the stick and felt the jolt of bodies, he pictured himself atop a garlanded float sixty years from now, a proud veteran of this heroic struggle on the streets of Gastonia on the night the Loray strike came to an end.

A voice called his name, and he saw Tom pushing his way through the crowd, his pistol drawn and pointed toward the sky. He tripped over something and fell to the street, squeezing off a shot that ricocheted against the blacktop and caromed into the night. The crowd dispersed at the sound of the gunshot, and Tom got to his feet and pointed his pistol at the strikers, who were fleeing in all directions.

"Stop!" Tom yelled. "Police!"

Albert gave chase, the stake raised over his head, but Tom caught him and spun him around.

"What the hell happened?" Tom asked.

"I was attacked," Albert said. He shook free of Tom's grasp. "And I didn't have my goddamned gun! They could've killed me, Tom!"

Tom looked up, scanned the crowd, the majority of which was headed up North Loray Street in the direction of the tent colony and union headquarters.

"Who attacked you?"

"All of them, damn it. Every single one of them. They could've killed me."

Tom looked up the street at the backs of the fleeing strikers, then broke into a run behind them. Albert didn't know what else to do, so he followed. He could hear Tom screaming something but he was too far behind him to hear what it was.

The moon had risen fully, and beneath its light Albert watched as dozens of people scattered through the tent colony on the west side of the road. Oil lamps swung from posts, casting an eerie yellow light and throwing long, thin shadows against the white canvas tents. He heard voices, screams, women's calls for men to get their guns and go out to the road. They were being attacked.

Up ahead, electric lights burned inside the union headquarters. The door opened and slammed shut, opened and slammed shut again. Loud voices came from inside. Someone extinguished the lights one by one, and the building and the night around it fell into darkness.

Tom was still running, so Albert ran too. His side pained him, and he held his hand cupped against it to stave off the ache, the hot dogs and candied apple and whiskey gathering in the back of his throat. He wanted to stop, catch his breath, but he feared being left behind. Tom slowed as he drew closer to the union building. He held his pistol with both hands, held it pointed at the door, only ten or fifteen yards away. Sirens wailed in the distance. Albert knew the rest of the police department would be there soon, and in his drunkenness and exhaustion he couldn't decide whether or not that was a good thing.

"Come on out of there!" Tom yelled, his gun still drawn and pointed at the door.

"Go to hell!" a voice said from inside.

Tom took a running leap and kicked the door. It didn't budge. There was laughter from inside.

"Go to hell!" another voice said.

The sirens were behind Albert now, and beneath their noise he heard the sound of tires coming up the road. He turned and saw two police cars pull into the gravel and skid to a stop. Their doors flew open, and officers scattered, two of them running behind the building. Aderholt climbed from the driver's seat of his automobile, and Albert felt his stomach lurch in his throat. His mouth flooded with bile.

"What the hell, Roach!" Aderholt yelled. "What the hell are you doing here?"

Albert turned and looked for Tom to make sense of what had just happened, hoped he'd be able to explain the past few minutes in a way that made some kind of impression on the chief, that displayed some of the bravery and honor that Albert believed he'd shown.

"We were attacked!" Tom said. He held his gun down by his side and rubbed the knee of the leg he'd used in trying to kick in the door. He nodded toward the building. "They're holed up inside here."

Aderholt looked from Tom to Albert.

"You been drinking, Roach?" Aderholt asked.

"No, sir," Albert said. "I just wanted to come down here and help out."

"Help with what?" Aderholt said. "What could you have possibly helped with?"

He brushed past Albert, walked up to the building, and knocked on the door.

"Beal!" he said. "Beal, if you're in there I suggest you come out now and have a word with me. We'll get this all ironed out so nobody gets hurt."

They all waited. Albert looked toward the tent colony on the other side of the road. The oil lamps had been snuffed out. Clouds had gathered. The night had grown darker without his realizing it. He wished he had his gun, considered whispering to Tom, asking for him to give it back, but he was afraid of the chief discovering that he still carried it.

"Beal?" Aderholt said. He knocked again, stepped back, put his hands in his pockets. He waited, appeared content to do so all night.

"They attacked us, Chief," Beal said from behind the door.

"Well, open up and let's talk about it," Aderholt said.

Whispered voices followed by hushes came from inside. There was the sound of something heavy sliding across the floor. Furniture, perhaps. The lock clicked. The door opened. A tall young man stepped out. He held a rifle with both hands, kept it pointed toward the sky.

"I want to talk with Beal," Aderholt said.

"I'm his emissary," the man said.

"Son, I need you to put that gun down," Aderholt said.

"I'm on the union's private property," the man said. "I got a right to hold this gun. I got more of a right to hold this gun than y'all have to be standing here right now."

"Send Beal out here or we'll need to see about coming inside," Aderholt said.

"You're going to need a search warrant," the man said.

"To hell with a warrant," Tom said. He stepped forward and reached for the door, but the man blocked his way. Tom grabbed the barrel of the man's rifle.

"No, Tom," Aderholt said. He reached for him, but the man pushed Tom, and he fell back and sprawled on the grass. "No!" Aderholt yelled again, but it was too late. Tom raised his pistol and fired one shot that caught the man in the stomach. He dropped his rifle and fell forward. He reached for the door frame, and caught himself before he hit the ground.

The shot echoed down the street. It was followed by the sound of the windows being broken from the inside with the barrels of shotguns and rifles. The wounded man managed to pick up his rifle and open the door. He disappeared inside the building.

"Now hold on," Aderholt said, but his words were swallowed by a shotgun blast.

The windshield in one of the police cars exploded. Everyone scattered in different directions. Albert fell to his belly and crawled along the ground to where Tom was crouched behind a car. Albert reached out, and Tom handed him his pistol. Albert's heart lifted. He'd never fired his weapon in the line of duty, and now he'd been given his chance.

Tom raised himself, leaned over the hood of the car, and fired at the building. Another blast from inside. Shot peppered the front fender and tore at the ground beneath the car. A tire hissed as air escaped.

"Goddamn!" Tom said. He laughed, looked at Albert, who sat leaning against the front fender. "We're in it now."

Albert peered over the hood. Rifle barrels protruded from the headquarters' broken windows. He fired, emptied his weapon. There was another shotgun blast, and what felt like fire ripped into Albert's arm. He fell back, felt blood soak through his sleeve.

"I'm hit," he said. He opened his gun, fed rounds into the cylinder, closed it. He looked over the hood, fired again.

A few last gunshots from both sides. The sound of more sirens in the distance. A car's engine fired nearby, then tires peeled off down the road. Footsteps as someone ran through the grass and then the gravel. Albert looked for Tom. He couldn't find him. He crawled around to the front of the automobile. His fingers plumbed his arm for the wound. His flesh was numb. He could smell his own blood.

"I'm hit!" he said again.

He heard the sound of someone moving toward him on the other side of the car. He raised his pistol and took aim at the figure as it revealed itself.

"Hold!" Tom screamed. "Hold!"

He collapsed beside Albert, fell against the car, out of breath. Albert looked down, realized that Tom had dragged someone along with him. It was Aderholt.

"Chief's hit," Tom said. "They shot him in the back. I think it's bad."

Aderholt turned his face toward Albert. His skin was white against his black suit and tie. He coughed. Albert could see where blood had flooded Aderholt's mouth.

"Why were you even here?" he asked. He coughed again. "Why?"

CHAPTER TWELVE

Hampton Haywood

Saturday, June 8, 1929

A loud pop in the distant night caught Hampton's attention. He opened his eyes and looked toward the window, waited to hear the sound again. The photograph of his mother and father still rested against the lamp.

Another pop, silence, then another. They were gunshots, volleys of them. He didn't know what kind of guns he was hearing, didn't know whether they were being fired in celebration or anger or defense. He thought of the picket Beal had planned. Hampton sat only a block from the mill, less than a half mile from the headquarters. He'd be able to hear shots from either location.

He sat up on the side of the bed. He considered going to the window and looking out, but something told him to remain seated. His first thought was that a mob had overrun the headquarters. He'd heard of the night back in April when vigilantes stormed the union's first headquarters on Franklin Avenue while the National Guard stood by and let it happen. ·

Footsteps echoed from the street in front of the boardinghouse.

Hampton reached for the lamp and extinguished it. Outside, the footsteps ran past the house and down the street. He listened until he couldn't hear them anymore.

Sirens wailed up on Franklin. Hampton was certain that something had gone terribly wrong. He tried to decide what time it could be. Midnight? Perhaps later?

The floorboards gave way under his steps like piano keys. He opened his bedroom door, revealing the dark hall and the landing at the top of the stairs. He opened the door a little farther and peered past the doorjamb. He listened to the crystalline ring of the house's silence. On the other side of the hall, a man named Stamp Dixon stood in the door to his own room in plaid boxer shorts and a white undershirt. Hampton had heard that Dixon worked as a bailer at Loray, one of the few jobs the mill offered Negroes. Hampton had never asked him directly, but it was clear that Dixon had no interest in either the union or a fancily dressed Negro from out of town.

The two men stood looking at one another across the hallway. In Dixon's gaze Hampton felt every misgiving he'd feared about his trip south. The man's face appeared stoic, but something in his eyes also portrayed disgust and disapproval. He stepped back into his dark room and closed the door quietly. Hampton listened as the lock clicked, listened to the springs give as Dixon returned to bed.

Hampton stepped back inside and closed the door, locking it just as Dixon had. The wail of the sirens still came from up around Franklin, and Hampton figured that whatever was making the noise—a police car or an ambulance—had parked at the scene.

What could he do aside from wait? After the anger he'd faced at the rally, he didn't feel safe leaving the house. He had nowhere to go, no one to take him in, no one to hustle him out of town, where he could catch the next train to New York. Sophia and Ella and Violet were probably miles away in Bessemer City. They wouldn't learn of the gunshots and the sirens until morning.

Loud voices rose from the street outside Hampton's window. He pulled back the curtain, kept his body in the shadows of the room, and looked out onto the street. A group of ten or so men walked quickly past the house and away from whatever was happening on Franklin. One of them stopped and looked back. The group continued on until another man stopped and spoke to the lone member who'd paused.

"Come on!" the man called out. "You want to go to jail?"

Hampton let go of the curtain. There was nothing he could do now but wait until morning.

HE KNEW HE must have fallen asleep because the noise he heard jolted him upright: a loud bang, followed by another. The sound of automobile doors slamming shut. He scrambled off the bed and went to the window, where he opened the curtains just wide enough for one of his eyes to look out on the street. Trees obscured his vision but he could see a vehicle parked in front of the boarding-house. He realized the sirens had stopped, but at what point he did not know. Then, on the porch downstairs, out of sight from where Hampton stood at the window, someone banged a fist against the front door.

He stepped, nearly fell, away from the window. He looked around for something with which to protect himself, but his room was nearly bare: the cot, the small table, the chair sitting before it. Nothing that would be any match for a gun or a knife or a gang of men like the group he'd seen on the street earlier.

There were voices downstairs. Whoever had been at the door was now inside. He could hear Miss Adeline's voice coming through the floor. The other voices he could hear spoke in low whispers, but Miss Adeline nearly yelled. He tried to discern if she sounded mad or confused or scared. He couldn't tell. He returned to the window and parted the curtain. The truck was still there. He thought of lifting the windowpane and climbing out, jumping to the ground. It was twenty feet, no more than that, but there was grass beneath. He pictured himself running down the street, cutting up through a yard, trying to hide in a crawl space beneath one of the small houses until the morning light allowed him to find his way to the headquarters, where he'd beg someone to help him.

The voices on the first floor had grown quiet, but now Hampton heard the creak of the stairs; then he heard footsteps coming up the flight toward the landing outside his room.

Like his father had done, Hampton decided he would fight with a fury fueled by fear and anger. He stomped across the room, the footfalls making him sound larger, stronger than he knew he would feel once he opened the door. He turned the lock as if chambering a round and threw open the door.

Miss Adeline's face collided with his chest. Her forehead slammed into his lip, drawing blood into his mouth. The old woman stumbled backward, collapsed, more out of shock than the violence of the impact. The oil lamp she'd carried skidded across the floor, snuffed itself out. Hampton looked down at the old woman, touched his lip, saw the blood, tasted it. He bent toward her, and tried to help.

"You got company," she said.

A woman's voice, then another, called to him from the back stairs. Already on his knees, Hampton pivoted and looked around the banister. Sophia stood at the bottom of the stairs, Ella beside her.

In what seemed to be one motion, Stamp Dixon turned the lock and flung open his door so that he had to stop it from slamming shut after it bounced against its hinges. He stood above Hampton, the light of his room behind him, tucking his undershirt into a pair of pants he struggled to button at the same time.

"You damned nigger," he said. He stepped out and grabbed Hampton by the collar, his other hand grasping at whatever it could find: Hampton's arm, his shirt, his pants' waist. Dixon pulled him toward the stairs, pushed against Hampton once his body teetered on the top step. Hampton felt himself going over, the small world of the boardinghouse's attic landing and then its narrow stairwell closing in around him as he tumbled head over feet to the story below.

As he fell, he scratched and kicked at the walls, did his best to stop himself before he reached the bottom, before he heard his neck snap, before the already dark stairwell was suddenly thrown into complete blackness. He caught himself halfway down the stairs, realized that he hadn't fallen as far as he'd thought. He was on his back, his legs splayed against the wall, the fingers of both hands grasping the stair rail's wooden spindles. Dixon stood in the hallway above. Beside him, Miss Adeline was on her feet.

"You damned nigger," Dixon said again. He raised his hand and pointed toward the street in front of the house. "I don't know what the hell's going on out there, but I know you and those white girls down there got something to do with it. I'm going to tell you right now to get gone. I'm calling the police. You ain't done nothing but made things worse. Nothing but that."

OUTSIDE ON THE darkened street, Ella and Sophia begged Hampton to get inside the truck, to hunker down in the floorboard, but he refused.

"What happened?" he said. "I heard gunshots, then sirens."

"It's Beal," Sophia said.

"He's shot?"

"No," Ella said. "There was a raid. Police were shot. Get inside."

"Where are you taking me?"

"Ella's got a friend who can help," Sophia said. She grabbed Hampton's arm and pulled him toward the open driver's-side door.

"I'm not sitting down in the floor like some boy," he said. He'd ridden into Gastonia crammed into the back of Reed's car. He didn't want to ride out of town the same way. He walked to the back of the truck, put his foot on the bumper, and climbed over the tailgate. He felt the truck give when Sophia and Ella sat down inside, heard them slam their doors. The engine fired. He lay on his back.

His mind tried to track the turns that Sophia took as she drove, but Hampton did not know the city well, certainly not beyond downtown and the Loray village. Headlights whipped by. He tried to sink his body as low as he could, tried to will the light from catching him. Above him, streetlights streaked by like comets. When the truck slowed in traffic he could hear people's voices, passing automobiles, horns honking, and the occasional siren off in the distance.

After a few minutes, Hampton sensed that they'd left the city. The sky darkened above him. The night grew silent. Sophia now drove without stopping, took curves without slowing. The truck creaked and rocked. Hampton closed his eyes, tried to steady himself, struggled to keep the dizziness from turning to nausea.

Sophia slowed the truck and pulled it to the side of the road. Where were they? In the country? A neighborhood street? Another town?

The passenger's-side door creaked open. He heard Ella's voice. "Excuse me," she said. "Excuse me."

"What you need?" a man's voice asked from the side of the road. Hampton made himself as flat as possible. He closed his eyes, waited.

"Do you know where Katherine McAdam lives?"

"Well, sure," the man said. "In the McAdam house."

"Can you tell me how to get there?" Ella asked.

"What are you girls doing out this late?" he asked.

"We need to see the McAdams," Ella said.

"Well," the man said. He spoke slowly, as if considering each word, as if considering whether he should be giving directions this late at night to two women alone in a truck. "You just keep going up Main Street here. And once you pass the big Baptist church you just take a right on that next road there. The McAdams live at the end of it. You can't see the house from the road, but it's back there."

"Thank you," Ella said.

She closed her door and they rumbled off up the road. The engine groaned when they reached the hill.

There were no lights on inside the house, but there was starlight and moonlight enough for Hampton to see that the house was large. He and Sophia stood in the yard and watched as Ella walked up the steps to the wide, covered porch and stood before the door. She knocked, waited, knocked again. A light came on in a window on the second floor. Another light came on in what Hampton assumed was the hallway beside a bedroom. The added light made it even clearer that the house belonged to someone incredibly wealthy. It was the nicest home Hampton had ever seen in person.

A porch light came on, bathing Ella in yellow. Hampton heard someone fumble with the door on the other side. He was tempted to step away from the light, return to the truck, and let Ella and Sophia take care of things without him becoming a distraction to the white people he was certain must live here. But before Hampton could turn away the door opened and revealed a middle-aged white man with a thin mustache. He wore a robe and a pair of spectacles, his eyes and his hair proof of the deep sleep from which he'd just awoken.

The man stared at Ella as he tightened the sash around his robe.

"Can I help you?" he asked. He looked past Ella to where Sophia and Hampton stood side by side in the dark yard, almost out of reach of the light coming from the house. Hampton was prepared for the man to ask them all to leave, to threaten to call the police, to go inside and return with a rifle or some kind of weapon. Instead he stepped out onto the porch and pulled the door nearly shut behind him as if shielding Ella's eyes from any valuables inside the house.

"Yes, sir," Ella said. She bowed her head slightly. Her voice had taken on a tone of nervousness and uncertainty that Hampton had not heard before. "Good evening, sir. I'm sorry to bother you so late. Is Kate at home?"

"Kate?" the man said. He looked at Ella as if the name confused him. "What's this about?"

"Well, sir, and again, I'm sorry to bother you like this, but I was hoping to speak with Kate."

"Richard," a woman's voice called from inside the house. The man pushed the door open and looked up as if he were looking toward the second floor. Hampton took a step forward, lowered himself a little, and followed the man's eyes. He saw a woman standing by the railing at the top of a wooden staircase. Her brown hair was pulled back in a bun, and she wore what looked to be a blue silk robe. "Let her in," the woman said.

"What is this, Katherine?" the man asked. "What's this about?"

"Let her in, Richard," the woman named Katherine said.

Richard stood as if uncertain of what to do, but then he opened the door just wide enough so that Ella could pass by him without the two of them touching. Ella raised her hand and gestured over her shoulder to where Sophia and Hampton stood.

"I've got friends with me," she said.

"Show them in, Richard," the woman at the top of the stairs said. "All of them."

Richard opened the door a little wider. Ella turned and offered a weak smile. She went inside. Richard did not look at Sophia or Hampton, but he stood there with the door ajar. Sophia moved toward the house, walked up the porch steps. Hampton followed her. When they entered, they found Ella had already ascended the stairs toward the woman. Hampton assumed that the woman at the top of the stairs must be Kate, but he could not imagine how Ella could know and trust someone so wealthy, someone who lived so well. The hardwood floors gleamed under the foyer's lights. A darkened hallway sat on one side of the staircase, leading to what Hampton assumed was the kitchen at the back of the house. To Hampton's left was a large dining room. He'd glimpsed a grand chandelier hanging over a long dining table as he'd passed through the front door. Oil portraits and old photographs, what looked to be daguerreotypes, hung on the walls. On his right, just inside the door, was a sitting room.

Ella and Kate stood whispering at the top of the stairs. The man named Richard pulled his robe tight around him again, refusing—perhaps unable—to make eye contact with Sophia and Hampton.

"Richard," Kate said. He looked up to where she stood on the floor above them. Ella was beside her. "Please offer our guests a seat, and then wake Claire and have her put on some coffee. There's cake in the cupboard. Please cut it." She turned away. Ella followed her. Hampton heard a door close.

Richard stared at the spot where the two women had been standing, then he lifted his hand and gestured toward the sitting room. Hampton followed Sophia inside. The room was dark, but he could see a long leather sofa and two sitting chairs. Richard turned on the light, and Sophia took a seat on the sofa. Hampton sat down beside her.

"Make yourselves comfortable," Richard said. He nodded, kept his eyes on the floor.

"Thank you," Sophia said.

Richard nodded again and left the room. Hampton listened as he walked up the stairs. The house was quiet. Then he heard Richard knock gently on a door and say, "Claire."

Hampton looked around the room. The two sitting chairs were on his right. Across the room, a low cabinet had been pulled away from the wall; one of its doors was open, revealing a stack of records. Hampton looked around the room, but he did not see a phonograph.

He'd almost forgotten that Sophia was sitting beside him, until he felt the warmth of her hand on top of his own. Her touch startled him. He looked at her.

"I'm sorry," she said.

"For what? There's nothing to be sorry for."

"For asking you to come," she said. "For convincing Weisbord to send you. It's my fault."

"No," he said. "If Beal were a better organizer—"

"It's my fault you came to Gastonia," she said, "not Fred's. But we're safe here. No matter what happened tonight, we're safe here."

Whispered voices floated into the room from the stairwell. People descended the stairs as quietly as possible, turned at the bottom, followed the hallway to the kitchen. Voices, louder now, came from the back of the house, accompanied by the sounds of cabinets and drawers opening and closing. Sophia and Hampton sat, holding hands, listening to the sounds of the people in the kitchen. Soon there was the smell of coffee brewing.

A few minutes later, Katherine rounded the corner and stood in the entrance to the sitting room. Ella stood beside her.

"Good evening," she said. "You must be Ms. Blevin." She stepped forward and reached for Sophia's hand. "And you must be Mr. Haywood." Hampton stood and took her hand in his, found her handshake firm and formal. His mind could not help but marvel at the impossibility of him touching such an elegant white woman in such an elegant home in the Carolina of the Klan and Jim Crow.

"Please, make yourselves comfortable," the woman said. Hampton returned to his seat on the long sofa. Ella walked around the coffee table and sat in the armchair closest to Hampton. "Ella, let me speak with my husband."

"Thank you, Kate," Ella said.

"Of course," Kate said. "Of course."

Kate turned and went down the hallway. Hampton heard her voice in the kitchen, followed by Richard's voice, which seemed louder, perhaps angry.

"She's going to help us," Ella said. She looked at Hampton. "She's going to get you on the next train."

Someone was coming up the hallway toward the sitting room. The shape of a woman filled the door, and Hampton, remembering that Kate had told her husband to "wake Claire," kept his eyes on the table before him. It was one thing to touch a married woman in her home; it was another to look her daughter in the face.

"There are milk and sugar here, if you'd like," a voice said. It seemed to belong more to a woman than to a girl, and Hampton knew that whoever had spoken was close to his own age. A silver tray was lowered toward the table; it held a pot of coffee, three cups with spoons, a carafe of milk, and a small bowl of sugar.

Hampton could not help but glance toward the woman's face. What he found shocked him enough that he could not stop himself from saying what he said next.

"Donna?"

Upon hearing that name in his mouth, the girl dropped the tray the last inch or so. It crashed to the table, the impact overturning the carafe of milk, spilling it onto the floor. The woman gasped at the clatter. She looked back and forth between Hampton's face and the milk that ran over the table and dripped onto the rug.

It was her, Donna, the girl from the train. Hampton was certain that she was the girl who'd wandered into the dining car in the middle of the night. The girl he'd made the mistake of speaking to when something told him he shouldn't. The girl who he'd feared had led to his lynching when Beal ordered him off the train in Salisbury just a few days ago.

Donna held his gaze. She appeared stunned.

"Donna?" Sophia said. She looked from Hampton to the girl.

Donna blushed a pale pink. "I'm sorry," she said. "I think you may have the wrong person. My name is Claire." She smiled, but Hampton saw her smile for the lie it was.

"Of course," he said. "I'm sorry."

"Who's Donna?" Sophia asked.

"I'm sorry," Hampton said. He looked at Sophia, then at Ella. "Someone I used to know. I just thought, I don't know. I'm sorry."

Claire now backed out of the room, nodded by way of goodbye, and then disappeared.

"Who's Donna?" Sophia asked again.

Just then came the sound of Richard's voice from the kitchen.

"This is unbelievable," he said. "That's the woman Claire met in D.C.?"

"Huh," Ella said. "I knew I recognized that girl." She reached out and turned over one of the coffee cups. She picked up the pot and filled her cup. She took a sip, swallowed loudly. Took another.

"What of it?" Kate said. "Who cares, Richard?"

Richard said something else, but she shushed him, cut him off from speaking.

A door banged open in the back of the house, and loud steps came up the hallway. Another door opened, closed. Richard appeared, a heavy blanket folded beneath his arm. He had changed out of his robe into a button-down shirt and trousers. His once messy hair was brushed back away from his forehead. He looked at Hampton.

"Let's go," he said.

"Where?" Hampton asked.

"To the car." He tossed the folded blanket toward Hampton. It landed on his lap, barely clearing the tray on the table.

"What's this for?" Hampton asked.

"To hide you," Richard said.

FOR THE SECOND time in less than a week, Hampton found himself in a white man's automobile in the middle of the night. This was the South about which he'd always been told, but he'd never been told about the kindness of mill owner's wives, the protective power of hillbilly women like Ella May, the willingness of a girl like Donna, or Claire, to shove the truth deep down into a place where they both hoped it would stay.

And now he was leaving this place, headed to Charlotte with money offered him by the McAdams to purchase a ticket.

"It doesn't matter where to," Richard had said. "Just get the hell out of North Carolina."

Hunkered down in the floorboard of Richard's Super Six, Hampton was leaving with nothing but the clothes he had on. The suit he'd worn down from New York was tattered and grass-stained after his fight with Beal. He reached around and touched his back pocket to make certain that he carried his wallet. It was there, but he remembered that he'd left the photograph of his mother and father by the lamp on the table back in the boardinghouse.

He sat up, tossed the blanket off him, and leaned over the seat. It startled Richard, and the Essex swerved sharply. Richard yanked the steering wheel in one direction and then in the other as he regained control.

"Go back," Hampton said.

"Jesus," Richard said. "You almost ran us off the road."

"Go back," Hampton said again.

"Go back *where*?" Richard asked. He slowed, turned, and looked at Hampton for a moment. "To my house?"

"No," Hampton said. "Back to Gastonia, to my room. There's something I forgot."

"Are you crazy?" Richard said. "You could be killed if we go back there. You'll be lucky if we're not stopped before we cross the river. We'll both be lucky."

"Go back," Hampton said.

Richard turned in his seat again and gave Hampton another quick glance. "It's too dangerous," he said.

Hampton threw his leg over the seat and attempted to climb over. Richard kept one hand on the wheel and fought Hampton with the other. The car swerved again.

"Sit down!" Richard screamed.

"Turn around!" Hampton said. "Now!"

"Damn it," Richard said. "What do you want? More money? I can give you more money." He fished his wallet from his pocket and handed it to Hampton. Hampton threw it onto the front floor-board.

"Keep your damn money," Hampton said. "If you drop me at the train station I won't do anything except come back to Gastonia, and it'll be morning by then. And if I'm stopped your name will be the first thing I say."

"They're going to kill you if they catch you," Richard said. "Strikers shot policemen."

"It's my life," Hampton said. "Drop me right here and I'll walk back. If anyone stops me I'll tell them I was visiting my friend Mr. Richard McAdam of Belmont, North Carolina, and his wife Katherine and his daughter Claire."

Richard slowed the automobile without saying a word. He turned around and drove back toward Gastonia.

From beneath the blanket in the backseat, Hampton did his best to offer directions to the boardinghouse.

When Richard finally turned onto the street where the boarding-house sat, he slammed on the brakes, and Hampton's body rocketed forward. His head slammed into the seat, and his neck forced itself down into his body with an awful crunch.

"The police are here," Richard said. "A lot of people. Stay down."

"Outside the house?" Hampton asked.

"Yes."

"Back up," Hampton said. For a brief moment, he contemplated throwing the blanket off him and opening the door. He'd run until he could either run no longer or until someone—the police, Richard, Sophia—caught up to him. "Can you turn around? Go up another street?"

"No," Richard said. "They've seen me. Stay down. He's got a rifle. Don't move."

Hampton felt the Essex roll forward. Its brakes squealed as it came to another stop. He heard Richard lower the driver's-side window.

"McAdam?" a man's voice said. "What in the hell are you doing up here?"

"Good evening, Mr. Epps. I heard there was some kind of trouble at Loray tonight," Richard said. "I thought I'd come up and see about it."

Epps. Epps. The name tumbled through Hampton's mind. *Percy Epps. Pigface.* He'd heard Sophia and Ella talk about him. The attorney for Loray, head of security. The leader of the Council.

"Trouble?" Epps said. "I'd say there's been a hell of a lot more than trouble."

"What happened?"

It seemed that Epps leaned away from Richard's open window. Hampton heard him talking to someone farther up the street. He strained to hear what they were saying.

"It's the communists," Epps said. His voice was closer, easier to hear. "Beal sent a whole group down to the mill tonight, got the night shift all stirred up. Aderholt and some of his deputies followed the picket back up to the union headquarters. They were fired on."

"Anyone hurt?"

"Oh yeah," Epps said. "Last I heard, it sounds like Aderholt isn't going to survive. They shot him in the back, McAdam. Damned cowards. They hit a couple of deputies too. A couple of the strikers were shot, but not enough of them."

"What's going on up the road here?" Richard asked.

"That union nigger from up north that I told you about," Epps said. "Police are looking for him. Goddamned Beal and the rest of them ran off somewhere, but they'll get caught. We're watching the trains in Charlotte and Spartanburg."

Hampton heard a third man's voice, but he couldn't tell what the man said.

"McAdam, this is Detective Randall," Epps said. "Senator Overman sent him down from Washington. He's been helping us out. Detective, Mr. McAdam is a member of our Citizens' Council. He's committed himself to breaking this strike."

Richard was silent, and Hampton squeezed his eyes shut as tight as possible and prayed to a God he hadn't prayed to since he was a boy. *Make him say something. Make him say something.*

"What's your role on the Council?" the detective finally said.

"Well, I just joined," Richard said. He stammered. His voice was higher than it had been earlier in the evening. "And I haven't really had the opportunity to get involved—"

"We could use you tonight, McAdam. And if you can put a call in—"

The detective interrupted Epps, asked him, "Did you call him to come here?"

"No," Richard said. "No. No one called me. I just heard something happened, and I came right down as soon as I heard."

"Well, I'm glad you're here," Epps said. He yelled something up the street, something about moving a car so that Richard could park. "Pull on up here."

"That's okay," Richard said. "I need to, I need to get home."

"But you just got here," Randall said. Hampton heard Richard slip the Essex into gear. "Why leave?"

"Yeah, McAdam," Epps said. "You just got here."

"And how'd you know to come here, to this house?" the detective asked. "The mill's a block over that way, and their union headquarters is across the boulevard."

"Yeah," Epps said. "How'd you know?"

"Okay, good night," Richard said. He put the car in reverse and they rolled back down the street. One of the men called Richard's name. He backed around the corner, stopped, and slammed on the gas pedal. They sped up the street behind the mill.

"Jesus, Jesus, Jesus," Richard said. "Jesus." Hampton heard him punch the steering wheel.

"They know, don't they?" Hampton said. He lifted the blanket, sat up in the seat. The lights from the mill burned above the northern tree line outside his window.

"They know something," Richard said. "I'd say they most certainly know something."

Minutes later, once Richard had reached the dark open road, Hampton turned and looked out the back window, saw a pair of headlights coming fast behind them. He squinted into the light and imagined his father staring into the cameraman's bulb in the seconds before his photograph had been taken for the first and only time in his life. Hampton would never see his father's face again. He'd come south to find him, and now he was leaving him behind for good.

CHAPTER THIRTEEN

Katherine McAdam

Saturday, June 8, 1929

Katherine had been alone in the house for what seemed like hours, and as the world outside began to lighten, she realized how long it had been since Ella had first knocked on the door, since Richard had gone downstairs to answer it. She had to remind herself that she wasn't alone in the house. Claire had gone up to her room not long after Ella and the woman named Sophia had returned to their truck and driven off into the night.

"You come back here if you need anything," Katherine had told Ella. "You find me, okay. Let me know." Katherine looked at Sophia. "That goes for you too," she'd said. "Both of you. I'm here."

Ella had seemed more relaxed after Richard had left with their friend Hampton. But now, with the house quiet and the sun preparing to rise and Richard still not returned, Katherine found it impossible to find the peace that Ella had shown.

She knew that Richard sometimes kept a bottle hidden in their closet, so she'd gone upstairs and felt along the top shelf where he kept his shoes, toes pointed out. The bottle was set in a pair of wingtips, and she closed her hand around its neck and took it down. She shook a cigarette free from the pack on the dresser and went downstairs in search of a glass and matches.

Instead of calming her nerves, the whiskey and the cigarette had done nothing but sour her empty stomach, and now she stood on the front porch staring out at the driveway, watching the night slowly give way to morning.

It was quiet. The only sounds were the calls of birds and the soft breeze that stirred the trees. Although she knew that another shift was about to begin down in McAdamville, that Edison's Dynamo No. 31 pumped like a heart in the belly of the mill, Katherine felt that she was the only person awake in the world. She wished that Richard were still asleep upstairs. Normally, if it were a weekday, he wouldn't stir for another hour yet, wouldn't rise and bathe and dress for the day until 7 A.M. By that time the world would be awake, and she wouldn't be alone, waiting, like she was now.

Her ears caught the noise of an automobile crawling up the hill. She recognized the sound of it. It was the Essex.

The car rolled through the driveway, its headlights off. Katherine caught a glimpse of Richard behind the wheel. He would not have expected to see her waiting for him on the front porch, and he did not look for her now. Instead he pulled into the garage just as he always did. Katherine all but ran through the foyer, down the hall, and toward the back door.

Richard had already parked and turned off the car by the time she called his name. He did not respond. Instead he closed the garage doors, laced a chain through the handles, and clicked a padlock shut. Katherine knew that something had gone horribly wrong.

Richard appeared ashen except for a dark spot above his right eye. When he drew closer Katherine saw that his face was bruised and his forehead bloodied. She gasped.

"My God, Richard," she said. "What happened?"

He brushed past her and walked up the hall to the front door. He extinguished the lights in the foyer, walked into the parlor, and drew the curtains over the window. He crossed the foyer and drew the curtains in the dining room as well.

"What's going on?" she asked. She closed the back door and walked up the hall. "What happened?"

"Turn the lights off in the kitchen," he said.

She leaned inside the door and flipped the switch. With the lights off the dawn outside seemed even brighter.

She found him standing in the parlor, drinking a cup of cold coffee from the tray Claire had left on the table.

"Richard!" she said. "What happened?"

He poured another cup, drank it more slowly than the first. She looked at his face, the bruised skin, the blood that had dried to a sticky brown. She wondered if he and Hampton had fought.

"Where's that boy?" she asked. "What did you do to him?"

"What did *I* do to him? *Me?* I drove him to the goddamned train station, Kate. Just like you asked!"

It was the tenor of his voice that reminded Katherine that Claire was upstairs. Claire had been away at school so long, that they did not stop to consider whether or not anyone could hear them when they fought. But they weren't alone now. She looked toward the foyer, pictured Claire lying awake in bed listening to the voices coming up the stairwell.

Richard seemed to know that he'd spoken too loudly. He sighed, ran his fingers through his hair.

"They're not still here," he said.

"Who?"

"Those damned women."

"No," Katherine said. "They left hours ago. Hours. Where have you been? What happened?"

He walked around the table and collapsed onto the davenport where Hampton had been sitting just a few hours earlier.

"I tried to take him to Charlotte, but he wanted to go back to his boardinghouse. I said no, but he threatened to go back whether I took him or not. And I thought it would be safer for us both if I just drove him." He looked up at her.

"There were police everywhere, Katherine. Percy Epps stopped my car. He had a detective with him. A Pinkerton, Kate. Do you know what that means? He asked me what I was doing there." He shook his head. "And I didn't know what to say because why in the hell should I have been there?"

"What did you say?"

"Nothing. There was nothing I could say, and they knew." He leaned forward and clasped his hands. "They knew something was wrong."

"What did you do?"

"I drove off. It was the only thing I could think to do."

"Where's Hampton?"

"I left him in Statesville," Richard said.

"Statesville?" She stepped into the room, considered sitting beside him on the davenport, but something stopped her. "What's in Statesville?"

"The train station, Katherine. Epps said they were checking trains in Charlotte and Spartanburg. Statesville was the only place I could take him."

She stared at him, wondering if she could believe him, if she should believe him. She remembered what she'd heard Richard say the night of Claire's engagement party about the child that Ella had lost. Katherine had been so disappointed in him that night. She wondered if he'd disappointed her again.

"Did you really take him to Statesville?" she asked.

He looked up, his face a mix of disgust and anger.

"Of course I did," he said. "Where the hell else would I have taken him?"

"Did you see him get on the train?"

"No," he said. "I thought the twenty dollars I gave him would see to his getting on the damn train."

She stared at him for another moment, finding herself desperate to believe him.

"What happened to your face?" she asked.

He touched his bruised cheek, put his fingers to the cut above his eye. The blood had dried tacky, and when he lifted his hand away he rubbed his finger and thumb together.

"Someone followed us," he said.

He reached for one of the cloth napkins on the table and dipped it into the water pitcher. He touched the napkin to his head, then looked at the watery, pink blood on the cloth.

"A car swerved around me and slammed on its brakes. Another car hit us from behind, ran us off the road. My head bumped the steering wheel."

Katherine remembered what Ella had told her about the Council, about her fear of being on the roads at night.

"Who was it?" she asked. "Epps?"

"I don't know," Richard said. "It could've been anyone."

"Is he all right?"

"Who?"

"The boy, Hampton. Is he all right?"

Richard tossed the wet napkin onto the table and stood.

"You keep saying 'boy' as if he's some child, Katherine. He's no child. He's twenty-five. He's an adult."

"So you talked to him?"

"Jesus, of course I talked to him," he said. "It's a long drive to Statesville. And we'd almost been killed, twice. Conversation was easy after that."

"What did you talk about?"

"Is that really important?"

"The strike?"

"What's important is that *we* never talk about this again. What's important is that Claire never mentions our visitors to anyone. Ever. I'll have someone in the mill shop look at repairing the car. No one can know about this."

He bent forward and picked up the napkin. He dipped it into the water again and held it to his forehead.

"You're a hero, Richard."

He closed his eyes and shook his head.

"Please," he said. "Please don't."

"You saved his life."

Richard walked around the table and stood in the middle of the room. Katherine saw how bruised his face was, how deep the cut above his eye. Whiskers darkened his cheeks. He looked tired and older than she'd ever seen him look before. She realized just how much of her life she'd spent with this man, and in the quiet of the house, the same quiet that she would hear forever once Claire married Paul and left them for good, Katherine understood how many years of her life still stretched out before her with this man by her side. She wanted them to be good years, empty of disappointment and sadness and this crushing quiet that had grown up between them.

"It's true, Richard," she whispered. "You saved him." She stepped toward him and took his hand. He let her hold it as if he could no longer bear its weight. She saw that he stared at the empty spot on the cabinet where the record player had been. Katherine felt his fingers tighten around hers.

"I wasn't trying to save him," Richard said. "I'm trying to save us."

GASTON TRANSOM-TIMES

JUNE 8, 1929, AFTERNOON EDITION

ADERHOLT SLAIN BY MURDEROUS STRIKE-GUARDS OF N.T.W.U.

Redoubled Effort to Apprehend Fred Beal

With the death of Chief of Police O. F. Aderholt earlier this morning after being shot in the back Friday night by assailants at the tent colony of the Loray strikers, county and city officials turned with redoubled zeal to the task of apprehending Fred Beal, organizer of the mob that led Chief Aderholt to his death and wounded several officers.

No trace of Beal's whereabouts has been found. The police worked during the night and into the morning to secure the arrests of other prominent members of the strike. Many suspects had fled the scene but were later apprehended. Velma Burch of Passaic, New Jersey, was arrested in a telephone booth in downtown Gastonia, phoning to New York. Sophia Blevin was arrested in Bessemer City at the home of Ella May Wiggins, a known striker. Wiggins was detained but later released when her alibi of nursing the sick wife of Richard McAdam, owner and operator of McAdam Mills, was corroborated by Mr. McAdam himself. Carlton Reed of New York City was arrested while attempting to board a train in Charlotte. Also arrested were the men who served as armed guards at the strike colony, namely Chesley Anderson of Gastonia, who has been identified by Deputy Officer Albert Roach as the man who shot Chief Aderholt. All are under arrest on charges of assault with a deadly weapon with intent to kill. With news of Aderholt's death, the charge is expected to change to first-degree murder.

The trouble at the tent colony began Friday evening among the strikers themselves. It seems that disparaging remarks passed between them and a group of Negroes. Rotten eggs and other missiles were hurled, followed by a sort of free-for-all fight. Some say that the strikers themselves called the police department to help allay this quarrel.

When the police officers arrived on the scene, a voice was heard to yell, "Shoot the——officers." After being wounded, Chief Aderholt spent the night in serious condition at the Gaston Sanitorium as he fought for his life with his wife and children by his side.

However, at about seven o'clock this morning convulsions set in as a result of the puncturing of his lungs by gunshot. A short while later the chief suffered a cerebral hemorrhage, accompanied by other convulsions, and the end came shortly after 10 o'clock.

This great man will be mourned by many, and we will never forget his bravery. Nor will we forget the perpetrators of such a heinous crime that robbed him of his life.

LABOR DEFENDER

JULY 1929

SMASH THE MURDER FRAME-UP!

Defend the Gastonia Textile Workers!
14 SOUTHERN TEXTILE STRIKERS
(Members of the National Textile Workers Union)
CHARGED WITH MURDER FACE THE ELECTRIC CHAIR
8 OTHERS FACING LONG PRISON TERMS

The police of Gastonia, upon the direct orders of the mill owners, attacked the workers' headquarters and their tent colony, fired shots into the tents, where women and children were sleeping and began shooting at the strikers and beating them with their guns. In the struggle which followed, Chief of Police Aderholt was killed. All the organizers and leading strikers, members of the National Textile Workers Union, have been arrested on a murder charge. The workers have been driven from their tent colony.

DEFEND THE RIGHT OF THE SOUTHERN WORKERS TO ORGANIZE!

RUSH ALL FUNDS to the NATIONAL OFFICE of the
INTERNATIONAL LABOR DEFENSE
80 East 11th Street, New York, N.Y.

International Labor Defense,
National Office: 80 E. 11th St. NY.
I enclose $_____ for Gastonia Defense.
I further pledge $_____ per week.
Name _____
Address _____
City and State _____

A RALLY HAS BEEN SCHEDULED IN GASTONIA, NC
ON SATURDAY, SEPTEMBER 14
TO PROTEST THE TRIAL OF OUR INNOCENT BROTHERS AND SISTERS.

WORKERS OF THE WORLD, UNITE!

GASTON TRANSOM-TIMES

FRIDAY, SEPTEMBER 13, 1929

Since June we have mistakenly believed ourselves rid of the Communist scourge that ordered the murder of Police Chief Orville Aderholt and the shooting of a number of brave officers in June at the Loray Mill. We found and arrested cowards like Fred Beal and other of their leaders and put them in jail. We tore down their tents. We demolished their headquarters. We thought we had flushed the Bolshevists from Gastonia and sent them packing to the dark slums of New York and New Jersey. Recently we learned that many of these same godless Bolshevists have relocated to Bessemer City, proving that even a snake with a severed head can still bite, can still spread poison, can still kill if given the chance.

Word has reached us that a great rally in support of the jailed Communists is to be held tomorrow in downtown Gastonia, a place that has had its fill of anarchy and bloodshed. Is more blood to be spilled? That is impossible to know, but if blood is to be spilled it must not be the blood of innocent, God-fearing Americans. If blood must be spilled, let it be the blood of those who seek to harm us, let it be the blood of those who murdered our beloved Chief Aderholt and wreaked havoc upon our peaceful city.

Tomorrow, we ask that every citizen—every husband, father, brother, officer, veteran—do everything in his power to confront these Communist agitators as they arrive in downtown Gastonia. We do not seek or desire violence, but we will not back down if violence is brought to our door. We will not allow more of our people to be murdered. We will not stand by quietly as our society is infiltrated once again.

PROUD AMERICANS, STAND WITH US TOMORROW AND HELP US PUT DOWN ANY INSURRECTION THAT SEEKS TO OVER-THROW OUR GOVERNMENT AND ALTER OUR WAY OF LIFE.

NOW IS THE TIME FOR ACTION.

NOW IS THE TIME FOR BRAVERY.

NOW IS THE TIME TO STOP THIS NIGHTMARE BY ANY MEANS POSSIBLE.

NOW IS THE TIME TO DO YOUR DUTY.

Advertisement Paid for by the Council of Concerned Citizens of Gaston County

CHAPTER FOURTEEN

Brother

Saturday, September 14, 1929

It had begun, which is to say that it had begun again, on the evening he'd seen Ella May Wiggins. At first he had been satisfied with the homebrew wine the monks made in secret and kept in the monastery's kitchen pantry. The brothers grew the grapes in an extensive system of arbors that threaded through a sunny glade in the middle of the woods not far from campus. A small, gurgling creek snaked along beneath the vines, the green tendrils often trailing in the water. It was not a secret place, but it was secret enough to remain unmolested by the college men and uninvestigated by the local police.

Even after more than a decade of experimentation, the brothers had not yet mastered the art of fermenting grapes, and the wine that often resulted from their efforts bubbled with a yeasty carbonation. At night, Brother would lie burping in his cot in the monastery's basement, the glaze of mild drunkenness having settled over him, the tiny chair he balanced on his chest rising and falling with each breath and belch. He'd stare into the darkness and ask himself what had first caused him to accept a drink after so many years, what caused him now to accept them still, what led him up the stairs from the basement and into the kitchen at night long after everyone had retired, what evil thing whispered in his ear and told him where to find the empty Mason jars to hide the wine.

His heart had been shrouded in a once-forgotten guilt since first laying eyes on Ella back in the early summer. Since that night his waking moments had been shadowed by dark memories of a wasted time that he had tried to put away. The rot and loss of his life, which Brother had kept behind him for so many years, now threatened to suffocate him. Many times he'd thought of cutting a length of rope from the workhouse and walking into the woods in search of a suitable tree with a limb that appeared strong enough to support his weight and long enough to keep his feet from the earth as his body thrashed above the ground. And then, one afternoon, he'd been cleaning Father Gregory's cell when he peered beneath the old man's bed and found it: an old, seemingly unused Winchester 270, a dusty box of ammunition resting beside it. Finding the rifle gave him a new thing to think about during the night as he lay awake: he saw himself kneeling in the middle of the maze of arbors, the grapevines stirring in the breeze above him, the mouth of the rifle's barrel propped beneath his chin, his outstretched arms balancing the length of it, his thumb resting on the trigger.

And then, one day, the wine was no longer kept in the kitchen pantry. The monks no longer offered him discreet pours during meals. He wanted to ask about the missing wine, but he knew they suspected him of stealing what they had once so freely offered. Instead of taking the length of rope from the workhouse, he took a thin strip of wire and used it to pick the lock on the sacristy's door inside the basilica. The wine there was used for communion and therefore authorized by law, shipped from Rome, and corked inside bottles.

Throughout the hot, violent summer the monks followed the events of the strike and discussed it often. Brother knew of Chief

Aderholt's murder, the apprehension of Fred Beal and others, the destruction of the tent colony, Ella May's ascendance to strike leader after the Local moved to Bessemer City. He tried to keep her from his mind, but his awareness of her, especially her proximity to him, pushed him toward drink, and after months of drinking the bubbly homebrew the smooth, rich communion wine was a revelation. By September he had begun making near-daily trips to the basilica, which was often unlocked and unattended, especially in the early mornings before Mass.

Although it was mid-September and roughly three hundred students had returned to classes two weeks earlier, Brother did not encounter a soul that morning when he walked to the basilica. The empty Mason jar in his pocket bulged against his thigh like a tumor he was afraid of cutting free.

Inside the basilica his steps echoed along the floor and lifted to the arched ceiling thirty feet above. Over the main altar, a statue of Mary, Help of Christians, stared down upon him with loving, forgiving eyes, the Christ babe held aloft in her arms. He passed beneath her gaze and walked between the monks' pews toward the sacristy that sat in a walled section behind the altar, which offered him ample cover while he picked the lock. But when he turned the corner he found a new latch and padlock securing the door.

He stepped back, stared at the new lock, imagined the monks speaking of the missing communion wine in quiet voices, their conversations ceasing upon his appearance. Of course they had noticed it. Of course they had considered him. Brother assumed that one of the younger monks, perhaps Father Elian, had come the evening before and used a hand crank to drill holes in the door for the latch as his spectacles slid down the bridge of his nose. The padlock key probably lay hidden somewhere in the monastery, and Brother's mind cycled through all the probable hiding places, but there were too many for him to consider beginning a search, and there was simply no way a search could go unnoticed, especially since it was clear to Brother that they suspected him of being the thief.

He passed beneath the statue of Mary again, stopped in front of the altar, and stared down the center aisle of the basilica. Dust motes floated through wafts of light that beamed through the small windows on the doors that kept the morning outside. The confessionals sat in the shadows on either side. To his right, in the Blessed Sacrament Chapel, the light from the red candle wavered in its sconce. A wooden crucifix hung on the wall, the face of Christ downturned.

If someone had discovered him they would have believed that he had fallen at the feet of Jesus in prayer, but Brother did not pray. Instead he picked at the lock on the tabernacle box with the scarred bit of wire, the chair he wore around his neck swinging like a pendulum before him. His hands sweated, his fingers shook. The light from the red candle licked the floor around him. He did not know how much wine the monks had blessed and set aside for the communion of the homebound and those who might need last rites at a moment's notice; all he knew was that the lit red candle signaled that the wine was inside.

He opened the box and peered inside, saw the crusty loaves and the glass pitcher, the dark wine catching the flickering light. He took the Mason jar from his pocket and unscrewed its lid, picked up the pitcher, and poured the wine into the jar until it overflowed the sides and ran through his fingers. He set the near-empty pitcher back inside, closed the box, and stood, stuffing the capped Mason jar back into his pocket.

He walked along the shadows of the basilica's west wall. Above him the morning sun illuminated the stained-glass windows that portrayed the lives of saints: Bernard, Patrick, Boniface. He'd almost reached the back wall of the basilica when something made him stop: the sound of feet coming up the steps outside, the basilica's front door creaking open.

Brother opened the door to the small confessional closet, stepped inside, and pulled it to behind him. It squealed, the noise of it echoing along the basilica's floor. Brother closed his eyes tight and tried to slow his breathing. The footsteps continued into the basilica and stopped nearby. Whoever it was knew he was there. He was surprised to hear a woman's voice.

"Father?" she said. She waited. "Father? Are you there?"

In his old life, Brother had asked this same question of God many times, and now he wanted nothing more than to offer this woman the same silence that God had always offered him, but she was persistent, and the more Brother tried to slow his breathing the more difficult it became. He swallowed, ran his dry tongue over his teeth.

"Yes, child?"

"May I give confession?"

Inside the darkened closet, Brother placed his hands over his face and pressed his fingers into his eyeballs. He stayed that way until his breathing slowed.

"Father?"

"Yes, child," he said. "Yes."

He listened as she opened the door and stepped inside, settled herself only inches away from him. He slid open the screen that separated them from one another, stared down at his lap, did not raise his eyes to her. He pictured her as a dark-haired woman of middle age who smoothed her dress over her legs when she sat down, who wiped at the corners of her eyes where tears had already collected.

"Bless me, Father, for I have sinned," she said. "It has been three weeks since my last confession." She waited.

He eased the wine-wet Mason jar from his pocket, careful not to drop it. He unscrewed the lid as quietly as possible, tipped it toward his lips. A drop of wine spilled onto his white shirt, blossomed like blood gushing from a wound. He took a sip. "Go ahead, child," he said.

"I am weak," the woman said.

Her northern accent surprised him. He took another sip of the wine. "We are all weak," he said. "We are all human."

"I am weak because I fear my husband," she said. "I remain silent while he commits violence and leads others to commit violence. And I know more violence will be committed today." He heard her stir and resettle herself. "And I fear that someone might be killed."

Brother took another sip from the jar. "Have you gone to the police?"

"The police?" she said. "They can't save her."

"Who is she?"

"That singer at Loray," she said. "That woman Ella May."

CHAPTER FIFTEEN

Ella May

Saturday, September 14, 1929

Ella was alone in the struggle now; at least it felt that way. Fred Beal and Carlton Reed and several other strike leaders remained in jail, charged with Aderholt's murder. Sophia and Velma had been arrested and then freed for lack of evidence. They'd both left town, Sophia heading home to her parents in Pittsburgh, Velma back to New Jersey. Sophia had promised Ella that she would return as soon as possible, but Ella couldn't wait for her, especially after the collapse of the Gastonia Local. She'd acted alone in opening the office of the Bessemer City Local, which she'd organized as an integrated branch of the National Textile Workers Union. Most of the members were from Stumptown, but a handful of Gastonia strikers had joined. Others had returned to Loray or moved on to other mills.

Today's rally in Gastonia had been organized by the national office. Party officials would be there, as would workers from mills in other parts of the state, all to show support for Beal and the jailed strikers. After how he'd treated Hampton and thwarted their attempts to integrate, Fred Beal was the last person Ella wanted to support. But she could not risk running afoul of the national office. The money Kate had given her was running out. She'd been able to piece together some kind of life from the meager funds that dripped down from New York, but she knew it wouldn't last forever, because the strike wouldn't last forever. Her only choice was to keep going, to try to recruit new members, to keep working to shut down the mills, to keep insisting that the union's demands be met. If it worked, her life would change. She could go back to the mill, feed her children, take care of them if they got sick. If it all fell apart, she didn't know what would happen.

It seemed that summer had only recently come to a close, but the morning had begun cool and breezy. Ella wore John's old jacket with the knowledge that it would be too warm to wear it by noon. She and Lilly stood with Violet and Iva on the side of the Kings Mountain Highway at the top of the mud road that led down into Stumptown. She'd been able to recruit two drivers with trucks to carry them into Gastonia for the rally. Aside from a fee of five dollars, the drivers had only one stipulation: no guns.

The drivers, both of them farmers, one from Kings Mountain and one from Shelby, stood by their trucks, smoking cigarettes and speaking in low voices. Occasionally, one of them would look back at Ella as if making certain she was still there, was still willing to pay the men for this job. The rally was scheduled for noon, and the strikers were set to leave at 10 A.M. At this moment it was just Ella and Violet and the girls standing out by the road, but Ella knew others would come.

"I'm cold," Lilly said. She cupped her hands together, huffed her hot breath into them.

"It'll warm up," Ella said. "And if it don't you can make a fire in the chimney. There's plenty wood."

"I don't know how," Lilly said.

"Of course you do. It's just like making a fire in the stove," Ella said. "Otis knows how. He can do it. Tell him I said to do it."

"Okay," Lilly said.

Violet stood behind Iva. She had her arms around her younger sister's shoulders to keep her warm. Violet's eyes were closed. She hummed a tune. Iva stared at the two drivers smoking by their trucks. Violet stopped humming, opened her eyes, looked over at Ella, gave her a weak smile.

"Thank you," Ella said.

"For what?" Violet asked.

"For sticking with me through this. I bet you didn't know what you were getting into."

"Don't matter what I knew when," Violet said. "I'm in it now."

Ella felt Lilly's hand find its way into hers. The girl leaned against Ella, put her cheek to her stomach, stared down at the road. Ella's belly had begun to grow round, but she was still thin enough that John's old coat was able to hide it. She wondered what Lilly would think when she discovered that her mother was pregnant again, that there would be another mouth to feed by the time winter arrived, that this new child, like the rest of her children, would not have a father to claim as its own now that Charlie had finally disappeared.

"I thought you said you weren't going to Gastonia no more," Lilly said. "I thought you said that."

"I won't," Ella said. "Not after today. Today's the last day."

"But I don't want you to go."

"Well, sometimes we don't get what we want," Ella said.

"I want to go with you."

"No, you can't go."

"But I want to."

"I need you to stay here," Ella said. "Look after the babies. Tell Otis to make that fire. I'll be back."

"When?"

"This afternoon or tonight, one. Soon as I can."

"Iva gets to go," Lilly said.

Violet stopped humming and opened her eyes. She looked at Lilly, and then she looked down at Iva.

"Says *who* you're going?" Violet asked her.

"Mama said I could," Iva said.

"She ain't never said that." Violet looked up at Ella and shook her head. "She never said that."

"Shoot," Iva said. She kicked at a rock. It rolled into the grass. "Thanks, Lilly. Thanks a lot."

Ella let go of Lilly's hand and turned the girl's shoulders so that they faced the road that led down into Stumptown.

"Go on home," she said. "Check on those babies. I'll be back soon."

"I don't want to," Lilly said. She raised her face to Ella and reached for her hand again, looking as if she might cry. "I'm scared for you to go."

Ella didn't want to admit it, not to herself and certainly not to Lilly, but fear had dogged her heart all night long and into the morning. She knew the primary fear was the fear of futility, the suspicion that nothing she could do today or tomorrow or the day after would change the events that comprised the course of her life and the future of the union.

Less than an hour later enough bodies had arrived to fill the back of one of the trucks. Ella and Violet watched as colored women and men came up the road from Stumptown and white women and men came across the field from Bessemer City. By 10 A.M. fifty or so had gathered, plenty of bodies to make for a tight ride to Gastonia.

"I hope you know what this means," Violet said.

She and Ella stood by the bed of the last truck, a man inside helping others get settled into spots. They'd all be standing during the trip. That was the only way for them to fit.

"I hope it means something good," Ella said.

"It does, girl. This is your doing."

"Everybody else done it," Ella said. "All I did was ask them."

Violet smiled and climbed up into the truck.

Ella walked up the road and stopped in between the two trucks. She stepped into the grass on the shoulder so that she could see most of the people standing in the truck beds and most of them could see her.

"I want to thank all of you for coming," she said. "I'd like to be doing something else on a Saturday, but this is what we have to do, so we'll do it." Someone whistled from the lead truck. A few people clapped. Ella stopped speaking for a moment, looked up the road toward Bessemer City, and recalled what it had meant for her only five months ago to walk this road alone to the crossroads of West Virginia Avenue. What it had meant to wait for strangers to pick her up in an automobile and carry her to her first union rally. Who had that woman been? Who was she now?

She looked back at the two trucks and saw Violet's face peering out at her from in between the slats. "I didn't join up in this union to be no kind of leader," Ella said. "But the police and the bosses have either locked up our leaders or run them off somewhere. So, like I said, I ain't no kind of leader, but I'm going to lead you now, and I need you to listen to me.

"We're about to leave here and go into town, where there are going to be hundreds of people, maybe thousands. Some of them are going to want us there, some of them aren't, but there's only two kinds of people you need to be on the lookout for today: the ones holding guns and the ones holding cameras. There ain't no need to say a word to either of them, no matter what they say to you. We're there to be seen. Let somebody else give interviews." She smiled, tried to fight it, but found that she couldn't stop. "Let somebody else get shot at."

"I'm proud to stand alongside all of you," she said. She looked at Violet. "I'm proud to be with my friends."

She walked to the back of the second truck, where Violet waited, her hand outstretched. Ella took Violet's hand, climbed up, and stood beside her. The driver came around and slammed the tailgate shut. The engine fired on the first truck, then the second.

They sang a few songs that everyone knew, and then Ella sang "Two Little Strikers" and "All Around the Jailhouse," both of which she'd written after Aderholt had been killed and the strikers arrested in June. She'd sing a line and the rest of the people in the truck would repeat it, and they carried on that way while they grew closer to Gastonia. The day warmed as the sun climbed higher. Ella shrugged off John's old coat and put her hands in the pockets of her dress to hide her belly.

The caravan crossed the bridge into Gastonia. Ella felt the truck slow and come to a stop. They waited.

"What's going on?" Ella asked. "Why we stopping?"

One of the men in her group climbed the slats on the side of the truck and peered over and saw that the other truck had stopped as well. The engine still ran, vibrating the floor and sending tremors through Ella's body. She heard voices, then shouts.

The truck jolted backward, and Ella stumbled. She would have been tossed over the tailgate had Violet not grabbed hold of her arm. The truck reversed itself, driving backward across the bridge slowly as if the driver were uncertain of what was happening up ahead.

"Other truck's backing up too," the man who'd remained posted atop the slats said. "Looks like we're turning around."

"We shouldn't be turning around," Ella said. "Ain't no reason to turn around."

But once they'd crossed the bridge and parked on the shoulder, with the other truck having passed them en route back to Bessemer City and the driver of Ella's truck having turned back toward home too, she was able to see what had caused them to stop. On the other side of the bridge, a cluster of parked automobiles blocked the road. Dozens of men stood holding rifles. She narrowed her eyes and did her best to recognize their faces; she thought she may have recognized a few.

"Damn," Ella said. She slapped the tailgate as hard as she could, hard enough to hurt her had she taken notice. "Damn, damn, damn."

She wanted to jump out, run around to the front of the truck, flag the driver down, and tell him to turn around. They'd find another way into the city.

The truck rounded a bend, and she could no longer see the roadblock that was now a mile or so behind her. She turned to Violet.

"We can't go back to Bessemer," Ella said. Terror had gripped Violet's eyes. She nodded, and Ella knew without her admitting it that Violet did not agree.

Ella pushed her way toward the front of the truck bed. She'd bang her fist on the roof of the cab, order the driver to stop, ask him what the men at the roadblock had said, and sort through their options. She'd made it halfway to the front when there was the sound of a car speeding past, followed by the force of its passing as it rocked the truck on its axles. A woman beside Ella screamed and grabbed on to Ella as if she feared falling. The next sound Ella heard was the crunch of metal hitting metal.

"They're running them off the road!" a man called out, but Ella could not see to whom the voice belonged, did not know who *they* or *them* were. The people surrounding her broke into a panic, and when she looked for Violet she saw another black car behind them just before it struck the rear of their truck, slamming them into the truck in front of them.

At first Ella thought it was the violence of the accident that caused her to stumble and lose her balance, but when she saw the sky give way to trees and then earth she understood that the truck had been overturned, and she found herself caught in a web of arms and legs and bodies, all of them screaming and trying desperately to untangle from one another. She struggled to free herself, calling Violet's name over and over but getting no response.

She'd gotten to her feet by the time the first gunshots rang out, and she knew that what she heard were not backfires from an engine. None of the strikers had brought weapons, and she could not understand why someone would be shooting at them. But the sound of the blasts scattered the people who'd toppled from the overturned truck, and they ran past Ella. When she looked toward the other truck in their caravan she saw strikers streaming over the sides and pouring from the tailgate. Before she knew it she'd crossed the road and was stumbling down a hill toward a shallow stream. More gunshots rang out.

She didn't know why she was running. She was certain that some kind of mistake had been made, that some confusion had spun events into motion and would eventually unwind them. Her shoes splashed through the stream, the hem of her dress snagging for a moment on a fallen branch.

Sprays of blue and purple wildflowers grew along the water, and as she ran past them Ella marked their beauty, thinking what a strange thing it was for her to notice them in such detail at this moment. She did not know who ran in front of her or beside her or behind her, but she was aware that the dirt had blackened and hardened, and she discovered that she ran through the first rows of a cotton field, the bolls exploding in white puffs all around her. There were more gunshots behind her, and she wanted to drop to her knees and take shelter, but the field was open and the cotton plants low, and there was nowhere else to go.

So when she heard someone call her name from the road behind her, she knew for certain that she was being invited back to the scene of the accident. She knew that something would be explained to her that would make clear that a mistake had been made. She heard her name again. She stopped running, turned, and held a hand to her eyes to block the sunlight. That's when she saw the glint of steel, followed by a shot that tore into her chest and knocked her back into the cotton.

It was quiet now. The sky above her was blue, with soft spreads of clouds. The sun was warm on her face, the earth cool against her back. She wanted to sigh, but she found that her lungs would not let her take a breath, so instead she closed her eyes and opened them slowly, turned her gaze to the rows of cotton she lay between.

She didn't realize how brisk the day had been until she watched the breeze move through the cotton, turning it this way and that, her eyes taking in the bright white bolls where they clung to the branches. She felt her heart slow, something warm and comfortable overtake her. She wanted to reach up and touch one of the bolls, to feel its softness against her fingers, perhaps hold it to her cheek, but she found that she could not lift her arms. Instead, she spread her fingers so that they opened across her belly, the roundness of which she was just barely able to register. She lay with her eyes fixed on the cotton, pondering the tiny life inside her that she would never meet.

Look at that cotton, baby, she thought. What a small thing. What a small, little thing.

CHAPTER SIXTEEN

Brother

Saturday, September 14, 1929

The streets around Loray were choked with police, no sign of strikers or a picket line or the outside agitators the newspaper had warned of. Brother drove the abbey's Model T truck along Franklin Avenue, Father Gregory's rifle resting on his lap, the box of shells on the seat beside him. He'd sat inside the confessional until he was certain the woman had gone, and then he'd fled out the front doors into the sunlight. In the orchard across the street, he'd seen Father Gregory on his hands and knees gathering apples into a basket. He'd found the keys to the automobile on the hook in the kitchen where they always hung.

He pulled to the corner across from Loray. A policeman stood speaking with men in suits. They looked like reporters. Brother opened his door and called to the policeman.

"Where's the rally?" he asked.

The policeman frowned and stepped off the curb toward the truck. "Why?" he asked. "You from out of town?"

"No," Brother said. "I work with the monks at the abbey."

"Oh," the policeman said. "I'm sorry, I just thought." He looked north, down the street in the direction of where the strikers' head-quarters had sat just weeks earlier. "We shut it down. No protests today."

"What about the Bessemer City group?"

"They stopped them at the bridge."

"Who's *they*?" Brother asked.

"I don't know," the policeman said. He smiled. "Just *they*."

He headed west out of Gastonia for the open highway that led to Bessemer City. As soon as he crossed the bridge he saw dozens of cars and trucks parked on the side of the road. A truck had tipped over and come to rest on its side in the field below. Men stood along the road and stared down at the truck. Most of the men were armed. In the field, black and white strikers sat bloodied and shaken. A few of them dared to walk back toward the road, the bravest of them screamed taunts at the armed men.

Brother parked the truck and took up the rifle, chambered a round, and stuffed more into his pockets. He felt and heard the ammunition clink against the Mason jar, and he pulled the jar loose and tossed it onto the floorboard. He climbed out of the truck and shimmied down the bank toward the field, where people stood in groups, some attending others who appeared injured. He searched each face for Ella's, but he did not see her. He reached a creek that cut through the field. He stumbled, and fell on the mossy rocks. The rifle slipped from his hands, and he got to his knees and felt around in the water until his fingers found it. He stood, then raced toward the high cot-ton on the other side of the creek.

He found her lying in the dirt between rows of cotton, the front of her dress soaked in blood. Her open eyes stared toward the sky. Brother knelt beside her, searched her throat for a pulse, placed his ear against her chest in the hope of hearing a heartbeat or feeling her lungs expand with breath. He stayed there, his head to her chest, the tiny chair coming to rest upright above her heart. Brother watched the chair, waiting for it to be disturbed by anything but the wind, but it did not move. He sat up, looked down at Ella's face, tried to picture her as the girl he'd met all those years ago in Cowpens, the girl who'd swindled him for pork rinds and Coca-Cola to satisfy Miss Myra's curiosity about the young woman in the wagon with the newborn baby.

Now, sitting by Ella's body in a cotton field miles away from the place he'd first seen her outside the general store, he recalled Miss Myra's questions to him where she'd stood in the doorway to the bedroom of John Wiggins's dogtrot. "Oh, Verchel, what are we going to do with them? With you?"

While he did not have an answer then, he had one now. He knew what he had done with himself, what all of his drunken hours with John Wiggins back in Cowpens had done to Ella and her children once Miss Myra had discovered how he spent his afternoons. The family had been forced out of town in the middle of the night. Miss Myra had forced him out as well. All he had wanted was to marry a good woman and be a good man, and he had tried, but he had failed. Seeing Ella again after all these years had given him another chance, and he'd failed at that as well. He slipped the necklace over his head and removed the tiny chair from the leather strap. He tucked it into Ella's pocket.

He heard the rustling of footsteps. A young colored woman appeared in the next row, her chest heaving from running. She looked at him for a moment, and then she looked down at Ella's body, covered her mouth with both hands, and screamed.

CHAPTER SEVENTEEN

Lilly Wiggins

Monday, December 26, 2005

I begged her not to go, Edwin. I was so young, and it was so long ago that it seems like I shouldn't remember, but I do. I can remember feeling like it was all over after the policeman had been killed and so many of them had been arrested. I just remember thinking that it was unnecessary for her to go because it had all ended.

We were standing out there in the road, watching the people load up into these big trucks. Well, they seemed like big trucks at the time. I remember telling Mother, "I don't want you to go." And she said, "Well, I have to, and I will." And she did. If someone had come along at that moment and told me that I'd never see my mother again, I think I would have believed them. I've always believed that so much about my life was decided right at that moment.

Mother sent me home, Iva and me both. Iva was sore because she thought it was my fault that she didn't get to go with them. But I didn't care what she was sore about. I was too afraid.

Iva had gone home to her house, so, an hour or so later, when I saw her coming down the road screaming as loud as she could, I knew something had gone wrong. She was screaming, "Hey, Lilly! Hey, Lilly!" and I remember standing on the front porch and wondering what she was going to tell me once she arrived. But as she got closer I was able to hear her more clearly. She'd been screaming, "They killed her. They killed her." And of course I knew exactly who they'd killed.

The two trucks in which she rode were attacked by an armed mob. Dozens of people witnessed it, but no one claimed to know for certain who had shot her. The police ended up arresting a few men, but Loray bailed them out and paid for their legal defense. They were all found innocent. I doubt it surprised anyone. It didn't surprise me.

The day after her funeral, the preacher who'd been hired by someone in town to preach her service came to pay us a visit. Mother hadn't stepped foot in a church in years, and I suspect they were afraid that someone from the union would want to lead the service. They'd all had enough of the union by then, so someone paid the Presbyterian preacher to do it.

The preacher wasn't done with us yet. He showed up with his wife, and they made us pack up the few things we owned and told us we were going on a trip. What they didn't say was that we were going to Barium Springs, the Presbyterian children's home outside Statesville. And what they definitely didn't tell us was that the preacher's wife had planned on keeping Wink. We didn't know that until they dropped us off that evening. It was like another death, Edwin. We didn't see him for years and years, and by the time I finally found him he had no memory of me or Mother or Rose or your father. He was a stranger by then, and I was a stranger to him.

The orphanage was nice, and we should have appreciated it more than we did because we had no other option. For the first time in our lives we had everything we'd ever wanted— school, clothes, shoes, food—but we'd lost something of ourselves. We were used to living outside, used to coming and going whenever we pleased. We'd never had anyone "in charge" of us, and it took us a long, long time to get used to it.

At night, after all the girls in my room had fallen asleep, I'd sneak outside through a window and climb down the gutter and drop to the ground in my bare feet. I'd wander around out there until near sunrise, and then I'd sneak back inside. That was the only time I felt like I was back home in Stumptown, the woods alive with night sounds right outside my window, the spring babbling like a voice not far away.

I got braver and braver, wandered farther and farther away from the home, stayed gone longer than I should have. Sometimes I'd be sweating and out of breath when the time came to get out of bed in the morning. Oh, I thought I was slick, thought I was getting something over on all the other girls and my teachers too.

I was never scared to be out there alone at night, until I heard the cry for the first time. It sounded like the scream of a woman who feared for her life, and I hate to use a cliché, Edwin, but it made my blood run cold. I thought for certain that some poor girl was out there in the woods being murdered. I would not hear it for a few nights, and then I would hear it every night for a week.

You may already know what it was, Edwin, especially because we heard it tonight when we were standing outside your house. It was the roar of a panther, but I didn't know it at the time. I didn't know what it was, not until the home's new pastor told me.

He was an old man, and I can't remember his name. I was drawn to him because he sounded "mountain" when he spoke the same way Mother sounded "mountain" when she spoke. He was from Cullowhee, and when I found it on a map I saw that it was close to Bryson City, and I knew Mother had spent time there as a little girl.

I never told the pastor that I snuck out at night. I've never told a soul except for you, so I hope you can keep my secret. I did tell the old pastor about the screams I heard at night that came from the woods behind the home, how I'd hear them every night for a while and then go weeks without hearing a thing at all. I asked him what he thought it could be.

He told me a story about growing up in the mountains, about how his grandfather would take him bear hunting at night, and sometimes they'd hear the scream of a panther up in the hills, and his grandfather would say, "That's the sound of a heartbroken woman calling for her lost babies to come home."

I asked him if it could really be a panther that I'd been hearing, but he told me he didn't think so. He told me they lived up in the mountains and that there were fewer and fewer of them now, and perhaps soon there wouldn't be any at all. But then he stopped, and thought about it for a second. He said, "Well, with all the logging and the waste and the mudslides, I reckon we could've forced her down the mountain to visit us all the way out here."

I've hung on to that after all these years, this idea that the lumber companies forced the panther from the mountains just as they forced Mother into that wagon bound for Cowpens. I've hung on to the idea that the sound of that woman calling her lost babies home was the sound of Mother looking for us. After that, when I heard it at night out in the woods, I'd close my eyes and chant over and over, "I am alone, and you are alone. I am alone, and you are alone." I know it's silly, but I still feel that way, and I found myself saying the same thing over and over on the drive home tonight after hearing that panther's cry from down at the zoo.

But here's what I wanted to tell you, Edwin. This is the reason I wrote you this letter tonight.

We'd been at the home for three years or so when that old pastor came to my class one day and told me that I had a visitor. I was fourteen years old, and I'd never had a visitor before. Not a single one. All of the things of my life were housed in those buildings there at Barium Springs. It felt as if the world outside were a place that no longer existed. I had no ties to it, so the idea of the world coming to visit me was exhilarating.

The visiting room was a high-ceilinged, drafty room just off the main foyer. I can picture the sunlight streaming in through the tall windows, the ceiling fans stirring the air far above. When I arrived there was no one in the room except for a black man who sat at one of the small tables. He wore the uniform of a Pullman porter, if you can picture it, and he looked familiar, like someone I had met before. I looked up at the pastor, unsure of what I was supposed to do with this stranger.

"I'll be out here in the foyer should you need me," the pastor said.

The porter looked up and smiled at me, and not knowing what else to do, I walked to the table and pulled out a chair and sat down across from him. We stared at one another like we were waiting for the other to start speaking, to explain exactly why we were sitting across from one another in the visiting room while my class learned algebra without me.

"You've grown up," he said. He smiled. "And you look like her."

"Who?"

"Your mother," he said.

"You knew her?" I asked.

"Yes," he said. He reached into his pocket and pulled out an old envelope. "Do you remember your mother's friend Sophia?"

Of course I remembered Sophia. She was one of the strike organizers from up north somewhere. She was a beautiful girl, and anyone who had ever met or had even seen her would never forget her. But she was trouble, and I have always felt that she brought trouble with her.

"This is from her," he said. He slid the envelope across the table. "She wanted me to give this to you. I'm sorry it's taken me so long to make it here. I've thought of coming to see you many times when I passed through Statesville, but I never found the courage to get off the train."

I picked up the envelope and looked at it, and then I looked at him.

"Why are you afraid to get off the train in Statesville?"

"I don't know," he said. "Bad memories, I guess."

I opened the letter and spread it out right there on the table. It was written in pencil, the handwriting so faded it was nearly illegible. I've still got it, though, and you can still read what it says.

Dear Lilly,

I hope this letter finds you well and happy. I was devastated by your mother's death. I loved her and respected her more than I can put into words. I promise to carry on her work of seeking justice and inspiring humanity and bringing together people of all races, for these are the reasons they killed her. Her death will not have been in vain. I send my best to you, Otis, Rose, and Wink.

With all my love,
Sophia

"I brought something else too," he said. "Something Violet wants you to have." He reached into his pocket and removed a tiny wooden chair. He set it on the table. We both stared at it.

"What is it?" I asked.

"I don't know," he said. "Violet found it with your mother. She wondered if it's yours."

"Do you know Violet?"

He smiled. "Yes," he said. "She's my wife."

The chair wasn't mine, Edwin, and I knew it didn't belong to Rose. We'd never owned a proper toy in our lives, and certainly not something as fine and detailed as this piece of dollhouse furniture. But I took it, and I've held on to it.

I looked down at Sophia's letter and read it again. In the room above us, chairs scraped across the floor, and I knew my class had just ended and it was time for lunch, but I wasn't hungry. I wanted to stay there with this man, ask him every question I could think to ask, but I couldn't think of what to ask first.

"Your mother saved my life," he finally said. "She was a hero. Not just to me, but to a lot of people."

Edwin, I'm eighty-seven years old, and to this day that's the only kind thing I've ever heard someone say about my mother. I didn't doubt him for a minute, though. I knew it was true. I know it's still true.

There is an old saying that every story, even your own, is either happy or sad depending on where you stop telling it. I believe I'll stop telling this one here.

Afterword

The Last Ballad is based on the life and tragic murder of Ella May Wiggins and the events surrounding the Loray Mill strike that occurred in my hometown of Gastonia, North Carolina, in 1929.

Ella May was born in east Tennessee in 1900 and married a man named John Wiggins in 1916. The couple soon left the mountains for Cowpens, South Carolina, a small town upstate where Ella worked on a farm and then in her first textile mill job. The couple and their growing family were eventually lured across the North Carolina line by the hope of financial security offered by the dozens of mills in Gaston County, which had come to be known as "the combed yarn capital of the South," the town of Gastonia leading the way as "the city of spindles." Over the next several years, Ella and John bounced from mill to mill in Gaston County before settling in a predominately African-American community called Stumptown outside Bessemer City. John soon abandoned the family.

By the spring of 1929, twenty-eight-year-old Ella had lost four of her nine children to pellagra and whooping cough, diseases that disproportionately affected the poor. She earned $9.00 for a seventy-two-hour workweek at American Mill No. 2, one of the few integrated mills in the county. In April, when she heard about the Loray Mill strike seven miles away in Gastonia, Ella walked off her job and joined the National Textile Workers Union, a labor organization of the American Communist Party. That summer she wrote and sang protest songs that were later performed by Woody Guthrie and recorded by Pete Seeger. She traveled to Washington, D.C., and confronted North Carolina senator Lee Overman about labor conditions in southern mills and the plight of working mothers. She integrated the Gaston County branch of the National Textile Workers Union against the will of local party officials and members, opening the union to her African-American neighbors and former coworkers. In effect, Ella became the face of the Loray Mill strike and the voice of organized labor in the South. She was a workers' rights advocate at a time when mill owners openly scoffed at federal labor laws, and she was a feminist and civil rights leader decades before these terms were staples of the American progressive movement.

A violent and unpredictable atmosphere surrounded the strike that summer. On the night of June 7, 1929, Gastonia police chief Orville Aderholt was shot and killed during a raid on the union's headquarters. Although there was intense speculation about what had caused the raid and who had fired the shots that killed Aderholt, dozens of strikers were arrested and charged with the police chief's murder. Nine men would stand trial that fall.

On September 14, Ella and other Bessemer City strikers were in a convoy of trucks headed to a rally in Gastonia in support of the jailed strikers when a gang of men rumored to have been hired by the Loray Mill set up a roadblock and fired into the trucks. Ella was shot in the chest and died at the scene. Dozens of people witnessed the attack, but the six men who were arrested were found innocent of Ella's murder. The Loray Mill paid for the men's legal defense.

Ella's children were whisked away to an orphanage near Statesville, North Carolina, where they would remain until their eighteenth birthdays. While Ella's murder and the events of the strike made headlines around the world, her name and legacy were slandered in newspapers across the state.

In 1935, the Firestone Corporation bought the Loray Mill and changed its name, and the story of the strike and the murders of Orville Aderholt and Ella May Wiggins disappeared from history.

I know this because I grew up in Gastonia, North Carolina, and I never heard a word about Ella May Wiggins, Orville Aderholt, or the Loray Mill strike until 2003 when I enrolled in graduate school in Louisiana. This despite the fact that my mother's maiden name is Wiggins, and despite the fact that my grandfather Harry Wiggins at twenty-two years old worked in a South Carolina mill only a few miles from where a woman who shared his last name was murdered; despite the fact that my grandfather would eventually move to Gaston County and retire from millwork there; despite the fact that my maternal grandmother Pearly Lucille Owensby Wiggins was born in Cowpens, South Carolina, in 1914, just a few short years before Ella and John arrived. But I was not alone in my ignorance. My mother and father, both born in mill villages not far from where Ella May Wiggins lived, worked, and was murdered, had never heard of her either. Anyone who remembered the violent summer of 1929 must have remembered it in private and spoken of it in whispers.

I know little of my parents' childhoods in the mill villages. My mother has talked of my grandmother's work in the carding room and of my grandfather's work as a supervisor. She has told me stories of going with my grandfather to the mill on Sundays when it was closed and she was allowed to explore while sipping an RC Cola. My father, who passed away before I finished this book, told me stories of working the register at the mill store as a teenager while the store's manager pushed the dope wagon through the mill during the afternoon shift.

One story my father told me not long before he passed away has stuck with me. He grew up in the Esther Mill village in Shelby, North Carolina, which is about twenty miles west of Gastonia. When my father was a child, his mother and father would go to work and leave my father's older sister in charge of him and his younger brother. According to my father, he had been hanging on to a nickel for weeks, trying to decide how he would spend it, when one day he dropped the nickel between the planks of the porch floor. He could peer between the boards and see the nickel on the ground below, but he could not reach it. There was talk of using a hammer to pry the boards loose, but the house belonged to the mill, and he and his siblings were afraid of damaging the house while trying to retrieve the money. They eventually moved out of the house, but my father said he had spent the rest of his life thinking about that nickel and what it could have bought.

This book is for Ella May and her children. This book is for people like me who learned of her bravery and her family's loss much later than we should have. This book is for Orville Aderholt, a man who, by all accounts, was virtuous and fair. This book is for my grandparents who were born on farms and saw hope in the mills. This book is for my mother and father who were born in mill villages and dreamed of the suburbs. This book is for everyone who is still reaching for nickels.

Further Reading

In researching the life of Ella May Wiggins, the events of the Loray Mill strike, and the evolution of mill culture I relied on the following resources.

Corn from a Jar: Moonshining in the Great Smoky Mountains. Daniel S. Pierce. Gatlinburg, TN: Great Smoky Mountains Association, 2013.

Documenting the American South. Audio interviews with textile workers. University of North Carolina-Chapel Hill. http:// docsouth.unc.edu.

Gastonia 1929: The Story of the Loray Mill Strike. John A. Salmond. Chapel Hill, NC: University of North Carolina Press, 1995.

Gastonia Gallop: Cotton Mill Songs and Hillbilly Blues: Piedmont Textile Workers on Record: Gaston County, North Carolina 1927–1931. Various Artists. Old Hat Records, 2009.

The Great Smokies: From Natural Habitat to National Park. Daniel S. Pierce. Knoxville, TN: University of Tennessee Press, 2000.

Linthead Stomp: The Creation of Country Music in the Piedmont South. Patrick Huber. Chapel Hill, NC: University of North Carolina Press, 2008.

Martyr of the Loray Mill: Ella May and the 1929 Textile Workers' Strike in Gastonia, North Carolina. Kristina L. Horton. Jefferson, NC: McFarland and Company, 2015.

"Mill Mother's Lament: Ella May, Working Women's Militancy, and the 1929 Gaston County Strike" (master's thesis). Lynn Haessly. Thesis copy available for in-library use at the University of North Carolina-Chapel Hill. 1987.

Millhands and Preachers. Liston Pope. Westford, MA: Yale University Press, 1942.

A New South Hunt Club: An Illustrated History of the Hilton Head Agricultural Society 1917–1967. Richard Rankin. Mount Holly, NC: Willow Hill Press, 2011.

Proletarian Journey: New England, Gastonia, Moscow. Fred E. Beal. New York: Hillman-Curl, 1937.

Textile Town: Spartanburg County, South Carolina. Betsy Wakefield Teter, ed. Spartanburg, SC: Hub City Writers Project, 2003.

Acknowledgments

A grant from the North Carolina Arts Council provided time to write this novel, and a residency at the Weymouth Center for the Arts and Humanities provided space for it to be written.

Thank you to the people whose eyes and hands touched these pages: my in-laws, Eugene and Jo-Ann Brady; my mom, Sandi Cash; Christian Helms; Thomas Murphy; Lydia Peelle; Mark Sundeen; Mitch Wieland; and Reggie Scott Young.

Thank you to the people whose ideas and encouragement pushed these pages forward: Marc Baldwin; Joseph Bathanti; Margaret Bauer; my brother Cliff Cash and my sister Jada Cash; Jim Dodson; Clyde Edgerton; Ben Fountain; Gail Godwin; Mark Koenig, the executive director of the Wilmington Railroad Museum in Wilmington, North Carolina; Kevin Maurer; Miwa Messer; Lucy Penegar; Daniel Pierce; Richard Rankin; Ron Rash; Ketch Secor; Brad Shipp and VariDesk; Shelby Stephenson; and Daniel Wallace.

Thank you to the many wonderful people at William Morrow/ HarperCollins Publishers, past and present, especially Jessica Williams, Liate Stehlik, Emily Homonoff, Chloe Moffett, and Tavia Kowalchuk.

Thank you to my publicist, Sharyn Rosenblum, who always finds the way, and my editor, David Highfill, who always finds the vision. David, I have no doubt that this book was as difficult to edit as it was to write. Your support has meant everything.

Thank you to Nat Sobel, Judith Weber, and the entire Sobel Weber team. Nat, I'll never be able to thank you enough.

Thank you to my students and colleagues in the Mountainview Low-Residency MFA program for sitting through years of me reading excerpts of this novel while I kicked the can farther and farther down the road.

Thank you to the University of North Carolina-Asheville for changing my life in naming me writer-in-residence. It's good to be home.

Thank you to the librarians and booksellers who sustain the creative, intellectual, and civic life of our nation.

An enduring thank you to my family: Mallory, this novel, like everything good in my life, is a testament to your grace and love. I write about strong women because I'm in love with one, and our daughters will grow into strong women because their mother is one. Early and Juniper, you have given me more joy than I deserve, and I will spend the rest of my life earning the love of hearts as pure as yours.

My dad, Roger Cash, was born in a mill village in Shelby, North Carolina, in 1943. He left this world in 2016. The glory of his life and the tragedy of his loss are in these pages.

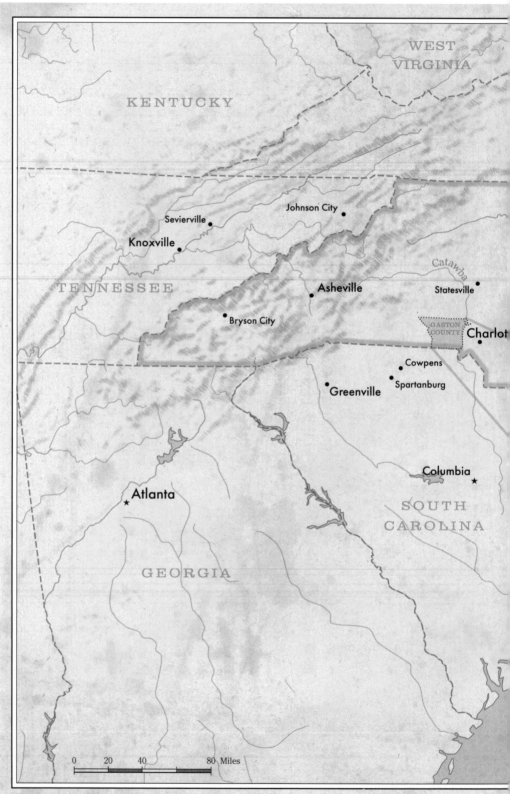